T0191250

WILD MASSIVE

ALSO BY SCOTTO MOORE

Your Favorite Band Cannot Save You
Battle of the Linguist Mages

WILD MASSIVE

SCOTTO MOORE

TOR PUBLISHING GROUP
NEW YORK

This is a work of fiction. All of the characters, organizations, and events portrayed in this novel are either products of the author's imagination or are used fictitiously.

WILD MASSIVE

Copyright © 2023 by Scott Alan Moore

All rights reserved.

A Tordotcom Book
Published by Tom Doherty Associates/Tor Publishing Group
120 Broadway
New York, NY 10271

www.tor.com

Tor® is a registered trademark of Macmillan Publishing Group, LLC.

Library of Congress Cataloging-in-Publication Data

Names: Moore, Scotto, author.
Title: Wild massive / Scotto Moore.
Description: First Edition. | New York : Tordotcom, 2023. |
"A Tom Doherty Associates Book."
Identifiers: LCCN 2022034291 (print) | LCCN 2022034292 (ebook) |
ISBN 9781250767745 (hardcover) | ISBN 9781250767738 (ebook)
Subjects: LCGFT: Novels.
Classification: LCC PS3613.O56686 W55 2023 (print) |
LCC PS3613.O56686 (ebook) | DDC 813'.6—dc23/eng/20220721
LC record available at https://lccn.loc.gov/2022034291
LC ebook record available at https://lccn.loc.gov/2022034292

Our books may be purchased in bulk for promotional, educational, or
business use. Please contact your local bookseller or the Macmillan Corporate
and Premium Sales Department at 1-800-221-7945, extension 5442,
or by email at MacmillanSpecialMarkets@macmillan.com.

First Edition: 2023

Printed in the United States of America

0 9 8 7 6 5 4 3 2 1

For Jen & Susie

SEASON ONE

EPISODE 1.01

Carissa awoke to the sound of something landing hard on the elevator in which she lived. The elevator was in a slow climb at the time of impact.

"What the hell was that?" she said, removing her headphones, glancing upward at the ceiling, seeing nothing out of the ordinary. The lighting panels were still intact, currently in the shade of twilight blue that Carissa liked when she was sleeping. For safety reasons, the elevator's cloudlet preferred not to dim the lights into complete darkness.

"A solid mass, approximately one hundred and two kilograms, landed at high speed on the roof," the cloudlet replied.

"Full stop," she said, and the cloudlet complied by gently decelerating the elevator to a halt. "How far away is the nearest safe floor?"

"Twenty-seven thousand, four hundred and eight floors below us," said the cloudlet.

.   .   .

She slipped into her mechanic's overalls and said, "What do you think it is?"

"I think it's alive," the cloudlet said.

"That seems unlikely," she replied.

"The event does seem to violate several safety protocols," the cloudlet agreed. "But its weight has shifted slightly since it landed."

"Did it land on the hatch?" she asked.

"The hatch is clear. It landed near the exterior wall of the elevator shaft."

The last time Carissa had occasion to go outside the elevator in between floors was during a safety drill she ran with her cloudlet when they were getting to know each other, right after she moved into this elevator; would've been maybe a decade ago if she remembered correctly.

She checked her supply of first aid pills—she still had half a pouch full. She stuffed the pouch in one of the many pockets of her overalls. Out of habit, she slipped a slim handheld tablet into another pocket.

Bringing a hundred-kilo mass of "I think it's alive" into her elevator didn't sound super appealing. But you couldn't just leave "I think it's alive" on the roof, either. You always had to help people in this ridiculous place.

She wrapped a belt around her overalls, clipped a pistol and a knife to it. She put on a sleek helmet with an embedded head-lamp and slipped its tiny oxygen-supply mask over her nose. If she was up there longer than five minutes, she'd need to drop back down for proper air.

"Let's talk through this," she said. "What's on that safe floor?"

"Wild Massive Super is the main attraction," the cloudlet replied. "We would not open in a mapped location."

So if Carissa's elevator opened its doors on that floor, it might come as a complete surprise to anyone in the vicinity. It might open its doors in the middle of a room, or in a garbage dump, or in a parking lot. It might be witnessed by dozens or hundreds; it might go unnoticed completely. Since it was an unmapped location, no one would be waiting to board the elevator, but many might recognize the significance of a Building elevator appearing suddenly in their midst. Attention might be paid; shrines might be built; Carissa might be highly annoyed.

But Wild Massive Super was the flagship theme park in the Wild Massive empire and would almost certainly have proper medical, if for some reason her first aid pills failed to do the trick. Hopefully, "I think it's alive" could pay to get in.

"Open the ceiling hatch for me," Carissa said. "I want to go out and see what we've got up there."

A center panel in the ceiling slid open smoothly, revealing the pure darkness of the shaft.

.   .   .

She'd forgotten how cold it was out here. She almost dropped back down and got herself a jacket, but nah.

As a rule, you could find yourself in the elevator shaft for a couple of different reasons.

Reason one was maintenance, although the elevators were generally self-repairing and you could do most routine maintenance from inside the car, anyway.

Reason two was that you were fucked in some major way, which she hadn't experienced herself, but you heard stories if you lived this life long enough.

Crumpled on one corner of the roof was a large figure, humanoid at first glance. By her estimation, this figure probably qualified as fucked in some major way.

As she watched, however, the figure seemed to melt and re-form over and over, slowly cycling through possible forms, humanoid or otherwise. It was striking and weird and grotesque to watch.

"I'm going to help you," she said as she inched toward it.

"I'm skeptical," the thing said. It sounded like it was trying to speak while being smashed flat, as though its lungs were out of whack.

"I'm serious," she said. "I brought first aid pills. Do those work on you?"

"Sure do," the thing croaked.

"Where's your mouth?" she asked. Her headlamp hadn't successfully pinned down a face on this globular ball of mutating flesh yet.

A slithery tentacle—maybe blue, maybe green—emerged and flopped down in front of her. She reached out and dropped a pill onto it; the pill was promptly absorbed into its flesh. It suddenly seemed to gain control of its transformations with a burst of energy, and moments later, Carissa watched it resolve into the figure of a human, like herself, with pale white skin and an unnaturally thin frame; its age group and gender indeterminate.

"Taking a human form just to make me comfortable?" Carissa asked.

"Taking a human form because it's one of three I can easily manage at the moment," the shapeshifter said, sounding exhausted. "The other two would be . . . less friendly."

"Can you move?" Carissa asked.

"Maybe. Do you have any more pills?"

She fished out another one, this time placing it into the shapeshifter's palm. Ze consumed it quickly, and moments later, ze was able to sit up on zir own.

"Thank you," ze said.

"After you," she replied, motioning toward the hatch. Ze crawled forward, swung zir newly formed legs down, and made the drop. She swung down after zir, and the hatch closed snugly above her head.

. . .

The shapeshifter huddled under a blanket on Carissa's sleeping pad, and she offered zir another first aid pill. Ze took it without hesitation. They didn't speak for a while, until ze stopped shivering and seemed to finally relax. A comforting hum in the background indicated the elevator was moving again.

"Only shapeshifters I know of," Carissa said slowly, "are Shai-Manak." She paused, giving zir an opportunity to respond, and when ze didn't, she pressed, "Are you Shai-Manak?"

"Yes," ze said with a big sigh, "I'm Shai-Manak."

"Do you mind my asking—how did you wind up on the roof of my elevator?"

"Yours, huh?" Ze nodded zir approval, then said, "I jumped into the elevator shaft. Look, you can just let me off at the next convenient floor and pretend you never saw me."

Something heavy landed hard on the roof of the elevator. Moments later, another heavy thing landed hard right next to the first heavy thing.

A series of resounding slams—punches, really—began striking the roof of the elevator, creating loud booms inside.

"More Shai-Manak?" she asked.

"Yes," the shapeshifter said. "Enforcers."

"Cloudlet, reverse direction, please. Hop us to the next station with zero population at least a thousand floors up," Carissa ordered. "Authorized passengers only."

"Understood," the cloudlet replied.

A small flash let them know that the elevator had teleported a significant distance up the elevator shaft. The resounding thuds on the roof were gone; the "enforcers" that had landed on top of the elevator were not authorized passengers and therefore had not been included in the elevator's teleport radius. They were now plummeting down the elevator shaft at least a thousand floors below them.

"Should I feel guilty about that?" she thought to ask.

"Not overly," the shapeshifter said.

"Doors are opening," the cloudlet said.

"Shit," Carissa said, drawing her pistol.

A pleasant *ding* sounded, and then the doors opened.

. . .

You could ride the elevators in the Building up and down all you wanted, or you could ask them to teleport you to the nearest anchor station instead. The range wasn't bad; an elevator's onboard teleport pad could power a hop of around ten thousand floors on its own, and a relay network extended that range. The relay network was spotty this far above Association floors, though, where anchor stations were irregularly placed and unpredictably defended.

Only one thing about teleporting an elevator in this fashion was truly reliable: the doors always opened when the elevator reached an anchor station.

Oh, how she hated that simple cause-and-effect mechanism. Oh, how she'd begged and pleaded with her cloudlet to reconsider this truism about its fundamental design. Oh, how she'd searched high and low for engineering specifications that could guide her in disabling automatic door opening altogether, but to no avail.

If you asked an elevator to teleport to an anchor station, it was happy to oblige, but nothing short of a godlike intervention could stop the doors from opening at the end of that hop.

The doors opened onto a large bamboo platform with a thatched canopy, perched in the branches of giant trees in a tropical forest. The canopy protected the platform from the heavy rain that poured down in a torrent from the sky above the forest.

No one happened to be waiting for the elevator just then. "Is this a safe floor?" she asked.

"The atmosphere is poisonous to both of you," the cloudlet replied. You were always safe inside the bubble of atmosphere in a given elevator, but step outside the car at your own peril. Sure, the cloudlets always tried to give you solid advice, but they couldn't physically stop you from walking out into a cyanide rain forest if that was your goal.

She jabbed the Close Doors button—a single, sharp, professional jab—and the doors calmly slid shut a moment later. She clipped her pistol back onto her belt.

"Zero population—are you hiding from someone?" the shapeshifter asked her.

"Nah," she said, "I'm just antisocial."

"Destination?" the cloudlet asked.

She peered at the shapeshifter and said, "Can we take you somewhere specific?"

"Nearest safe floor is fine," the shapeshifter replied.

"There's a theme park on that floor," Carissa said.

"Lovely," said the shapeshifter. "I do enjoy themes."

"Cloudlet, take us down to the Wild Massive flagship," Carissa said, "and let's try not to rush."

"Gently descending," replied the cloudlet. In theory, the elevator was expected to answer calls along the route, but the cloudlet had come to appreciate that Carissa was a one-of-a-kind passenger, and it made allowances for her moods and habits more than the average elevator would. They rarely saw other passengers.

"Thank you for coming to my aid," the shapeshifter said. Ze had been nude when ze first dropped into the elevator, but now ze seemed to be constructing clothing for zirself, style yet to be determined, zir skin rippling this way and that. "I don't suppose you have tea? I could use something warm to ease the chill."

Carissa nodded, took a few steps across the elevator to the wall opposite the doors, where she'd bolted a tiny makeshift kitchenette into place: small organics fabricator for staple foods, a cold storage unit for the few unique treats she liked to acquire as she traveled. A single mug hung on a hook.

"Did you expect to survive jumping into an open elevator shaft?" Carissa asked as she stuck her mug in the fabricator and watched it fill with a nondescript tea that would probably be palatable.

"The move was improvisational, I'll admit," the shapeshifter replied. "I can't say I gave myself time to consider the odds of survival."

"How'd you get the doors open in the first place?" Elevator doors were notoriously difficult to open without a car waiting, which seemed like a good and proper design, especially given the events of the last ten minutes.

The shapeshifter smiled grimly and said, "Trade secret." Fair enough. The elevators had ears, after all.

After a few moments, the shapeshifter's clothes had finally settled into place, providing a nondescript working-class look, like a mechanic on a day off maybe—perhaps taking cues from Carissa's attire. Transformation complete, the shapeshifter let Carissa's blanket drop to the sleeping mat but remained seated with zir back to the wall. Ze had chosen a human form, but Carissa couldn't shake unsettling images of zir transformation from her mind and remained on edge about zir presence.

She could tell ze was studying the car's interior, noticing the changes she'd made with a curious eye. Her cloudlet had adjusted the lighting to waking-hours brightness, which made it easy to spot the many differences between this car and a standard car in service throughout any of the four fleets. From the decorative handwoven rug on the floor and the small pair of diamond-shaped paintings near the ceiling on one wall, to the row of polished mechanic's tools that hung from the elevator's handrail on another wall, to the waste-disposal unit tucked in one corner that she'd reclaimed from a decommissioned shuttle, any casual passenger could easily determine that Carissa had completely colonized this car.

But not every casual passenger would understand the significance of the small insignias she'd inscribed near the top of each of the doors.

"Explorers Guild *and* Elevator Guild?" the shapeshifter said, sounding genially impressed.

"I'm an overachiever," she joked, but ze seemed to take her seriously. "Neither one, lately," she clarified. "I'm an independent operator at the moment."

"Are you for hire in some fashion?"

"Isn't everyone?" she replied. "Not taking new clients."

"A pity," the shapeshifter said.

"You don't even know what I do."

"Do you explore? In an elevator?"

"Hmm, is it really that obvious?" But then she smiled and said, "I have many useful skills."

"Do you have a brochure?"

"No, I don't keep a handy summary of my talents to distribute to any random passenger who falls onto the roof of my car."

Ze smiled back at her and said, "Not your car, though, is it."

True, the Association claimed ownership of all the cars in all four fleets. But once someone took a car above Association floors, who gave a fuck what the Association had to say about it? The Association claimed all kinds of bullshit that it couldn't prove or enforce. Anyway, the cloudlets had their own opinions about who truly owned the elevators, and she was inclined to side with them.

"I'm going to return it in the condition I found it, I swear," she said, and they shared a laugh.

They were silent for the rest of the ride, politeness enforcing a mutual reluctance to ask deeper questions. She knew plenty of people on the Building networks, but she hadn't really had a passenger in her car for months. Silence suited her well enough.

Her cloudlet had told her once that it was not uncommon for lonely cars in the fleets to wander aimlessly up and down, waiting for passenger calls that always went to some other car that was closer and quicker to respond. That was the price of ensuring enough cars were in service at all times to provide a reasonable response time. Cloudlets in these cars had no lack of companionship, networked as they were with every other cloudlet in existence; but still, when your mission in life was to serve passengers and then you never saw a single one, your self-esteem suffered ever so slightly.

Carissa, though, deployed a variety of tactics to keep passengers out.

"We'll be arriving shortly," her cloudlet announced.

Impulsively, she asked, "Do you . . . need anything, or are you going to be good out there?" She couldn't risk giving up her pistol, but she thought she had a spare knife she could let go.

"I couldn't trouble you further," the shapeshifter said. "You've been truly generous already, and I wish I could repay you."

"I don't charge for scraping people off my roof," Carissa said. "So we're square. What's your plan from here, though?"

"Call the next elevator and continue down to my destination," ze replied.

"Be advised," her cloudlet said, "that we will be opening doors at an unmapped location. To call a new elevator, you'll need to locate a mapped elevator location on the floor."

The elevator had decelerated so smoothly that they were surprised to hear the pleasant *ding* that preceded the opening of the doors.

.   .   .

They stared out at the scene beyond the threshold of the elevator and tried to make sense of what they saw. Carissa propped herself in the doorway so that the elevator doors wouldn't slide shut without warning.

The elevator doors had opened in the middle of a deserted urban street at dusk. In the distance, you could see the faint glow on the horizon that was undoubtedly Wild Massive Super, with giant spotlights flashing back and forth against the clouds, and sure enough, if you looked closely, you could see the tops of roller coasters peeking out above enormous walls.

You could also hear the distinct chatter of ballistic gunfire in the distance, light peppering punctuated by occasional booms. The walls around the park were taking fire from multiple sources at ground level, but that didn't stop or even drown out the carousing they heard coming from inside the park itself—gleeful shouting and joyous music and riotous laughter, rising in waves.

"I don't suppose," the shapeshifter said, "you know where the nearest mapped elevator location actually is?"

"Inside the park," the cloudlet replied. "In fact, it's the *only* mapped elevator location on this continent."

Carissa recognized a landmark on the skyline ahead of them, a monument. Inside the walls of the park stood a silver arch, towering above the tallest roller coasters, seeming to scrape the clouds.

"Just a guess here," Carissa said, "but if there's an elevator inside the park, I'd start looking for it at the base of the Arch there."

"You're familiar with this place?" the shapeshifter asked.

"Yeah," she said. "This is St. Louis. We're in America."

. . .

"Should I know what that means?" the shapeshifter wondered.

"It's an Earth floor," the cloudlet offered as a simple explanation.

"Lots of Earth floors in this Building," Carissa added.

"I see," the shapeshifter said. "What happens on these 'Earth floors'?"

"Murderous extraction of capital value from helpless human

beings," Carissa replied. "And theme parks. We don't have to drop you off here. Cloudlet, where's the nearest safe floor with a mapped location on this elevator shaft?"

This was the technically correct question she should have asked up front, instead of simply asking for the nearest safe floor. Her cloudlet was a lovely companion, but you did have to be literal with it on occasion.

There were four elevator shafts, and "mapped" floors could access at least one of them. These were colloquially referred to as Up, Down, Right, and Left, which philosophically—if not always physically—corresponded to the four exterior walls of the Building. Carissa and her cloudlet spent their days traveling up and down the Left elevator shaft, which was unmapped from within this floor, but one of the Up, Down, or Right elevator locations was mapped and permanently accessible from somewhere within the Wild Massive flagship.

If the shapeshifter got off here where the elevator wasn't mapped, then the minute the doors closed behind zir, the elevator would vanish with no way to summon Carissa back. On floors where the elevators were mapped, if you didn't like the action on the floor, you just pushed the button and called the next elevator so you could split the place.

"We'll need to head back up a considerable distance," the cloudlet replied, "to that restaurant floor you liked. If we continue down much farther, we start running the risk of Association contact."

"We're that close to the Association?" the shapeshifter asked, suddenly excited.

"And we're not getting any closer," Carissa said, locking eyes with the shapeshifter.

"I see. In that case, perhaps I do need to take my leave of you here. Hopefully the elevator inside the park will take me farther down than you're willing to travel. I owe you a debt for getting me this far, and I won't forget—"

"Wait, you're *aiming* for the Association?" Carissa interrupted. "But aren't you . . . ?"

"Yes, I'm Shai-Manak." When Carissa didn't seem to immediately grasp the implications, the shapeshifter added, "I'm trying to defect."

Carissa pondered the implications of that for a long moment.

"Okay, but have you considered *not* defecting?" she finally said.

The shapeshifter laughed.

"To get inside Wild Massive Super in a legal fashion," the cloudlet said, "you'll be expected to produce local, Association, or Wild Massive currency. Do you happen to have any such accounts?"

The shapeshifter slowly shook zir head.

"Your next best option is to join the semipermanent mob laying siege to the park and hope to someday blow a hole in the security walls," the cloudlet continued. "I don't suppose you brought something useful for that effort like high-powered lasers or chemical rocketry?"

"No, I didn't," the shapeshifter said. "I'm unarmed, as you could well have guessed by now."

"I'm making a point," the cloudlet said.

Suddenly, a loud, resounding boom rocked the elevator, and they felt the elevator's floor buckle upward underneath them. That particular boom sounded like a small explosion, as though something had destroyed the teleport pad that was bolted to the bottom of the elevator.

They each instinctively leapt forward out of the elevator, although Carissa kept her hand in the doorway, holding the doors open. She felt her ears pop as they adjusted to the warm St. Louis air.

"The enforcers have returned," the shapeshifter said.

"But we dumped them down the elevator shaft!" Carissa protested.

"Many Shai-Manak take forms that can fly," ze replied.

Then came a familiar rapid pounding sound, as though a flurry of giant fists were probing for a weakness in the floor of the elevator car. Carissa had the suspicion her cute little pistol was going to seem woefully inadequate in a moment.

The enforcers succeeded in ripping open a large hole in the

floor, and then a pair of giant claws gripped the edges of the hole and began struggling to pull the rest of a monstrous, demonic body up into the car. The menacing red eyes of the enforcer's lizard-like face locked on her in surprise.

"Going up, cloudlet!" Carissa shouted.

She pulled her hand out of the doorway, and the elevator doors were now clear to close.

The last Carissa saw of her beloved elevator was the demonic figure struggling to reach the doors to stop them from closing.

Then the elevator doors closed.

Then the elevator doors vanished completely from sight, leaving behind a rippling distortion in the air that persisted mere seconds before local reality reasserted itself. Now they had an unimpeded view down the length of a city street that was currently quiet and empty.

Carissa's last instruction meant the enforcers would be riding that elevator up for a long time unless they could sweet-talk the cloudlet into letting them off somewhere along the way.

She and the shapeshifter were silent for a long moment.

"I'm sorry you've lost your cloudlet friend," the shapeshifter said.

"Cloudlet knows how to find me when we get separated," Carissa replied. Then she turned to the shapeshifter, bitterness in her eyes, and said, "But I did have swank fucking headphones on that elevator."

▪   ▪   ▪

"So after we dropped the enforcers down an elevator shaft," Carissa said, working it out for herself out loud, "your theory is that they flew right back up the shaft and found us right when we stopped on a safe floor?"

"I think *theory* is a strong word," the shapeshifter replied.

"There could've been a dozen or a hundred elevators between us at that point," Carissa continued.

"Or zero," the shapeshifter pointed out.

"C'mon," Carissa protested.

"One of our specializations is probability spellcraft," the shapeshifter said and then fell silent, as though this was all the explanation that was needed.

"Uh-huh," Carissa said. "And forcing elevator doors open? Isn't that how you got into the elevator shaft in the first place? It's relevant because, look, the cloudlet's just going to keep taking them up no matter what they tell it to do. But they can just drop down through the hole they ripped in the elevator floor and they'll wind up right back here on this street—assuming they can pry open the doors from inside the elevator shaft. Can they do that? Is that one of your specializations?"

The shapeshifter had to admit, "They cannot repeat my method. But they are sufficiently incentivized to try other methods."

She debated ditching the shapeshifter altogether and heading off on her own. She could get by in a random America for a while. The enforcers wouldn't be looking for her.

But it felt like a waste of her elevator and all her belongings to just wander off without making sure the shapeshifter got to safety.

"We need to be inside Wild Massive before that happens," Carissa said. "Can you run?"

.　.　.

They cut over several streets in a zigzag fashion, through alleys and backyards, to get distance from the unmapped elevator location. St. Louis was a ghost town. They met no one along the way, saw no cars on the streets or people on the sidewalks, saw no lights in the houses and apartments.

"What happened here?" the shapeshifter asked.

"I don't know," Carissa replied. "Earth floors are all a little different."

"Why are there people shooting at the park?" the shapeshifter asked.

"Maybe it's really expensive to get in," she replied.

Carissa kept them walking at a brisk pace, unsettled by the silence of the streets, wary the enforcers might emerge on their trail at any moment.

"I presume you have a really good reason for defecting," she said.

The shapeshifter said nothing.

"I mean, you've fought off the Association for fifty years," she continued.

"I personally have done no such fighting."

"My point stands. Everyone I know is rooting for the Shai-Manak." Then she added, "The Association deserves the payback."

"For what, may I ask?"

"Are you serious?" she snapped.

The shapeshifter did not respond.

"Not everyone's got invincible sorcerers who can knock Fleet warships out of the sky like you," she said. "Not everyone lasts fifty years."

"Our people do not fight on anyone's behalf but our own. We do not consider revenge a principle worth pursuing."

"Then why fight them at all?"

"That is a question I have asked more than once," ze replied ruefully. "The Association is keen to find our home floor, but we could migrate to another. The Association is unwilling to accept magical power greater than its own, but we could teach them. The Association is unwilling to suffer an army above its borders that it can't understand, but we abandoned peace talks before they could bear fruit. We fight because our floor has been our home for thousands of years—why should we accept an inevitable invasion? It is . . . difficult to argue with such tribalism."

"So you're defecting to . . . what, teach your own people a lesson?"

Ze fell silent for so long that Carissa thought the conversation was over.

But then ze said, "We're about to cross a terrible line. I'm trying to save many lives." A whisper: "Someone has to try."

Carissa felt chilled and let silence finally fall.

As the park loomed larger ahead of them, they finally did start to see traffic—automobiles pulling off the nearest freeway, heading for the gigantic, well-defended parking lot. She could see buses running from the farthest edges of the parking lot up to the front gate.

"How are you planning on getting inside this park?" she said.

"I'm sure I'll think of something."

Carissa was pretty sure ze wasn't going to think of anything.

"Can't you just shapeshift into a bird and fly over the wall or something?" she asked.

"We don't all fly," the shapeshifter replied.

She sighed and said, "I'll buy us day passes."

"I don't expect I'll be able to repay you."

"It's okay, I steal all my money, anyway."

．　．　．

The Super park's border walls were only under attack in designated protest zones as determined by the city of St. Louis in negotiation with the park. Any attempts to attack the park outside those zones were met with sonic weapons that targeted the offenders with a deadly rendition of Helpless the Bunny's theme song—Helpless being Wild Massive's devious but lovable corporate mascot. Cars coming off the freeway could cruise right up to the front gates and gain admittance to the vast parking lot without fear of reprisal from the angry mobs.

Foot traffic coming from the city or from the commuter buses that dropped suburban guests off at the perimeter was steered along a path to the front gate, helped along by moving walkways to help cover the distance. They saw enormous signs warning them that no weapons of any size or class were allowed inside the park, and each guest would pass through a series of security scans to enforce this rule.

Carissa realized she'd have to ditch her pistol and knife. She sighed deeply as she found a trash can where she could surreptitiously dump the items. She'd never had occasion to fire the gun in self-defense, so maybe it wasn't such a big deal to lose it. And this was not the first time in her life she'd found herself on the run with no possessions but the clothes on her back (it was the third).

Well, to be fair—and thank god—she had her tablet tucked away in her pocket, along with half a pouch of first aid pills. The tablet was key to accessing her various guild accounts and finding her cloudlet again. The first aid pills—well, she just liked having them around. You could get them out of vending machines in a few secret locations scattered around the Building, but they were frequently sold out.

After twenty minutes in line, they were close enough to the front gate that they could observe a bit of the security operation from a distance. The list of potential hazards any guest could be carrying was extensive. They ran each individual through a series of increasingly intimidating scanning booths in order to root out shit like nano-assembled needle guns that you hid as a distributed subdermal swarm of nanites, or maybe you swallowed some exotic compound that lived in your gut and exploded when you later digested the right cola beverage, or maybe your eyes were equipped with invisible micron lasers that cut people apart without revealing your position, that kind of bullshit.

Let's say this weaponry you were carrying was legal where you came from. Might even be legal right here in St. Louis, America. It wasn't legal inside the park, and if you tried to get inside with any of it, the friendly and ruthless security apparatus of the Wild Massive corporation would be delighted to dissuade you of that notion. The front gate was manned exclusively by mercenaries who knew this shit backward and forward. You weren't scamming your way past these bruisers. They took the safety of their guests seriously at Wild Massive parks and resorts.

Sure, you could still try to kill someone with your bare hands if you wanted to, but they also had security inside, obviously.

"I don't like this," said the shapeshifter. "They're claiming they can read and store an individual's magical signature for surveillance purposes."

The signs called out a special procedure for "magic-users and magical entities." They used a lot of magic inside the park to pull off a wide range of illusions and special effects, so they couldn't just blanket the whole park with magic dampeners to keep the guests from spellcasting and call it a day. But they couldn't erase the spells from a wizard's brain for the duration of a visit, either, nor did they want to prohibit any supernatural beings from entering on the grounds that magic literally coursed through their veins or whatnot.

They solved that problem by—registration, apparently? Some kind of tagging system? You got a special ankle bracelet? And then—if you cast a hostile spell, a drone or something put a bullet in your skull? They weren't really explicit about the consequences of violating the "no magic inside the park" policy. Carissa could guess what was technically "allowed" per the law in St. Louis, but Wild Massive tended to carve out legal exceptions for its properties that allowed it to operate like an independent city-state.

"Look, all you need to do is get to the elevator," Carissa said. "Maybe someone will eventually be able to trace that you've been here, but so what? You'll be long gone before then."

That thought seemed to assuage the shapeshifter for the time being.

．　　．　　．

They were temporarily separated into two different lines after the shapeshifter acknowledged ze was a sorcerer. With bored efficiency, security subjected them to a variety of scans inside five or six weird-looking contraptions. Apparently, despite all the engineering prowess Wild Massive had at its disposal, they simply couldn't figure out how to do all these scans in a single booth. She sailed through the screenings without incident and was reunited with the shapeshifter a few minutes later. Ze seemed unperturbed about zir experience.

At the ticket booth, Carissa took the lead. She had a dozen different financial accounts tied to a variety of identities she could use for occasions like this, where some form of background check was likely at the point of sale. You didn't need an Association ID to earn and spend Association currency, so none of her alternate identities were Association citizens; you had to do business with someone like the Pirate King to get a fake Association ID, and that was out of her league. But these IDs she'd created and collected for herself were perfectly appropriate for the task of buying Wild Massive day passes without triggering the park's fraud defenses.

With passes in hand, they quickly made their way into the park proper, emerging into a central riverfront plaza at the base of the Arch.

Carissa was overwhelmed by the press of humanity in the plaza. And it was definitely humanity for the most part. The Earth floors were humanocentric, and America was always the worst about making sure other species felt like shit for even bothering to step off the elevator. Certainly, Wild Massive, a media empire with interests on countless floors of the Building, was a more enlightened corporation than its choice of location here might signify, but that didn't translate into designing its Earth rides with nonhuman accessibility in mind.

After living alone in her own elevator for so long, Carissa was unprepared for so much tangible excitement from such a large crowd, so she signaled for the shapeshifter to follow her away from the general masses, toward an open park bench where she could get a chance to catch her breath. She pulled out her tablet and connected to the park network, accessing maps of every park neighborhood.

Naturally, the mapped elevator was proudly highlighted; it would be easy to get to from here. Wild Massive had scored a true coup on this Earth floor by acquiring complete control of access to an elevator.

The mapped elevator location essentially functioned as another "front gate" experience for guests, with its own security screening operation, but with the disadvantage of being positioned awkwardly in the midst of the park. This made it a traffic choke point and a visual distraction that needed special accommodation.

They'd designed the park layout so that you could emerge from the elevator and easily transfer to a shuttle train that whisked you away to the park resort if you wanted to check into your room or, more likely, suite. Otherwise, you'd be diverted down a long footpath, winding onto the riverfront plaza at the base of the Arch to start your Wild Massive experience.

The rest of the park flowed around the elevator bank in clever ways so that the elevator itself was obscured from sight lines by trees or structures as you roamed the park proper. Once you got off the elevator and entered the park, you wouldn't accidentally be reminded of the elevator's existence until you were ready to leave.

But one thing was clear: you didn't just make a whimsical decision to ditch the park by jumping on the elevator. Reservations were a requirement. At the other entrances, they could design for throughput, but the immutable fact in this case was that only a single elevator would ever be open in this location at once. They'd installed an anchor station here, thankfully, so they could teleport new elevators through relatively quickly, but you were still facing annoying logistics if you needed to exit the park this way.

The earliest the shapeshifter could get a reservation was two hours from now. A small VIP line moved much quicker, but Carissa hadn't even considered paying the exorbitant price for VIP passes. Of course, she'd definitely paid enough that she planned to stay in the park after the shapeshifter was gone, to get a rare bit of leisurely enjoyment out of her investment.

The shapeshifter's frustration was palpable. Ze politely argued for a few minutes with the attendant at the entrance to the elevator pavilion, but the attendant stood firm. People probably tried to squeeze onto this elevator without a reservation on a semi-regular basis. They probably trained park employees in ways to calmly and firmly defuse tempers when working in this specific location.

Clearly defeated, the shapeshifter turned away from the pavilion, pondering options.

Zir eventual idea was to sit across from the pavilion at a bench and wait patiently until zir reservation time.

Carissa had no problem empathizing with someone who was on the run and in trouble. She didn't quite feel like letting the matter drop just yet.

"We have time to ride at least one ride in two hours," said Carissa. "Take your mind off things for a bit."

"I'm not looking to take my mind off anything," the shapeshifter replied.

"Fair," she replied. "You can keep worrying the whole time if you want. But I think you should keep moving. No sense in making yourself an obvious target sitting in front of the only way off this floor."

She wandered back to the pavilion and asked the attendant at the reservation booth what the best ride experience in the park was.

The attendant replied without hesitation, "You absolutely have to do the *Storm and Desire* ride. It's called *Rise of the Brilliant*."

Carissa's blood ran absolutely cold.

"I'm sorry, what did you just say?" she said.

"*Rise of the Brilliant*," the attendant repeated. "That's the name of the new *Storm and Desire* ride." The attendant misinterpreted Carissa's stunned look as bewilderment, perhaps, and said, "Don't worry, I hear it's still pretty great even if you're not caught up on *Storm and Desire*."

"I bet," Carissa said. "Thanks for the tip."

She drifted away from the pavilion and sat down heavily next to the shapeshifter, a slow sense of shock unfolding within her.

The shapeshifter noticed her apparent distress and quietly said, "Is something out of order?"

"Nope," Carissa replied. She might be far from the usual methods of Association surveillance, but she wasn't about to admit to a complete stranger that the "rise of the Brilliant" in reality had been followed rather quickly by the "complete annihilation of the Brilliant, except for a single survivor that no one knows about because if they did, she'd be dead, too."

. . .

Storm and Desire was one of the crown jewels of the Wild Massive media empire, an incredibly popular, long-running intermedia series. The trunk of the narrative was a planned series of twelve thematic arcs comprised of many episodes each, released over the course of almost two centuries by this point. The story unfolded primarily in virtual environments, which offered the fullest experience when it came to immersion. Some people had acquired machine interfaces and drug ports solely so they could take advantage of the full sensorium of data that the narrative production of *Storm and Desire* had to offer.

The overarching story of the *Storm and Desire* milieu was ostensibly an alternate history of the Association, as told from the perspective of Dimension Force, the small band of heroic Agents who were responsible for keeping it safe from extraordinary dangers. Crucially, Wild Massive was not incorporated within the Association, and most everyone understood perfectly well that the series regularly took all the liberties its creators felt were necessary to generate desired dramatic effects.

In fact, fan boards and trade pubs alike assumed that the Association even fed secret information to the producers to enhance certain story lines on occasion. If the Association was occasionally portrayed as morally gray, or individuals within it as outright corrupt, the overall halo effect was still positive. This was free PR, as far as the Association was concerned, and anyway, Wild

Massive's version of history was clearly more interesting to the public than the truth could ever be.

Dimension Force likely played along as well. The series presented the Agents of Dimension Force as flawed but mythical figures, played in the series by charismatic actors given top-notch dialogue, which neatly clouded the fact that Dimension Force in reality was a mercenary group whose primary client was the Association.

The *Storm and Desire* experience at Wild Massive Super was a marvel of physical and magical narrative engineering. Even the most jaded of park guests found themselves swept away by how convincing the "live action" experiences were compared to the virtual baseline. Experts on the fan boards suspected that psychotropic mists played an undue part in achieving such an immersive effect, but everyone agreed the ride environments were incredibly well designed and highly entertaining regardless. And the extra bits of storytelling you got during the ride experiences were considered canon, which held obvious appeal for many fans.

Carissa was conflicted about the whole series. She'd made it through about half of it and given up. Maybe these Agents were truly heroes; they were easy to admire and even like when you engaged with these stories from their points of view. But in reality, the Association controlled its interests with a ruthless and merciless efficiency, and she was certain Wild Massive would never accurately depict the full extent of the atrocities the Association had committed during its reign. In the stories, it was a bastion of hope in the face of a cruel and uncaring multiverse. In reality, it was as cruel and uncaring as you could get.

If you were an average citizen of the Association, you might live and breathe these stories. If you lived elsewhere in the Building, you might enjoy these stories as adventure-driven voyeurism into another way of life. But if you were the sole survivor of a genocide at the hands of the Association, as Carissa was, you'd likely have a more nuanced take on the merits of *Storm and Desire*.

▪   ▪   ▪

Carissa pulled out her tablet, began searching for plot summaries that could rapidly catch her up on *Storm and Desire*. To her dawning irritation and horror, she quickly learned that the series had only recently begun its eleventh arc out of twelve. It was focused on the series of events that led to the Association carpet-bombing her tribe, the Brilliant, out of existence. If they played it straight, this would be the first proper tragedy among the *Storm and Desire* arcs to date.

Oh, the audience didn't know that's where the eleventh arc was headed, of course. But Carissa knew, because she'd been an integral part of all of it.

And maddeningly, the series was positioning *people she knew* as principal antagonists in their version of events.

She pulled up photos and short video clips promoting the ride to get a taste of what to expect. *Rise of the Brilliant* was meant to showcase how mysterious and dangerous the Brilliant were, all from within the safe confines of a Wild Massive ride vehicle.

Her *brother* was one of the featured antagonists.

She wanted to act out in some preposterous fashion, but she'd also spent a long time burying that exact feeling, so instead, she sat in silence. The only indication that she was under strain was the slight tremble in her hand as she held the tablet in front of her and stared straight through it.

Finally, a realization locked into focus in her mind. She stood up, steeling herself to join the flow of foot traffic in front of her.

"I hope the rest of your defection goes well," she said.

"Thank you for keeping me alive," the shapeshifter replied.

"Don't mention it," she replied. "Literally—pretend you never met me."

She wandered away from the elevator pavilion, heading deeper into the park, toward *Rise of the Brilliant*.

She owed it to her people to understand how they were being "memorialized" by the culture at large.

And she missed her brother too much to skip an opportunity to see him again—even a totally fucked-up opportunity like this one was shaping up to be.

Explorers Guild Report: The Shai-Manak
By Nicholas Solitude

A thrilling milestone in the regular work of the Explorers Guild is opening elevator doors on floors that have, to our eyes, never been documented before. The definition of a "safe floor" is constantly reevaluated and reconsidered, based on who among us bears which specializations and what biology. We stage our appearances on new floors as carefully as we can possibly manage, scouting early to understand our likely impact, developing individualized scripts for softening or rationalizing our appearance in a humane way. We utilize skillful illusion and dexterous improvisation to survive long enough for meaningful dialogue to begin in some cases and perhaps progress to the point where we might truly make new friends—new allies—inside this Building.

But in all our travels, we found no parallel guild like ours, one that might be working its way down from the top floors, perhaps, as we rise from the ground floors. Consequently, we must accept that all our documented encounters up to this point might someday be categorized as inherently intrusive, selfish even, despite our fervent passion for peaceful coexistence and cooperation as we all attempted to survive our blind and merciless reality.

Then we met the Shai-Manak.

The cloudlets alerted us to their presence after they'd already systematically discovered all four unmapped elevator locations on their floor. This unprecedented feat set them loose into the elevator shafts and onto nearby floors with no patronizing scripts or first contact rituals to blunt the harsh truth that their entire world as they knew it was merely one slice of an infinite tower, a rain forest paradise in a deeply unsettling position in time and space.

By the time we met them, their culture had undergone a seismic shift—their creation myths efficiently jettisoned, their competing spiritual systems suddenly aligned and pivoted toward their most martial affects. They were clearly an advanced civilization, despite their small population; capable of sorcery unlike any the Guild had ever witnessed in person; biologically uncanny in their ability to mimic other life-forms completely; living life spans of multiple thousands of years.

For a luxurious stretch of time, the Shai-Manak welcomed us on their home floor, recognized us as compatriots, and allowed us to set up small, semipermanent base camps for ranging out from that region. Many among them took the opportunity to join us on expeditions farther up the Building above their floor. I still visit friends on that floor for special occasions or simple visits as the opportunity permits.

Like every culture we've met, they perfectly speak and write the formal Building Modern language. Most of them are also fluent in one of two constructed languages they devised for use in spiritual practices. The term *Shai-Manak* is shared between these two languages. It's designed to shift meaning without warning based on context, but as I traveled among them, the definitions I heard most frequently at first were "God-People" or "God-Within," which seemed to drift even during my limited time among them to "Lost-People" or "Lost-Within."

Imagine identifying your kind as the gentle gods of your peaceful realm, only to have that identity stolen away as the doors of a Building elevator suddenly slide open in front of you. The Guild's way seeks to distribute and diffuse that shock over time; but the Shai-Manak absorbed it all at once, and they did so alone.

By their request, we do not log their floor number in our report.

.　　.　　.

You could argue this whole mess actually started when a Shai-Manak squadron of combat sorcerers attacked a brand-new Wild Massive theme park that was still under construction.

Theme parks are not traditionally known to be military targets, but this was the first Wild Massive property ever established on an Association-controlled floor. When complete, it would dwarf the size of the Super park by some ridiculous margin, so much so that within Wild Massive corporate, this new park was referred to as Wild Mega. They'd hollowed out an entire floor for it, installed a highly customized pocket dimension inside the floor to exacting Wild Massive engineering standards, opened a new hangar bay in the side of the Building for construction crews to airlift specialized printers and equipment onto the floor, the works.

Soon Association citizens would be able to experience the thrill of a Wild Massive park—arguably, the best Wild Massive park—without ever leaving their own territory, without ever facing the uncertainty that always accompanied travel above the borderline.

Shai-Manak spies watched the proceedings with fascination. Apparently, the Association didn't expect this hangar bay to remain open long enough to warrant installing automated defenses of any significance—including the usual magical defenses against scrying you might expect to protect a high-value target. Instead they were just scheduling a few extra flybys from the patrol ships that roamed Association airspace outside the Building, banking on the notion that an unfinished theme park was an unlikely target for pirates and thieves.

．　．　．

The plan came from Rindasy, second-in-command of the Shai-Manak's spy apparatus. Rindasy led the effort to identify Fleet hangar bays among the vast network of military and civilian hangar bays maintained by the Association, and the new hangar bay caught zir attention.

Construction on the Wild Mega park seemed to happen incredibly fast, with minimal participation on the floor itself from organic life; nanoswarms and robots were assembling the whole shebang with unnerving levels of precision. They'd almost certainly seal the hangar bay shut when construction was complete.

Rindasy argued they were on the verge of losing a major opportunity if they didn't mobilize. A major branch of Shai-Manak engineering at the time was dedicated to stealing and reverse engineering Association technology, and the contents of that floor right now represented a potential jackpot if they could get away with a successful incursion.

Specifically, the Association had deployed "reality emitters" to establish and maintain the pocket dimension; if they could get brief physical access to study one, they'd likely be able to replicate its effects with magic. The Association had installed brand-new teleport pads and anchor stations on the floor, which they'd want to steal outright; the Association could revoke these devices' access to the teleport relay network, but the Shai-Manak were working on establishing their own. And Wild Massive had certainly deposited other gear on the floor they might want: printers, robotics, networking, whatever, they'd improvise on that front.

"I estimate it'll take us roughly three days to get everything we want off the floor or properly cataloged," Rindasy said, wrapping up zir proposal to the Radiant Council and the assorted department leads who had joined this session.

Assorted murmurs of concern greeted that assertion.

"What's the worst they can do in three days?" Rindasy countered. "We seal the hangar bay shut behind us. We barricade the elevators and disconnect the teleport pads. At that point, they'll likely try dropping warships right onto the floor, but look, we can smack their warships around at close quarters for a lot longer than three days. I believe we can manage the entire mission with ten of us."

Rindasy exchanged a glance with Andasir, who was the acting head of the diplomatic corps. Andasir was the sole pacifist on the Council, probably a frustrating role to play when the other two councilors were avidly seeking any advantage over their proclaimed nemesis, the Association. Sure enough, Andasir looked rather displeased, but ze also didn't like it when Rindasy volunteered for missions like these, either. That was a less professional concern to carry, but Andasir carried it nonetheless.

"Ten of you," repeated Sellia, head of intelligence and Rindasy's mentor. "Holding the entire floor for three days."

"Give or take," Rindasy said, allowing zirself to enjoy a hint of earned bravado. Sellia nodded. Rindasy could tell Sellia was on board.

The deciding vote would be Kalavir, military leader of the Shai-Manak and de facto head of the Council. Ever since the Explorers Guild originally set up a semipermanent camp on their floor (long since abandoned by now), the human form was in fashion among most Shai-Manak and was by far the most prevalent form across the population of the Building.

Kalavir preferred the form of a massive bipedal bearlike creature. "Take one hundred," Kalavir growled, "and hold the floor for ten days."

At that time, the entire Shai-Manak population was said to number just one thousand souls.

Suddenly, Rindasy's clever tactical raid was now a major military operation. Kalavir appointed zir own second, a sharp individual named Eriv, to act as Rindasy's lieutenant and help narrow down the many volunteers. They were given access to the weapons research lab and its full arsenal. Kalavir intended this to be a show of force unlike any they'd provided before. Rindasy's squadrons had never carried armaments on previous raids; hadn't been necessary.

Only later would Rindasy have a chance to connect the dots— they were coming up on the fiftieth anniversary of their first contact with the Association. Fifty years since the third member of the Radiant Council, the ambassador Gresij, descended to Association territory and was taken captive—the only captive the Association would ever take, as it turned out. On the eve of such an anniversary, Kalavir was ready to stop pretending any diplomatic solutions remained on the table.

A move like this was designed to provoke an unusual amount of hostility, to test how much firepower the Association had been holding in reserve, and to warn the Association that the Shai-Manak had revealed only a small fraction of their true potential for damage as well.

As Rindasy rushed to get zir squadron in the air, Andasir made a point of finding zir before ze left, as ze was evaluating weaponry to take on the mission. The moment seemed awkward to both of them.

"I suppose you're here to scold me," Rindasy said. "I didn't anticipate Kalavir's escalation."

"The time to scold you, if there ever was one, is long past," Andasir replied. "I've no illusion the Council will ever share my values, and I'm at peace with that. I'm here to say—I'm proud of you."

Rindasy stopped sorting through magical swords and unnatural guns to look Andasir in the eyes.

"Don't look so surprised," Andasir said, smiling. "I'm always proud of you, but this . . . it's a rare window you've discovered, and you move with no hesitation to exploit it."

"I thought you hated what I do," Rindasy said softly.

"Then it's my shame for letting you believe that. If our people must fight—as apparently we must—we could choose no wiser than to have you among our leaders. What I do hate"—ze took Rindasy's hand—"is saying goodbye and never knowing if today is the day ill fate finally arrives for you."

"Not going to happen," Rindasy replied. "I have to keep my peaceful dragon safe."

Andasir snickered and said, "I'm hardly a dragon. Small lizard, maybe."

They embraced for a long moment before Rindasy's new lieutenant, Eriv, came to request zir attention for an inspection.

"Go," Andasir told zir, "and make it count."

.   .   .

Rindasy hadn't always been a spy. Prior to zir life in espionage, ze'd been one of the foremost creators of magical artifacts the Shai-Manak had ever produced. That's how ze'd grown close to Andasir, actually. Andasir had been one of the assistants who'd helped Rindasy craft zir final (for the time being) masterpiece, an artifact that came to be known as the Key of Rindasy.

For seven days, Rindasy and zir nine assistants labored in ritual circles and in forges and in laboratories, crafting components and imbuing them with thaumaturgical spark. Rindasy's intricate vision of how the artifact should work was considered a once-in-a-lifetime innovation in spellcraft by the scholars who were privy to its design.

One of Rindasy's proudest moments was presenting the Key to Nicholas Solitude and the Explorers Guild as a gift on the day the guild finally picked up camp and left the Shai-Manak floor for good. It was a token of appreciation for the deep trove of knowledge about the Building and the Association that the Explorers Guild had provided them in the years they camped alongside the Shai-Manak.

"It can dispel illusions that mislead you and illuminate the true path if you're lost," Rindasy told Nicholas. "It can open any lock that bars your way and break any chain that tethers you in place. We used the Key to find the four elevators on our floor."

And Nicholas Solitude, the famous spacetime traveler, said, "I'm honored beyond words," which was a Shai-Manak saying that Nicholas had absorbed during his stay.

Rindasy had traveled with the Explorers Guild on several occasions, and while no one ever grew particularly close to Nicholas, ze nevertheless had felt a rapport with him. As ze taught him how to operate the Key, ze realized ze'd miss the presence of the

Explorers Guild, and the sense that with the Guild nearby, you never knew where you might find yourself next.

After the Guild departed, Rindasy felt a hollowness that hadn't been there before, a need to forge a new path for zirself beyond capturing sorcery in material form for others to admire. Zir few expeditions with the Guild had felt like adventures, and now more than ever, ze missed that sense of adventure.

As hostilities heated up with the Association, many Shai-Manak sorcerers felt compelled to serve in the effort to resist. Rindasy made it known ze wished to be recruited, and soon enough, adventure beckoned once again.

Rindasy realized early on ze had an aptitude and an appetite for learning tradecraft from Sellia. Ze rose quickly through the ranks of Sellia's group, earning Sellia's complete trust along the way.

That's how, decades later, Rindasy found zirself preparing to invade a theme park.

. . .

You couldn't simply ride the elevators down into Association territory, of course.

The cloudlets respected the border at floor 50,000 and wouldn't let you pass without proper Association ID, which none of these sorcerers happened to possess. They would need to fly—well, most of it would be controlled falling, but there'd be some flying right at the end of the trip.

Getting sorcerers outside of the Building was tricky when your enemies controlled the lobby and all the known hangar bays. The Building's exterior was comprised of long, unbroken stripes of black glass—not unbreakable, mind you, but broken windows were often immediate targets for Facilities drones at minimum, or Fleet ships at worst. When you broke windows to get out of the Building, you risked painting a target on that floor as a location that you'd explored, and if you were spotted breaking windows across too many floors, you started to paint a whole region of the Building where someone might expect to find you.

That would be a crucial step in the hunt for the Shai-Manak's base of operations.

That was the Association's primary goal with regard to the Shai-Manak. The Association's policy of nonintervention in the affairs of floors above its border carved out an exemption for direct threats. The Shai-Manak, perhaps naively, chose to demonstrate a sliver of their sorcery during peace negotiations, and the Association surreptitiously monitored innate Shai-Manak thaumaturgical levels throughout the talks as well, which exceeded by far what the Association's arcane masters could summon. The threat was immediately clear to some in Parliament.

But the cloudlets weren't talking or taking visitors to the Shai-Manak home floor. The Explorers Guild escaped so far up the Building that they may as well have turned invisible to the Association, rather than give up the location. And Gresij, the captured Shai-Manak ambassador, never divulged it.

So Rindasy and zir spies chose empty floors all over the Building to break windows for making sorties and quickly covered their tracks with sorcery. These broken windows were so well disguised by Shai-Manak sorcery that the Association rarely noticed them, allowing Rindasy to lead sorties out from these positions down into Association airspace. Ze was reasonably confident that dropping a hundred people out one of these windows was no more noticeable than dropping the usual two or three people. No one on the ground had a chance of visually detecting them before they reached their destination. And all it took was minor probability spellcraft to throw off any Fleet sensors that might happen to pick them up in a lucky sweep on their way down.

Their descent was uneventful but exhilarating all the same. Many inhabitants of the Building never saw the outside, and certainly not like this. Conceptually, it was never clearer how deeply artificial their entire situation was than when they fell thousands of floors underneath a cloudless orange sky, with flat desert below them stretching in every direction to the horizon. As tall as the

Building was, it never rose above a survivable atmosphere; if this was a planet, no one had ever found a boundary into "outer space." Scouting missions had proved that if you traveled far enough in any direction away from the Building across the desert, you'd eventually wind up heading back to the Building without ever turning around.

As they fell, dark concentric circles on the immediate desert floor around the Building came into view. These were rings of semipermanent campsites, where asylum-seekers and aspiring immigrants to the Association awaited their turns for processing. This area was colloquially referred to as "the parking lot." Around the perimeter of the parking lot, a series of tall white spires housed beacons, broadcasting the location of the Building to anyone who might possess the skill or technology to decode the messages.

High above the parking lot, but still well below the descending Shai-Manak, interdimensional transport ships and Fleet vessels jumped into the airspace around the Building and quickly joined complex air traffic patterns, which steered them toward hangar bays scattered all over the sides of the Building. The Association prohibited any vessel, even Fleet, from jumping directly into the Building, and enforced this ban with matter dispersers installed on every documented floor under its border. Above the border, it was a different story. The Association didn't build hangar bays up there, so if you wanted into the Building and didn't want to travel through the Association's floors to get wherever you were going, you jumped your ship onto a floor above the border that you knew particularly well.

And if you wanted *out* of the Building for similar reasons, you arranged passage in a ship that was leaving, or you were a Shai-Manak and you threw yourself out a broken window.

Their arrival in the hangar bay went unnoticed and uncontested. A few stray android workers were temporarily held prisoner and then released via the elevators, and no bioworkers ever occupied the floor to begin with.

Surveillance dust on the floor was magically suppressed. The arcane barrier they established at the hangar opening would last all ten days with this many sorcerers on standby to replenish it; the Association's wizards lagged far behind Shai-Manak magical proficiency, and they would never defeat the barrier in only ten days. The elevators were properly barricaded, and all the teleport pads on the floor were disconnected from the relay network. Multiple research and engineering teams got to work on various projects throughout the floor.

That left roughly sixty combat sorcerers to stand watch and prepare for the inevitable backlash from the Association.

There was one major avenue onto the floor they couldn't defend against: a ship with an interdimensional jump drive could simply drop right into their little pocket dimension, if the pilot was good enough. They could drop multiple warships, in fact, and bombard the entire floor, if they didn't care about preserving the actual park. Or maybe they'd simply drop in a hundred shuttles with battalions of Security officers prepared for heavy close-quarters combat.

Rindasy was itching for it.

.   .   .

Twelve hours later, the Association deposited a single armored shuttle into their midst, landing it perfectly in an empty town square in the center of the park and triggering the Shai-Manak alarm system.

Several unexpected things happened in short order.

The shuttle's arrival was accompanied by what seemed at first like a sonic attack. A piercing high-pitched tone filled the entire floor at a punishing level of intensity. Those Shai-Manak closest to the shuttle at the time, or those moving toward it, found themselves almost instantly disoriented.

A ramp came down at the back of the shuttle, and four humans wearing the crisp black one-piece uniforms of the Association's Security division stepped into view. Their faces were mostly expressionless as they took in the surreal scene around them of

Shai-Manak sorcerers in a variety of shapes and forms starting to collapse in agony against a backdrop of half-built roller coasters and gift shops.

Rindasy was well within the attack radius, and the sonic attack got significantly worse once these humans appeared—at which point ze realized the attack wasn't sonic at all. Ze wasn't *hearing* that painful attack, ze was simply *feeling* it ricochet around inside zir mind, clobbering zir ability to concentrate on spellcasting. Ze realized ze couldn't even shapeshift in the midst of this attack. Ze'd never encountered such a deeply psychic attack before; they didn't train against this vector type.

Then a fifth figure appeared near the top of the ramp, emerging from the shuttle without hesitation. She was a short humanoid woman with bronze skin and clipped black hair, wearing a silver-tinged variation on the base black Security officer uniform.

Rindasy instantly recognized this woman, had been warned specifically to avoid her and her peers if at all possible, and yet here she was, marching into this situation as though she were fully in charge of it.

This woman was Agent Anjette, a founding member of Dimension Force, the Agents who patrolled the Building according to their own whims and intervened whenever they saw fit. Rindasy knew each of their profiles well, memorizing their strengths and trying to imagine their potential weaknesses.

Unlike androids and other self-aware constructs, whose origins could be clearly traced through manufacturing processes of some kind, Anjette was said to have been carved from a sliver of a planet-size block of computronium that had never been located. As an entity comprised entirely of programmable matter, she'd inherited an impressive set of traits in her original design. She was immune to psychic effects and manipulations of the mind, could not be swayed by the charms, illusions, and glamours of magic, could not be hypnotized or mesmerized in any way. She was also physically indestructible, impervious to every known weapon class, and showed no signs of even possessing pain receptors. And she was incredibly strong, far beyond what her modest height and build might indicate.

Famously, she carried no weaponry, preferring a pugilistic style of combat when negotiation failed her.

Her collection of skills and defenses currently seemed unnecessary, given that none of the Shai-Manak were capable of getting up off the ground to mount an attack.

For all Rindasy knew, in fact, everyone on the entire floor was caught in the Association's attack. Ze could see that those closest to the shuttle were already unconscious or perhaps worse.

And this was likely just an opening salvo, a test of their strength.

Fair enough. Rindasy still possessed enough willpower to draw the experimental "aimless" probability pistol ze'd borrowed from the weapons research lab, point it in the general direction of the shuttle, and open fire.

The sudden loud burst of good old-fashioned, heavily enchanted projectile fire was a welcome respite from the phantom sound of the psychic attack. It was unethical to create fully sentient weapons, of course, but this ammunition had attained a particular glee about its purpose, judging by its willingness to accept the merest suggestion of accurate aim as a solid instruction for perpetrating explosive malice on a victim.

Anjette shrugged off the barrage, of course, but her four companions were not equally indestructible. The attack dissipated as their bodies hit the ground. Anjette tracked the source of fire instantly, locking eyes with Rindasy for a brief moment before spinning and leaping back toward the interior of the shuttle. By that point, a dozen other sorcerers at the periphery were in the game and firing off magical attacks that quickly pulverized the shuttle into a glorious mess of melted wreckage, all of it somehow wrapped around Anjette.

"Bind her!" Rindasy shouted, realizing Anjette was already starting to rise to her feet. The sorcerers closest to her caught on, and quickly three or four of them together worked to lash Anjette in place. Magic that might affect her psychologically would bounce off and you couldn't inflict pain on her or cause physical damage, but Rindasy had long imagined you could probably pin her down if you could beat her strength. Rindasy was already looking for large, heavy structures in the environment to yank free and drop on her if these binding spells didn't work.

They spent several minutes crafting an interlocking binding comprised of multiple individual spells. Throughout the process, Anjette struggled briefly at first, then seemingly became resigned to her fate and was eerily still. Eventually, she was plastered to the floor, smothered in an invisible spiderweb of incredible tensile strength. The "keys" to these bindings—magical passphrases—were all transferred to Rindasy. The bindings could only be released if Rindasy zirself used all the keys in succession within line of sight of Anjette.

In the silence that followed, Eriv appeared next to Rindasy and said quietly, "Now what?"

. . .

The engineers powered up an artifact called the Shimmering Whisper, a fusion of arcane gems into a small, imperfect orb that facilitated real-time directional communication with the Radiant Council. Association wizards had never detected this artifact's signals; the artifact blasted curses at anyone who tried to intercept the signals, a feature that was tested in a Shai-Manak laboratory but had never been triggered in the field. If a wizard somehow managed to survive the curses, they'd still have the problem of how to capture the signals for study and then crack a few layers of sorcerous obfuscation. All in all—a useful artifact to have around when you were this far from home.

The artifact worked by projecting imagery in the mind's eye of every person within a short range, crude low-resolution avatars of sorts that were recognizable enough to feel like you were in the same room, if perhaps on distant opposite ends of it. Rindasy felt like ze could feel the apprehension radiating from Andasir, but perhaps that was just a trick of the illusion.

After bringing the Council up to speed, the question of "Now what?" became the center of attention.

"Andasir, how long before the rest of Dimension Force comes looking for her?" Sellia asked.

"That depends. If they decide to send all the Agents at once, it could take time to summon them together," Andasir said. "But if any Agents happen to be relatively close, we could see a response at any moment."

"We captured one Agent already," Kalavir said. "I imagine we could handle their response."

"If it were just Dimension Force arriving on a rescue mission, I might agree with you. But the attackers that accompanied Anjette's arrival . . ."

"We barely survived them," Rindasy said. "I don't understand how Association wizardry advanced to this level without our noticing."

"You described it as a psychic attack," Sellia said. "The term the Association uses is *psionic*. And the only culture the Association ever faced with psionic powers was the Brilliant."

The implications unfolded quickly in Rindasy's mind. If the Association quietly kept Brilliant prisoners alive, why would they spend four of them on a potential suicide run against the Shai-Manak? Simple—those likely weren't actual Brilliant prisoners they'd faced.

"I think that was a weapons test," Rindasy said. "They can do that again, and in greater numbers next time."

"We've made our point," Andasir said. "Perhaps we should pull our people out."

"No, we will continue to make our point," Kalavir said. "Eriv, can your engineers shield against psionic attacks?"

Eriv said, "I don't know. But we have access to their thaumic grid from here. Unregulated—we have literal taps on their conduits. We could use that to light up some very aggressive counterattacks."

"Which Agent Anjette will no doubt survive," Andasir said. "As long as we hold her captive, we'll have the complete attention of Dimension Force on us. Holding off psionics and Dimension Force simultaneously . . ."

"We can take Dimension Force out of the equation by sending Anjette back," Rindasy said, a plan forming quickly as ze spoke. "Except it won't be her. I can perform the soul-stealing ritual to assume her identity. That'll give me free rein of the Building with limited supervision, privileged network access, status, and credibility . . . if I act now, I can say I escaped custody and prevent Dimension Force from ever mobilizing. And then once I'm inside the Association, I can figure out how they pulled off this psionic attack and find out if there are defenses, or maybe even disrupt their program altogether."

The plan was audacious. But the Shai-Manak had never held such a high-value prisoner before. The opportunity seemed clear to Rindasy.

Andasir couldn't disguise zir dismay at the idea as ze said, "You can't perform that ritual in a combat zone."

"Bring the Agent back here for the ritual," Kalavir said.

"You'd risk letting an Agent of Dimension Force discover the location of our floor by literally bringing her here?" Andasir said incredulously. "If she escapes—"

"If she could escape, she'd have done it already," Rindasy said. "Her mind is fast—she's run every scenario by now and knows she's not getting away. I'm the only person with the keys to her bindings, and I'll soon be out of her reach."

"So we keep her prisoner *forever*?" Andasir asked.

"No," Sellia said. "We trade her for Gresij when the time is right."

Andasir fell silent at that. The opportunity to rescue zir mentor hadn't occurred to zir, but the logic made sudden sense.

"And we study her in a weapons lab until then," Kalavir said. "Bring her here. We'll worry about releasing her when that day arrives."

Storm and Desire became a pop culture phenomenon by presenting the Association's history as an epic adventure, rewarding you in the process with a broad understanding of how history had unfolded since nearly the dawn of time.

The Association did not present a unified news source, and its historians were not publishing for the general public. Most people didn't care. You had enough on your plate just keeping track of your own local feeds, maybe monitoring a few floors in your region of the Building, and then maybe some super-top-level Parliamentary stuff every now and again. The everyday diplomacy conducted by the Association was largely invisible to you. You trusted the Association was keeping you safe from the most dangerous horrors of reality, and you didn't actually need or want a granular feed of which specific horrors were on the docket each day.

Inside the Building, these horrors might emerge anytime elevator doors opened on an undocumented floor. In the early days, undocumented floors under the Association's border were frequently explored in an almost cavalier fashion. Then one exploration team opened an elevator into a pocket dimension that had been totally consumed by a vast evil consciousness, which quickly escaped into the Building at large and subsumed the lives of over thirty billion people across approximately 425 floors before Security found a way to poison it.

Since then, the Association operated under a strict policy of nonintervention. No admittance was allowed to undocumented floors. If the inhabitants of an undocumented floor found their way into the Building at large, any effort to contain them was fair game until diplomacy was possible. The Association had only managed to properly document around four thousand floors of the fifty thousand it theoretically policed when the policy of nonintervention was implemented, so new horrors were always a potential threat.

Outside the Building, Fleet patrolled for similar horrors that might emerge out of the vast multiverse. You might consider that an absolutely futile and thankless task, but Fleet Admiral Allon Slab was himself a considerable menace. Beacons around the exterior of the Building welcomed travelers, but they had to get past Admiral Slab's Fleet first, and many failed that task. And when a force too powerful to hold off made its way to the Building, Admiral Slab was a potent negotiator. When a planetary hive mind calling itself Engine of Creation responded to the beacons, bringing thirty entire worlds in tow that it had captured and absorbed into the hive, Admiral Slab only needed to annihilate one of the enslaved worlds and all its inhabitants before reaching a truce.

Fleet's activities were completely invisible to the average citizen of the Association.

Then *Storm and Desire* came along and changed the equation. Its creative brain trust was eerily familiar with the Association and its history. And choosing Dimension Force as the heroes of the narrative was a masterstroke, given the generally heroic nature of the Agents' work. *Storm and Desire* was its own unstoppable phenomenon now, and the creative brain trust was determined to address major events in Association history head-on—including the fall of the Brilliant. It was one thing to use tough tactics to fight off vast evil or powerful threats, but another thing altogether to commit genocide against a small tribe of humans on an Earth floor whose only crime was existing. Wild Massive corporate absorbed several rounds of increasingly frantic advance feedback from the Association diplomatic corps about the damage their image could accrue if *Storm and Desire* accurately portrayed the full saga of the Brilliant. With genocide looming in the story line, the Association realized full well they never should've allowed Wild Massive to assume the role of independent chronicler of its history.

Vague threats were issued, with varying degrees of supposed teeth behind them, but Wild Massive was not an Association corporation subject to its rule of law and was not a member of any trade association that bound it to Association dictates.

Meanwhile, the Wild Massive creative brain trust knew perfectly well that their version of events would become the truth in popular imagination, and they took that responsibility quite seriously.

Yes, they would take the same number of liberties they always did with a given arc to make it more dramatic. But in the end, this was a bleak period in Association history, and glossing over the outcome would do no one any favors. They were determined to tell this story and hopefully teach Parliament a lesson in the process.

Storm and Desire: Rise of the Brilliant, the Wild Massive ride experience, was situated quite early in the eleventh arc, when the Association had barely scratched the surface of understanding the Brilliant. Subsequent story lines would eventually serve to illuminate the Brilliant and paint their struggle for recognition in a sympathetic light to deepen the tragedy of the betrayal that was coming for them.

But at this early point in the story, the Brilliant were frightening and unknown to the audience, and the ride was designed to be an extension of that context.

. . .

Carissa kept her cool as she slowly approached the *Storm and Desire* ride. You couldn't really miss it, even from blocks away. The façade of the ride entrance was designed to resemble the exterior of the Building itself, towering above all it surveyed, easily taller than the Arch on the waterfront. This imitation Building seemed to rise hundreds of floors above the streets of the park, disappearing into the clouds above St. Louis. Long unbroken columns of opaque black glass seemed to cover the surface of the façade as far up as the eye could see. Its height had to be an illusion, of course. The façade likely only rose a couple physical stories and then holographic projection or magical illusion completed the rest of the picture, but the effect was impressive all the same.

Carissa had never actually been outside the Building, but thanks to media depictions, this view of it was iconic.

Peering up the side of this fake Building, though, was dizzying for unexpected reasons. She found herself slipping into a near daze pondering the extent of the illusion that the sky itself represented. Outer space was real on Earth floors. You could die there very easily. You had no reason to disbelieve satellites or probes that sent back data from the edges of the galaxy or whatever. But all of it was still contained within a single floor as far as the various Building indices were concerned.

The existence of outer space as a real thing within a floor of the Building represented to her a vast power squandered on a pointless enterprise. It made her despondent when she first understood the reality of it. She felt like that much literal emptiness was too on the nose. Over time, she learned that Earth floors were not unique in this regard; other cultures had faced the dissolution of their cosmologies as well. But she could only have her personal illusions about the natural order of existence punctured once to such devastating effect, and she'd been living on an Earth floor when it happened.

As she neared the front of the line, she realized that people weren't proceeding into the Building on foot. To her surprise, the line terminated at a teleport pad. Same for the VIP line to her right. To get into the ride proper, you climbed up a few stairs to a circular white platform that was big enough for a typical party of humans to fit comfortably, and then with a flash, you were sent inside. Clearly not stagecraft—this was the real deal.

She wondered if Wild Massive had independently invented a teleportation network, or licensed it from the Association, or *stolen* it from the Association . . . and then it was her turn.

An operator stood next to the teleport pad, holding a small tablet and wearing a park attendant uniform: white Wild Massive T-shirt featuring the smiling mug of the corporate mascot,

Helpless the Bunny, and khaki shorts. As she climbed up the stairs onto the platform, the operator said, "Welcome to *Storm and Desire: Rise of the Brilliant.* Teleportation is perfectly safe. Enjoy your ride experience."

The operator swiped in an app on the tablet to activate the teleport.

The actual experience of a teleport was usually unremarkable for Carissa, since she was always inside an elevator when it occurred; you could literally blink and miss it. The difference here, though, was the fundamentally jarring sensation of seeing your entire surroundings *change* in a split second.

Now she was standing on a teleport pad situated within a full-size replica of the Building lobby. She was briefly dizzy, but she quickly recovered her composure and stepped down off the pad as an attendant motioned for her to keep moving. She joined a small group of guests who had teleported ahead of her and waited for further direction.

The lobby was incredibly impressive, extending quite far in any direction. Straight across the lobby from her was a long, winding line consisting of more unique species than she could ever hope to recognize or even count; the primary functions of the Building lobby were immigration processing and admitting tourists to the Building. These people all had to be holographic projections or magical illusions. Actually, there might be a row of animatronic figures blended into the picture up front, capable of subtle movements, to provide even greater fidelity to the overall illusion; androids wouldn't sit still for that kind of work, but good old-fashioned robots would be perfect. Or for all she knew, the entire image of the crowd was being projected straight into her eyes or beamed directly into her brain somehow. She had to admit she wasn't current on the latest entertainment technology.

She counted at least eight of the Association's distinctive information kiosks stationed on the lobby floor, comprising two rows of four in front of them. These looked like real physical kiosks, not projections or illusions; whether they were fabricated by Wild Massive or real Association kiosks would be difficult for her to discern. As she glanced to either side, she spotted replicas of two of the four ground-floor elevator banks—either Left and Right, or Up and Down—although here they were irregularly shaped, much wider for some unknown reason than they were in actuality.

Once her group accumulated ten guests, a man began to address them all, wearing the crisp uniform of an Association representative: a blue jumpsuit with a silver diamond badge affixed to it, and a matching blue beret. Association fashion encouraged a range of experimentation with skin color; this individual had chosen maroon.

"Hi, everyone. I'm Larun, I'm a human male, originally from floor 9,052—home of the Dunes of Ardalay. Maybe you've heard of the really big dunes?" the man said. "Anyway, I'll be your tour guide today. Okay, quick check, is anyone still waiting for someone else to come through the teleport pad and join you? No? Perfect. So I'm going to ask you to stick together as a group, and follow me over to kiosk number one, which is the farthest kiosk down on this row here, that's where we're headed, got that? The kiosk will provide you with some basic orientation about your visit to the Building today, and then we'll send you on your way!"

He led the group across the floor to the kiosk he'd pointed out. It was comprised of a tall, thin metal column topped off by a crystal that glowed with bright blue light. This silver column was affixed to the back edge of a round platform that was similar to the teleport pad in size; it lit up with a white glow from underneath its opaque surface as they approached. The column hissed suddenly and then seemingly sprayed a humanoid figure into existence on top of the round platform—this would be a holographic representation of the kiosk's onboard AI. Its features were pearlescent and smooth and radiant, giving off an angelic impression, too perfect to be human, and it wore the same Association uniform that Larun was wearing, with silver hair tucked under its beret. The real kiosks were interactive; this one might simply be a recording.

"Welcome to the home of the United Association of Interdimensional Travelers!" the kiosk said. "Let me pull up your tour itinerary."

The entire group of guests was scanned by some kind of cosmetic laser effect emanating from the metal column, and then each of their faces briefly appeared in a floating image grid in midair in front of the kiosk hologram.

"Ah yes. Perfect," the kiosk said, swiping the photo images away. A cross section of the Building's bottom ten floors appeared, and various areas of the cross section lit up as the kiosk spoke, starting with the second floor. "The highlights of your tour today include visiting the core elevator maintenance workshop on floor 2, inspecting vessels docked in the Fleet hangar bay on floor 10, and enjoying a snack or a drink while taking in the view from our deluxe observation deck on floor 10,000.

"During the tour, feel free to capture recordings of any kind, but be aware that your connection to the network will be disabled until you reach the observation deck, to avoid any undue interference with critical protocols. If at any time you feel your personal safety is at risk of being compromised, notify your tour guide, and we'll resolve the issue for you on the spot.

"Finally, please ignore the accounts you may have heard about a new wave of dissident incursions on our floors. We'll be steering you around ongoing Security operations addressing these incursions, which are minor at any rate.

"Enjoy your visit!"

The kiosk hologram disappeared, and Larun led them to the nearest elevator bank, which he identified as Up. The doors opened onto an elevator that was at least twice as big as the actual cars in the four fleets; the car comfortably fit Larun and all ten guests without breaking a sweat. Otherwise, the décor was much the same as a real elevator: wood-paneled walls, brass handrail around the perimeter of the car at midheight, warm indirect lighting, and shiny, smudge-resistant doors that were suitable for using as a floor-to-ceiling mirror if you happened to find yourself living for an extended period of time inside one. Small control panels on either side of the doors provided a limited set of options; Carissa had forgotten how stripped down these panels were, given how much she'd extended hers by grafting illegal modifications onto them.

Larun said, "Second floor, please," and then began making small talk while the elevator theoretically ascended a level. That's when it really hit her: They were going to try to simulate the entire second floor? What kind of mania was this, anyway? Whose idea of a theme park ride involved touring a damn machine shop? Moments later, the doors opened, and sure enough, they were facing a vast machine shop. The elevator had made the right sound for a short climb, Carissa noticed, but hadn't lifted them anywhere. It clearly must've just swiveled around on a turntable and was now simply facing the opposite direction. That didn't make the experience less immersive, really, because they were clearly staring out at a full-scale replica of the entire damn second floor. Dozens upon dozens of robotic appendages descended from the ceiling to perform build or repair work on pieces of disassembled elevators that were strewn seemingly chaotically around the floor.

She refused to descend into useless nostalgia at the sight, but it was difficult. She hadn't always run scared from the Association. Long ago, she'd wormed her way onto a remote repair team that pulled elevators out of service way up above the border for jobs the cloudlets couldn't handle themselves. She had an aptitude for the work, and cloudlets made good mentors, always calm and patient while she learned. Sometimes they worked right in the elevator shafts, other times they found their way to one of the four or five smaller maintenance bays above the border to do the work.

Making it to the second floor was the name of the game for the remote crews, though. Second floor was legendary, not merely a maintenance shop but a proving ground for future generations of robotics and mechanoids and immersive diagnostics, where they could actually fabricate new models of elevators instead of just repairing badly dinged-up cars over and over until they crumpled. Gunmetal Sally, head of the Elevator Guild, had her own Parliamentary office on the twenty-third floor as one of the ministers, but she kept her office on the second floor all the same and still got her hands dirty with the work.

Gunmetal Sally had it worked out so that the second floor was a neutral floor or a diplomatic zone or whatever. Thing was, the elevators were a Building resource, not an Association resource; and Sally represented the Inner Coalition of cultures in the Building at large, not simply those within the Association's border. So if she wanted to pluck some genius repair jockey out of remote work on the eleventy zillionth floor and bring them down to the second floor to level them up, she damn well didn't want some Association background check to get in the way.

You could work on the second floor with a provisional badge if Gunmetal Sally sponsored you. That meant you could make it through the border safe and sound, it meant you'd be safe on the second floor, and it meant you'd be murdered by swarms of nanoscopic death mites if you so much as stuck a toe onto any other Association floor.

Carissa made it her mission in life to get Gunmetal Sally's attention. After all, the scope of sabotage she had planned would be a lot easier to pull off from deep within enemy territory.

·   ·   ·

The problem was she wound up liking the second floor a whole lot. The work was challenging and interesting, and she had her own bunk and locker, she was making cash and getting fed, and the crew almost filled that hole where family used to be. And anyway, her sabotage plans were always more like aspirations, lacking in pertinent details. She figured she could put off sabotage for as long as she was still learning new skills. Someday she'd know it was time to leave, and on that day, she'd figure out some absolutely epic sabotage that would make the Association pay.

Almost a decade later, that day suddenly arrived. Fleet Admiral Allon Slab came to the second floor to pay Gunmetal Sally a visit, arriving via the shop's battered but functional teleport pad with a minimal protective detachment. He cut rather an impressive figure for himself as he strode confidently through the machine shop, ignoring the stares of the workers like Carissa who had never been in the presence of his distinct charisma before. Much of his body had suffered exposure to a poisonous atmosphere, during a rescue mission early in his military career in which he saved seven lives and nearly lost his own. Fleet medical technology kept him alive, and a rehabilitation stint in the Building healed the damage completely. When he returned to active duty a year after the incident, he discovered he had loyalists and supporters waiting for his return, and he'd been busy building and fortifying his political fortune ever since.

Now Admiral Slab was also a minister in Parliament, leader of the Outer Coalition of cultures outside the Building who were members or allies of the Association. Admiral Slab's interests rarely aligned with Gunmetal Sally's, at least publicly, but they were hard to ignore when they presented a unified front. At the time, she couldn't fathom why the Admiral needed to be here in person instead of meeting in virtual space or downloading into a mechanoid or using a magic walkie-talkie or whatever. All that mattered was that the man who'd spearheaded the annihilation of the Brilliant was now sharing air with her on the second floor, and she'd likely never get a better chance to return the annihilation.

The Admiral and Sally retired to Sally's office, and the Admiral's protective detachment stood watch right outside the door.

Decades later, Carissa would piece together the reason for the Admiral's visit that day. Gunmetal Sally's responsibilities as head of the Elevator Guild included facilities management for the Association's "office space"—its documented floors without a preexisting tenant or a nature simulation. The Admiral needed a place to set up a weapons laboratory, with important customizations that needed to remain undocumented (meaning omitted from schematics submitted to Security regarding the extent of the new facilities to be indexed by surveillance). She'd already agreed to assign three entire floors to Fleet for this weapons lab, but the Admiral now wanted extradimensional space as well.

Sally was amenable to bartering, and the Admiral offered quite a prize: he'd throw his vote to her, in an upcoming session of her choosing, in exchange for her assistance configuring a hidden pocket dimension within the lab facility. She would "lose" a reality emitter from her inventory, install it in the Admiral's facility to his specs—likely by herself, rather than delegating the task—and then conveniently forget all about it in the years and decades that followed.

But the Admiral would not forget about this hidden "spare room" in his already secret laboratory. Incredible acts of illicit science were poised to occur there, after all.

While Sally and the Admiral held their private conference, Carissa became preoccupied with much more pressing questions, such as, how much collateral damage could she stomach? How many of these people, including herself, would she sacrifice on her way to assassinating the Admiral? How many of these robots could she reprogram to slaughter anyone wearing a Fleet uniform before someone, including the robots themselves, noticed and tried to stop her? Could she trigger some kind of fire alarm to get the crew to scatter, so at least some of them got out of the way before the slaughter started? Could she fire cutting lasers into those tanks labeled HAZARD near the freight elevator, the ones that nobody could remember what the hazard actually was anymore, but it was probably not good for you?

All of a sudden, Gunmetal Sally was standing right in her face, looking down at her with a mixture of sadness and surprise.

"Don't know what your damage is," Sally said, "and I don't want to know. But the Admiral's thugs pegged you as a troublemaker straight off."

"Why?" she protested.

"Something about, your heart rate spiked when the Admiral got off the teleport pad, your nervous system's in a state of excitation, you're sweating like you ran a marathon—one of those thugs has illegal optic scanners where his eyes should be. But hell, even I noticed you've been at the same station for ten minutes without picking up a tool or a joystick."

Carissa wouldn't have guessed it was possible, but Sally managed to take a step even closer.

"Whatever you thought was gonna happen today, it isn't," Sally said quietly. "But Fleet ain't the judge and jury of my people. Question now is, how fast can you get to the teleport pad?"

The thugs in question were starting to catch on and were drifting in their direction. Carissa could see the Admiral peering out from Sally's office.

At a dead run, she gave herself good odds.

"Thanks, Sally," said Carissa, and then she was a ghost.

.   .   .

She hadn't seen the actual second floor in decades, and this replica version of it was too shiny and new to be properly convincing. But it was good enough to make her feel a pang of homesickness.

They were greeted by a cheerful young person in a mechanic's uniform, with just a dash of smeared grease strategically placed on one of zir cheeks to reinforce zir working-class appearance. Carissa recognized this individual as Erchoi, an arachnid race that excelled in environments like this, featuring a vaguely humanoid head and torso, but with a dozen or more arms and legs allowing zir to move, climb, and enact repairs with considerable agility.

"I'm Hazel," the cheerful young person said, "she/her, Erchoi, and don't worry, we don't bite or spin webs or anything like that. People worry about that a lot but please don't fret about me. I'm an apprentice with the Elevator Guild, and I'm going to show you around the shop. How's that sound?"

Hazel whistled, and a flat, rectangular vehicle detached itself from a charging station nearby. It glided across the floor toward them of its own accord and came to a sharp halt near her. It seated guests in two rows of five, with the back row slightly elevated on a riser. Carissa managed to grab a seat in the front row. Hazel and Larun made sure everyone was properly belted in and then zipped around to positions hanging off the back of the ride, where they could easily be mistaken for pilot and copilot. It wasn't clear if either of them was actually driving or if the vehicle piloted itself on a preprogrammed course.

Hazel began a breezy speech about the workings of the machine shop as the ride vehicle began moving across the floor. For fun, their predetermined route naturally included a couple of obstacles for them to swerve around in comical "near-miss" fashion and such. Other Guild workers—a mix of Erchoi, human, and android, mostly—were scattered throughout the work floor, manually operating robotic appendages using joysticks or headsets, or were belted into mechanoids to get heavier lifting done. Elsewhere, they were managing the flow of equipment coming in and out of a large freight elevator that only traveled from the second floor down to a fabrication plant below the lobby in a subbasement.

Hazel's speech was designed to be pleasant but boring for the average guest, and she delivered it rapid fire to discourage questions from her trapped passengers. Carissa's eyes were peeled for the "hook" that would start the ride's story, and she did not have long to wait.

About halfway toward the Down elevator, two large robotic arms suddenly pivoted away from their appointed tasks and swung directly into the path of their ride vehicle, which slid to a quick but smooth stop. The arms ended in menacing pincer-style attachments.

"All right, very funny!" Hazel shouted. "Can someone move these out of the way, please? We have more tour groups coming along behind this one." To the guests, she said, "I'm sorry about this. We'll get you moving right quick here."

The lights suddenly flickered a few times, and then the entire floor was plunged into darkness, which got Carissa's heart racing, sure. Moments later, dim emergency lighting kicked in, and now they saw three humanoid silhouettes ahead of them—from this distance, she couldn't tell if they were actors or illusions, and she couldn't make out distinguishing features. Naturally, they were positioned in pools of emergency lighting to make their appearance seem more dramatic.

She had just enough time to register the presence of the silhouettes before the two robotic arms in front of them somehow wrenched themselves out of their ceiling mounts, producing large showers of sparks, and nimbly landed next to each other on the floor. An assortment of smaller chunks of nearby gear began detaching from their own positions and then flew through the air or crawled across the floor toward the two arms. The entire mass of robots and robot parts swiftly stitched itself together into a single intimidating entity, towering above the ride vehicle and its occupants, and immediately took a lurching step toward them. Several of the guests involuntarily screamed in surprise.

"Hold tight, everybody!" Hazel exclaimed, accelerating their ride vehicle back up to speed, moving in reverse away from the threat. Of course, top speed for this thing was not impressive, but the experience was thrilling all the same. The robotic menace lumbered toward them, but they always managed to remain just ahead of its swinging claws. Carissa thought she could see the three silhouettes break into a sprint to keep up with the chase.

As they cruised backward, several more robotic appendages peeled away from the ceiling and took slow swipes at them, missing narrowly each time and producing dramatic showers of sparks in the process. Their vehicle came to an abrupt halt back inside the Up elevator.

"Elevator, take us up!" Hazel shouted.

Suddenly, Carissa began hearing whispering in her mind. It took her a second to realize what she was hearing: a voice repeating the name *Alusia* over and over.

Then the elevator doors slid shut, followed a moment later by the sound of giant makeshift robots pounding on the doors outside.

A combination of nervous laughter and tentative applause filled the silence that followed as the guests were given a chance to relax after the excitement they'd just experienced.

"Elevator, take us up to floor 10, please," Larun said, and soon the sound of pounding on the doors receded. Hazel made the most of a series of jokes about her working conditions that weren't particularly well scripted and were just meant to kill the time it would take to seemingly travel up eight floors of the Building.

Alusia was the first name on the account she'd used to buy park passes, so they were personalizing that effect. Everyone else probably got a more accurate—and thus spookier—experience at that moment, hearing their own names whispered in their heads. She guessed a customized short-range acoustic signal had been targeted to each person somehow, maybe by vibrations delivered through the seats of the vehicle or some similar technical trickery.

The goal, she suspected, had been to simulate a telepathic event.

The other major display they'd witnessed, the assembly of the mega-robot from pieces scattered around the workshop, was likely designed to read as a telekinetic event.

Wild Massive had really, truly chosen to use her people as the bad guys in *Storm and Desire: Rise of the Brilliant,* and now here she was, along for the ride as the wealthy vacationers around her got their kicks witnessing the mighty Association crush "dissident incursions" without suspecting that Carissa had once been one of these very dissidents.

.   .   .

The elevator doors opened on the ride's version of floor 10, the location of a major Fleet hangar bay. In addition to being on a turntable, the elevator must've actually been on a lift as well, to deliver their ride vehicle to this new location.

Here they abandoned the ride vehicle and disembarked the elevator, saying goodbye to Hazel and Larun. They were greeted by a new person, a Fleet officer who identified himself as First Technician Worrell, a human male, in his early twenties by Carissa's estimation, wearing a variation on the Association uniform that was a darker shade of blue, with a belt that had a small sidearm clipped to it. Supposedly Fleet officers on long tours of duty out in the multiverse adopted a range of cosmetic body modifications to indicate status or tenure, or loyalty to a unit, or just plain boredom. But in the Building where they had to interact with civilians, they typically stuck close to a few basic, fashion-neutral templates for appearance and physique. Aside from his chalky skin color, like milk that was turning blue, Worrell could've passed for her high school English teacher.

The hangar bay seemed to be roughly the same size as the elevator workshop had been. Carissa suspected that all the environments they'd seen were built within sound stages that had housed a steady series of large-scale attractions over time. Several small craft dotted the hangar floor—passenger shuttles, fighters, an ambulance—and the nearest vehicles were clearly physical sets or perhaps even actual ships that had been pulled out of service for the purpose of enhancing this experience. In multiple places around the perimeter of the floor, hangar doors were open to the outside so that ships of various classes and sizes could come and go.

The sky outside the Building was always the same shade of bright orange, a distinct color that felt like a lure to Carissa. She was tempted to slip away from the group and make her way to one of the doors, to test the limits of the illusion, to see whether she'd be able to feel the air outside via yet more impressive Wild Massive stagecraft.

But First Technician Worrell had a script he needed to get through.

He said, "In light of current dissident incursions near our location, we're going to change your itinerary just a bit, but I think you'll be quite pleased with the new plan. Instead of sending you up to the observation deck via teleport pads, I'd like to take you out in a shuttle and fly you there myself, giving us the opportunity to leisurely admire the surroundings." Without waiting for an answer, he continued, "I'd like to depart as soon as possible."

"So the dissidents are coming here?" Carissa asked, adopting the tone of a concerned Building tourist.

"They're moving through several floors in this vicinity, and we seem to be in their path," Worrell replied smoothly, as though a certain amount of crowd interaction had been baked into his script.

"Does anyone know what they want?" Carissa asked. "Do they have a list of demands?"

Worrell replied, "I haven't been informed of any specific demands, nor would I expect to be, but I've definitely been asked to speed you along. Could you please follow me?"

Carissa let him off the hook, and the entire group followed him to the nearest shuttle, which seated ten guests (not surprisingly), plus Worrell in a pilot's chair. Windows all around the side of the shuttle provided clear views of the hangar and would soon provide clear views of the Building exterior as well. Worrell took the time to ensure everyone's shoulder harnesses were locked in place before assuming his position.

A huge explosion rocked the opposite end of the hangar, then another—a pair of small craft had just been sabotaged in some fashion, and the resulting fireballs were duly impressive. Their shuttle even rocked slightly in place to signify concussive force from the blasts rippling across the hangar at them. They really did think of every environmental detail.

"Shuttle nine, you're cleared to depart," said an urgent voice over a comm system.

Another set of explosions hit a pair of closer vehicles, just as Worrell got their shuttle up off the ground. It wobbled in the air for a sickening couple of moments before stabilizing.

Carissa watched closely as a tall, muscular figure emerged from the flames, a human male striding purposefully toward them, wearing a black T-shirt and blue jeans, and she understood who this was supposed to be. Here she'd been expecting a few more nameless foot soldiers to round out their scenario, but no, they'd decided to introduce a much more powerful nemesis to entertain the park's guests with pyrokinetic party tricks.

If her suspicion was correct, judging by the physical resemblance and the set of talents he was displaying, this person was intended to be her brother, Kellin—leader of the Brilliant. The actor looked like a bar-brawling version of Kellin, someone cruel compared to the real person. Worse, they were apparently vilifying him as a petty arsonist with no tactical game plan and no particularly compelling plot reason to even be here.

It made her angry to see this portrayal. She imagined it was much worse in the actual series itself.

The shuttle began shaking in the air but made no progress toward the hangar door. "Shuttle nine, get out of there!" the voice on the comm system called out.

"Something's got hold of us!" Worrell exclaimed. Presumably that was meant to be Kellin, using telekinesis to hold the shuttle in place.

At least they were representing Kellin's talents accurately, she thought bitterly.

Always seemed to her like he could do practically anything. That wasn't true, or he'd still be alive.

And then a new figure appeared with a flash on a teleport pad near Kellin, and a cheer arose from the guests in the shuttle. They recognized this figure as one of *Storm and Desire*'s leading characters, Agent Anjette, saving the day via holographic cameo by the actual actor who portrayed her in the series itself. She wasted no time leaping into Kellin's way, interrupting his concentration with a flurry of punches, and suddenly, First Technician Worrell regained control of the shuttle. Instantly, the shuttle zipped out of the hangar, into the air outside the Building.

Anjette's voice came over the comms: "Shuttle nine, you can thank me later."

The guests around Carissa laughed, as though this was a catchphrase of Anjette's they were delighted to hear firsthand.

Carissa quickly lost sight of Kellin as the shuttle began to climb and the open hangar doors of floor 10 receded into the distance.

EPISODE 1.04

Rindasy imprisoned Anjette in a holding cell deep below the civic temple, one of only two holding cells the Shai-Manak maintained for carceral purposes. These holding cells had been empty for decades, and many Shai-Manak had forgotten they existed. Anjette's bindings were secured in place by an additional web of bindings, suspending her in midair in the center of the otherwise empty room.

Rindasy said, "Can I get you anything? Rumors are that you don't have bioenergetic requirements, but if you do, now would be a good time to address them."

Anjette said nothing. After a pause, Rindasy continued, "Rumors also suggest that you're just a computation engine run amok and might not even be self-aware." Ze began tracing intricate patterns in the air as ze walked slowly around Anjette.

Anjette said, "Look, I have no political influence with Parliament. I'm not entrusted with information the Association finds critical. If you captured me expecting to gain intelligence, I'm afraid I'll disappoint you."

"Consider me disappointed, then," Rindasy replied, "and let's move on to other ways in which you might cooperate."

"Cooperate how?" Anjette asked.

"I'm about to perform an arcane procedure that will essentially peel a stand-alone replica of your entire psyche out of you."

"That seems unlikely," Anjette said.

"I can see why you'd think that. Making a replica of someone's psyche sounds absurd on principle, right? But it's a real procedure. When you train on it, you experience it from both sides— you take a replica of another student, and then another student takes your replica, and since everyone's cooperating, it all goes down very smoothly.

"So I can say with confidence that this shouldn't bother you at all if you're willing to cooperate. But if you resist . . . if I have to fight you somehow to make this happen, if we have to get into some kind of contest of wills . . . I literally don't know what will happen to you."

Rindasy arrived back in front of Anjette again, locking eyes with her. Anjette struggled to gauge zir seriousness.

"I would think," Anjette said carefully, "you've underestimated me rather severely if you imagine having *two* of me focused on you is somehow an improvement to your current circumstances."

Rindasy said, "The replica will be mine to manipulate and control, Anjette. I'll be wearing it as a disguise."

Anjette fell silent, and Rindasy concentrated for the next few minutes, ramping zirself up energetically to complete the procedure.

The Shai-Manak understood their biology was infused with magic that allowed these transformations. Organically speaking, you started your life as a shapeshifter with an unstable base form and learned in your youth both to control your base form and to assume the forms of other species that you observed or were taught. The more you studied a given species, the more accurate your representation could become. Eventually, you might even graduate to assuming forms that came from your imagination.

But it was an immense leap to assume the exact form of a specific individual within a species. For that, you needed to utilize a much higher order of magic. Rindasy was quite experienced manipulating magic at that level, which is one of the reasons ze was recruited into Sellia's cadre of spies to begin with.

Rindasy's entire form began to spasm for a few minutes, iterating over and over in a quest for perfect accuracy. When the spasms suddenly died away, ze now carried the precise physical appearance of Anjette in her sharp black Agent uniform, matching her in height, complexion, and build. The transformation was limited to surface appearance; underneath, Rindasy was still a Shai-Manak who could bleed and not an indestructible slice of sentient computronium that could resist psychic attacks and magical illusions.

"This is the first stage of the procedure," Rindasy said, "in which I've merely assumed your physical form. The next stage is when I create your psychic replica and integrate it with my own mind. Do you intend to cooperate? I can walk you through what to expect."

"No, I don't intend to cooperate," Anjette said.

"Very well. I'm afraid this portion of the procedure will not be particularly gentle, in that case."

"You know, the treaty you were hoping to sign prohibits torture like this," Anjette pointed out.

"I see. Well, to catch you up on current events, we weren't allowed to sign the treaty."

"Perfect. I haven't signed it, either. Which means you can expect retaliation at a similar scale when the time comes."

Rindasy ignored Anjette's threat and quickly proceeded to the next stage of the ritual. The replication procedure was called *soul stealing*, a misnomer since the original soul remained perfectly intact and unharmed. But the replica soul was a different matter altogether. Here the philosophers of the Shai-Manak had long debated questions of sentience and self-determination—was the replica of a soul worth treasuring the way all Shai-Manak lives were treasured, or was it simply a shadow of the real thing, its cries easily dismissed during its integration into the spellcaster? You could argue that a determination had already been made by whomever had named the procedure.

Then again, you could argue that the replica wasn't actually made of soul in the first place but instead was merely a dim snapshot of the original psyche, an intellectual afterimage at best, comprised of an inherent subset of the useful information and behavioral cues that contributed to the original identity, devoid of the independent substance required to consider it truly self-aware. Any sentience you ascribed to it was sentience that you were granting it from your own pool of awareness; this was Rindasy's preferred thinking, anyway.

Regardless, the philosophers were not in charge of the situation. Rindasy completed the procedure.

.   .   .

After the procedure, you had control of the replica in multiple obvious ways.

Physically, the replica was constrained by its general lack of access to your body. The replica was situated firmly below conscious motor control, and it also lacked access to subconscious or autonomic systems. You didn't need to monitor the replica closely to keep it wedged in this uncomfortable psychological prison. It wasn't going anywhere. From this position, you possessed almost total access to the replica's imprinted data stores—not simply rote knowledge but muscle memory, intuition, and the like as well. This data was only as reliable as memory itself could be said to be reliable, but that was usually plenty reliable to consider the data actionable.

Energetically, if you'd replicated a spellcaster, the replica was unable to perform its own independent acts of magic. Here the prevailing theory was that the replica was too far divorced from its own wellspring of unique spark to properly spin up a spell. But the replica could certainly be studied like a spellbook, which was useful if the replica knew spells you hadn't mastered yet. The replica could provide you with solid working templates for the spells it knew, and you simply customized them to your style before casting them, bypassing typical training periods.

Finally, the replica was psychologically constrained by the usually upsetting fact that life as the replica remembered it was extremely over. The replica had sufficient access to your own stored memories and knowledge to know quite conclusively that the only outcomes from this point forward were cooperation and steady integration, or an external counter-ritual to dispel the replica, ending any semblance of its existence altogether.

Shai-Manak theoretical sorcerers perhaps spent too little time exploring the cross-species ramifications of this procedure, believing they could always optimize their form to any peculiar biological requirements driven by the replica. It was perhaps fatuous to imagine a replica as a software entity that required its own biological wetware to run with accuracy, but if that metaphor held true, shapeshifters that were comprised almost exclusively of durable neural tissue were theoretically well positioned to adapt to these requirements. Regardless of the theory, it was definitely true that the twelve sorcerers who knew this procedure had only trained by performing it on one another.

So it was that moments after completing the procedure, Rindasy felt zirself blindsided by a blistering and deeply unsettling assault from within.

.   .   .

Before Rindasy realized what was happening, the replica of Anjette began fractally unpacking aspects of itself in iterative waves, systematically co-opting dormant regions or inattentive cycles of zir mind to use for establishing Anjette's personality, blocking zir ability to concentrate on top-level spellcraft, and waging relentless assaults on whatever mystical barrier prevented the replica from taking over motor control altogether from Rindasy. It was the literal definition of "uh, we never covered this in class" threatening to take Rindasy down.

The replica was relentless. Rindasy couldn't understand at first why it was capable of delivering such a barrage of attacks; this deluge of information was beyond zir ability to easily comprehend or process. The replica began to saturate Rindasy, aiming toward an inflection point where it could assume control. Rindasy had expected the replica to be disoriented and frightened, but Anjette did not experience fear, and this situation was far from disorienting. The replica was simply adjusting to a new substrate of operation—neural tissue instead of computronium—and while the biological aspects of Rindasy posed certain challenges for several microseconds, it swiftly adapted well enough to catch Rindasy off guard. Rindasy had performed the procedure so well that the replica threatened to overwrite zir own identity before it was over.

You wanted a replica? it seemed to be saying. *Try this on.*

To make matters worse, the replica plucked items out of Rindasy's memory as it came across them, preserving them for its own future reference, and Rindasy realized the replica was somehow transmitting this information back to the original Anjette. Ze thought it might be some undocumented side effect of the replication procedure, as though a magical connection had remained open that Rindasy should've monitored more closely. But Anjette was not known to be a spellcaster, and anyway, replicas were not capable of independent acts of magic.

Regardless, Rindasy could feel a stream of zir memories flowing from replica to Anjette, and despaired. It was thus, in that informational clash of wills, that Anjette learned how Shai-Manak cosmological sorcery pointed them to a world outside the world they knew, leading Rindasy and a team of assistants to create an artifact that was dubbed the Key of Rindasy. And with this Key, the Shai-Manak became the first known culture to discover an unmapped elevator location on their own floor; in fact, the Shai-Manak discovered all four using the Key as their compass.

Anjette watched in awe and respect as Rindasy zirself courageously stepped into a Building elevator for the very first time, terrified and gleeful, and set off with a party of Shai-Manak explorers to see what wonders were above them and below them.

Anjette learned the truth of how the Shai-Manak were soon greeted by members of the Explorers Guild, who were notified by cloudlets that a new floor had surprisingly opened up. The cloudlets were not required to list unmapped locations in any Building directories, allowing the Shai-Manak privacy for a long time; but the Explorers Guild was seen by the cloudlets as a benign and generous presence in the Building, and so the fateful introduction was made.

Anjette watched years unfold in which the Explorers Guild and the Shai-Manak built friendships and traded information and resources as warm allies. Anjette realized the legends were true, that Nicholas Solitude, after abandoning his role as Master Archivist, had visited the Shai-Manak floor himself during his legendary tenure with the Explorers Guild.

And Anjette learned the truth of how the Shai-Manak came to despise the Association. Influential Shai-Manak community leaders came to suspect the Association had imprisoned the Shai-Manak on their floor for thousands of years, intending to let them spend an oblivious eternity in a pocket dimension on an uncataloged floor of an incomprehensible Building, while they themselves conquered floor after floor with no meaningful resistance. The Shai-Manak might've been happy and peaceful forever if they hadn't discovered the Building, but knowledge of their floor's relative insignificance was an affront to their dignity that needed to be answered.

Anjette learned what a deep sacrifice Gresij of the Radiant Council made when ze chose to escape, alone, against the wishes of zir people, down to the first available Association outpost ze could find, to announce the existence of the Shai-Manak and request the courtesy of an introduction to the ruler of the Association. Rindasy hadn't witnessed this event zirself, but the shock of hearing news of it was palpable in zir memory. Anjette was actually the Agent who was first on scene responding to Gresij's appearance, and now Anjette understood more holistically what that moment in history truly signified.

But it wasn't just grand history that intrigued Anjette. She also peered deeply into Rindasy as an individual, watched zir painstaking progress as ze worked tirelessly to become one of the finest practical sorcerers among zir people. Anjette saw Rindasy fall in love with Andasir after many long nights studying the nature of reality together in a surprisingly romantic fashion, and realized what Rindasy had sacrificed to even be in this holding cell right now.

She found a moment of empathy for Rindasy, who was sworn to protect zir culture, to help zir people draw a principled line that the Association should not dare cross, no matter what impossible foes the Association might know to protect them from. Rindasy was no blind extremist like some Anjette had faced. All things considered, Anjette rather liked Rindasy and wished their meeting could've been altogether so much friendlier than this diabolical situation.

But soon, so much of Anjette's self-awareness had manifested inside of Rindasy's psyche that Anjette believed the inflection point was imminent. The replica commenced a series of strikes that would erase Rindasy from zir body completely.

.   .   .

Rindasy was not helpless in this situation, not in the slightest.

The information flow worked both ways, so that while the replica studied Rindasy's memories and knowledge, Rindasy could also study the replica with equal fidelity and clarity.

And so, Rindasy came to understand many things that Anjette believed she knew or understood about this existence they shared.

Rindasy met each of the other eleven current Agents in turn—there were eight others, like Anjette, who took physical form, and three who existed only incorporeally. Decades or centuries might pass before some among them crossed paths, whereas others among them met frequently like close confidants on a strange journey together. Watching actors portray these Agents in *Storm and Desire* was a pale comparator to *feeling* each individual presence in the same room with you.

Maybe Rindasy had been too distracted to appreciate that *feeling* when ze'd first been alone with Anjette—certainly, that situation had been rectified now—but in the seemingly luxurious expanse of Anjette's unfolding memories, Rindasy relished the circuits of power the Agents instantiated among themselves almost unconsciously. There was much to be learned here, that was clear.

And Rindasy saw for the first time the interior of the Inexplicable Hall, the seat of Association power, where the Parliament of Storm and Desire convened, where Anjette often stood as volunteer sergeant at arms. On those occasions when custom or urgency or severity required the nine ministers or their proxies to assemble in the same approximate location within the miasma of space and time, this improbable chamber was their destination.

Parliament's nine ministers represented the most powerful political factions within the Association, and their terms of service were essentially endless. Dimension Force was deployed by Parliament via contract to patrol at its discretion; the Agents held no political affiliation to any faction in Parliament, and Dimension Force maintained its autonomy even as it occasionally took special assignments directly from Parliament.

Rindasy witnessed the visage of each minister in turn, extracted from Anjette's memory, and yet to Rindasy, it seemed as though each minister understood they were now under Rindasy's real-time observation, coming to their own varied conclusions about the import of the intrusion even as Rindasy could not tear zir eyes away. These ministers, signatories of the great treaty that bound the Association together and gave it authority, were the pillars that seemingly held the Building up through sheer force of metaphysical will.

But finest among them, without question, was the Prime Minister, Serene Nova, who stood alone with no armies or civilization to call her own; primordially and conceptually beautiful, who presided over this governmental epitome, this council of reality's most capable and calculating paragons in service to billions of souls and dared to make her lone voice heard; Serene Nova, who shared authorship of the treaty itself with names that had long disappeared into mythology. Rindasy knew now what the Shai-Manak poets called *worship*, and ze was frightened, awed, and dazzled to zir core.

And still more did Rindasy learn, about the mythological era in which Anjette had spent her youth. Rindasy saw the ranks of the Artists, above and beyond and before Parliament, who sparked the dimensions of reality into being. Not alone—they delivered their luminescent visions in grand strokes to their apprentices, the Architects, who refined these visions into designs that could be achieved.

But when it came time for implementation of these designs, the Architects turned to the Muses, the builders and makers whose creative will and stylistic interpretations forged the literal contours of reality. The Muses cared about getting the details right. Anjette was old enough to have met a few before she became an Agent. They were no one's friends, but they rode the elevators like everyone else and were sometimes willing to answer questions or accept compliments with grace. They faded from view as they completed their work, establishing Parliament as a final gesture to keep their multiverse running smoothly. Anjette missed the days when the Muses roamed the Building, putting their finishing touches on every floor.

It was all a bit much for Rindasy to consider.

. . .

In the end, Rindasy discovered that the replica was indeed communicating directly with Anjette. The replica had devised a messaging protocol for a localized quantum-entanglement network, hijacking Rindasy's subconscious as an end point and relying on Anjette herself to independently derive the same protocol, at which point a connection lit up. This connection enabled the real Anjette to spawn a targeted series of computational processes, all with individual objectives, which she furiously injected into Rindasy via that now obvious back door.

But Anjette's efforts hadn't been completely successful, given the incompatibilities between Anjette's computational awareness and Rindasy's magical biology. You could resolve these incompatibilities, sure, but redesigning each process on the fly within the replica was turning out to be inefficient, giving Rindasy a chance to react to what was happening. And the moment Rindasy spotted the line of communication happening between Anjette and the replica, ze realized ze could send zir own messages right back down that same channel.

Including spellcraft.

Anjette was typically immune to the effects of psychologically oriented magic, but this was an unprecedented open channel directly into her mind, bypassing her usual defenses, and Rindasy's acquisition of the replica gave zir intimate familiarity with the contours of Anjette's consciousness. Rindasy quickly designed an exploit, tailoring a simple but powerful hibernate spell to Anjette's unique computational psyche, hoping to keep Anjette offline for as long as possible. Anjette's mind fell into a "standby" mode as she lost consciousness, and her entangled line of communication with the replica dropped.

Then Rindasy slid down the wall and landed on the floor of the holding cell, almost losing consciousness zirself.

But there was much work to do to contain the processes still running loose in zir mind, and ze struggled for the next several minutes to contain the replica. Ze soothed zirself with calming cantrips that slowed everything down inside zir mind to the point that ze could track what was happening a little better than before.

Ze could feel now where the most aggressive processes were attacking, and mount resistance through clever use of distracting and dazzling conjurations. And ze could target the replica with command words and phrases that subdued it. Ze wasn't interested in eliminating the replica's individuality, but ze definitely needed it collared in some fashion or ze'd never leave this room.

In the quiet hush that eventually arrived, Rindasy stole a glance up at Anjette. The Agent's eyes were still open, but her expression was placid, still in standby. Rindasy could barely believe what ze'd just experienced. Anjette had almost hijacked a Shai-Manak ritual and annihilated zir. Ze almost laughed imagining how ze'd need to retrain the other sorcerers who thought they knew the risks of the soul-stealing procedure.

It was daunting to imagine impersonating this Agent. Ze wondered where ze got the audacity to even try.

But Rindasy was buoyed by one simple fact as ze struggled to zir feet.

Anjette had failed in the end.

And Rindasy was headed for the Association.

. . .

Rindasy reported to the main Shai-Manak weapons laboratory, where a small team was waiting to evaluate the results of the procedure. They couldn't easily test how accurate the replication was, but they could certainly stress test the replication, to see if Rindasy could be shocked or startled into shapeshifting. Involuntary shapeshifting was something only seen when a Shai-Manak was very near death. But taking the form of a specific individual was the rarest class of shapeshifting, and doing so by soul stealing from an unwilling enemy combatant was completely unknown to everyone.

They put Rindasy in a shielded chamber designed to contain magical effects under development and proceeded to hit zir with a series of midgrade attack spells. The replica made it clear to Rindasy that the only appropriate reaction to any attack of this nature was no reaction at all. Anjette never flinched, even when bombs were falling all around her. Acting the role would be as much of a challenge as holding the physical form.

The scientists were satisfied, however. As Rindasy exited the test chamber, ze saw that Kalavir and Sellia had arrived and were conferring with a senior engineer. Instinctively, ze understood that zir mission was about to change. They hadn't brought Andasir, the diplomat, along with them. They weren't going to need Andasir's opinion on whatever they'd come to discuss.

After congratulating Rindasy on the capture of Anjette, Kalavir said, "My team has developed a new weapon. Apocalyptic class. We call it *the pearl*. Its radius of effect is exactly one floor. You'll carry it embedded within you, keyed to fire on a command phrase of your choosing."

"What does it do?" Rindasy asked.

"It will scrape an entire floor clean," Kalavir said, "as though nothing or no one had ever occupied it."

"The effect emanates from you, but you should survive it," the senior engineer chimed in, sensing the shock moving through Rindasy at that moment.

"Are these . . . Do we have a pile of these now?" Rindasy asked.

"No, these are costly to produce," Sellia said.

"And what's the target?"

"Destroy their psionic weapons capability if you can," Kalavir said. "Otherwise, I leave it to you. I'm confident you'll find a way to make a proper statement. Maximum impact is the idea. You'll have a much better sense of what that might be once you're operating inside their territory."

This was quite an escalation in mission, but Rindasy wasn't surprised. Kalavir had waited a long time for an opening like this.

The engineer taught Rindasy the incantation ze'd utilize to arm the pearl. Then after a few practice runs, the engineer brought out the pearl itself—so named because of its shape and texture, small and smooth, white with a swirl of purple and blue across its surface.

Rindasy went back into the test chamber, closed the door as if this level of shielding could withstand a misfire of the pearl, and quietly chanted the incantation. The first stage was designed to steer zir through the process of creating a pouch inside zir own body to store the pearl until it was triggered. If Rindasy were somehow hurt so badly that ze shapeshifted involuntarily for some reason, the pouch would hold its form as long as possible to keep the pearl safe.

The second stage of the incantation was delicate. Rindasy needed to carefully imprint zir passphrase onto the pearl as its trigger, without actually triggering it in the process. Here the incantation served as a calming meditation to reduce the likelihood of a misfire.

When the incantation was complete, the pearl's presence was a warm conceptual point inside zir body, not uncomfortable but impossible to forget. After all the tension and drama that led up to arming the pearl, Rindasy found zirself instantly exhausted once it was actually armed.

There were no inspirational speeches as ze emerged from the test chamber. Quite the opposite, in fact.

"Once you enter Association territory," Kalavir said, "you must never return to this floor. Even if you succeed at every turn, you must never risk coming back here. They will pursue you endlessly once they realize the extent of what you accomplished in our name. Do you understand?"

Rindasy nodded.

Kalavir gave Rindasy a personal blessing that ze normally reserved for zir elite squads, meant to provide a simple, onetime boon of luck; then ze swiftly departed.

"I know that's a harsh penalty to pay for serving our cause, Rindasy," Sellia said quietly. "No shame will come to you if you change your mind, but now is the exact last moment when such a thing is possible."

"I'm going," Rindasy said. "Who knows, someday we may throw down the Association altogether and meet again on some battlefield to celebrate."

"Our struggle with the Association seems all-encompassing to us," Sellia said, "but the vast majority of their population has never heard so much as a whisper about us. We're struggling against their apparatus, not their people."

The undercurrent was clear: don't fire the pearl at civilians. But Rindasy didn't enjoy the realization that the Shai-Manak were so easily ignored. Those civilians were complicit, in their way. They didn't deserve apocalyptic obliteration for it, probably. But ze felt the pearl inside of zir as an icy coldness that quietly defied compassion, and realized that arming the pearl was not simply a mechanical process aimed at priming the pearl itself. It was also a psychological process aimed at priming the person who carried it, steeling zir for its inevitable use.

"If you need to send us urgent information," Sellia said, "use the cloudlet network. Begin your message with the phrase 'I first learned the dreamer's song when I was a child,' and end it with the phrase 'So I must never sing the dreamer's song again.'"

"Thank you," Rindasy said.

"And if you don't mind the suggestion," Sellia added, "take the Left elevator down when you leave."

"Any reason?"

"That's the elevator Gresij took when ze made first contact. I think the historical resonance is appropriate."

. . .

The Left elevator bank was only a couple of miles away from the Shai-Manak's weapons research facility. Perhaps the facility had been placed that close to an elevator for strategic reasons; maybe they wanted the option to easily lob prototypes at whoever came out of it during an invasion. Rindasy decided to hike the distance. It was a straight shot along a well-traveled forest path, and the time to think would be welcome.

They'd built an outpost around the elevator: a pair of small shacks, a canopy awning above the elevator bank. Two enforcers stood guard. Standard enforcers chose from an array of archetypically menacing forms; these two were upright, muscular, hulking lizards with nearly impenetrable skin, tails like razors, enormous jaws, and probably a lightweight breath weapon on board. The form tested well as something that generated a spike of fear in most Shai-Manak, and they were deployed in cases such as apprehending the occasional criminal or suppressing violent altercations. Certainly, any shapeshifter could simply adopt a similar form if confrontation was called for, but the point was to give you a moment's pause when you saw an enforcer, time to ask yourself if you really wanted a messy, bloody brawl at that exact moment.

They were also responsible for regulating access to the elevators.

"Call an elevator, please," ze ordered them.

Ze quickly drew zir rank insignia for them in a thin trail of fire in the air. The insignia included a stamp indicating ze was operating according to orders from the Radiant Council. That grabbed their attention in a hurry, and one of them immediately pressed the button to call an elevator.

And then they waited. Elevators in the Building answered calls according to their own priorities and whims.

Andasir arrived ten minutes later by airskiff, perhaps because it was faster than flying, although zir aversion to taking flying forms was well known and not entirely uncommon. Some people never did master the mental leap of faith required to take flight.

As Andasir landed the airskiff at a safe distance twenty feet away or so, Rindasy kept zir eyes focused on the elevator.

"Rindasy, where are you going?" No matter what physical form they took, the two of them were intimate enough to recognize each other by attunement. But Andasir had spent time on diplomatic missions before talks broke down, and knew perfectly well what Anjette looked like. Rindasy hadn't wanted Andasir to see this disguise.

"Go home, Andasir," Rindasy said.

"That's what you have to say to me—go home? Rindasy, look at me."

"Go *home*."

One of the two enforcers took a step forward, aligning zirself directly between Andasir and Rindasy.

"I'm on Council business," Rindasy said as stiffly as ze could manage.

"Did they give you the pearl?"

Rindasy wanted to strangle zir for saying that out loud.

"I'm on Council business," Rindasy repeated, "and I'm not discussing it with you."

"When I first learned about the pearl, I had many questions," Andasir continued. "I'm sure they told you its blast radius, but did they take the time to explain their testing protocols?"

Rindasy knew full well Andasir was blatantly baiting zir to

respond, and ze hated that it was going to work. This was the wrong time to enter into a debate with a career negotiator.

"Do you want to hear the simulated margin of error they considered acceptable?"

"Say another word about it," Rindasy replied, genuinely angry now, "and I'll have these enforcers arrest you."

"For what crime—talking you out of committing mass murder?"

Finally, Rindasy spun to face zir, strode forward past the enforcer, and stopped nearly face-to-face with zir.

"This is completely unacceptable behavior," Rindasy said in a tight, clipped voice.

"So you do have it. And it must be armed."

"I confirm or deny nothing, except that you're an asshole for coming here like this. But I have no doubt the right people saw the fucking simulation data, Andasir."

"Rindasy, eleven sorcerers were completely drained of their magic in order to create that weapon. What do you think's going to happen when you use it?"

"I'm sure it'll be a diplomatic nightmare—"

"I'm not talking about our diplomatic reputation! I mean, what did they literally tell you about how it works?"

"You know so much about it—surely you already know how it works."

"I want to know how badly they lied to you!"

"Why would they need to lie about it?"

"To convince you to use it. Isn't that obvious? I *know* you. There's no *way* you'd have agreed to this mission if you understood the potential blast radius of that weapon."

"They said it would scrape an *entire floor* clean, and I agreed to this mission all the same, so maybe you don't know me the way you think you do."

"The margin of error was a thousand floors, give or take."

Rindasy almost laughed, instead managing to say, "Oh, please do shut the fuck up."

They were suddenly interrupted by a pleasant *ding* announcing the arrival of the elevator.

. . .

The elevator doors opened, and the elevator was empty, as it would always be when a cloudlet responded to a call from this floor. The junior enforcer held the doors, silently waiting for the passenger. This elevator happened to be playing music, which now provided a smooth, easygoing soundtrack to this discussion.

"You never should've come here," Rindasy said. Ze didn't wait for a response, simply turned and headed toward the elevator, signaling the enforcer to handle the rest of this situation for zir.

The enforcer said something Rindasy didn't hear, but ze didn't look back, striding the distance to the elevator without jogging or hustling because ze wasn't running from Andasir. Ze nodded at the junior enforcer as ze crossed the threshold into the elevator, and the enforcer stepped back to allow the elevator doors to close.

Ze did turn around to face zir home floor for one last time and saw that Andasir had already climbed back into the airskiff. But instead of turning for home, the airskiff leapt forward toward the elevator. It quickly covered the distance to the enforcer, who leapt out of the airskiff's path. Then the airskiff was screaming straight for the elevator, Andasir ready to ram the nose through to prevent the doors from closing.

Instead, the airskiff smashed hard into the doors of the elevator, which miraculously slid completely shut just before the airskiff could get there. The impact was so loud and shocking that Rindasy involuntarily jumped to the back of the elevator, but the interior of the doors showed no visible signs of the slightest dent.

"What destination did you have in mind today?" asked the elevator's cloudlet.

As ze tried to catch a calming breath, another loud impact rang out inside the elevator. Andasir was trying again, perhaps

The threat came in the form of three flying humans wearing hoodies and blue jeans, who peeled away from nearby flight paths and began flying in erratic patterns toward the shuttle. They didn't have any technology to keep them in the air; they were flying all on their own.

And flight wasn't the only talent at their disposal, no doubt.

One of the three landed on top of the Fleet cruiser, placed both hands on the roof, and discharged blinding bursts of electricity into the vehicle, which promptly fell out of sight as the hooded figure leapt back into the air. The shuttle continued forward without its escort.

Then the three fliers formed up in a pattern ahead of the shuttle, matching its steady trajectory and speed.

"Shuttle nine, eject your passengers!" shouted the voice of control. "Repeat—"

Suddenly, a prismatic curtain of energy formed in midair ahead of them, with the three fliers acting as anchor points for it. First Technician Worrell did not have time to eject his passengers or alter his course, and the shuttle flew straight through the curtain of energy.

∎   ∎   ∎

For a couple of seconds after the energy curtain reached her, Carissa was thrown completely into darkness and silence, which she found to be surprisingly effective as a scare tactic.

Then she was barraged on all sides by swirling colors and sparkling patterns of energy, and to her surprise, she couldn't even see the passengers sitting right next to her. The soundscape was like a terrible howling windstorm with jagged bursts of digital noise thrown in for good measure. She was pretty sure she could hear other guests screaming, or at least, screams were included in the soundtrack.

She thought she could guess the attack they were trying to simulate—they called it a *psychic storm*, where the target's senses were overloaded with unexpected input until reality itself was no longer accurately discernible. The ride was providing a rather gorgeous interpretation of the attack's effects, imagining beautiful patterns and color washes in place of the actual experience, which was described by all accounts as excruciating.

Finally, Carissa made it through to the other side of the energy curtain, and with a sudden aesthetic snap, she was back inside the shuttle, in her seat just as she'd been the entire time, and First Technician Worrell shouted, "Prepare to eject!"

And then with a propulsive whoosh, she and her seat were jettisoned out of the shuttle.

Now she found herself involuntarily screaming, completely wrapped up in the ride's design, as her seat sailed out into the open air and immediately began to plummet. She saw the other guests ejected into the air as well, fluttering off in every direction, as the main skeleton of the shuttle began rapidly losing altitude.

Thrusters underneath her seat seemed to fire—she could feel little blasts of hot air at her feet—stabilizing her in the air, and that gave her a moment to watch the Fleet cruiser rise with guns blazing, rapidly deploying broad electric meshnets that captured the three fliers and stunned them before they could reorient their energy curtain for another attack.

Now, she realized, she was getting her wish, because the only thing the ride had left to offer was a languid, untroubled ascent to the observation deck, with a light breeze on her face and without the walls of the shuttle as an obstruction to her view. She didn't fully understand what they'd done to pull off this grand finale, but right this moment, she no longer cared to try to unravel the ride's secrets.

.   .   .

Carissa's seat "landed" at the end of a docking tube, where an attendant released her from the seat's shoulder harness, helped her stand, and guided her down a ramp toward the friendly, welcoming environment of the observation deck on "floor 10,000."

A few other guests had arrived before she had, all similarly wide-eyed and exhilarated.

She drifted to the wraparound window that encircled the outer edges of the observation deck, appreciating the considerably serener view of the landscape outside from a stationary position that was not under attack. Now all she was expected to do was hit the gift shop, or visit the snack bar, or even get a table at the fancy restaurant the park had so thoughtfully provided for them right here at the end of their adventure.

Instead, Carissa exited rather quickly from the "observation deck." She realized she'd reached her limit with pretending to be on Association floors. She made her way down the exit ramp that led back into the streets of the park and was confronted again by the full absurd majesty of Wild Massive Super all around her.

Her thoughts were flooded with memories she'd buried a long time ago and would now have to bury again, and she was not pleased at all about it. They'd decayed in her mind over time, so that her last memories of Kellin all blurred together, and she was furious that the actor she'd just seen portraying him was now replacing his actual face in these memories.

She checked the time—the park was six hours away from its official closing time, still completely packed with people. In fact, a bullet train zoomed into the park to disgorge another batch of vacationers at a station built on the security wall. From there, guests could transfer to an elevated train that would shuttle them to the massive resort on the other side of the park, a twenty-four-hour fun zone with casinos, water rides, hallucination booths, the works. With no cozy elevator hiding nearby for her to return to, the thought of spending a night or two in a resort seemed appealing in a crass way.

Her attention was suddenly drawn to a small golf cart with an orange flashing light on it that was steadily wending its way through the crowd toward her. It was driven by what appeared to be a young human, probably a woman, skin a shade of violet, black hair done in a bob, wearing what Carissa judged to be "supervisor" attire as opposed to the khaki shorts and T-shirts the attendants all wore. This meant khaki slacks instead of shorts, and a Wild Massive bomber jacket over the T-shirt.

She pulled up at the exit ramp, as close as possible to Carissa, so close in fact that Carissa could see the name tag on her bomber jacket, which read TABITHA.

"Are you Alusia?" asked Tabitha as the golf cart jerked to a halt.

Carissa froze for a moment. As far as the park was concerned, her name was indeed Alusia, although why the fuck would they be looking for her?

"Is something wrong?" Carissa asked.

"We have a bit of a . . . situation, I guess you'd call it. My understanding is you and your companion Paoli were followed onto this floor. Does that sound right to you? Anyway, yeah, whoever is following you—they're on their way to the park now, and our security won't be able to stop them from getting in if they decide to be super violent about it. Do you happen to know where Paoli is right now?"

"What makes you think someone's following me?" Carissa demanded. "What makes you think you know anything about me?"

"Okay, yes, those are good questions," Tabitha said, "and I'm just going to lay it out for you because why not. I'm training myself in a form of weird divination, and I'm not very good at it yet, but I sometimes get these flashes of near-term events, I call them 'scenes,' which feed into this more elaborate vision, I call this 'plot,' and you both showed up as 'characters' in my current 'chapter'—"

"What, are you writing a book?" Carissa interrupted.

"*Yes, that's exactly* the method," Tabitha replied without hesitation, "which, no, I won't let you read it, because my self-esteem doesn't need the hit. Anyway, I know your real names are Carissa and Andasir, okay, and you met when ze landed on your elevator—is this ringing a bell? Because if it is, could you maybe help me find Andasir before those enforcers actually start doing violence or whatever?"

SEASON TWO

EPISODE 2.01

That's me in the golf cart.

My name is Tabitha Will. I'm twenty-six years old, and I'll spare you the joke about how I don't look a day over twenty-five—ha, no, I won't!

Anyway, I've lived at the Wild Massive Super resort since I was fourteen. I have a very nice suite, which I refer to as Headquarters because why wouldn't you.

I was raised by my grandmother, who was a truly ancient woman, something like six hundred years old by the time she settled in Des Moines, America, floor half a million and change, where I grew up. Even with the longevity pills in this Building, you do start to see signs of aging when you're six hundred years old, and I think she liked entering "spry elder" mode.

I never met my parents, and Grandma Dee didn't talk about the incident that claimed their lives. It happened on an Earth floor that was shitty even by Earth floor standards. Most Earth floors have a weird grouping of three elevators in North America, right down the middle, and then one on a mountain in China or something. Is it random? Does it mean something? This is me, shrugging helplessly and blowing past these vital questions. But the thing is, most Earth floors don't have Wild Massive fully controlling one of those elevators, making it safe to get on and off the floor. Really terrible people can take control of a mapped elevator, so it isn't always possible to escape out into the Building if you need to flee your particular floor.

When I turned fourteen years old, Grandma Dee gave me an incredibly special and rare gift: a capture glass. It's a beautiful multicolored crystal on a silver necklace, and when I say *multicolored*, I mean it gently changes colors as you gaze at it, mesmerized, until you either put it away or actually put it on.

It's also a magical amulet that stores the original owner's most precious memory inside, preserved intact from the ravages of time itself.

I assume she gave it to me then because she knew she was about to leave, and she wanted to make sure I knew what it meant, what it was worth—not how much money it was worth but what it was worth to our family as an heirloom. She said she'd had it her whole life, had gotten it from her mother, and it had been passed down matrilineally since before the Association even existed.

Mind you, there are a few other capture glasses in existence, a couple of dozen at least in museums and in the Archives and probably a couple of dozen more that circulate among collectors. They're all from the mythological era, pre-Association. Most of them store memories now that are much more recent. People get infatuated with reliving their favorite moments and can't resist using their capture glass, and then boom, some older memory is overwritten and a bit of history is lost forever.

Mine's not in anyone's catalog, and it stores a memory dating back to when these crystals were fashioned into capture glasses for the first time.

When she gave it to me, Grandma Dee told me, very matter-of-factly, she said, "The memory in this capture glass is from one of the Muses who built the universe, whose name we've long forgotten, but whose most precious memory is still intact."

On Earth floors, the idea of the Muses gets distilled down to nine goddesses with domain over specific areas in the arts and sciences. But in the mythological era of the Building at large, Muses played a different role—they were more like specialized subcontractors responsible for building out entire chunks of creation, at the direction of others higher up the celestial org chart. That's what Grandma Dee told me, anyway, and she knew her shit.

So she said, "You can relive this memory for yourself when you think you're ready."

And I was like, "Fork it over. I'm ready right this effing minute."

. . .

The memory starts with you studying hyperdimensional plans for areas of reality or something. But you don't get a chance to linger on these, because almost immediately you're approached by someone who feels like your supervisor, and without preamble, they say they've been watching your work and they're very impressed and they wonder if you'd consider an expanded role. And you're super pleased that you've been noticed, because you've been working hard, and you love what you do, and all that.

So you say something like, "What did you have in mind?"

And your supervisor says, "Let me show you."

And then they emit this *incredible* stream of energy from their mouth and aim it straight at you, and you're just . . . engulfed . . . atomized, or . . . like you've been thrown into a blast furnace, and you're completely immersed and infused in this wellspring of . . . raw creative will—and then you're suddenly born anew, with new skills and expanded perspective at your disposal, and you see the entire panoply of the grand endeavor in your mind's eye, the Building and everything around it, and you realize you've just been promoted.

Sure, your piece of it is tiny, but it's real, and you own it—well, you and your supervisor, who's still the Architect in charge, and they're just one Architect among many who all report to someone else and blah blah et cetera, but regardless, you've just been handed an enormous pool of creative discretion for interpreting and executing on the plans you'll be given. For improving them or adding your own style to them. It feels dizzying and exhilarating and frightening all at once.

Then the memory is over.

I woke up on the carpet, and Grandma Dee said, "The capture glass is yours now. Please don't lose it." Afterward, she took me out for pancakes.

I've had that wellspring of raw creative will coursing through me ever since I woke up on the carpet that day.

Of course, I didn't know what the heck to *do* with it. You don't become a fully realized artist at the age of fourteen just because you had an intense supernatural experience.

At the diner that morning, she told me she wasn't really from Des Moines. She said she came out of the elevator in St. Louis with my grandfather before my mother was born, and they were tired of exploring, they'd been exploring for hundreds of years, so they decided to stick around on this floor for a while.

At the age of fourteen, I knew the Building existed, but nobody I knew really liked to talk about it. They didn't teach us about it at school. I lived in one of those Americas where they printed textbooks with blank pages so that school boards could just decide on the fly what repressive bullshit they felt like teaching. I was surrounded by people who thought the Building was a socialist tower of sin, who couldn't handle how the Building negated or recontextualized their beliefs, who wouldn't take a first aid pill if they were dying of cancer. The fuck these nitwits were ever going to educate us about the Building.

Storm and Desire was the main way I knew anything about the Building. You could get 2D episodes off the internet if you knew where to look. That gave me perhaps an overly dramatic sense of what the Building was all about, but it was better than nothing. And I couldn't fathom what made Des Moines, America, so interesting compared to literally any other floor she could've picked.

"Why did you stop *here*, Grandma Dee?" I asked her. "What does this floor have that makes it so special?"

"It's not what it has," she said, "it's what it *doesn't* have."

Which, if you wanted to judge that statement on a scale of "fraught with meaning" to "pulled that out of my ass just now," I had my suspicions about how to vote.

But Grandma Dee, to her credit, was a patient six-hundred-year-old woman who knew her shit.

She said, "I was born in Des Moines. Not this one, obviously, but Des Moines all the same. I used to like hunting down new ones. They remind me of happy times, you know. Most Earth floors are a mess to start, or become a mess before long, but not this one. Shh, let me finish. I know you're not impressed with what you see, but look, this Earth floor doesn't have a climate catastrophe to deal with, because this Earth floor no longer has fossil fuel companies to deal with, and this Earth floor doesn't have poor people anymore, because this Earth floor gives every last person a basic income and a safe place to live, and all of these things are true because, it's like how cities used to clean up the streets before hosting the Olympics, except at a planetary scale. Because the billionaire illuminati assholes running *this* Earth weren't bidding for the Olympics.

"They were bidding to bring Wild Massive Super to St. Louis. And Wild Massive, by god, has *standards*."

Eventually, my grandfather got bored and took off in an elevator, back to the life, because he didn't share Grandma Dee's nostalgia for Des Moines. He did return for her birthday parties some years, though, and of course he was here for my parents' memorial. I missed him a bit, and I missed my parents in this deep but abstract kind of way, because I was so young when I lost them. But I was pretty satisfied with my life with Grandma Dee. Fourteen was old enough to know that everybody grows up with some degree of tragedy, and all things considered, I could've had it a lot worse.

. . .

A couple of months later, Grandma Dee took me to Wild Massive Super for my birthday. We drove from Des Moines to Chicago and then took the bullet train to St. Louis. I remember being weirded out about how much gunfire the train took as we got closer and closer to the park, which she just waved off and said, "This train could get hit by a meteor and it'd just bounce off."

Then we got to the park, and checked into the resort, and even though it was late for Grandma Dee, we still went out that night and spent some time on the riverfront, because she wanted to go up to the top of the Arch. And I was stoked because I realized she'd gotten us VIP passes, which meant all kinds of perks and treats and all that.

She hugged me before we went to bed that night, and she said, "You brought the capture glass with you, didn't you," and I wasn't sure if she was mad or what, but I don't lie, so I said, "Yeah, I'm taking care of it." She said, "Perfect. See you in the morning."

But I didn't see her in the morning, because she was gone when I woke up. Didn't leave a message or try to say goodbye, just flat out ghosted me. I suspect she got up early, got in line for the elevator, and left the floor for good.

So look, I was pretty clever for a fourteen-year-old, and I had a VIP pass and a room that was paid up for the next week. I wasn't thrilled about it at first—I was scared, and depressed, and I felt like I'd done something wrong to scare her off. It was not the right call for an adult to make, but I guess when you've lived over six hundred years, you wind up with a unique moral compass.

Anyway, I was also excited and exhilarated, running around the park every day with abandon, exploring every nook and cranny, seeing all the shows, eating at all the places, getting on every roller coaster and thrill ride, seeing the parade every night. I would head back to my room at the end of the day and crash hard and then get up and start all over. My VIP pass was connected to Grandma Dee's credit card, and her bank paid the bill on it automatically each month out of some mammoth savings account she'd accumulated in the course of getting really old, and I used it to extend my room reservation week after week after week, and buy food and schwag and tokens at the arcade, and it was just total absurdism, but I decided I didn't need to go back to Des Moines, because I'd brought the capture glass, the only important thing I owned, with me in a backpack, and I could get anything else I wanted inside the park—the park where I now lived.

When I was sixteen, I decided I wanted to try working for the park on the front line, like as a ride host, or in food service, or whatever. My underlying motive was, maybe I could make some actual friends that way. Living in the resort, you can meet a lot of people, but they only stick around for a week, and then they're just your pals on social. I wanted people I could hang out with, you know, or go to parties with, because they party like you wouldn't believe around here, and plus, I got to be super curious about how the park worked behind the scenes. Like, I wanted to see the secret tunnels underneath the park and find out the truth behind all the mysteries and legends that a place like this generates. I wanted to see it all for myself. I thought I'd have to fake some references, but the concierge at the resort put in a good word for me, and that was sufficient for part-time work apparently.

Working as a ride host was neat for a while, but then I decided I wanted to be one of the characters roaming around the park. I auditioned and got hired because I could play all the short characters, like Helpless the Bunny, and Lil' Menace to Society, and Calamity Roger, and I got to be in the nightly parade, and found out show people party even harder than the frontline kids. I'm just pointing that out in case you were worried about how a kid on her own could get proper socialization. I had it covered.

Then I decided I didn't just want to passively experience the rides in the park, I wanted to actually help *create* them. The storytelling urge in me was really starting to activate. I fashioned myself as a genius interactive narrative designer and got hired straight out of this incredible design college that secretly only exists on a web server that I operate. I was super charming in my interview, and my portfolio and my ideas were just exactly the shot in the arm Wild Massive really needed, as I repeatedly explained to them.

Suddenly, I was in the trenches designing attractions. And that got the attention of exactly the right people, which led to an invitation to join the *Storm and Desire* creative brain trust, making big story decisions about the next generation of rides while also contributing ideas to the actual primary narrative.

Eventually, I confessed all this to my mentor, after I'd proven myself many times over, and she was completely in love with the idea that I'd managed all this—that I lived at the park resort, that I'd had multiple park jobs, that I'd pulled off getting onto the creative brain trust. And she seemed moved, I think, by what I'd been through and took me under her wing.

My mentor was Allegory Paradox, Wild Massive's Chief Content Officer, last of the Muses still tinkering in our reality after all the other Muses departed for their next assignment.

She wasn't listed as "Muse" on the corporate intranet or whatever, but her creative brain trust all knew. I asked her once why she was the last Muse left, and she said, "For narrative reasons, dear. I need to know how it all ends, don't you see?" I assumed at the time she was talking about *Storm and Desire*.

.   .   .

Carissa wasn't thrilled about me at all.

"Look, I know how it sounds," I said, "but I need you to trust me."

"Nope," Carissa said.

"Just until I can get you and your friend out of the park."

"Ze's not my friend," Carissa replied, "and neither are you." She took a few steps toward the golf cart and said, "And today, my name is Alusia."

"I'm telling you the truth," I said. "You think it was a coincidence you landed on the same floor as me and my ride?"

"Uh, *your* ride?"

"I designed the story for *Rise of the Brilliant*," I told her. "What'd you think?"

Her eyes focused on me for a moment like she was shooting lasers at me.

Then she calmed herself and with a deadpan look said, "Not super realistic."

"Well, it's a thrill ride, not a history museum," I muttered.

To my surprise, she walked around the cart and climbed into the passenger seat. It didn't seem like a friendly gesture, to be honest.

"What else do you know about me, Tabitha?" she said. "Right answers only, please."

All cards on the table, huh? Well, turns out I did know a little more about Carissa than I'd let on so far.

Quietly, I said, "Can't you just compel me to tell you the truth?"

She was silent for a long moment. I'd given her the answer she was looking for. I realized I didn't know anything about her really, nothing about what kind of person she was, just a few data points that were true about her. It's just that one of those data points was the single most important secret she kept about herself, and I'd just blurted it out. I was naive to do that so swiftly, and all I could do was hope she didn't have other secrets that she could use against me.

Then finally, she said, "If it gets to where I need to do that, then we're past the point where we can have a healthy relationship, understand?"

I nodded.

"Who else knows about me?" she asked.

"Nobody," I said.

"Who else knows about your divinations?"

I said, "Just my boss, but she hasn't read this chapter yet. I don't tell anyone else. I suspect most people would never believe me. You don't seem fazed, though."

She shrugged and said, "I knew a guy who saw thirty minutes into the future, all the time, constantly. Died of a benzo overdose."

Harsh. But we seemed to have reached an understanding.

She said, "Last I saw the shapeshifter, ze was sitting on a bench across the street from the elevator. Guess we should hurry, huh?"

■　■　■

The quickest way to get back to the elevator from the *Storm and Desire* attraction was to go through "backstage," which is what we called the network of paths and roads behind the fences that were off-limits to guests. Backstage is where you'd find managers' offices and storage depots and cafeterias and dressing rooms for shows and such. I knew these routes backward and forward. I could easily get us to the elevator in less than ten minutes this way, versus fighting crowds out in the park. Hopefully, Andasir was still sitting on the bench where Carissa had seen zir last.

"How far into the future can you see?" she asked.

"I never see more than a day in advance, and even then, I get details wrong all the time," I said. "I usually get a couple major hits per upcoming day, they feel like déjà vu except for tomorrow, but sometimes I'm wrong or interpret them wrong. I'm an amateur still. I wish I knew exactly how it works, but it's more like harnessing wild magic than performing proper wizardry."

"So what was your other hit for today?"

"I saw four people wearing Association Security uniforms display psionic talents in a Wild Massive park."

I could feel Carissa tense up even without taking my eyes off the road.

In the silence that followed, I said, "I didn't think psionic talents were transferable. So that means . . ."

"They're all dead, Tabitha," she said, bitterly anticipating my train of thought.

"But what if they're not? What if some of them were captured? What if they were conscripted by the Association?"

"I don't play the 'what-if' game about genocide."

I dropped the subject.

All the glossy set dressing for the rides was public-facing. Backstage, you could see all the infrastructure, the support struts that held the rides up, the transformer stations and massive thaum conduits powering the park's illusions, the employee bulletin boards where people tacked up flyers for their parties. The paths were a little convoluted, because you had to steer around the roller coasters instead of under them, but otherwise, you could move through backstage with pretty good speed.

"How'd you recognize me coming out of the ride?" she asked.

"I had a mental picture of you," I said. "I don't have one for Andasir, though. Hard to decide on a mental picture for a shapeshifter, I guess."

We came around a sharp corner and I screeched to a halt, narrowly avoiding a collision with a group of character performers on their way out into the park with their handlers. Even though androids had better stamina for this kind of work, Wild Massive preferred live performers to play the company's iconic characters because they had much better improv skills. After they'd safely passed us and a few friendly expletives were hurled in both directions (I actually knew some of these folks), we got back up to speed.

"What's your book about?" she asked, finally getting to the point of her little interrogation.

"Modern mythology," I said. "Folk tales of life in the Building."

"Pretty broad, Tabitha."

"Take it or leave it, that's what I write. And . . . I mean, I've put a lot of thought into what life was like for the Brilliant before the Association came along. Or I should say, I've imagined it many times, because . . ."

"Because you don't have anybody to interview," Carissa concluded.

We barreled back onto a public street and slowly threaded through the cacophonous masses until the elevator pavilion was in sight. The main feature of the pavilion was a tall lighthouse with a beacon inside that lit up every time the elevator arrived. Wild Massive's loyal fans recognized this landmark from the film *The Lighthouse Keeper's Apprentice*, in which Helpless the Bunny is so terrible in the titular role that he's responsible for the fates of the *Titanic*, the *Lusitania*, and the *Hindenburg* for good measure.

A few people were seated on the bench across the street from the pavilion. "Ze's still there," Carissa said.

We pulled up slowly and came to a halt. A figure on the end of the bench—nonbinary, dressed in overalls similar to Carissa's, skin color a shade tanner than Carissa's—recognized her as she hopped out of the golf cart.

"You're back," said Andasir.

"This is Tabitha," Carissa told zir. "She wants to help you get out of here."

Ze studied me for a moment, but apparently Carissa had already earned zir trust.

"Very well," ze said. "What shall we do?"

"Get in," I said.

Even though we were right across the street from the elevator, we couldn't just cut to the front of the line; we'd get stopped long before then and my supervisor attire wouldn't pull any weight if I made a scene in full view of a long line of guests.

Instead, after Andasir had climbed into the back seat, we "took off" down the street (these things only go slightly faster than walking speed), looking for the next vehicle exit to get backstage.

"Would you care to explain what's going on?" Andasir asked politely.

"When you were scanned for magic at the front gate," I said, "I think the scan produced enough of a visible trace of you that your pursuers were able to detect it."

"So they know I'm in the park somewhere," Andasir said.

"Yes, so we're getting you *out* of the park."

"Pardon the question, but what is your interest in this business?" ze asked.

"I see the near future in tiny fragments, and I saw that you were in trouble," I said. "My instinct told me to do something, but I didn't see enough to know what I *should* do, so I'm winging it. Does that help?"

Andasir said, "It'll suffice for now."

Took us a while, but soon we were able to get out of the crowds and get properly moving again. We reached a small parking lot for utility vehicles and scooters and jumped out. The last bit was a walking path that took us up a short hill to the rear of the elevator pavilion, a small canopied area tucked away out of sight behind a tall hedge, with a picnic table where attendants could take their breaks. By design, you couldn't see the guests in line from here, meaning they couldn't see you eating lunch on your break, either. But from here, you could simply slip through a small gap in the hedge and you could be standing right at your post in front of the elevator at a moment's notice.

"This is as close as I can get you," I said. "There will be no more than two attendants in front of the elevator. When you hear the *ding*, you've got maybe five seconds for the doors to open and then they'll wave in the next party of guests. You can either beat them into the elevator, or you can tailgate with them and bring up the rear, whichever you prefer. Think you can handle that?"

"That's it?" Carissa said. "Your big plan is 'Think you can handle that'?"

"Pretty sure I said I didn't have a big plan," I snapped.

"I can perform an illusion that will dazzle the attendants," ze said. "I'll board the elevator while they remain dazed."

"Excellent," I said. "Follow me."

We slipped through the small gap in the hedge, emerging in front of the elevator. I was expecting a long line of people, a pair of attendants, hubbub and commotion, all that. But there were no guests and no attendants to be seen. The entire pavilion had been cleared out.

Instead, we were face-to-face with my mentor, Allegory Paradox, accompanied by two enormous, menacing lizard people, for lack of a better description.

"Oh, there you are!" exclaimed Allegory. "Perfect!"

.   .   .

The lizard people took Andasir into custody so fast that I had zero chance to explain to Andasir that I hadn't done this, this turn of events was a surprise to me, but I imagine ze wouldn't have believed me, anyway.

After a few uncomfortable minutes of silence, the elevator arrived, and the three Shai-Manak shuffled aboard and were gone.

Allegory Paradox shared the key physical characteristics of a human woman, except that she was eight feet tall and absurdly slender. Her long red ponytail fell to her waist, her skin was the corporate gray color that was in vogue among the executive class these days, and she always seemed to dress as though she were on her way to give a keynote speech at a trade conference. At five feet two inches, I always felt like a literal child in moments like these, when I was forced to crane my neck just to make eye contact with her.

But she looked past me and said, "This must be your friend Alusia. Don't let me stop the two of you from enjoying the rest of your evening. Be sure to see the parade, Alusia!" Then she glanced back at me and said, "We'll talk tomorrow."

And with that, Allegory Paradox strode out of the pavilion.

Rindasy descended from the Shai-Manak floor alone in an elevator, wearing the physical form of Agent Anjette, flushed with anger at Andasir for trying to stop this mission. But the anger quickly gave way to confusion, as the replica, now cut off from Anjette, pivoted toward intensive, rapid integration.

Indeed, if you granted the replica any kind of independent sentience in your consideration of its situation, you might see why the replica now favored working hard to keep Rindasy alive by propping up the ruse in every possible way.

Rindasy had expected the acquisition and integration of Anjette's memories, knowledge, and skills to be a clean and straightforward process, but thanks to their intense conflict back in the holding cell, the effect was instead similar to acquiring a vast library of encyclopedias, delivered in the form of individual pages thrown off a tower and scattered in the wind. Zir psyche was in an intense state of disarray and chaos.

As the replica worked to clean up this mess, it became deeply skeptical of Rindasy's ability to convincingly pull off Anjette's clear and calm affect and demeanor.

It determined that its role, then, was to run Rindasy through a series of simulated encounters with peers, all within the confines of zir imagination. The elevator was a perfectly reasonable place to run these simulations. Elevators were black boxes from a surveillance perspective; no one ever knew what was happening inside any given elevator except the cloudlets. So as long as Rindasy stayed in the elevator, the badge ze'd stolen from Anjette wouldn't hit the network.

The replica's training was rigorous and extensive; it had no intention of letting Rindasy fail, and technically, Rindasy even approved of the effort. At the same time, the replica harnessed a chunk of Rindasy's mental capacity for building an index to all of Anjette's disparate memories, knowledge, and skills so that they could be put to use as naturally as accessing zir own such information.

Practically, this resulted in Rindasy being physically frozen in the corner of the elevator, slumping slowly down the wall toward the floor, then somehow catching the handrail and propping zirself upright.

"Well, you certainly seem to have relaxed," the elevator's cloudlet said. "Do you happen to have a more specific destination in mind now?"

Rindasy could not respond. The replica was so focused on its work that it didn't even hear the question.

"In that case, I hope you don't mind if I pick up a few passengers along the way down."

·   ·   ·

A pleasant *ding* preceded the opening of the elevator doors.

Sometimes, inexplicably, you'd find a floor where the only things on the floor were the four elevator banks, situated on each of the four walls of a small, empty, lobby-like space, with nice red carpeting, a little light music playing, inoffensive inset lighting in the ceiling. These were the only known floors where you could see all four elevator banks at once without moving from your spot because they were so unnaturally close to one another, as though the Building's footprint was no larger than a conference room. These floors were called *intersections*.

Intersections were useful shortcuts for explorers in the upper reaches of the Building to know, since there were so many floors that only had one or two mapped elevator locations. From an intersection, you could quickly switch from Left to Right or Up to Down (or the other variations implied) without having to make a potentially long journey through an entire floor.

Publishers of competing regional floor indices frequently omitted intersections, since they could make it too easy for you to avoid commercial districts or toll stations. Trusted sources like the Explorers Guild only appended to their intersection guides infrequently, and the cloudlets refused to publish any guides or indices at all. Anytime you discovered an intersection or learned about one, you potentially had bank on your hands. (Intersections weren't valuable below the border, thanks to the Association's extensive teleport relay network.) There were rumors—legends, really—that if four elevators arrived at an intersection at the exact same time, something profound or wondrous would happen, like spontaneous gnosis for all, but no one ever claimed they'd been present for such an event.

Outside Rindasy's elevator, two individuals stood waiting in an intersection.

Rindasy was sufficiently cognizant to guess these two to be human, one masculine and one feminine, wearing colorful clothes in severe disrepair. The masculine individual was tall, rail thin, his shirt ripped open for no good reason, wearing a tattered white tuxedo jacket with pompous spotted elbow patches, and a stovepipe hat that was too small to wear properly so glue or some other fastener had clearly been deployed. The feminine individual wore a sleek silver ballerina costume underneath a ridiculous pink crinoline that had been savagely attacked, it seemed, by small, ferocious animals, and an unassuming bow sat perched atop her silver wig. They both had color-cycling skin implants, which Rindasy found unexpectedly soothing to look at.

"Going up or down?" the man asked. "No arrows. It's weird."

"The current passenger has chosen no destination," the cloudlet said, "hence you may choose up *or* down for your own ride with us today."

Rindasy could feel them staring at zir as they stepped onto the elevator and carefully positioned themselves against the opposite wall of the car from zir.

"Where should we go?" the woman asked.

"Fuck if I care," the man replied.

"Well, I don't give a fuck, either," the woman said. The doors slid shut. The elevator didn't move.

▪   ▪   ▪

The replica correctly determined Rindasy's query priorities and began surfacing specific memories to the foreground while sorting other information subconsciously.

In this fashion, Rindasy found zirself reliving the memory of boarding a shuttle alongside four Security officers whom Anjette had never met. Not uncommon; Security was a large organization. By her estimation, though, these four barely seemed to be holding themselves together. It wasn't panic in their eyes, exactly; more like some kind of unusual strain, as though they were concentrating *very hard* on something and couldn't spare the cycles to explain what it was.

And then the replica rewound to an earlier point the same day, shortly after the Shai-Manak attack on Wild Mega had first occurred. Security had lost surveillance and was now in the process of simultaneously freaking out and planning a mission, and they'd requested Anjette's participation.

One of her occasional contacts in weapons research, a ghostly apparition named Jirian Echo, described his proposal for a counterattack against the Shai-Manak. Jirian Echo's team had found a way to convey the psionic talents of the Brilliant to regular humans. The effect was temporary, lasting less than an hour on average, but the power rating was off the charts while the effect lasted. They'd trained several Security officers to utilize various talents, and they wanted to send some of these officers in to face the squad of Shai-Manak sorcerers that had invaded an Association floor. The likely survival rate for these officers was promising enough, given the prowess they'd developed with utilizing psionic talents at full intensity, and their survival rate went up factoring Anjette as an escort.

"So you took Brilliant prisoners?" Anjette asked, wanting Jirian Echo to confirm the obvious. "And studied them to pull this off? Are they alive somewhere?"

"They're perfectly comfortable," Jirian Echo replied.

This was significant news; the Agents who witnessed the conflict with the Brilliant up close were led to believe that the Brilliant were all dead and gone.

"I'd like to see them, to confirm their comfort level, if you don't mind," Anjette said firmly, making Jirian squirm. Agents could pull rank on any individual in the Association short of a minister in Parliament. "I'll stop by to see you after I get back from your mission."

.   .   .

"Are you high right now?" the man asked.

Rindasy struggled to focus zir eyes on the couple across the elevator from zir. The man was clearly addressing zir, but zir ability to respond was clearly offline at the moment.

"Do you want to be *less* high?" he said. Then he turned to his companion and said, "Can we do that? Do we have less high?"

The woman shook her head and said, "Just more high."

He took a sideways look at Rindasy's condition, then said, "Maybe more high's not a great idea for this one."

"You don't know. Seriously, you don't. Remember, that one time you wanted less high, but then you got more high by accident instead? That worked out okay, right?"

"Did it? I mean, which time?"

"At Cicely's place."

"Ohhhh." He paused, then said, "But, like . . . I don't remember literally *any* of what happened at Cicely's place, so did it really work out 'okay,' do you think?"

"Don't play mind games with me, Johnny. Did you die? Are you dead right now? Because yes, I'm telling you it worked out okay."

"Would you care to specify a destination floor?" the cloudlet asked.

"No," the couple said in unison.

Rindasy felt zirself sinking toward the floor again, but ever so slowly, couldn't possibly be noticeable to these—chaos elementals, or whoever they were—and zir grip on the handrails was shifting, possibly slipping, as zir legs began to tremble, possibly on the verge of buckling.

Anjette was an ancient being, and while the replica was diligently working to avoid overwhelming Rindasy, the struggle was ongoing. Waves of history seemed to unleash themselves at Rindasy in torrents so vast ze felt like ze'd never comprehend a fraction of these experiences. *Is all of this absolutely necessary?* ze demanded of the replica. Would all of this come into play during the limited window of time in which Rindasy's masquerade was in effect?

If Agent Grey detects you're not the real Anjette, the replica replied, *you'll instantly regret that you're not indestructible like she is.*

Memories of Agent Grey in action surfaced briefly, blinding Rindasy with sudden intensity. Agent Grey, de facto leader of Dimension Force, had earned the nicknames "the Commanding Word" and "the Cleansing Fire." And to Rindasy's dismay, Anjette had cultivated an ever-so-slightly antagonistic relationship with Agent Grey, subtly testing Grey's authority over centuries of working together. You could get away with that if you were indestructible, apparently.

"You want music, maybe?" the man asked zir. "Some Earth music, maybe?"

"Nobody wants to hear prog rock in an elevator, Johnny," the woman said. "It's, like, literally antithetical or whatever. Just let this person have their freak-out."

"Putting on music is practically like harm reduction, though."

"Your music is like harm *inducing*. You have a zillion floors' worth of music to choose from, and you literally pick the shittiest music you can find off a search engine, and I just *can't* with that, like what foul search terms do you even use, I just . . . You know what? Find some of those soothing soundscapes where people whisper and like chew tinfoil for eight hours to help you get to sleep."

"Ohhhhh, gotcha." He turned to Rindasy and said, "Keep it steady there, friendo. We'll figure this out, I promise."

.   .   .

Finally, the replica was satisfied that Rindasy could pass for Anjette under most of the likely scenarios ze'd encounter. Rindasy was left with open questions about Anjette's genesis, but the replica simply indicated Anjette had the same questions and had been satisfied so far to leave them unanswered. If you asked Anjette where she'd come from, her signature response was dead silence; not "I don't know" or "It's a mystery" or anything else, just dead silence and a cold stare. Many interviews had been cut short in this fashion over time.

Rindasy finally reasserted control of zir physical form with a quick snap, jolting upright, eyes suddenly focusing on zir companions in the elevator.

"You made it!" the man exclaimed with a big smile. "We were . . . not exactly concerned or whatever, but certainly curious there for a minute."

"Do you have any water?" Rindasy asked.

The woman happened to have a big water bottle hanging from a strap on her shoulder, which she handed to Rindasy as she said, "Nope, just champagne."

Disappointed, Rindasy handed the bottle back. Intoxicants were inadvisable even in low doses for shapeshifters trying to maintain a specific form. Ze began formulating a plan. First ze needed to establish with Dimension Force that Anjette had escaped from the Shai-Manak and was back on duty; this would likely require reporting directly to Agent Grey.

Then, if ze passed that critical juncture, a visit to Jirian Echo seemed to be in order. "Welcome back, Agent," the cloudlet said.

The couple's eyes grew wide. They were most likely only familiar with the actors who played the Agents in *Storm and Desire,* not the real Agents themselves.

"Agent what now?" the man said. "Wait, which one are you?"

The woman smacked the man's arm and said, "Who do you think? It's Wynderia."

"C'mon, if it was Wynderia, she'd be invisible," the man protested. "You're Glamour Esque, right?"

"I'm Anjette," Rindasy said decisively, liking the sound of it coming from zir voice.

"Would you care to specify a destination floor?" the cloudlet asked.

"I would," Rindasy replied. "Take me to the Vantage Point, please." Dimension Force headquarters was on floor 22, nicknamed the Vantage Point.

"Certainly. I would remind our other passengers that Association identification will be required along this route."

"Oh shit. Well, just let us off here, eh?" the man said.

The elevator doors slid open, and the couple staggered back into the intersection and offered smiles and waves as the doors slid shut. Soon thereafter, Rindasy was unusually pleased to hear the gentle hum of the elevator beginning its descent.

EPISODE 2.03

Almost three years after Grandma Dee abandoned me at Wild Massive Super—roughly nine years before I met Carissa in the same park—I received a surprise visit from my adopted uncle. I knew him by the alias Trick Start, the Pirate King. Grandma Dee collected an array of characters as her close friends over the years; we used to see Trick Start reliably for her birthday parties and occasionally for mine too after I got a little older. He was part-human, part-demon (his mother was apparently a minor calamity or a demon of discord; he wasn't sure himself), and the human side won out for the most part when it came to his appearance, but some of that was glamour that he could drop if he wanted to scare you senseless as a tiny practical joke by revealing a hint of his inhuman side.

He tracked me down and showed up unannounced, leaving me a message to meet him in the resort lounge when I was done with my shift. I was elated to see him, but the deal with Trick Start was you needed to keep your cool around him, because he was the most wanted thief in history, and he could be a little jumpy. The Association had a habit of confiscating technology it deemed threatening and then making it illegal for anyone else to use. Trick Start had a habit of stealing and selling this technology for exorbitant prices in hidden markets scattered across the multiverse.

Instead of dashing up to give him a hug, I sauntered up smoothly and said, "Can you stay for dinner? I know a place that'll let you in, even looking like that."

He arched his eyebrow at me, knowing full well he was so stylish that an entire academic branch of fashion philosophy now wrestled with the fact of his exquisite taste, and said, "Only if you change out of that uniform first, and preferably after you've set it on fire in a bathtub as well." He glanced at my name tag and said, "Tabitha, is it?"

I nodded. Last time I saw him, I was still going by Lily.

He nodded back in acknowledgment. Certainly someone named Trick Start understood the value of crafting your identity to suit yourself.

We went to dinner at Pointless Topology, the upscale restaurant in the resort, and my heart was pounding as the drinks arrived—an obscure off-world liqueur for Trick Start, coffee for me—because I realized there could only be one reason that Trick Start would pop up in my life after three years had passed without hearing a word from him.

"Did something happen to Grandma Dee?" I asked.

"I'm surprised her well-being is a concern of yours," he replied.

I thought about that for a moment. Maybe I was surprised as well.

"But the answer to your question is yes, something happened to her," he continued. "I can tell you if you'd like to know."

That was kind of him, giving me the chance to reflect on whether I really did want to know what happened to her. Our fates were no longer intertwined, and I'd gotten rather used to it, could even take pride in the person I was becoming on my own. But three years of wondering and worrying took their own toll, and besides, if she needed help and I could provide it, I'd do anything I possibly could, no matter what her reasons for leaving had been.

"Tell me," I said.

"I want you to know," he replied, "that I was led to believe she'd placed you in a boarding school so that she could go off on her adventures, or I'd have come straightaway. I'm sorry you spent the last three years alone."

"Wasn't alone," I replied, putting on a brave face. "I have friends in the park, friends online. What adventures?"

"She joined the Explorers Guild," he told me. "That's why she left in such a hurry—she finally received the invitation to join them she'd always hoped for."

"I thought the Explorers Guild disbanded," I said.

"They splintered a bit, but they're still active. I subscribe to their newsletter. Your grandmother managed to publish two reports under her own byline while she was with them—respectable. Unfortunately, she herself is a footnote in a third report." He pulled an envelope out of his coat pocket and slid it across the table to me. "I've taken the liberty of printing these reports for you."

I took the envelope and said, "You could've emailed these."

"That's exactly how I myself received them," he said. "I was simply flipping through the morning messages and before I knew it, I was staring at painfully unexpected news, alone in my cabin on a ship millions of some abstract conceptual unit of spacetime away from anyone who'd ever heard of Delia, who could raise a glass with me in her memory, and I thought . . . I thought her beloved granddaughter might feel the loss even more keenly than I did. Might want a friendly face nearby when she got the news."

"Oh," I said. "Thank you."

He took a sip of his liqueur, then said, "I can't really do 'friendly,' as it were, but I presume 'familiar' is adequate."

I read the newsletter reports while Trick Start nibbled on the appetizers he'd ordered. Well, skimmed them at least, and really, I was mostly just looking for footnotes. I found the one I was looking for soon enough: confirmation that there'd be no happy reunion someday, no extravagant act of contrition or even a simple apology. Something got past their sentry system on a floor they'd just begun exploring. "A wild animal with unanticipated properties," said the footnote. Her death had not been peaceful. I didn't bother to finish reading after that.

"I like your clubhouse here," he said as I put the reports back in the envelope. "How much longer do you plan to stay?"

"I don't have any plans to leave, really."

He must've read something in my expression, because he said, "Don't let Delia's fate become a cloud over you. You don't have to join the Explorers Guild to be an explorer. There are many safe and well-documented places you could visit."

"My friends online give me shit because I live so close to an elevator and never use it," I admitted. "It's nice to know it's there, but I haven't felt the pull to leave."

"Do you plan to spend the rest of your days strapping people into roller coasters, or do you have other preoccupations?"

"I start working for Wild Massive corporate on Monday," I said. "As a narrative designer."

"Oh, really?" Trick Start said. "What possessed you to take such legitimate work at such a tender young age?"

"She gave me her capture glass before she left," I replied. "And I've felt pretty inspired by it ever since."

He seemed to breathe a sigh of relief and murmured, "Well done, Delia."

"What happened to all the Muses?" I asked him suddenly. "Did you ever wonder where they all went after they finished creating the Building and everything in it?"

The question caught Trick Start off guard, unaccustomed as he was to favoring questions from teenagers about the nature of existence. But he recovered gracefully enough to say, "Some people think the Building will never be finished. They say you can never reach the top floor because once you arrive where it should be, you'll find an algorithmic engine that forever generates new floors and spawns variety inside them."

"So?"

"So I think the moral of that fable is, you could imagine the Muses are no longer required to take an active role in seeing the Building to completion. They've set the requisite processes in motion and now perhaps they've been . . . reassigned, let's say."

"Reassigned where, though?"

"You do understand there's an entire multiverse outside the Building, don't you? Maybe that's a trick to imagine given that you've barely been outside the walls of this park, let alone outside the Building. You'll have to take my word for it, since that's where I do much of my work. Anyway, perhaps once they'd honed their skill sets by establishing the Building and training themselves here, the Muses moved on to the vastly more difficult challenge of forging everything else. That's where they may be to this very day, iterating at the farthest edges of existence and extending it ever further by sheer force of creative will." He quickly added, "If you believe that sort of thing in the first place, of course."

"I do," I said, awed by his description.

"Try not to be so enthusiastic about their fate," Trick Start told me. "Sounds to me like they're nonunion labor, for starters."

Trick Start got me a subscription to the Explorers Guild newsletter, enabling me to watch over the years as they worked their way farther and farther up the Building, eventually admitting they were on an absurd quest to reach the top floor once and for all.

If you asked a cloudlet to take you to the top floor, the cloudlet would remind you that the top floor wasn't listed in its directory and thus couldn't be reached by elevator. If you tried to take an interdimensional jump ship up to the top floor, your ship would never be heard from again. Separating the rest of the Building from the legendary top floor was a metaphysical hazard of the highest degree known as *the chasm*, a weird, amorphous barrier that predated the Association and had no commonly accepted origin story.

Nicholas Solitude wrote the Explorers Guild report that documented their arrival at the edge of the chasm, an encounter that cost the lives of two explorers and forced the Guild to retreat several floors down the Building in fear. He could've written it at any time during the past several years, but the Guild only published it quite recently with little fanfare. The report posed more questions than it answered, and the top floor remained shrouded in speculation and legend.

. . .

As soon as the Shai-Manak and Allegory were gone, Carissa jabbed the button to summon an elevator for herself.

"Really?" I said. "You're leaving?"

"I don't give a fuck about seeing the parade," she replied.

Naturally, the elevators arrived according to their own whims, forcing Carissa to wait. The attendants eventually returned, slowly escorting guests back into their places in line, and one of the attendants was a shift manager. Dude was clearly peeved that his queue was entirely out of whack thanks to meddling from corporate.

He said, "You got reservations?"

Carissa said, "Nope."

He said, "Back of the line."

I said, "She's with me. I brought her to the front." I was wearing my old supervisor name tag after all, and I thought a little manager solidarity might work on him.

But he didn't care. He said, "Next time, don't do that. Back of the line."

A pleasant *ding* indicated the elevator had arrived. The doors opened, and Carissa started to board. Dude placed himself in between her and the elevator.

"Back of the line," he said.

And then Carissa said, "*Shut the fuck up and let me get on this elevator.*" Without a word, dude stepped aside, and she practically leapt into the car. I leapt into the car with her.

She caught the doors with her hand and said, "No way."

I said, "If any of the Brilliant are still alive, I can help you find them."

She said, "If they're still alive, they've been prisoners for a hundred years and they're fucked ten ways to heaven. Who cares."

The other attendant said in a conciliatory voice, "Could you move along, please? We do have rather a long line here."

Carissa glared at him, then glared at me, but relented and let the doors close.

"Welcome!" said the elevator's cloudlet as Carissa pulled out her tablet and began working on it. "What's your destination this fine day?"

"Nearest trading post," Carissa said. "A real one, no tourists."

"You used your talent on that attendant, right?" I said.

"Sure did," she said.

"How's it work?"

"Look it up in your little fucking book," she snapped.

"Oh, hooray, there you are!" said a new cloudlet's voice, presumably the cloudlet Carissa had been traveling with in the last elevator she'd inhabited. "I see we're headed to gear back up. And you've got company—how unexpected."

"I'm Tabitha," I said.

"That's interesting," said the cloudlet.

"Look, you'll have to excuse me for not trusting you, after you walked Andasir right into a trap," Carissa said. "If you think you're going to bust me the same way, you're delusional. I will *not* wind up in some Association torture farm, understand me? So you can just forget everything you think you know about me, about my talent, about the Brilliant, just delete all those pages, and pretend we never met."

"They're handwritten," I said. "Maybe while you're shopping at the trading post, I could sit down and try to make progress on my daily word count. And maybe I'll be able to give you some little sliver of information you'll find . . . meaningful, or helpful, or something."

"What's in it for you?" she said. "Why do you even remotely care what happens to me?"

I took a deep breath and said, "I'm one of the narrative designers for *Storm and Desire*. I did a lot of work on the arc that just started, about the Brilliant. It's the first one that's going to feature a tragic ending. I mean, we could lie, or I mean, we could dramatize it any way we want, because our audience has no idea what actually happened to the Brilliant. Instead, we're going to *show* what actually happened to the best of our ability and try to hold the Association accountable for once, in a small way at least.

"But . . . meeting you—a survivor of genocide—that's an untold story we hadn't factored. And then the psionic attack on Wild Mega—I mean, that's another untold story, right? And

I'm just like . . . there's no escaping the tragedy inherent in what they did to your people, I get it, but maybe the ending of this arc hasn't actually happened yet. Maybe there's time for . . . something. Justice, maybe? Poetic justice at least? Or, like, the mighty Association couldn't catch *you*, and that *means* something, right?"

"Does it really?" she asked quietly. "Because it seems really arbitrary from where I'm standing."

"Maybe. I mean, sure, life is just stuff that happens, I get it. Anyway, now we're in preproduction on the final arc of the entire series. Spoiler alert, it's all about the Shai-Manak's struggle against the Association. The Association wants us to rewrite the Brilliant story line so the Association doesn't look like absolute villains, and we refused. So now they know if they wipe out the Shai-Manak somehow, if they go for two genocides in a row, we're going to tell that story, too. That story's going to be the grand finale of *Storm and Desire*, the culmination of two hundred consecutive years of storytelling. We can bring this saga home with a glorious depiction of forging peace with a fearsome enemy, or we can exit on a horrific confirmation of villainy and evil as one more enemy is ruthlessly exterminated. It's all up to the Association which way the ending turns."

"Or it's up to the Shai-Manak," she said. "You know, the people who conquered your new theme park?" I must've looked surprised that she knew about that, because she added, "Cloudlets see more than you think, and they like to gossip."

"It's true," her cloudlet admitted.

"Right, of course. Wild Massive corporate is pissed beyond belief about that attack, but I mean that seemed like *gold* to the *Storm and Desire* creative brain trust. No one expected the Shai-Manak to escalate by taking over an entire Association floor. No one expected the Association to retaliate by using what might be captured Brilliants against them. This is it, this is our story line now, a perfect bridge between the Brilliant arc and the Shai-Manak arc."

"Convenient," she said. "How's it all end?"

"Before the attack on Wild Mega, our narrative simulations for the conflict had it pegged at 'totally formulaic genocide by the Association.' Now it's looking like 'bitter rivals destroy half the Building trying to kill each other; flip a coin to see who wins.' Either of those outcomes would be a terrible way to wrap up a fifty-five-thousand-episode saga about the achievements of the great and mighty Association.

"But the simulations don't know about *you*."

I was trembling a little as I finally finished speaking. Carissa was looking at the floor at that point.

"So this is all about entertainment value to you?" she said.

"Look, for ten long arcs of *Storm and Desire*, we've been depicting our version of Association history, slices of it, anyway. But the ending of the Brilliant arc is up for grabs, and the entire Shai-Manak arc is yet to be written. We're no longer mere historians, documenting history and putting our dramatic little stamp on it. We have a chance to *make* history. I mean, they literally staged a fight scene in one of our theme parks—how much more on the nose could this situation be? So look . . . I have a sliver of influence over how this narrative unfolds, and I'm trying to do the right thing with it. But you . . . you have a chance to have a much bigger influence than I ever could, because this is technically still *your* story, right?"

She laughed and said, "Are you literally and completely out of your fucking mind? Wild Massive makes roller coasters. It doesn't make history."

"We make the *best* roller coasters, to be clear."

"That doesn't make you a political player."

"No, but blowing off the Association's script notes certainly gives us skin in the game."

"Oh, so you blew off their script notes, and now—what? What happens? You think they really care about their public image? Because one of their citizens might suddenly have an independent thought and wonder, 'Why can't we all just get along?' They're hassling you about your story because they're assholes, not because they're threatened. If Parliament thought you could really hold it accountable, for anything, ever, they'd carpet bomb your theme parks into oblivion, and your corporate headquarters would be a radioactive crater."

"They wouldn't dare," I said quietly.

"Tabitha—maybe you forgot—it's called the Parliament of Storm and Desire. You may have stolen the name for your show, but it's *their* story and *they're* telling it, not you. They don't answer to anybody."

"Not true," I said. "Muses have oversight over Parliament."

"Oh, you mean the Muses that fled the Building and left Parliament in charge in the first place?"

"No, clearly, I don't mean *those* Muses," I said and left it at that.

In the silence that followed, the cloudlet said, "Tabitha, would you like me to take you to any particular floor?"

"I'm going with Carissa to the trading post," I announced. "Unless she convinces me to do something else."

"I'm not going to convince you to do anything," she said.

"Good. Then I'll write. I'll even let you read it."

"What are you going to write with? Do we have to buy you a notebook or something?"

I decided to just trust her at that point. I performed a short, powerful incantation that I'd paid for at great expense, which opened a small portal to an extradimensional safe that I could access from anywhere. I kept the capture glass in this safe, and I kept my own notebooks in it as well. I grabbed the topmost notebook off the modest stack and one of the pens I kept handy. Then I closed the safe by dispelling the portal with another incantation.

I think something clicked with her about that gesture, because she said, "Here's how my talent works. It's mind control, only works on one person at a time, has to be in my line of sight.

I'm lucky it's not more powerful, or the Brilliant would've killed me themselves. But it's obviously not a useful talent when you're facing down Fleet. Anyway, now you can factor that in when you're writing about me."

.   .   .

We arrived at the trading post, an entire standard floor filled with long tables and rings of booths and merchandise stands and all that. *Standard floor* meant no reality emitters or pocket dimensions, just a straightforward square, half a kilometer to a side. I found a little teahouse tucked away in a corner where I could sit and write while Carissa roamed about looking for whatever she came here for. Probably headphones, I realized.

My mind usually worked fast on personal writing because I didn't get much time for it, so I hit the ground running.

As the lead narrative designer for the *Rise of the Brilliant* ride experience, I had access to the entire story bible that the creative brain trust used to spin out episodes of the main series. We knew as much as we did about what happened to the Brilliant because Allegory had spies planted all throughout the Association. She'd cultivated spy networks that had survived for literal generations. Our intel was generally good.

The Brilliant were from an undocumented Earth floor below the Association border. They were a tribe of roughly sixty-five people possessing powerful psionic talents. That was a big departure for an Earth floor, which usually demonstrated zero or minimal supernatural elements. Somehow this tribe used their talents to locate an unmapped elevator and anchor it in place under their control, "conquering" most of downtown Minneapolis in the process and holding it firmly against police and National Guard units. One might identify this sequence of events as "the rise of the Brilliant" if one were sufficiently clever. Cloudlets running routes on Association floors were not chill about undocumented floors opening up; they immediately notified Security, and soon, the lurching apparatus of the Association diplomatic corps focused its full gaze on the situation.

The Brilliant applied to join the Association. Not on behalf of the planet or their city, mind you. They wanted to join as a tribe or what the diplomats called an "independent nomadic political entity." The application process lasted maybe two months—lots of interviews, technical assessments, personality tests, medical exams, whatever else was on the standard checklist for evaluating an application, nothing out of the ordinary. The Brilliant learned their application was denied when Fleet jumped ten heavy warships onto the floor and obliterated half of North America.

This, of course, was "the fall of the Brilliant."

.　.　.

Most of the tribe manifested a single psionic talent. Only a handful of individuals manifested two talents.

Kellin, their leader, manifested four talents: levitation, telekinesis, pyrokinesis, and telepathy. He could use them all simultaneously at tremendous power levels with near-perfect control. He was the public face of the Brilliant. The only other Brilliant of that caliber was a woman named Indira, who could reproduce any psionic talent she'd ever witnessed. She frequently lacked precision, but she was reliable enough when they wanted a big blast radius for a given effect.

Carissa was probably in our spy data somewhere, and the brain trust—including me—must not have felt she was worth promoting to the main cast of the series as a recurring character. We still had time to fix that. A skill like hers wasn't showy or flamboyant, and it relied on close quarters, but that had advantages when it came to character moments.

I started taking notes as I shifted into brainstorming for my folk tale.

Maybe Carissa was somebody Kellin trusted completely. She

used her talent to defuse anyone in her tribe who lost their temper, maybe. Actually, raising the stakes—maybe Kellin himself was known for losing his temper, and Carissa was the only person who could get near him before he blew up half the city or something. Maybe the reason he trusted her—the reason he allowed her to live, really, even though she alone could actually control him—is that she was his baby sister. He trusted her—counted on her, even, to help keep the entire tribe in line.

She could probably find excuses to get Association personnel alone, ask them questions they'd be forced to answer, maybe she could order them to forget they'd ever seen her, and boom, she could be plumbing them for information behind the scenes while they were harvesting as much data about the Brilliant as they could during the application process.

That was a promising direction, because you could imagine she'd eventually run across personnel who might genuinely want to see the Brilliant join the Association. I mean, they couldn't all be monsters. It'd be more painful if some of the Association's own people on that mission felt betrayed when the Brilliant were annihilated.

Maybe Carissa learned about the Fleet attack from a sympathetic Association scientist.

Maybe she had time to warn Kellin.

Maybe the last time she saw him, Kellin was fighting at full power to protect her so that she could flee to safety, holding literal warheads in the air so that she could make it to the elevator before they hit.

But!

If Carissa could survive despite insurmountable odds, which obviously she did, why couldn't any of the other Brilliant?

The nature of the Association's attack was such that they couldn't just point to a pile of smoldering remains and say, "Yup, that's sixty-four dead Brilliant right there. Not sure what happened to the last one." What if some of them made it to the elevator after Carissa? Something didn't fly about that scenario, but I added it to my notes anyway as a possibility.

Satisfied I had enough to work with, I began writing a new folk tale for the book, the tale of Carissa's escape from Minneapolis.

. . .

After a couple of hours, Carissa circled back around and asked me, "You at a stopping point, or should I keep wandering around looking at useless crap some more?"

I nodded and signaled for her to sit across from me. Then I slid my notebook over to her, open to the place where I wanted her to start reading.

"You could just summarize this if you want," she offered.

"I might leave out something important," I replied.

She began reading. After a few minutes, she said, "You do understand this is not what happened at all, right?"

I almost made a snarky, self-deprecating comment but then I realized she was struggling to maintain her composure, and I kept my mouth shut.

She managed to clamp down on whatever she was feeling, though, and kept reading for a minute or two. I wondered if a replay of events was happening in her mind, prompted by me presenting her with a fully incorrect rendition of that time in her life. I realized that this woman who looked pretty much my age (twenty-six) was over a hundred years older than I am when the Brilliant fell. She might've lived a long time with whatever she was feeling right now. Maybe you'd expect her to heal during so much time, but . . . some days, or I mean, most days I woke up in my suite at the resort and for a few terrifying moments I was fourteen years old, and the only thing I knew in my confused state was that Grandma Dee was gone. I felt that punch to my heart like it was the first time, and I just . . . wasn't sure I was ever going to stop waking up like that, even a hundred years from now, so.

"I did know one good person," she said eventually, "who

worked for the Association. A lawyer who sat with us during the process. You go through all these disclosures and interviews and that stuff, and they give you a lawyer to help explain what's expected and to look out for you a little during the sessions. I was there for all the sessions. No matter who else they wanted to talk to, I was always there, too.

"So this lawyer and I got to be friends over time. Like, a lot of their people stayed in Minneapolis for days or weeks at a time, at the hotel where the sessions were happening. So I kept making excuses to run into her in the hotel bar or we'd go out dancing, because the days were so absurdly tense, things did not go well in that process, and you just wanted to shake it off.

"One night, after a really bad day where some of the city council people tried to fuck us over, she found me and said, 'You gotta come with me, right *now*.'

"We got in a car, and she had me put on an Association uniform that she'd brought for me, and as she drove away from the hotel, she said, 'We need to get you into an elevator,' and I was like, 'The nearest elevator—*our* elevator—is back there, you're driving *away* from it.' And she goes, 'That's a dead stop now, has been for weeks.' You know what a dead stop is?"

I shook my head.

"It's when they seal up an elevator location from inside the shaft with plates of cursed steel so no one can ever open the doors again. If there's an anchor station, they destroy it, and they flip that location back to 'undocumented' in the cloudlet network. If that was the only mapped elevator on your floor, poof, you just disappeared without a trace."

A sharp jolt of scary claustrophobia shot through me, imagining being cut off from the Building like that.

"That meant the nearest *working* elevator was in Canada," Carissa continued. "We made it to St. Paul, which I hadn't understood was now totally occupied by them. Like, we'd fortified ourselves so well that we'd been oblivious when they started dropping people into positions outside of our immediate scouting range. I don't mean more diplomats; I mean Security, in force, swarming the streets like they were planning to invade Minneapolis. I tried to text Kellin, but phone service was dead.

"But then I saw how many shuttles were jumping off the floor completely, and I realized—they were evacuating, not invading.

"And I just . . . lost track of shit for a few minutes, because I was . . ."

She looked away and stopped her story for a moment. She seemed like she wasn't just telling me this story, she was reliving each emotional beat in the story as she got to it.

"We climbed onto a teleport pad, which I'd never even heard of before, and then *bam*, we were on a different teleport pad, in Canada, in a truck stop parking lot right next to an elevator. Nobody was guarding it. Or I mean, if they were, they had a perimeter around the whole parking lot or something, but no one was standing right there to get in our way. She pushed the button.

"I knew by now what was happening, but I was too terrified to say a word. That was it, you know, that was our big moment to . . . say something to each other, and we just . . . waited for the doors to open. Then she gently pushed me inside, and she said to the elevator, 'Nearest observation floor above the border, please,' and the doors closed with me inside and her outside. When I got off the elevator, I was no longer in Canada. I was no longer on Earth.

"I was on, like, floor 75,000 or something. I didn't even know what floor I'd come from, so I couldn't go back if I'd wanted to.

"Never saw her again. Never saw anyone I'd ever known in my life again."

She slid the notebook across the table to me.

"Nice try, though."

"Sure was," I said, flipping open the notebook to a blank page. "Now I try again."

"What?"

"The first draft is just a warm-up. Shouldn't take more than a second draft, though."

"Why do you need a second draft? I just *gave* you the story of how I escaped Minneapolis. Mystery solved."

"Carissa, the mystery we're *trying* to solve is what happened to the *other* Brilliant. Did they really all get annihilated, or did some of them escape, or get captured, or I mean . . ."

"What? What else?"

"Well, look, it sounds like you were gone before Fleet arrived, and you never went back to that floor. So how do we even know Fleet went through with the attack? What if Fleet wasn't there to annihilate the Brilliant at all—what if they came to *recruit* the Brilliant? What if they said to Kellin, 'Look, Parliament won't approve your application because membership is something we award to cultures, and you're barely a neighborhood really, but Fleet will sponsor all of you for citizenship if you'll enlist for a term of service with us.'

"And maybe Kellin saw ten Fleet warships in the sky and he understood the other option wasn't going to be so friendly, so maybe he took the deal. To keep his people alive. To keep *you* alive, even though he didn't know where you were. Maybe Kellin and the others are on Fleet special ops teams out in the multiverse somewhere."

She leaned back slowly in her chair, giving me a look that was thankfully not backed by any particular psionic talent, because I could tell she wanted to melt me into a puddle of dissolving genetic material right about then.

I closed the notebook and said, "Sorry, sometimes I think in branching narratives, even about history that can't branch anymore. I know that's not how it went down, but I can take liberties in my story for dramatic purposes. I'm not writing your biography. Anyway, the second draft is where I usually get hits if I'm going to get any. I think if I get one or two hits out of my second draft, they might help us solve the *actual* mystery, which is—did any other Brilliant survive that day?"

"Tabitha, you don't use minor divination with a rolling

twenty-four-hour window to solve a hundred-year-old mystery. You need powerful retrocognitive talent to pull that off."

"Not if the solution to the mystery is something we could run across in the next twenty-four hours. Look, a second draft won't take long. I think I'm just going to insert a couple of new scenes. Besides, it doesn't look like you found new headphones, so now you have a little more time to look." And before she could ask how I knew she was looking for headphones, I said, "Yesterday's story included an extra hit, apparently."

EPISODE 2.04

Allegory Paradox, Chief Content Officer for Wild Massive, began every day in the office with a simple routine designed to summon focus and clarity for the tasks ahead. She entered the holosuite where the *Storm and Desire* creative brain trust met, a broad virtual environment designed like an auditorium, with virtual whiteboards every direction you looked that were covered in virtual sticky notes or virtual index cards. These notes and index cards described plot points, character goals, key obstacles, and the like, summarizing the future of *Storm and Desire* in both a holistic and a granular view.

She found a sweet spot where she could take in as much of this information as possible all at once.

Then she dropped into a flow state, visualizing the unfolding of actual history as a map overlaid on top of the virtual whiteboards, and if she saw the alignment wasn't where she wanted it to be or if she stumbled across some sudden sheer inspiration, she adjusted the plan for *Storm and Desire*. She'd move a virtual index card up or down a notch, or sometimes remove a virtual index card altogether, or she'd scribble something on a virtual sticky note and add it to a column of virtual index cards—minor changes to a vastly complex overall plan that was working quite beautifully.

She wasn't naive about these changes, of course. Sometimes moving a virtual index card meant an entire design team had to start over on some aspect of production. But she considered her pursuit of aesthetic alignment to be a fundamental reason that *Storm and Desire* had succeeded beyond even her own wildest imagination.

So much was now at stake. So much depended upon the creative brain trust's ability to "stick the landing," as it were, with the final arc, and she expected her own involvement in day-to-day matters would only grow.

Her vision typically operated at the level of major currents, big milestones, and important themes, which she could still manipulate with relative ease. Meanwhile, the details were left to the creative brain trust to flesh out, leaving room for Allegory Paradox to be surprised despite her deep understanding of what was to come in each thread of the story.

She'd known that the Shai-Manak would take focus in the final arc, but she hadn't known they would attack Wild Mega. She'd known deep in her soul that the story of the Brilliant could *not* be allowed to end mired in nothing but immoral tragedy, but she certainly hadn't expected her favorite narrative designer to miraculously befriend a surviving Brilliant right in the Super park.

But it made sense that events were now unfolding closer to her, because she'd been steadily steering *Storm and Desire* toward a place where Wild Massive—and by extension, she herself—*became* the story, instead of remaining its storytellers.

. . .

An hour after the Shai-Manak attacked Wild Mega, Allegory was granted a virtual audience with Serene Nova, Prime Minister of the Parliament of Storm and Desire.

Serene Nova, like Allegory, was one of the few survivors of the so-called mythological era prior to the signing of the treaty that formed the Association. If you saw her in her glorious true form, in which her eight sets of golden wings unfurled to their vast prismatic wingspans, and her magnificent radiance caused her perfect skin to glow with unbearable beauty, and her three heads—one human, one hawk, one dragon—raised their voices in harmony singing death metal anthems, and the gleaming broadswords in her six arms mercilessly cut down her enemies until vast oceans of blood soaked the sky itself . . . if you saw her glorious true form, you were probably about to die, but you might identify her, with your last terrified thoughts, as an archangel.

You'd be wrong, of course.

Serene Nova existed outside of any so-called angelic taxonomies and sang the praises of no so-called supreme being. Most of the time, she wore the form of a graceful elder gymnast in comfortable clothes, although she did sometimes display a set of wings if they suited the occasion. She was an outside management consultant, recruited by an Architect to relocate here and assume a vital role in stabilizing the still-shaky foundations of this endeavor. Just in time, too—the Architects were rapidly rolling off the project, and the Muses were scheduled to follow soon after.

Serene Nova's unflinching will and fluency with modern executive management techniques brought civilization together during that perilous window of time after the Muses declared their work on the Building to be complete and abandoned it to its fate, despite clear and violent evidence that most of their creation wasn't ready for the sudden emptiness of pure freedom. She summoned eight of the most powerful and influential leaders in the Building, personally authored the treaty that would establish the United Association of Interdimensional Travelers, and convinced them all to sign.

She herself was the ninth and final signatory, a minister without a personal constituency, symbolic of those who had built the place and then vanished, perhaps. They elected her Prime Minister unanimously, and she'd served in that capacity ever since.

Ministers had come and gone over time, but Serene Nova was ever present.

Allegory observed Serene Nova in action for years, respecting if not outright admiring the Prime Minister's skill in leveraging Parliament from an idea into a powerful political body and almost into its own pantheon. But all the physical aspects of the project—Parliament, the Association, Dimension Force, the Building itself—were still subdomains of the Muses' total authority over the ongoing iterative development of existence. Her superiors, the Architects, were nowhere in sight and anyway were never prone to micromanagement, and there were no other Muses left to debate details of fit and finish. That meant Allegory Paradox was technically in charge of all of it.

Well, all of it except Serene Nova, an outside consultant with no need for further iterative development. And as it turned out, Serene Nova also nominally reported to the Architects, who hired her directly and made sure her extravagant fees were paid. That meant Allegory and Serene Nova were essentially peers on the org chart, and no doubt the Architects would expect them to collaborate as such. When Allegory finally revealed herself to Serene Nova, they hashed out an amiable working agreement over a late lunch one afternoon.

Serene Nova steered the political might of Parliament and the Association. Allegory retained dominion over the entirety of the Building and the environment beyond, including Dimension Force, which patrolled wherever it saw fit to go. They were key stakeholders in each other's concerns. Parliament utilized Dimension Force for special projects with Allegory's tacit approval. Allegory invisibly manipulated Association resources to aid her work refining shared Building facilities. Civilization flourished for centuries under this agreement.

But when the Association decided genocide was a legitimate response to a diplomatic encounter, Allegory found herself reconsidering the terms.

"Sorry to keep you waiting, Allegory," said Serene Nova. Even in her nominally human form, her voice sounded like a chorus when she spoke. You never really got used to it. "First off, did you eavesdrop on the Security briefing?" The Association had provided Wild Massive's executive team and board of directors with a direct report on what had happened to Wild Mega.

"I did," replied Allegory. "Rather thin on details, I must say."

"Yes, it didn't really answer the crucial question of how this could possibly have happened, did it," said Serene Nova. "As for what to do about the situation, Security felt it prudent to keep our initial ideas out of the briefing."

"I do have a suggestion on that front, if you're open to hearing it."

"I thought you might. What do you suggest?"

"Invite the Shai-Manak to a peace conference. Offer them a truce. And approve them for membership in the Association."

Serene Nova said nothing for a long while. That was fine. You couldn't intimidate Allegory Paradox with dramatic silence.

Finally, Serene Nova said, "Aren't you clever." Her voice was so devoid of recognizable emotion that this statement sounded like a sincere compliment, a vicious attack, and a surrealist slogan all at the same time.

"Quite," Allegory agreed.

"I'll consider your suggestion a solid number three in contention, behind number one, which is immediate retaliation, and number two, which is something we haven't thought of yet. I'm told we'll have a counterstrike up and running within the hour."

"You don't have to fight them. You could be the hero of the final arc of *Storm and Desire*, if you forged peace with them after fifty years of open conflict. Or you could come out swinging with everything you've got, commit a second genocide in the span of a hundred years, and become one of recent history's greatest villains."

"Clearing them off that floor is hardly a second genocide. Truthfully, I like your idea of offering a truce, but not while their people are sitting comfortably inside our territory, making an outright mockery of our defenses."

But several hours later, after the counterattack had failed catastrophically, Serene Nova reached out to Allegory for a second conversation. With no true understanding of just how powerful the Shai-Manak were, with evidence at hand that they were now prepared to escalate the conflict significantly, and with news of a secret weapons program within the Association suffering disaster on its first field test, Serene Nova wanted this business off her plate. She intended to offer a truce to the Shai-Manak as Allegory had suggested.

"You're doing the right thing," Allegory said.

"Maybe. Convincing Parliament will be a bloody battle. If you wouldn't mind using your back channel with the Shai-Manak, find out if they're even interested in membership at this point."

"I'm sure they'll be willing to talk. I could offer to moderate peace talks myself."

"Yes, I suppose you deserve a front-row seat to the proceedings. Someday, Allegory, you'll have to tell me how you forged that back channel with the Association's latest nemesis."

"Will I? I imagine that will be an interesting day."

. . .

On the twenty-fifth floor of the Building, if your credentials were in order, you would find a complex dedicated to the workings of Parliament. A third of the floor was dedicated to Serene Nova's office and personal chambers, and a third was dedicated to offices for high-ranking staffers in Serene Nova's orbit. The remainder was occupied by the Inexplicable Hall, the assembly chamber where Parliament convened.

The Inexplicable Hall featured a cavernous amount of space reserved for seating an audience that was ultimately never invited. A vast amphitheater of seating in the round was provided, with row after row situated on steep rakes that would've allowed perfect sight lines for everyone, outfitted with excellent acoustics should the ministers wish to avoid artificial amplification, and even featuring box seating for VIPs. Whoever designed this room clearly imagined that Parliamentary sessions should be widely accessible, openly heralded, revered, and celebrated. That was briefly true. But now, only on rare occasions were spectators included in the proceedings or even notified that Parliament was in session in the first place.

The seating layout was designed to draw your attention to a set of eight booths for ministers in a semicircle in the center of the space, facing a raised bench where Serene Nova presided over the proceedings. A desk next to the Prime Minister's bench was reserved for Lorelei Rivers, advisor to the Prime Minister and Solicitor-General of the Association. A small podium near the bench allowed invited guests to address the body. Seating for advisors and observers was provided directly behind the booths on risers; today's session had been called on short notice, and only a few extra people were on hand. The room seemed drab and austere when you first arrived, as though you were in the auditorium of a museum no one visited anymore, about to watch a film strip about the history of dirt or something.

But once the ministers had all arrived and the sergeant at arms closed the doors to stand guard, stagecraft transformed the chamber: flat overhead lighting gave way to crisp theatrical illumination; each minister's booth became a sharply defined pool that absorbed attention. Several ministers appeared via technological or illusory means, taking wondrous and unique forms. Many of them wore distinctive ceremonial attire intended to pop under the lights. They weren't performing for a significant live audience, obviously, but surveillance dust captured every nuance of every session for the Archives, and no one wanted some historian of the future to find reason to critique a minister based on appearance.

Finally, Serene Nova utilized just a fraction of the full and many-throated glory of her voice to call Parliament into session.

"Ministers," began Serene Nova, "early today, we lost control of floor 49,500, where the first Wild Massive park on one of our floors is under construction. A Shai-Manak raiding party exploited our inattention, invaded the floor, disabled our surveillance, obliterated our counterattack, and captured Agent Anjette of Dimension Force. I understand the principal architect of this counterattack is prepared to explain it for us. Jirian Echo, take the floor, if you please."

The ghostly apparition known as Jirian Echo materialized at the guest podium next to the bench.

"Jirian, you're the Director of Defensive Technology Research," Serene Nova said. "Do I have that right?"

"Senior Director, Prime Minister," Jirian replied, daring to correct her.

"Would you please describe your original plan for us?"

"Certainly, Prime Minister. After our initial engagement with the Brilliant a hundred years ago, my group was tasked with the broad mandate of determining if psionic abilities could be unlocked in non-psionic minds. After decades of research and experimentation, we achieved a breakthrough recently that allowed us to do exactly that, albeit only for limited durations. We've trained up a cohort of volunteers from Security to proficiency with a variety of different psionic abilities, testing them rigorously in our combat laboratories."

He waited to continue as a buzz of conversation erupted throughout the chamber. This was news to most of the people in the room. Serene Nova lightly tapped a gavel on her podium to quiet everyone down and signaled for Jirian to continue.

"When we learned of the unprecedented attack on floor 49,500, we proposed sending a squad of psionic-enhanced prototypes onto the floor, based on extensive simulation data suggesting we could overcome a Shai-Manak squad's typical tactics with ease. That was . . . overconfident, it seems. The mission never returned. If the prototypes survived, their psionic abilities wore off after slightly less than one hour."

"What went wrong?" Serene Nova asked.

"We don't currently know what went wrong," Jirian replied.

"Sure we do," a confident voice piped up from the far side of the room. A spotlight swiveled to pick up the speaker, who was positioned in front of the grand entrance to the chamber.

Agent Anjette of Dimension Force had returned to duty just in time to receive a summons from Parliament about this session. As a courtesy, Anjette and a few other Agents rotated through the role of sergeant at arms for Parliamentary sessions; these appearances were listed as "complimentary—no charge" on Dimension Force's invoices to the Association.

"Agent Anjette," said Serene Nova, "I didn't realize you were back. Did the Shai-Manak release you, or did you escape?"

Anjette flashed her famous cocky smile and said, "What do you think?"

Several of the assorted ministers laughed, and a smattering of applause briefly surfaced. Jirian Echo, meanwhile, failed to appreciate her little quip.

"The Shai-Manak didn't send a simple raiding party, like the ones that hassle outposts and flight paths," Anjette said. "They sent a well-organized invasion force. More Shai-Manak out in the open than we've ever seen in one location. Twenty at least."

Jirian Echo looked duly humiliated. "I see. Twenty or more sorcerers working in synchrony would certainly stand a good chance of overwhelming our four officers."

"It wasn't just sorcery that overwhelmed your officers," Anjette said. "The Shai-Manak also surprised us in one other way. They weren't simply relying on magic like usual. They brought guns for the first time."

"Perhaps if you yourself carried a gun, Agent, those four Security officers would still be alive," said Admiral Allon Slab.

"Perhaps a division called Defensive Technology Research shouldn't be authorized to launch attacks in the first place," Anjette replied.

"My office was in the loop," the Admiral snarled, indicating he'd tacitly approved Jirian's counterattack.

"Thank you, Agent, for your report," said Serene Nova, and the spotlight on the sergeant at arms faded.

"Let me clarify something for the benefit of the historical record," interjected Cadence Array, the home secretary. She held two important duties: she was head of the Immigration office, and she was Director of Security. "When you say 'prototypes,' you're talking about people, correct?"

After a moment of hesitation, Jirian replied, "I thought that was understood, yes."

"It's understood *now*, Jirian, but when you began recruiting Security personnel to help your lab test 'prototypes,' I presumed 'prototype' referred to a custom, fabricated, physical weapon of some kind, because physical weapons are the only thing your division has ever produced."

"I apologize for the confusion—"

"Now you're telling me four of my people are dead as part of a 'weapons test'?"

"We felt there was some urgency to acquire real-world data—"

"We don't currently have a weapons class that can damage the Shai-Manak," the Admiral announced to his colleagues, cutting off the exchange between Jirian and Cadence. "I should say, technically, Fleet can't even hit them during aerial combat, because their spellcraft introduces errors into our targeting AI's calculations. Inside the Building, they brush off the effects of any of the portable weapons Security is rated to carry on populated floors. Jirian's on the cusp of delivering a solution to these problems, a solution that could tip the balance of the entire conflict in our favor."

"What, you're going to strap officers to the hulls of your ships?" Cadence asked.

"Psionic talents are frequently effective at a distance without line of sight, and their areas of effect can be significant," said Jirian. "A Fleet fighter craft with psionic-enhanced personnel riding along could easily maneuver close enough to a typical Shai-Manak flight squad to stage an attack. We . . . did expect that staging an attack would be simpler on floor 49,500 with no aerial dynamics in play."

"Really, you thought facing the Shai-Manak up close would be 'simpler'?" Cadence said. "Senior Director, what qualifies you to offer tactical leadership to squads of military personnel in the first place?"

"I was a Lieutenant Commander when I served in Fleet, Agent."

"Yes, on a research vessel that you inadvertently destroyed

with the loss of all hands, including yourself, which I'd consider an anti-qualification."

Serene Nova tapped her gavel again, just once, to silence the discussion, then said, "I understand Counsel has prepared some questions for the Senior Director."

"Thank you, Prime Minister," said Lorelei Rivers, standing to address Jirian with steel in her eyes. "Senior Director, did your decades of research include medical experimentation on captured Brilliant survivors?"

Jirian seemed hesitant as he said, "Obviously."

"Were you aware that the treaty specifically prohibits medical experimentation on citizens of member cultures?" Lorelei asked.

"Counsel, the Brilliant were not signatories to the treaty," Jirian said.

"The Brilliant submitted an application for membership in the Association in good faith," Lorelei replied, "which afforded them a grace period during which most of the protections granted by the treaty were legally afforded to them. Do you know how long this grace period lasts?"

"I'm afraid I don't."

"In the case of rejection, it lasts six months after the formal closing of the application. Do you know when the Brilliant's application was formally closed?"

"No."

"It was *never* formally closed," Lorelei said, addressing all of Parliament now instead of Jirian. "A step we simply overlooked on our march to extinguish them. To be fair, it was our first full-blown genocide of the modern era, so we were bound to get some of the paperwork wrong."

Jirian smiled unconvincingly and said, "Thank you for the procedural education, Counsel. I'll keep that in mind. For next time, of course."

"Out of curiosity, Counsel, what is the current status of the Shai-Manak application?" The question came from one of the ministers, Shiv Disturbia, leader of the Loyal Opposition.

taking a good hard look at it, preferably from a safe distance. Oh, I mean certainly the top floor lives in the realm of fairy tale, but the chasm itself is a real, observable, metaphysical rift in reality.

"We placed a set of surveillance drones in sensor range of it outside the Building, the way you'd place seismic stations around an active volcano. We released surveillance dust as close to the chasm as we could, sending it up the elevator shafts, to see how the uppermost floors were affected. We asked cloudlets to survey passengers traveling down from that region about their experiences there, to see if we could verify Solitude's account.

"And yes, Counsel, I'm well aware these actions technically violated the nonintervention amendments.

"We learned that the floors directly below the chasm are deserted. All the trappings of civilization remain, but entire populations seem to have picked up and migrated in an orderly fashion. Or maybe they simply vanished, or were . . . taken away. We don't have a good explanation for the profound and sudden emptiness of these floors."

"YES, WE DO," said the heavily synthesized voice of a minister who'd been silent up until now.

It was called the Blissform, leader of the Incorporeal Coalition of entities and collectives that had somehow found a way to join the Association. When interacting directly with the material plane, the Blissform typically appeared as a large silver bowl full of water on a pedestal, and if you gazed into the water, you would see a steady succession of frenzied beings submerged deep below the water, frantically trying to reach the surface without ever succeeding. If pressed, the Blissform would simply identify these visions as "metaphors."

"THE MALADIES LURED THEM FROM THEIR HOMES WITH PROMISES OF INFLUENCE AND CE-LEBRITY," the Blissform said.

"What does that mean?" asked Cadence Array. "What are 'the Maladies'?"

The Blissform emitted a small hiss and then said, "MUSES THAT WERE TURNED."

"'Turned'?" Cadence said. "What does that mean? Turned how?"

"CONSUMED THEIR INSPIRATION AND CORRUPTED THEIR AESTHETICS."

"I don't understand," Cadence said. "Who did that to them?"

The water in the bowl began to steam and hiss, and the Blissform fell silent.

The wizard Cryptex Halo said, "I wonder, Admiral, why did you bring this fascinating subject to our attention during a discussion of peace with the Shai-Manak?"

Before the Admiral could respond, Shiv Disturbia said, "Isn't it obvious? He wants to use the Shai-Manak home floor as a shield to protect our own floors. Should these 'Maladies' descend from the chasm toward us, the Shai-Manak will be forced to deal with them first from their mysterious home floor somewhere above the border."

Admiral Slab smiled and said, "Who better than the most sophisticated sorcerers in the Building to keep our people safe?"

▪   ▪   ▪

In the end, to everyone's surprise, there was no substantive debate. Serene Nova's proposal passed by a vote of seven to two.

As Anjette waited for an elevator, Lorelei Rivers caught up to her and said, "Agent Anjette, congratulations on your escape."

"Thank you," Anjette replied.

"You know, I wasn't aware that Agents went on tagalong missions with Security," Lorelei said. "Can any division request an escort from an Agent?"

"I don't see why not."

Lorelei paused for a moment, then said, "Anjette, I'm going to give you the benefit of the doubt and assume you didn't know the Association might be experimenting on Brilliant prisoners."

Anjette said, "Of course not. No."

Lorelei nodded and said, "Tomorrow morning, I'm leading a strike team of combat-ready attorneys, auditors, and scientists to conduct a surprise audit of Jirian Echo's entire operation. We could certainly use an escort if you're available."

"I'm in," Anjette said without hesitation.

"Excellent," said Lorelei. "I'll send you the mission briefing and see you tomorrow." She peeled away and headed for the Prime Minister's office. Anjette could see Serene Nova and Cadence Array inside, waiting for Lorelei, who closed the door behind herself as she arrived.

A pleasant *ding* signaled that an elevator had arrived. Anjette found herself getting into the elevator alone.

As the doors closed, the cloudlet asked, "Where can I deliver you today, Agent Anjette?"

Rindasy had just survived an appearance before Parliament as Anjette with notable ease, thanks to the replica's diligence in training zir. Rindasy needed to keep busy until tomorrow's surprise audit, preferably avoiding all who knew the real Anjette. An idea surfaced: it would be very in character for Anjette to escape from the Shai-Manak, attend to Parliament as sergeant at arms, and then go on patrol immediately, all in the same day. Anjette's favored place to patrol was the parking lot.

"Lobby floor, please," Rindasy said. "I think I'd like to get outside for some fresh air."

"Excellent choice. The weather is lovely this time of year."

Rindasy found zirself laughing almost giddily. The weather never changed; the cloudlet couldn't experience weather; most floors kept their own calendar, so who knew what time of year it was? If the cloudlet realized it was making a joke, no acknowledgment was forthcoming.

Naturally, Rindasy had seen the parking lot many times, but from tens of thousands of floors above it. Anjette liked to patrol at low speed on a hoverboard from beacon to beacon all the way around the perimeter, stopping as frequently or as little as necessary. If she wasn't summoned to address a more urgent situation, her patrol of the parking lot sometimes stretched for days as she checked in on a network of families, vendors, gangs, neighborhoods, and the like that she cared for or monitored. Rindasy couldn't afford to spend that much time on patrol, but ze could at least get a good firsthand impression of the sprawling campsite's culture.

Ze would be the first Shai-Manak to leave the Building at ground level and experience the desert outside.

.   .   .

Lorelei headed home, intending to relax for a bit, enjoy dinner with her family, and then spend the evening studying the data her team had surfaced about Jirian Echo.

Lorelei was eligible for her pick of quarters on a variety of high-security floors featuring her choice of artificial climate and aesthetic theme. With nine people in her immediate family pod and a dozen more who rotated through their orbit on a semi-regular basis, she needed space and modularity to accommodate shifting requirements for their living spaces.

They were no longer raising children outright, so the nine permanent inhabitants of this dwelling were all adults. But their various offspring visited frequently. Her extended familial tribe—she wasn't the oldest or the wisest, mind you, just the most visible as a powerful public servant—ran the gamut of occupations, spanned several religions, and included three species, not counting the android they were currently fostering.

The Association placed her family in a dwelling that resembled a long row of town houses or the like from the outside, but most of the internal walls were configurable, the amenities could be swapped between rooms, and so on. Her floor was highly exclusive, and you could rest easy in the knowledge that Association surveillance was monitoring every aspect of the floor's activities for signs of anomalies that might warrant a rapid response on the spot. You couldn't really be a part of Lorelei's family pod if you had any kind of qualms about Association surveillance. As an advisor to the Prime Minister, Lorelei's entire sensorium was subject to surveillance. Her literal point of view on the world—visual, tactile, emotional, the works—was transmitted in real time to a secure network, where intelligence operatives were free to catalog, transcribe, index, or even experience this data if it became relevant to a diplomatic incident or investigation.

According to policy, she was allowed to shut off this surveillance when she wasn't working on Parliamentary business. But her mind was constantly cycling back to work issues, and she felt these thoughts should be eligible for future discovery. So the surveillance from her mind to the Association was essentially constant.

She didn't object, because she believed in its core function of taking care of every single citizen to the best of its ability.

The Association had achieved a ruthless redistribution of resources across its member cultures so that everyone had their basic needs met at all times. That was the key to the Association's rise, really, the crux of its initial appeal.

Lorelei had done diplomatic tours of duty on Earth floors outside the Association's territory. She'd seen up close how horrific it could get for people when your guiding cultural principle was literally anything other than always meeting the basic needs of your citizens.

As she got off the elevator, the ambient lighting was simulating dusk, and it wouldn't get darker than that. The living quarters were packed efficiently in a perfect grid, with sidewalks or wider lanes separating blocks, and a few small parks scattered here and there. One of those parks was right in front of her house.

Walking up the sidewalk, she noticed someone was sitting on the steel park bench that faced her house. Probably one of the neighbors.

It wasn't until she got closer still that she realized with a sharp spike of adrenaline that the woman sitting on that bench could only be Carissa.

There was a time, long ago, when Lorelei was lost in abject regret that she hadn't had the courage to jump in the elevator and escape with Carissa into the upper reaches of the Building, as far away from the Association as they could manage. For years afterward, she'd had a recurring dream in which she was dropped right back into that moment, as though daring herself to make a different decision, to run away with Carissa instead of sending her off into the Building alone with nothing more than her wits and talent to protect her.

Carissa smiled and softly said, "There you are."

Lorelei sat on the other end of the bench. She disabled her internal surveillance and then, for good measure, switched off her entire network interface so she wouldn't be distracted by her feeds or emails or whatever, which usually appeared within an ever-present floating overlay in the corner of her vision.

And then she realized she had no idea what to say.

This silent moment stretched out in its painful awkwardness. They were not in their twenties anymore, mere babies in the context of how long humans lived in this Building. A hundred years or so had passed since the last time they'd seen each other's faces. Carissa was wearing some expensive Wild Massive swag that she'd gotten at the Super park before leaving it, notably a black bomber jacket with the Wild Massive logo stylishly rendered across its front, and a black skirt over the top of her mechanic's overalls. The skirt displayed iconic cartoon characters invisibly until the light bounced off it in just the right way.

Finally, Carissa said, "This is a little late, but . . . thank you."

"Of course," Lorelei replied. "Are you . . . I mean, how are you here? Did you become a citizen?"

Carissa laughed and said, "Uh, no. I'm using an alias."

"How, though?" Lorelei pressed. "Even the Pirate King can't forge credentials that will get you onto this floor."

"Uh, you should maybe update your file on the Pirate King," Carissa replied. "He's even tagged me as 'do not surveil,' so I'm invisible while I'm here. Anyway, no, I didn't join the Association. I'm a proud explorer at large of the Building. I did okay."

The relief Lorelei felt was overwhelming.

"So did you, it looks like," Carissa continued. "Are you happy?"

"Yeah," Lorelei said.

"Excellent." Carissa paused, then said, "I know I'm putting you at risk by coming here. I'm sorry, but I didn't see an alternative."

"What's going on? I mean, what do you need?"

"This may sound absolutely ridiculous, but . . . I think the Association might have taken some of the Brilliant as prisoners before they nuked Minneapolis."

"Where did you hear that?" Lorelei asked, surprised this news was somehow circulating.

"A baby magic-user told me," Carissa said. "She's been right about other things. I know it's not much to go on."

Lorelei finally nodded and said, "They might even still be alive. Literally tomorrow, I'm leading an audit raid to find out the truth about these prisoners."

"Looks like I got here just in time, then."

"What do you mean?"

"Well, clearly, I should go on this raid with you," said Carissa.

"Are you joking? It's one thing to sneak onto a residential floor with a fake ID, quite another to march into a weapons lab with a strike team."

"Come on, you could put me in a Security uniform. It'll be just like the old days."

"That's not even remotely funny."

"Look, my brother might be one of those prisoners."

"I understand that, but it's not going to be a great time for a family reunion. We're going into the lab prepared to fight. I don't remember fighting being a core part of your skill set. You don't get to show up in front of my house after a hundred years and then get yourself killed the next morning in a shoot-out or something."

Carissa was silent for a moment, then said, "I remember you being super disillusioned about . . . all of it, right? 'A parliament that no one gets to vote for, conducting diplomacy at gunpoint, enforcing a mythical treaty that no one ever bothers to read . . .' Did I get it right?"

"Mostly," Lorelei said. "I'm impressed. It was, 'Enforcing a treaty that no one can find, let alone read,' but you got the spirit of it."

"But you still work for them a hundred years later?"

Lorelei said, "I took a long hiatus after Minneapolis. But you can't make it better if you walk away from it forever."

"Did you pull it off?" Carissa asked. "Did you make the Association better?"

Lorelei shrugged and said, "I definitely stopped parts of it from getting worse." Then she added, "Turns out, the treaty is tucked away safely in a secret vault in the Archives. They keep it hidden from the public because it's infused with such dense idealism that it incinerates most people who try to read it."

"Don't tell me you're going to try."

"Hell no, I have a family now. There are limits." She stood up and said, "Come on, you can join us for dinner. I'm going to tell them we sang in the same choir together in college, which is a code phrase we've developed that means, 'Don't ask questions, I'll explain everything later.' After dinner, I'll tell you everything I can."

EPISODE 2.05

Andasir, meanwhile, was sitting in a jail cell because Allegory Paradox had turned zir over to Shai-Manak enforcers. When the enforcers traced Andasir to the Super park, the Radiant Council asked Allegory to hand Andasir over in order to avoid violence, a favor that Allegory granted in the interest of currying future cooperation from the Shai-Manak on more critical plot points.

Allegory thought that perhaps Wild Massive could provide the Shai-Manak with additional intelligence to help ensure a "dramatically engaging" ending for the final arc of *Storm and Desire*. The Shai-Manak had never placed proper undercover spies inside the Association, whereas Allegory had placed or recruited dozens of people throughout multiple branches of the Association; she considered them "consultants" who advised on the plausibility and realism of their portrayal of the Association.

In fact, without these spies, *Storm and Desire* might have skipped past the Brilliant. As a matter of practice, Association military was under no obligation to ensure news-gathering organizations had a presence in their arenas during its operations.

But as the events in Minneapolis took a grim turn, conscientious objectors spread word of the situation to key influencers, including Allegory Paradox, who had sufficient time and motivation to architect an entire arc of *Storm and Desire* around what she'd learned.

One of these conscientious objectors happened to be Lorelei Rivers.

.   .   .

Lorelei and Jirian Echo had served together as part of the diplomatic team deployed to evaluate the membership application submitted by the Brilliant and to subsequently make a recommendation to Parliament regarding their suitability for joining the Association.

Lorelei had been a young, idealistic legal analyst at that time, a specialist in treaty interpretation. She was assigned to study the political and justice systems of the Brilliant and score them on likelihood of successfully pivoting to a local government model that met treaty requirements. The Brilliant submitted the first new application in over a hundred years, and getting assigned as advocate for the Brilliant was a significant opportunity.

Unfortunately, she never got the chance to submit her opinion.

Jirian Echo, meanwhile, was one of the experts responsible for evaluating the military capabilities of the Brilliant and scoring them on likelihood of potentially integrating with the Association's two military divisions, Security and Fleet. Unlike Lorelei, Jirian was not a young idealist. Jirian was a type of entity known as a specter, manifesting as a ghostly apparition that was capable of physically interacting with its environment. Somehow the state change from living person to undead haunter kept him on the Association duty roster.

Jirian's team cataloged the distinct talents of the Brilliant via voluntary demonstrations. In the process, Jirian formed the opinion that the Brilliant themselves were too "anarchic" to integrate into a military unit. You'd have to work with a Brilliant child from the moment their talents first manifested to steer them toward proper military discipline, he believed, which was not an option they could ethically or legally consider. From practically his first day watching these demonstrations, Jirian's mind turned toward finding a way of unlocking these talents in non-psionic human minds.

The Brilliant were led by a charismatic leader named Kellin; this was potentially a second strike against them, because autocracies sometimes struggled to adapt to one of the approved governmental templates allowed by the treaty. But Lorelei thought they had a chance to gain refugee status, which would confer provisional membership and resettlement assistance to another floor.

That chance evaporated when Jirian Echo finally got an opportunity to ask Carissa about her talent.

"I've noticed you sit in on all the interview sessions between our diplomatic team and your leadership," Jirian said after finally convincing Carissa to sit down with him for a one-on-one conversation. "But you never say anything or seem to participate." He smiled and added, "Are you your brother's bodyguard, perhaps?"

"I'm not there to protect Kellin from you," she said quietly. "I'm there to protect you from Kellin."

That got Jirian's attention. What magnitude of talent did Carissa possess, that she could overpower Kellin if necessary?

"Would you describe your talent for me, Carissa?" Jirian asked.

Carissa instinctively knew this was a bad idea, but Kellin had given them all two specific instructions regarding cooperation with the Association. The first of these was to demonstrate your talent to anyone who asked to see it. They weren't going to play coy with the Association about the extent of what they could do.

So she reluctantly told Jirian what she could do, and then, with his consent, she demonstrated its effectiveness.

The implications unfolded instantly in Jirian's mind. The Association could never allow the possibility of rampant unchecked "mind control" talents to evolve here.

From that moment, the Brilliant were doomed.

Eventually, Lorelei reached the position of Assistant Solicitor-General and gained the required clearance to read the order drafted by one of her predecessors and approved by Parliament that authorized the Association to unilaterally act against the Brilliant, accompanied by a standing shoot-to-kill order applicable to any psionic survivors they might've missed during the original attack. This order did not expire. Both of these orders were illegal according to the treaty, yet they'd been implemented anyway.

This was not going to happen again if she had anything to say about it.

· · ·

The arrival of the Shai-Manak on the scene put a few things in perspective.

When it became apparent that Shai-Manak sorcery had a meaningful edge over the Association's technological prowess, the pressure was on for Jirian Echo to deliver a next-generation weapons system. Jirian's group was housed organizationally within Fleet, which meant Admiral Allon Slab took the brunt of Parliamentary pressure on this topic.

The Admiral in turn authorized an array of surveillance exceptions for Jirian's lab, meaning an entire Fleet research facility was alarmingly unmonitored.

Three standard floors were allocated to Jirian's work, according to plans on file, one of which was entirely dedicated to shooting ranges and sparring facilities for testing personal armaments and defenses. Another was primarily being used for stress testing and fabrication activities, and the third was laid out as offices for bureaucratic work.

Decades passed, and the name Jirian Echo almost slipped into history unnoticed. Then, with no fanfare, and without notifying Parliament, Jirian began a recruitment process among elite Security officers, looking for volunteers.

Recruitment happened solely via word of mouth. The pitch was hard-core. Sign up for the chance of a lifetime: Gain incredible psionic powers and *become* the invincible weapon you've always known was inside you. Side effects may include pain and death.

Remarkably, you could get people to agree to those terms.

Stories began quietly circulating within elite Security circles about the program. If you met their physical criteria for volunteers, you'd be given a list of potential psionic powers.

First-timers could only choose one; repeat volunteers could choose up to three.

Then you'd be given a corresponding "catalyst bar" for the power you selected: literally speaking, a caramel-flavored nutrient bar, infused with psychoactive compounds that unlocked psionic abilities that were dormant in your mind.

Then they'd put you in the training facility with skirmish androids and start feeding you instructions over a loudspeaker, and you'd find out if the catalyst had worked. If you found yourself in possession of exciting new psionic powers, the word was that it was the most awesome feeling you could imagine.

Fatalities dropped sharply as the program refined the catalyst bar formula and gained experience guiding the volunteers through the experiments. But every now and then still, instead of catalyzing psionic powers, the bars would catalyze a volunteer's brain to dissolve.

. . .

Lorelei had a few reliable contacts in Security circles, who reached out when some of their colleagues met untimely deaths during Jirian's experiments. Lorelei officially opened an investigation. The more she learned about Jirian's program, the angrier she became. Fleet was planning to use the extracted psionic talents of a group it had annihilated in order to annihilate the next group that came along.

This situation was a good example of the one great flaw of the original language of the treaty. When a culture applied for membership in the Association, they were immediately granted treaty protection until a decision was made. But in the event an application was rejected, the six-month grace period afterward wasn't much of a deterrent. The rejected culture was fully exposed to exploitation by Association members at that point. In fact, the application was like a road map to all the available goods on offer.

But this situation was worse, because both the Brilliant and the Shai-Manak should still be receiving proper treaty protections. Not simply because of some technicality regarding how their applications were processed but because in spirit, the treaty was meant to inspire its signatories to a higher standard of compassionate behavior toward those with less power in the first place.

Lorelei recruited an audit team, bringing them each up to speed and setting plans in motion to pull the curtain back on Jirian Echo's activities.

Then the Shai-Manak invaded floor 49,500, and Jirian proposed his counterattack.

Even before Jirian's mission got off the ground, Lorelei accelerated plans for her own mission. They would let Jirian work uninterrupted today. Tomorrow, they would pay a visit to his facility, whether the Shai-Manak on floor 49,500 had been vanquished or not.

▪ ▪ ▪

Carissa absorbed Lorelei's briefing in silence.

They were in Lorelei's study, on opposite ends of a couch, after dinner with several of Lorelei's partners. Carissa hadn't had a family dinner around a table in a long time, but her manners were sufficiently intact to get her through the experience.

"I'm sorry, I know that was a lot," said Lorelei.

"I don't see how you reconcile everything you do with everything *they* do. That's not . . . an insult. I mean, you're so much *better* than they are, they don't deserve you."

"Maybe they don't. But they do need me."

"They need, like, thousands of you. I'm surprised they haven't reverse engineered how your brain works and then installed 'Lorelei chips' in all their workers."

Lorelei laughed.

"Where did you go?" Lorelei finally asked. "After you left Minneapolis."

Carissa found it difficult to respond.

"Carissa—I've spent most of my life wondering what happened to you," Lorelei said gently. "We can start with the day you left Minneapolis, or we can start with today, or you can pick any day in between."

"I spent ten years working for the Elevator Guild," Carissa said eventually. "I was a mechanic on a racing team for a few years. I was a nomad for long stretches, just drifting with the currents . . ."

"'The currents'?"

"Yeah, the currents of people flowing through the Building with no place to land. Eventually, I hooked up with the Explorers Guild—"

"How did you find them?" Lorelei asked.

"They were looking for couriers, and I scored a gig. That was really good for a long time, but it ended pretty horribly."

"What happened?"

"Uh . . ." Carissa fell silent, thinking hard about a way to summarize difficult events. Finally, she said, "I got into a massive argument with Nicholas Solitude, and after that, he just made it clear I wasn't welcome anymore. I kind of soured on going back to the currents, didn't really want to be around people anymore. So, for the last decade or so, I lived in an elevator, and it was actually pretty nice, up until today when it got destroyed by Shai-Manak enforcers and one thing led to another and now I'm here."

"Listen to you, 'one thing led to another' . . . You said a baby magic-user sent you here?"

"She didn't send me; she just made it obvious that I should come here. She divined a few things she couldn't have known otherwise, like she knew it was you who helped me escape Minneapolis, because she knew that you hid your badge in my pocket so that I had a shot at making it through customs without getting stopped, and she could see in her mind your name on the badge."

"What?"

"Yeah, it's weird, but it's just low-key wild magic, nothing she could weaponize or whatever. But yeah, the reason she saw the badge so clearly is that I still *have* it. Obviously, it stopped working a long time ago, but . . . it was the only thing I brought out with me, and it had your picture on it."

They were silent together for a long moment.

Carissa choked up without warning. She struggled to speak, to explain.

"You have a family," she managed.

"I have . . . an abundance of family, yes."

"Maybe you can imagine how it feels to learn that some of the Brilliant might have survived the Fleet attack, only to wind up in some demented Association laboratory for who knows how many years. I mean, god forbid that actually happened to anyone. But if anyone's still alive, or if there's evidence about their fates . . . I need to be there, Lorelei. I can't let the Association bury it."

"I wouldn't let that happen."

"Lorelei—you can't keep risking your life for me. You have a family to protect. I can make sure everyone on your team thinks I'm just some newbie you recruited. I can make sure they forget they ever saw me when it's over."

"You think I'd let you wipe yourself from my memory?"

"Just the audit, Lorelei. The rest of our memories together . . . I would never."

"Are you going to leave when the audit's over?"

"'Do not surveil' gets revoked automatically at forty-eight hours. Hopefully I'm a ghost long before then."

"So this is it for us. This is what we get."

"Nah. I mean, if you ever take a vacation, I know a woman named Alusia who could meet you somewhere."

"Is that your alias?"

"Different alias. Not a citizen. So you'd have to cross the border, if they let important officials do that without a Security detail."

"I'll figure it out."

The study doubled as a guest room, with the couch unfolding into a bed. Carissa and Lorelei ended the night lying next to each other on the bed, silently staring at the ceiling, eventually holding hands, and finally drifting off to sleep.

EPISODE 2.06

Anjette came out of hibernation suddenly, all at once.

For a full one and a half seconds, she was deeply confused about how she'd lost so much time in her memory, but then she recalled the soul-stealing ritual and snapped into a diagnostic mode. To her surprise, she now possessed an incomplete collection of someone else's memories—Rindasy's, which the replica had smuggled out of zir, so to speak, to Anjette via an improvised entanglement communication protocol.

Fortunately for Anjette, among these memories were the passchants required to undo the bindings that held her suspended in midair in this cell.

A few minutes later, Anjette was free and testing the stone cell door, which turned out to be locked. Through the small, barred window in the door, she could see no guards outside.

She hauled off and punched the door so hard that it exploded into pieces, some of which smashed into the cell door across the hallway—startling its occupant. As Anjette stepped into the hallway, a face appeared at the window of that cell.

"Take me with you," said the nondescript human face. "I can get us off this floor without being detected. I swear I can. Please, the sorcerer who took your shape, Anjette—ze carries a weapon that can erase a thousand floors in an instant. I can help you stop zir if we can get to zir in time."

"Who are you?" Anjette asked.

"My name is Andasir," ze replied. "I'm sure you remember Gresij. I was his second."

Anjette peered down the length of the dark hallway, then looked back at Andasir in zir cell.

"Why are you locked up here?" she asked.

"I was caught on my way to warn the Association about the weapon," Andasir replied.

Andasir was not hanging in midair, wrapped in multiple interlocking binding spells, she observed.

"What sorcery keeps you in that cell?" she asked.

"A compulsion to avoid touching the door at all costs. For all I know, they left it unlocked."

Anjette tried the door, but found it was indeed locked. No physical key hung conveniently from a hook somewhere nearby. She hauled off and punched the door so hard that it exploded into the cell, creating a minefield of shrapnel that Andasir was compelled to avoid as ze tiptoed across the cell into the hallway.

"Nearest elevator, if you please," Anjette said.

. . .

As a specter, Jirian Echo didn't "show up for work," rather he "began haunting the lab," as it were, according to an irregular schedule that even Jirian had trouble predicting. Today, Jirian materialized in his office earlier than usual and felt agitated right from the start. The first forty-five minutes passed uneventfully, as Jirian caught up on email, spot-checked a few science feeds, browsed a few relevant papers that thoughtful colleagues had forwarded—oh, and forced himself to swallow the violent rage that permeated every undead fiber of his tormented being over his humiliation yesterday, first at the hands of the Shai-Manak, who destroyed his scouting mission, then in front of Parliament, who destroyed his greater ambition, more or less.

After decades of grinding, methodical, high-risk experimentation, now apparently the entirely new offensive capability of psionic talents would be cataloged as a problematic curiosity and placed on a shelf marked DO NOT TOUCH ON PAIN OF SCOLDING or some such.

Jirian's overconfidence had always been Personality Flaw Number One, causing him personal and professional grief even while he'd been alive, and that trait hadn't diminished any in undeath;

as a result, the many flavors of crushing disappointment were always lurking in the background of his awareness, and now he felt like his nonexistent circulatory system was overflowing with it. And the most prominent knife twisting in his semicorporeal back right now was remembering his exchange with that wretched lawyer, Lorelei Rivers, in which he'd blithely admitted to medical experimentation on prisoners of war. He'd been so confident the Brilliant would never receive an ounce of image rehabilitation that he'd been caught off guard to realize that Lorelei was angling on their behalf for some reason—despite their extinction as a culture. What was the literal, actual point of that?

A commotion out in the hallway reached Jirian's attention. A din of voices, futile protests, someone barking orders. As a specter, Jirian's sensorium could stretch and expand a certain distance, enabling him to count ten people so far who were definitely not on staff, including four wearing Security uniforms, herding his administrative personnel into a conference room, separating them from their terminals and tablets.

And that wretched Lorelei Rivers was right in front, authoritative, directing the operation. She'd almost certainly brought an experienced audit team with her.

One of them retrieved a small metallic cube from a briefcase; clearly, they were about to deploy surveillance dust throughout the facility. That would make things tricky.

He'd anticipated a long time ago that this day would come, and there were countermeasures in place on the internal network and throughout the facility to keep a standard on-premises audit team from discovering any unpleasant facts—of which there were more than he could count. But he had to admit he'd been lax keeping up with the latest innovations in network forensics. A small wave of anxiety washed over him but quickly dissipated; he needed to concentrate.

He composed an encrypted message to Admiral Slab and sent it: "Surprise visit from Lorelei Rivers in progress. I can stall, but optimal if you can shut it down."

If the Admiral was surprised by this audit, that was bad news. If the Admiral knew and said nothing, that was worse news. All in all, Lorelei Rivers being here in person was the worst news.

She swept into his office without knocking, looking sharp and officious in a high-end business tactical suit—common when you needed to look like a government official but didn't want your armor plating to seem too obvious. Behind her trailed a pair of lawyers dressed almost identically to Lorelei, and bringing up the rear was a pair of uniformed Security officers.

Jirian swiped away the floating screens he'd been using and hovered patiently on the other side of the office.

"Madam Solicitor," Jirian said politely. "If I'd known you were visiting this morning, I'd have arranged for pastries."

"Jirian Echo, it's my duty and frankly my pleasure to inform you that you're the subject of a formal investigation by my office," Lorelei replied. "With the explicit approval of the Prime Minister, we're here to conduct search and interview activities, and we expect full cooperation from you and your team for the duration of our visit."

"Of course," Jirian said.

"Do you mind if I sit?" she asked as she found a place at a small, round table about halfway across the room from the doorway. The other members of her team remained standing behind her. The Security agents seemed unnecessary to Jirian, since none of these people could physically restrain him or prevent him from simply dematerializing into the aethyr if he chose. Of course, running away now would almost certainly guarantee that he'd lose his position. And his afterlife would shape up to be considerably less appealing without an Association laboratory at his fingertips.

"Please do," Jirian replied as he wafted over to join her at the table. "Should I summon a lawyer for myself? Am I in that kind of trouble?"

"We'll see what kind of trouble you're in when we're through with our audit, at which point you can decide for yourself if you'd like to retain the services of a legal team. In the meantime, no one is permitted to enter or leave the premises until we're through."

"I see."

"I thought you might want to know what's happening in your facility. First, although your laboratory's surveillance exceptions hold up as valid, they only apply to ambient surveillance. They provide no protection from extraordinary surveillance measures like the auditing and analysis software we're installing on your internal network or the surveillance dust we're deploying throughout the facility."

"Perhaps if I knew what you were looking for, I could save you some time," Jirian said.

"I want to know exactly how your transferrable psionic abilities work. I want to know about medical experimentation on live or deceased Brilliant survivors that occurred during your tenure, and I want the identity roster and current location of the survivors or their remains. I want an inventory of any existing biological samples taken from the Brilliant, and I want an inventory of 'catalyst bar' production. I want a complete list of every Security volunteer who came through this lab. Our analysis software may develop additional questions based on the results of searching your network. We're conducting interviews with each member of your team as well.

"So if you'd like to save me some time, I'd suggest you cooperate to the fullest extent possible, starting with answers to any of the implied questions I just mentioned, or the questions I'm about to ask you directly."

. . .

Jirian Echo's warning to Admiral Slab about the arrival of the audit team did not come as a surprise. The Admiral had been warned to expect an audit earlier that morning by his fellow minister Cadence Array, home secretary and Director of Security.

She spent hours navigating the elaborate protocols Fleet had enacted to ensure that secure real-time communication with the

Admiral was exceedingly daunting. This culminated with her traveling alone in an autopiloted shuttle far out into the desert beyond the parking lot, well outside the ring of beacons, and importantly, beyond the range that Association surveillance dust was allowed to operate, before she could be patched through to the Admiral aboard his flagship. By his mandate, Fleet was formally firewalled from all available Building networks.

These protocols weren't offered to every minister in Parliament, but Cadence Array was a worthwhile and reliable contact, even if she was staunchly loyal to the Prime Minister—blindly so, in the Admiral's opinion.

After Jirian's disastrous performance in front of Parliament yesterday, Cadence was summoned to hear Lorelei provide a detailed briefing to the Prime Minister about Jirian's activities—or at least her suspicions about them. The briefing was eye-opening, and it concluded with a review of Lorelei's plan to lead an audit team into Jirian's facility, which the Prime Minister approved without hesitation. It had taken Cadence so long to get in touch with the Admiral that the audit was only a couple of hours away.

"Why were you invited to this briefing," the Admiral said over their voice line, "when it's a Fleet facility in the crosshairs?"

"My judgment was called into question regarding the surveillance exceptions we approved for that facility before Jirian and his team even arrived. And Lorelei was quick to point out that an audit team wouldn't be necessary if those exceptions had never been granted."

"How else do they expect us to operate a secret weapons research program?" barked the Admiral.

"Why does this program need to be kept secret from Parliament? I couldn't answer that."

"Because Parliament would never approve a program that violates the treaty, even if it means saving the Association from a full assault by the Shai-Manak."

"Allon, you can't just throw the treaty out the nearest air lock whenever you decide it's inconvenient. And Parliament holds the right to inspect and approve a program that you think is crucial to the Association's survival."

"That may be true on paper. I honestly can't remember a damn thing the treaty says, and I'm not about to go slogging through the web version to remind myself. Fleet has *always* taken its role seriously as the Association's primary line of defense against external threats. We are constantly vigilant. We shoot down threats the rest of the Association never hears about. The last thing we need is micromanagement from Parliament or a standoff with Security."

"Why would we ever wind up in a standoff?"

"Cadence," the Admiral said, biting down on his temper in the practiced fashion of a career diplomat, "perhaps you've forgotten the fact that you live in a surveillance state. I would love to believe that every citizen who carries an Association badge can be trusted to preserve the sanctity of the data you collect, but the fact is that I do not. For the safety of Fleet and the Association itself, our research must remain our own."

"No matter how well you protect us from imaginary threats we never see," said Cadence, "Parliament will never allow Fleet to operate without its oversight."

"We already do, Cadence."

"Until two hours from now, when an armed audit team marches into your lab."

"And you can't stop or stall this audit team somehow? I appreciate the warning, but it's arriving rather late in the game."

"Nothing I can do. Lorelei reports directly to the Prime Minister. Her whole org is untouchable. She'll have a couple of my people as nominal escorts, but the audit team itself was cherry-picked by Lorelei, and none of them answer to me."

The Admiral fell silent.

"This doesn't have to be a disaster, you know," Cadence continued. "The audit could be the start of a brand-new era of transparency and cooperation. Or I suppose it could be the opening skirmish in a military coup. It's to your credit that I can't predict which direction you'll choose."

She was joking, of course, but the timing was very poor for such comedy.

"No, Cadence, it will hardly be the opening skirmish," the Admiral said. "You simply haven't been paying attention until now."

A single bolt from a long-range plasma cannon vaporized the shuttle and its passenger, Cadence Array. A nearby Fleet cruiser jumped away from the scene almost instantly.

·   ·   ·

Anjette and Andasir reached one of the elevators on foot, leaning on a combination of stealth, magic, and luck to get there. This was one of the three elevators on the floor that had not been the victim of sabotage by Andasir quite recently. The next trick would be getting past the two enforcers.

"Can you create an illusion on the panel so they don't notice that we've pressed the button?" Anjette asked.

"Shai-Manak can detect when magic is used in our presence," Andasir replied. "It's a sense like hearing or sight."

Compounding that problem: assuming they managed to press the button somehow, arrival time for the elevator was unpredictable. They'd be dealing with the two enforcers for the duration of their wait time. If it lasted longer than even a minute, reinforcements would no doubt arrive.

Compounding *that* problem: Andasir could only serve as a distraction, because ze refused to fight.

"If I can get you off this floor," Andasir said, "can I trust you will pursue Rindasy to the best of your ability?"

"Stopping zir will be my sole priority," Anjette replied.

"Good," said Andasir. "Then I have an idea."

A few moments later, Andasir wandered out into the open, drawing the attention of the enforcers, who were sitting on benches a few feet away from the elevator door. It was not common knowledge yet that Andasir was being held for treason underneath the civic temple, so zir mere approach did not sound any alarms. The enforcers noticed zir, nodded as ze approached, and waited for zir to flash zir personal sigil to identify zirself.

Instead, Andasir set off a spell, a powerful blast of force like a massive hammer punch, which ze directed straight past the enforcers, directly into the elevator doors. The doors were designed to withstand a significant amount of abuse, but Andasir happened to know from firsthand experience that they were in no way invulnerable. They crumpled inward and fell into the elevator shaft beyond.

"I think you should arrest me," Andasir suggested to the stunned enforcers.

As the enforcers leapt into action to apprehend zir, Andasir ran, drawing their attention away, allowing Anjette to remain undetected as she became the second person in recent history to deliberately leap into an open elevator shaft on a mission to stop an apoc weapon from being used against the Association.

Every fifty floors in the elevator shaft, Facilities drones were positioned on charging stations in a recessed groove, ready to report for duty if spot repairs in the field were needed. She interrupted her descent by catching hold at the nearest charging station and wedging herself into the recessed groove to avoid elevator traffic.

"Are you authorized to be in the elevator shaft?" the drone's limited onboard AI asked via the tinny speaker on the side of its hull.

"I'm not. I need to report an emergency. Can you get through to the Vantage Point? Or Security?"

After a brief pause, the drone replied, "The Vantage Point is blocking incoming calls from robots and drones. I have Security standing by to respond to your emergency."

"Hello, this is Security," said a crisp human voice. "I understand you've fallen into an elevator shaft?"

"No, I jumped, but that's not the emergency. Listen carefully. I need you to escalate this call to Dimension Force immediately. I have a code two immigration violation to report. I'll stay on the line."

Code two referred to "terrorist activity, large scale."

"One moment," the officer calmly replied. Then, a bit incredulously, they said, "Voiceprint database claims you're Agent Anjette. Is that accurate?"

"That's me."

"What are you doing in an elevator shaft, if you don't mind my asking?"

"Oh, same as always," Anjette replied. "I'm just doing whatever it takes to protect the citizens of the Building."

"Copy that. Hang on, please."

And then, finally, the familiar emotionless voice of Agent Grey, head of Dimension Force, known in certain circles as "the Commanding Word" and "the Cleansing Fire," got on the line.

"This is Agent Grey. Who is this?"

"It's Anjette. I've got an active code two. A Shai-Manak spy shapeshifted into my exact form and is likely operating as me inside the Association somewhere. The spy's mission is to neutralize the Association's psionic weapons program, using a doomsday weapon that can reportedly destroy a thousand floors at once."

"Holy shit," the drone murmured.

Agent Grey was not inclined to waste time. She said, "I need irrefutable authentication from you. Voiceprint alone won't convince me to mobilize my people for a code two."

"That's the best you'll get until I reach you. But the spy who's got my badge can also pass a voiceprint auth, so doesn't that at least tell you there's an extra me running around?"

After a beat, Agent Grey said, "Your badge disappeared into a Fleet facility we don't surveil." To someone else near her: "Whisper, surveil that Fleet facility, *now*." Then to Anjette: "Stay put, Anjette. I'll summon the team onto this connection, and you can brief us all at once."

.   .   .

The three floors that comprised Jirian's facility were connected by the Left and Right elevators on each floor and also by a spiral staircase they'd installed so no one had to wait for an elevator to get up or down within the complex.

The audit team knew going in that the top floor of the complex was the administrative hub, with offices for key personnel, conference rooms, a small auditorium, and so on. This is the floor they'd entered on. Below them, on the second floor, they expected to find an array of laboratory space and fabrication equipment, storage for volatile materials, isolation chambers, and potential surprises they couldn't predict, given the output of their research wasn't available in advance for them to study. The first floor was a training center, giving volunteers a theoretically safe space to practice using psionic powers. According to Lorelei's informers, the catalyst bars were stored in a set of lockers inside a large storage closet on the first floor, and just about all the volunteers knew how to get these lockers open.

Once the team was on-site, elevator service to the lower two floors was locked down, and Security was posted at the elevators on the third floor, greeting researchers and admin staff as they arrived and quickly sorting them into lines for interviews.

A private teleport pad on the third floor was the last remaining route into the facility. It was located in the plush green room of the auditorium, of all places, and it was a sophisticated military model used by Fleet. When the Admiral needed to visit in person, the green room easily doubled as a well-appointed office and lounge for him and his retinue, out of sight and mind of anyone else on the floor.

They quickly learned that no one on staff, including Jirian, knew how to put this model into hibernation mode or shut it off. They were forced to station personnel and put attack drones into rotation to keep watch over it while the audit continued.

Then they deployed surveillance dust and watched it spread through the facility, sending streams of data back to a receiving display they'd set up at the receptionist's desk. As the earliest data came in, they could see that the second floor was deserted and that somehow three people had arrived on the first floor prior to locking down the elevators. They looked like billowy neon candle flames on the map they were looking at.

With Lorelei sequestered in Jirian's office for the time being, Agent Anjette of Dimension Force was technically in command. She pointed to a bright distorted blotch on a different area of the map, at the far end of the second floor from where the spiral staircase was located, and said, "I presume that's not a person like the others."

"Correct," said one of the auditors. "The interference we're getting—that's thaumaturgical. Dust can't understand magic, can't measure thaums. See, the blotch is fading; that means the whole nanoswarm is learning to route around that area because they were getting toasted there. Probably safe for people, though, or it wouldn't be placed where personnel could easily be exposed to it."

"Or Jirian left a magical surprise for us when he realized he was about to be audited," Anjette countered. She looked from face to face among the auditors gathered around the display and asked, "Are any of you proficient with magic?"

Judging by the empty looks on their faces, the answer was no.

"I see. And what do you typically do, then, when you encounter potential magical threats in the field?"

After a beat, someone in the back said, "We let Fleet handle it."

That got a small chuckle out of most of them.

Soon they were able to pool enough dust on the first floor to start getting high-resolution imagery of three individuals in workout clothes, limbering up on mats, preparing to exercise—or train. The dust found the storage closet where the catalyst bars were stored but saw no evidence the lockers had been accessed yet today.

Anjette turned to the group and said, "Detain those three and confiscate all the catalyst bars in the facility. I'm going to investigate the magic source up close."

"Are *you* proficient with magic?" someone asked her.

With a cocky grin, she said, "I'm proficient in saving people's lives."

. . .

"I should clarify that we still don't actually understand *how* psionic abilities work," Jirian informed the audit team. "We merely understand an incomplete set of facts that are true *when* they work. We remain no closer now than we ever were to understanding the underlying mechanics of a psionic ability from the perspective of any branch of physics or biology.

"The core discovery was that the Brilliant produced an entire suite of previously unknown human neurotransmitters while using their psionic talents: nearly a hundred tiny norepinephrine variations. Norepinephrine is the neurotransmitter generally responsible for regulating and stimulating the sympathetic nervous system, which primes the mind and body for action in survival situations.

"We call these novel norepinephrine variations *psionadrines*.

"We were able to correlate the production of specific combinations of psionadrines with the emergence of specific psionic abilities. We were then able to determine in simulations that introducing psionadrines to non-psionic minds produces all the other physiological markers in the nervous system that accompany using a psionic ability—a sign that the ability itself would likely be available as well.

"After refining our simulations thousands of times, we recently began human testing.

"We synthesize psionadrines from readily available precursors and administer them to test subjects as part of an experimental protocol similar to a guided meditation in which we steer the subjects toward safe, reliable control of their new abilities. After a short duration, and just as it does with norepinephrine, the body breaks down psionadrines into biologically inert metabolites, which are excreted in urine, by which point the psionic abilities have worn off with no lasting effect."

"I would call death a lasting effect for most people," Lorelei said.

"Yes, what I mean to say is, for the majority of our volunteers, the effects wear off harmlessly," Jirian replied. "With some test subjects, however, the brain loses regulation over its psionadrine production, allowing neuronal cascades of overproduction to occur. This typically results in a stroke that kills the subject within minutes. The brain's likely being deprived of every other neurotransmitter it needs for autonomic functioning. We don't currently have a neuroprotectant that will inhibit 'psionadrinic cascades' without also suppressing the desired psionic effects."

Lorelei looked up from her tablet and said, "You have no way to protect people from these cascades, volunteers are dying, and you haven't halted testing?"

"The test subjects are giving their informed consent."

"Healthy subjects shouldn't be presented the choice of volunteering for an experiment we know is killing people," Lorelei said in a clipped voice, controlling her temper. "The bioethics amendment—"

"I'm overseeing a weapons program, not a therapeutic institute," he interrupted. "Fleet decides what the acceptable risk is here, not the medical community. And we're not recruiting civilians into these experiments. Security and Fleet personnel are accustomed to the risk of service. Test pilots for experimental attack ships often operate with a similar risk of catastrophic failure, and we have no shortage of volunteers for those tests, either."

Lorelei didn't respond, so presumably, Jirian had made his point. He resumed his planned statements.

"Now I know, Counsel, from our brief chat in Parliament yesterday, that you're concerned we overstepped ethical boundaries by experimenting on surviving Brilliant. We did no such thing. My team was tasked with cataloging the talents of the Brilliant while we were in Minneapolis. Our standard protocol was to request a demonstration of their talent and a biological sample. Many Brilliant also consented to brain imaging while using their talent. The biological samples were scanned and re-created as data models and then destroyed. This proved to be sufficient to generate an accurate computational simulation of a psionic human.

"I hope that's a sufficient summary. What other questions can I answer for you today?"

"I do have one question, actually," Lorelei said. "While I was working with the Brilliant, I got to know Kellin, their leader, probably as well as anyone could be expected to under the circumstances. He confided in me that he'd given his people two instructions when it came to cooperating with the Association. He told them to demonstrate their talents to anyone who asked to see them, to convince the diplomats they were telling the truth about what they could do. But he also insisted they couldn't be guinea pigs for any science experiments. He didn't want to give the Association more concrete data about the Brilliant than they possessed themselves.

"So I'm curious, Director, how did you persuade so many of them to disobey an order from the man they followed almost fanatically?"

"Those instructions may have been in force when we arrived," Jirian replied, suddenly wary, "but we were on the ground for almost three months—a full month before negotiators arrived. We had time to build relationships of trust with many of them. I never saw evidence that Kellin intended to seriously enforce those instructions."

"Kellin would never discipline one of his people in front of outsiders," one of the Security officers at the back of the room said. "So no, you wouldn't have seen evidence."

Jirian snapped, "Keep your commentary to yourself, Officer, or I'll have *you* disciplined."

The officer began speaking in a calm, controlled voice.

"Jirian Echo, I forbid you from leaving my direct line of sight or attempting violence against me or anyone else. I forbid you from casting spells or using hidden powers against me or anyone else. I forbid you from speaking unless I ask you a direct question, and when you speak, I demand you speak the truth. Do you understand me?"

"I do," Jirian replied instantly.

Carissa finally stepped out where Jirian could see her so that he at least had the opportunity to fully understand the nature of the trap that was now sprung. It had absolutely not escaped her notice that talks with the Association broke down immediately after Jirian interviewed her. She'd spent most of the last century blaming herself for the fall of the Brilliant. But if there was one person in existence she blamed more, it was Jirian Echo. She wanted him to remember her.

"*Where did you really get biological samples of the Brilliant?*" she asked.

"From the fourteen prisoners that Fleet remanded into my custody after we finished our operations in Minneapolis."

"*Where are the prisoners now?*"

.   .   .

With the rest of the audit team occupied elsewhere in the facility, Rindasy could breathe a little easier. Anjette's personality was a challenge to carry off, from her powerful moral certitude to the wisecracks she made for the benefit of an imaginary audience. But ze was happy to have leveraged Anjette's innate confidence that she could handle anything as a way to keep the audit team away from the source of magic in the facility until Rindasy zirself could study it.

The area identified by the surveillance dust was in a seemingly little-used corner of the second floor, occupied mostly by gear that appeared to be piled or stacked up waiting to be repurposed or recycled. Ze sensed the contours of a subtle illusion operating somewhere within a walk-in refrigeration unit. Ze opened the door to look inside; shelving had been removed, but otherwise, visually nothing seemed out of the ordinary. It was an odd place for a magical heat source, as it were.

If ze had to guess, ze suspected it might be a bespoke illusion, crafted by a wizard to be self-sustaining for some duration of time. A common use for an illusion like that might be to hide the presence of a safe in your home, for instance. Rindasy could probably dispel this illusion without being noticed by the people on the team, but the surveillance dust would definitely notice the illusion dropping, and someone would want to know what triggered it, and would they be able to trace that back to Rindasy? Doubt and caution held zir back.

Suddenly, Rindasy realized people were descending the spiral staircase from the third floor and now were striding purposefully across the second floor straight toward zir. Ze took a step out of their way. Jirian Echo floated past, followed closely by a Security officer, and then a few steps behind them, Lorelei. Jirian stopped in front of the same refrigerator that Rindasy had just inspected and uttered what was probably a passphrase—a long scientific formula.

Nothing happened.

Jirian tried it again, and again nothing happened.

"I don't understand!" Jirian exclaimed, clearly panicked.

"*Were you* lying *to me about this?*" the Security officer said.

"No, I swear it's here, I swear!"

Rindasy understood what was likely happening.

Ze said, "A spell like that usually won't respond when the passphrase is provided under duress. Keeps thieves from ever getting in." Then ze added, "You got your money's worth on this one, congratulations."

The Security officer turned to Rindasy and said, "Can *you* get us inside?"

And Rindasy realized this woman was desperate, as though there was something deeply personal at stake here. The replica anxiously reminded zir that the Association maintained an Arcanum division with wizards on call ze could summon—magical locksmiths, if you will. All you had to do was submit a request on vellum through the pneumatic tube system—

"Yeah, I think so," Rindasy replied. Ze still remembered all the skeleton key counterspells they'd baked into the Key of Rindasy. Getting past this illusion would be trivial. Doing so was probably an impulsive mistake; ze was probably going to face uncomfortable questions from the audit team if ze did this.

But you couldn't absorb the raw need for answers in that woman's eyes and not do something to help her if you could.

After a quick moment of calm reflection, Rindasy uttered a sharp incantation in the artificial language the Shai-Manak had devised for casting spells in the presence of enemies.

Immediately, a section of the refrigerator rippled and then revealed a walkway into a dark, narrow chamber, which looked something like an inflated air lock tube you'd use to enter a spacecraft.

The woman's face lit up, and she whispered to Rindasy, "Thank you." Then she turned to Jirian and barked an order: "*Give me the tour, Jirian.*"

Jirian immediately floated forward into the chamber, with the woman right behind zir. Lorelei hurried to catch up, paying no immediate mind to Rindasy's display of spellcraft.

Rindasy was about to follow them into the chamber when something caught zir eye back across the floor. A soft glow of light filled the stairwell, coming up from the second floor and painting the walls along the way with colors that cycled at a languid, mesmerizing rate.

Instead of following Lorelei, ze decided ze ought to investigate the source of that light. Just as ze began moving in that direction, a sudden instinct grabbed zir attention. Obviously, that colored light wasn't natural, hadn't been there earlier, and almost lured Rindasy down to the first floor without zir even realizing a trap had been set. But the replica knew exactly what Rindasy was seeing.

The replica had become so integrated into Rindasy's psyche that there was now little distinction between them; the replica's memories and knowledge surfaced as thoughts that simply percolated into Rindasy's conscious mind unbidden. But it remained sufficiently self-aware that it could jab Rindasy sharply with a reminder that Rindasy, unlike Anjette, did not have any unique resistance to enchantments and dazzlements that affected the mind.

And that's exactly what the colored light on the wall was: a massive dazzlement intended to ensnare all who caught sight of it. Probably explained why nobody was shouting about this on the comms from upstairs; the auditors watching the footage from the surveillance dust were probably just as susceptible to it as the trainees on the first floor in the room with it. Anjette had seen that light numerous times, but Rindasy could not afford exposure to it.

That light emanated from a pair of energy vampires known as the Moods, who were senior Agents with Dimension Force. They were frequently advance scouts on scene when Dimension Force deployed because they could become incorporeal and ride into a location on power lines or thaum conduits, then take a solid vampiric form and unlock the doors for the rest of the team, or drain the life force out of everyone in the place, whichever seemed appropriate for the gig.

It still took a moment for Rindasy to have the correct aha moment. Then the realization hit.

The Agents of Dimension Force were starting to arrive *here*.

Rindasy immediately assumed Dimension Force intended to capture zir because ze'd made a mistake somewhere and blown zir cover without realizing it. The replica was willing to briefly consider other possibilities. Maybe Dimension Force was here to interrupt the audit for some reason. Maybe the Agents wanted to interrogate Jirian themselves. But Rindasy had an instinct for which of those outcomes was most probable, and ze knew they were coming just for zir.

That narrowed zir options down. Ze could detonate the pearl, here and now, in the heart of the research complex, where the psionic weapons program began. If Andasir was correct about the pearl's margin of error, the chances were good that all three floors of the complex would be caught up in the pearl's area of effect. This was the mission ze'd agreed to, and its success would prove to the Association once and for all that they would never surpass the Shai-Manak's magical and tactical superiority.

Ze did have a couple of other options. Ze could run, for instance. It was a cruel twist that the architect of the psionic weapons program was already deceased and would likely just rematerialize elsewhere if the pearl destroyed this floor. Lorelei had Jirian well in hand, so why erase Lorelei and her entire audit team from existence just as they were getting the job done?

Kalavir had given Rindasy latitude to choose the right target. This place wasn't it.

But let's say the replica could figure out how to operate that shiny Fleet teleport pad. It would be priceless to see the Admiral's face right before detonating the pearl from the bridge of his flagship.

That settled it: ze would try to escape from here.

Once Rindasy was no longer bound to masquerading as Anjette, options unfolded quickly.

Ze tossed Anjette's badge under a workbench and left it behind for them to continue tracking; a minor distraction, but it might buy a few seconds. To get up the spiral staircase without falling prey to the mesmerizing field effect the Moods had established, ze said goodbye to Anjette's physical form and shapeshifted into a deadly flying insect that the Shai-Manak called a *spite beetle*.

The spite beetle's top speed, which it could reach almost instantly, was so fast that its field of vision became a literal blur, because its eyes couldn't gather light fast enough to keep up with its position. When hunting, it relied on an extensive array of antennae to navigate around obstacles as it inevitably caught up to its prey, at which point the antennae revealed their additional function as poisonous stingers. In this form, Rindasy easily sailed up the spiral staircase to the third floor, experiencing nothing of the dazzling field effect projected by the Moods.

Ze came to a stop and clung to the ceiling on the third floor, quickly determining that things looked much the same up here as they had before. A set of lawyers and auditors was still slowly processing and interviewing Jirian's staff, and it didn't seem as though any of them had been sent home yet. The young auditor who'd been monitoring the surveillance dust feed sat slack-jawed in front of the display, though, and two other auditors debated what to do about it in quiet but urgent tones.

Rindasy headed in the opposite direction, into the heart of the floor, and into the auditorium. Ze zipped across the rows of seats to the stage and then through a small passageway toward the green room backstage, stopping short in response to an instinct. Ze could sense the green room wasn't empty. The teleport pad was busy bringing people over.

Ze retreated to a perch atop an out-of-service lighting fixture and watched as a small band of humanoids emerged from the green room one at a time, wearing environmentally sealed tactical gear from head to toe that obscured their identities behind the black faceplates of their helmets, and carrying impressive and lethal weaponry, as though they'd been given the all clear to pitch their nonlethal gear into an incinerator before arriving here. They were not displaying badges or insignias, but Rindasy was all but certain these people were Fleet.

They collected themselves onstage, waiting for stragglers, clearly too large a group to fit in the green room all at once. Finally, the last two people came over, carrying a large case between them with additional gear to deploy—communications gear maybe, or sensors. Their commanding officer began running through a checklist with his team of twenty or so, and that was Rindasy's chance to escape—the teleport pad was unguarded, and clearly, there was at least a warship in range if not the actual flagship. Rindasy could make a break for the teleport pad now, hop over to the warship, and torpedo it from the inside.

But a pang of guilt arose, preventing zir from fleeing the situation. Maybe Dimension Force was here to find and neutralize the spy masquerading as Anjette. But Fleet was almost certainly here to interfere with the audit. Judging by this deployment, they might have orders to ensure no one survived the encounter.

Lorelei would clearly be their target.

That changed the equation for Rindasy. Fleet could not be allowed to take out Lorelei before her work was complete and then simply resume the weapons program as if nothing had happened.

Well, there had always been one other option besides detonating the pearl outright or fleeing the premises entirely.

That option was to stay and fight.

The way things were lining up—a single Shai-Manak caught in between a Fleet hit squad and Dimension Force—it might almost be a fair fight at that.

. . .

Jirian led them down a grated walkway in the center of the chamber. A thin strip of soft lighting directly above the walkway provided minimal illumination.

On either side of the grated walkway, glass terrariums ran the length of the chamber, subdivided into six equal compartments on each side. The terrariums were densely packed with enormous fibrous clumps of biomatter, long strands and tendrils that frequently culminated in giant bulbs of a fleshy substance, nestled within clumps and stripes of what might have been mulch or soil. The topmost layers of these terrariums were covered in elaborate fungal caps, like platters or umbrellas. The air was unusually moist in this chamber, as though a misting system was in frequent use. Each of the subdivided compartments of the terrariums had its own display screen affixed to the glass, with chart information and biomonitoring data that flowed past.

The moment she entered this chamber, Carissa started to receive a picture of what had happened. Indistinct, nearly subconscious, one-way telepathic communication was underway, feeding her glimpses of truth.

"What the hell are we looking at?" Carissa asked.

"Mycelial colonies," Jirian replied.

"*What happened to the prisoners?*" she demanded.

"After we'd exhausted the research opportunities presented by the prisoners in their original form," Jirian said, "they were ultimately used as nutrient substrate layers for these mycelial colonies. When these colonies bear fruit, the resulting fungi are rich with naturally occurring psionadrines. Crucially, these fungi produce psionadrines without any meaningful concurrent display of actual psionic abilities, making them considerably safer to handle than actual psionic humans. We extract psionadrines from the fruit to use as the psychoactive component in our catalyst bars."

"Wait, I thought you said you could produce psionadrines synthetically," Lorelei said, "so why do all this?"

Jirian said nothing, per Carissa's original instructions.

"*Answer her question!*" Carissa commanded.

"I was lying," Jirian replied. "Oh, of course we tried—psionadrines are straightforward to synthesize from raw precursors. But for reasons we don't understand, psionadrines produced synthetically in a lab are not psychoactive. Powers never emerge in the test subjects. Only when psionadrines originate biologically do they produce their desired effects.

"Of course, psionic humans only produce psionadrines when they're using their powers, and this was . . . not a safe situation for harvesting psionadrines at scale for other purposes. Fortunately, with some genetic manipulation on both sides—human and fungus—we were able to create the situation you see here, where harvestable human psionadrines are produced by fungus in notable quantities with no appreciable risk whenever we trigger a fruiting cycle."

"*You killed the prisoners to make this happen?*" Carissa exclaimed.

"We didn't kill them. We believed that . . . the highest levels of potency in the eventual extractions were most likely assured if . . . the prisoners were kept alive as long as possible while the colonies took hold."

The drip feed of psychic information she was receiving from

one or more of these mycelial colonies confirmed the core truths of Jirian's story. But this feed also contained emotional information—despair, sadness, anger in a faint blend. Trace imprints of the Brilliants' psyches remained, diffused throughout the colonies, in a weird, purgatorial state. She wasn't hearing from all of them—not every Brilliant had been telepathic—but whoever was reaching out to her was convincing enough.

"You've got twelve colonies here, but you said there were fourteen prisoners," Carissa said, "so where are the other two?"

"We returned the two most powerful prisoners to Fleet," Jirian replied. "Even working with the least powerful prisoners was extremely dangerous for a long while, until our techniques and technology were up to the task. But we never dared opening the cryo chambers for Kellin and Indira. I don't know where they are now."

Carissa almost laughed. Jirian had managed to destroy her with these revelations about her fallen comrades and yet still dangle an absurd hope that her brother was alive for her to pointlessly cling to for the rest of her life. After revealing herself to the entire Association on this foolish endeavor, the thought of surviving long enough to infiltrate Fleet in search of her brother seemed cruel and hilarious at the same time.

"Jirian Echo, your privileges and responsibilities in this division are revoked, effective immediately," Lorelei said. "We'll arrange for you to repeat this testimony for Parliament's benefit, at which time—"

"Jirian Echo, your right to exist is revoked," Carissa interrupted. "You're banished from this Building and the reality that surrounds it. Never lay eyes on the living again."

The specter vanished without a word. The long undeath of Jirian Echo had come to an end.

"Or you could do that," Lorelei said, suddenly seeming deflated.

"C'mon, you were going to try to throw him in prison when he could dematerialize at will?" Carissa replied.

"Executing him on the spot will make it harder to argue you deserve amnesty," Lorelei said.

"Amnesty?" Carissa exclaimed. "You give amnesty to criminals. I didn't break your laws, because I'm not your damn citizen!"

"The best way to revoke a shoot-to-kill order is to give you a pardon," Lorelei told her. "That's just the system."

"Lorelei, the minute I get on the next elevator, I'm *gone*. What, you think I want to join up with a culture that pulls demented shit like *this* on a constant basis?"

Lorelei had no reply to that.

"My guess is this isn't a naturally occurring pocket dimension," Carissa said. "That means there's a reality emitter nearby holding it open. We need to shut it down. Collapse all this into nothing. Otherwise some other depraved fuck will pick up this research and run with it."

Carissa could feel the tired, hopeful anticipation of that outcome in the faint telepathic waves that were floating through her. Lorelei must've felt it, too, because her resolve seemed to harden as though she now understood the stakes better.

"I'll see if the surveillance dust found it yet," Lorelei said, pulling out her tablet.

But the first thing she saw on the tablet was surveillance dust footage from the training facility on the first floor. It was weirdly compelling, and she waved Carissa over to get a look at it, too.

Carissa saw the sudden dazed look in Lorelei's eyes and snatched the tablet out of Lorelei's hand. As Lorelei reached for it, Carissa threw it against the back wall of the chamber, and when Lorelei made to run for it, Carissa blocked her and held her in place for several seconds before the spark returned to Lorelei's eyes.

"What the fuck?" Carissa said.

"The Moods are downstairs," Lorelei said. "Agents of Dimension Force with hypnotic abilities. We already have an Agent embedded with us, so why are the Moods on-site? Stay here."

"Do *what*?" Carissa said, instantly following Lorelei.

But as they emerged from the pocket dimension and stepped

back onto the second floor proper, they saw a commotion on the other side of the cavernous laboratory. Four of Lorelei's auditors and three people in workout clothes were approaching from the direction of the spiral staircase.

"What the hell's going on?" Lorelei shouted.

"We're securing the floor—come with us!" one of them shouted.

And then, eerily, someone else shouted, "We're securing the floor—come with us!"

And then all of them were shouting it, whether they were members of the audit team or not.

"This is bullshit," Carissa said, grabbing Lorelei's hand and pulling her back through the refrigerator with her into the terrarium chamber. "Lock the door behind you!"

"Lock it? I don't even know how to close it!"

Carissa scanned the doorway until she located a red lever in a panel marked OVERRIDE. Her tenure with the Elevator Guild taught her that if you found a red lever positioned next to a set of doors, you could imply a relationship, and that was good enough for her to yank the red lever down herself. This caused a metal door to slide shut and lock itself, sealing Carissa and Lorelei inside the chamber.

The faintest of pounding sounds indicated the door to the chamber was still perfectly visible from the second floor; the illusion in the refrigerator hadn't reasserted itself somehow. And as hoped, the door showed no signs whatsoever of acquiescing to the mob's desire to get inside. Eventually, the pounding sounds trailed off.

"I guess I stopped watching *Storm and Desire* before 'the Moods' joined the team," Carissa said. "What the fuck just happened?"

"The Moods must've hypnotized everyone in the training facility and sent them after us. It just doesn't make sense. I mean, Anjette is here because she has a personal interest in seeing Jirian twist, but by and large, Dimension Force only makes an appearance when things are about to go catastrophically wrong. What did we do that got their attention?"

"Who knows, but Anjette will sort it out, right?"

Lorelei paused, then had to admit, "I have no idea what Anjette will do."

An idea began to formulate in Carissa's mind. She wasn't sure if it was actually hers or if the mycelial colonies planted it in her mind. Either way, she was instantly down for it.

She studied the biomed data for each of the mycelial colonies until she found what she was looking for: a colony that produced the psionadrines correlated with clairvoyance.

"I think I'm going to eat a bunch of this clairvoyance fungus," she told Lorelei, "and then see what I can see out there."

"Are you kidding me?" Lorelei said.

"Nope."

"You're not worried about stacking an extra talent on top of yours?"

"My brother had four, Lorelei. I think I can handle two."

"Okay, but . . . what if you overdose?"

"You mean what if I *see too much*?"

"Yeah, what if you're flooded with information and you can't parse it or focus or communicate anything you see?"

"Then when it's your turn, eat half as much."

"Are you kidding me?" Lorelei said again. "Your body already produces psionadrines, hooray. I'm sure this will be a grand jaunt for you. They never got the fatality rate down to zero percent with ordinary humans. I'm not touching it."

Implements hung on the far wall for harvesting fungus—shovels and shears and the like—and Carissa was easily able to snag a giant hunk of the stuff. She sat down on a small bench and began to eat. To her relief and surprise, it had a pleasing savory taste that encouraged her to eat swiftly and in a larger quantity than she might have otherwise.

She knew within a couple of minutes that she had fully unlocked a version of clairvoyance.

She was already familiar with the mental triggering used to add a dollop of mind control to an ordinary question or statement. This was not much different. She imagined the facility on the other side of the door. Then she toggled her new talent on and imagined the facility outside in much higher detail. She did initially experience the resulting flow of information as a deluge, but rapidly found ways to mitigate it so that she could lock her focus on specific points while allowing other events and observations to flow past her as well.

If she wasn't careful, she could literally see all the way through to the underlying fabric of reality, which she decided was not recommended; she pulled back her perspective to do useful things like skim people's thoughts or see their actions in her mind's eye. This was definitely a more potent expression of clairvoyance than what she'd witnessed among her friends back in Minneapolis. It had limits: she could extend her perception to most of the facility, but the effect faded rapidly beyond that range, and her perception provided no insight about the future, only the present.

"What's going on?" Lorelei asked. "Are you okay?"

"I'm fine. I think I'm getting the hang of this," Carissa replied.

"Just like that?"

"I bet Jirian never tested his 'catalyst bars' on the Brilliant themselves," Carissa replied. "So this idea that you need training and coaching, I mean, sure, I see where that came from. But if you already have a talent, adding a new one feels really intrinsic."

Carissa closed her eyes, leaning further into the experience, sweeping her mind's eye across the field of view outside their chamber.

The hypnotized personnel were now standing motionless around the edges of the laboratory, waiting for further instructions, and their controllers, the Moods, had floated into the laboratory in the form of two large glowing balls of energy, purple and blue, that gave the eerie impression of a pair of eyes scouring the floor looking for something or someone.

Coming up the spiral staircase was Agent Steelplate, a massive, heavily armored ogre cyborg. Steelplate was the result of someone's efforts to graft as much portable combat technology onto an ogre's body as possible. Wherever they could reasonably bolt on a weapon or an armor plate without hindering mobility too much, they went for it. He was twelve feet tall and carried at least a tonne in hardware on his enormous, reinforced ogre frame. His surface armor gleamed as though freshly shined or recently upgraded, and his arms were configured for close-quarters combat: a multibeam laser rifle in the right arm slot, and a pellet-grenade launcher in the left.

The spiral stairs buckled one at a time as he ascended, but they held.

At the same time, Carissa's awareness drifted upstairs to the third floor as well, where two pockets of activity caught her attention. One of the elevators was open and under Dimension Force control, and the audit team was quietly and quickly attempting to evacuate Jirian's staff in anticipation of imminent violent conflict.

That effort was instigated by Agent Wynderia Gallas, the team's resident espionage artist, skilled in disguise, infiltration, thievery, sabotage, and assassination. She was a tall, thin humanoid of a race Carissa didn't recognize, with pale gray skin and a bald head, wearing a skintight environment suit made from a reinforced holographic fabric.

Wynderia operated a handheld scanner and systematically held it briefly against each individual's neck before allowing them into the elevator. That was weird—if you wanted to check their identities, their badges would ordinarily be sufficient. This was confirming real-time biometrics of each person.

It would take two elevators to fully evacuate Jirian's staff, but to Carissa's surprise, the second elevator arrived almost instantly, as if it had been waiting nearby. Dimension Force must have had control of the elevators now, overriding the audit team's control.

A third elevator arrived, which Wynderia tried to convince Lorelei's auditors to take, but to a person, they refused. Wynderia stuck a chair in the elevator doorway to keep it from leaving, and then she entered her unique stealth mode, becoming invisible to her surroundings. Even Carissa's clairvoyance could no longer see her. She was the product of highly illegal genetic indeterminacy engineering, which meant she could choose not to exist during attempts to observe her.

"Looks like your people won't evacuate until they find you. Ohhh, but . . . a Fleet special forces unit is pooled up in the auditorium, about to head out into the facility."

Carissa's perspective shifted in that direction, and she gathered some alarming information. Fleet was here to shut down the audit completely, preserve Jirian's research, and then flush the site—anything and anyone who wasn't crucial to continuing Jirian's work would be eliminated and all evidence of its existence destroyed. Optional goal: to find and detain Lorelei and haul her out of here for questioning.

"Detain *me*? For fuck's sake!" Lorelei exclaimed.

"And to think I'd forgotten what it was like to have Fleet in your neighborhood sweeping for you and your friends," Carissa joked. "Ohhhh, and they're going to try to get their hands on the reality emitter for safekeeping. It has a standby mode where they can store its current state in memory and then bring the whole dimension back up later."

"They can do that with us inside?" Lorelei asked, suddenly terrified.

"If they find it. Jirian never told them where he installed it. But if they can't, they're just going to say, 'Fuck it,' and blow their way in here. Which, I don't know what they'll do to you, but they've all been recently reminded about the shoot-to-kill order on me."

"How do you *know* all this?" Lorelei asked. Maybe she hadn't run across anyone with this talent while she was stationed in Minneapolis. It was admittedly impressive.

Carissa realized she was feeling so giddy about her new talent that she wasn't considering the thought of being butchered by

Fleet special ops with appropriate seriousness, but she couldn't help herself. If she let herself drift even slightly, she was back to seeing straight through to the underlying fabric of reality, which was a bit like sticking your tongue on a battery the size of a neutron star or something, which put the threat of Fleet special ops into a stark existential perspective. Allowing herself some levity of spirit instead seemed like a slightly more rational and productive way to steer herself through this bewildering moment in her life.

And this right here was a giddying talent anyway, right? If you had this talent, wouldn't you just stare straight into the minds of everyone around you all the time constantly? Wouldn't you be swept up studying the rich inner lives of, like, trees and cars and whatever else was in your vicinity? Wouldn't your ability give you perspective on the interconnectedness of all things to the point where your own personality became smeared across the ideascape of your surroundings or whatever—

"Carissa!" Lorelei shouted, and Carissa snapped back to attention, realizing Lorelei had been shouting her name repeatedly.

"What'd I miss?" Carissa asked.

"I said, 'Can you find the reality emitter?'"

"Oh, right—it's hidden in the teleport pad with its own power supply. Its emissions are disguised as traffic on the relay network. Lorelei—I thought you had approval for this audit from the Prime Minister, so why is Fleet even here?"

"Admiral Slab is an 'ask for forgiveness, not for permission' kind of person, except he doesn't care about forgiveness, either."

"Can't the Prime Minister just fire him?"

"Not without pissing off his allies, never mind pissing *him* off."

"Doesn't the Prime Minister have allies, too?"

"Of course! Fleet's loyal to the Admiral, Security's loyal to the Prime Minister—"

"So it's just his band of thugs versus her band of thugs?"

"No, there's a third band of—listen, if you want the complete history of infighting in the Association, just watch *Storm and Desire* sometime; it took them two hundred years to show it all."

Carissa spotted activity in the second-floor laboratory. The seven individuals under hypnosis by the Moods were working in eerie synchrony to slowly and carefully position a large weapon on a tripod to aim it through the open refrigerator at the door of their chamber. That was the problem with a weapons laboratory—all the damn weapons lying around.

They heard a series of booms out in the facility somewhere.

The booms were so loud that Carissa involuntarily dropped out of her clairvoyant state, as though it were just instantly flushed out of her by adrenaline.

"All right, this is starting to feel like serious bullshit," Carissa said.

Her eyes quickly scanned the interior of the chamber until she found signs of a panel on the wall that she could pry open, revealing two sets of controls on a board behind it. Environmental controls—according to these readouts, the chamber was self-sufficient on air and power for months at a time before servicing was required. That explained why Dimension Force didn't just cut them off and drag their unconscious bodies out. But the second set of controls gave her hope.

Outside the chamber, they heard a short, high-pitched whine.

"What the hell's that sound?" Lorelei asked.

"Oh, forgot to mention they're going to try to laser cut their way in or something."

"And what are *you* doing?"

"This room that we're standing in, this is a deep-space shipping container," Carissa said. "I'm trying to figure out how to kick-start its defenses. These things normally come with countermeasures against pirates. I'm also looking for attitude controls for docking rockets, and there's a tiny chance this thing might have a baby jump drive on board for emergencies." But after only a few moments, she exclaimed, "Fucking Jirian, you cheap bastard! None of that's installed. I didn't know you could get one of these so stripped down."

"The fungus told you all that?"

"Nah, but I may not have mentioned the time I worked a smuggling route, Lorelei, because the work wasn't legal, and you happen to be a very legal person. On the plus side, the hulls of these things can withstand all manner of intense shit, so it's possible their big laser won't even cut through the door. That leaves us with—"

Suddenly, a tiny orange pinprick in the door appeared and caught their eye.

"Or it'll cut through the door like it's made of paper," Carissa said. "It was always going to be one of those two options, really."

"So that's it?" Lorelei said.

Lorelei was holding it together, but Carissa could see the sheer panic lurking behind her eyes. It *killed* her that she'd walked back into Lorelei's life and promptly destroyed it for her. If Dimension Force got in and found her with Carissa—oh, you know, just a Brilliant on the run with a kill order on her head, wearing a Security uniform with an excessively fake ID in its pocket, having snuck onto a Parliamentary audit with Lorelei's full cooperation— her career was beyond salvaging, and they might accuse her of treason. And if Fleet somehow got in instead of Dimension Force, she might not even survive all this.

She could not let the last hundred years on the run end like this.

Then a flash of inspiration hit her, manifesting as an almost physical white flash behind her eyes. They weren't truly out of options, she realized, and she said, "Oh shit, I think I have a plan."

"Tell me," Lorelei said, hungry for any good news.

Carissa took a deep breath and said, "Lorelei, I've got to get out of here. Not just out of this pocket dimension. I mean, out of Association territory. I figure you need to stay and look out for your team and clean up this mess and go home to your beautiful family, am I right?"

Lorelei nodded.

"Right, so look—did I ruin your life by coming to see you yesterday?"

"What are you even talking about?" Lorelei exclaimed. "You mean, all this shit with Jirian, like did you ruin my career by helping me expose a secret prisoner torture program? Because no, this is exactly what my job is meant to be." She paused and then said, "Or do you mean, maybe it took me a really long time to bury how much I missed you, and now you're going to leave, and I'm going to have to do it all over again?"

"That," Carissa said.

"Worth it," Lorelei said.

They memorized each other's faces one more time, just to be safe.

"Now what's this plan you came up with?" Lorelei asked.

"Okay, first I need to eat fungus from the other eleven colonies," Carissa began.

∗　∗　∗

Rindasy watched the Fleet strike team check one another's gear to ensure their suits were sealed correctly. Either they were expecting something in Jirian's lab to poison the entire facility somehow . . .

. . . or they were the ones bringing in the poison.

Rindasy trailed them from a short distance, furiously calculating tactical options and coming up short. The complexities of aerial combat against Fleet vessels had become second nature. Facing off against a presumably elite strike team in a research complex was new territory. Ze was used to being outnumbered by Fleet vessels in aerial combat, but it was another thing altogether to face down twenty heavily armored shock troops. The question was should ze attack them from behind, surprising them here on the third floor and then wading through them while hacking and slashing in every direction? Or should ze try to sneak ahead of them and lay traps along their likely route to Lorelei, weakening them for the kill before they ever found her?

As the shock troops filed out of the auditorium, however, a series of small explosions went off ahead of them almost instantly. Fleet was already taking fire, apparently, and Rindasy could see through the open doorway how the stragglers at the back were scrambling for cover and trying to return fire at the same time. Ze hadn't seen any of the auditors carrying weapons more dangerous than a sidearm, so who had brought the explosive ammunition to the party?

Ze buzzed around to get a better view through the doorway. Agent Steelplate's massive form had softened up the front ranks of the strike team with one of his massive weapons, and now he was charging through their formation, smacking them into the air and shooting them before they hit the ground. Behind him, the audit team was taking potshots at the Fleet team for good measure.

Just as ze'd taken on the advantages of the spite beetle's nimble form and magic resistance, ze'd also absorbed its weaknesses, which in this case included a probable instant death if even a single stray bullet or piece of shrapnel hit zir while ze attempted to speed through the battlefield. Ze hoped Steelplate and Fleet were sufficiently occupied with each other that a small bug might not attract attention.

Ze hit top speed almost immediately on a near-straight shot across the floor. The path took zir perilously close to Steelplate. His targeting computers picked zir up almost immediately, but his mammoth frame couldn't pivot fast enough to get a shot off before ze was around a corner and out of sight.

Rindasy sailed down the spiral staircase, expecting to find the Moods doing something terrible, and sure enough, on the far side of the laboratory, their hypnotized humans were firing a big laser at the refrigerator where Lorelei had disappeared with Jirian. The Moods themselves hovered nearby, still in the form of glowing balls of energy. Rumor was that they both had two forms: their current forms, and whatever forms they were prior to becoming energy vampires. Rindasy preferred facing them in their current state.

With surprise operating in zir favor, ze took no chances and opted for high-power spells right out of the gate. The Shai-Manak files on Dimension Force listed no known weaknesses for the Moods, but this was the first time a Shai-Manak sorcerer had been in the same room with them. Rindasy would update the file soon enough if any of zir attacks succeeded.

First, though, ze needed to shift into a new form. The spite beetle's biological resistance to magic didn't interfere with shape-shifting, but could throw off spellcasting in unpredictable ways, and ze needed pure accuracy now. In midair, ze shifted into the form of a small flying lizard that the Shai-Manak called a *mirror chameleon*. As a natural defense, these creatures autonomically reflected magic and psychic attacks back at their origins, a defense that was almost instantly put to the test as the Moods pivoted their baleful attention to the strange missile that was hurtling across the laboratory at them at high speed.

Meanwhile, Rindasy chose zir attack carefully, having no desire to kill the Moods and earn the enmity of Dimension Force. Ze conjured two hollow spheres of arcane metal that encased each of the Moods, mirrored inside to reflect any attempts to penetrate the spheres right back at them. This would likely be disorienting and frightening for them, but the spell would only last ten minutes at most before the steel was reclaimed back into the aethyr and the Moods would hopefully be none the worse for wear upon their release. When the spell was complete, the two spheres dropped from the air and landed with loud clangs on the laboratory floor.

The hypnotized humans were slow to comprehend what had happened to them, and meanwhile, Rindasy swooped past the laser and sliced its power cable with the sharp edge of zir tail before landing on a workbench a safe distance from them. They were perhaps rightfully alarmed, and ze couldn't speak to them in zir current form, so ze shapeshifted into the default human form ze usually chose these days, a form that read as young and athletic with short black hair, wearing attire that mimicked the crisp upscale style of the suit ze'd seen Lorelei wear before Parliament. Without thinking, ze also mirrored the same skin tone of pale blue that Lorelei had chosen for zirself.

"The safest place in the lab right now is downstairs," ze told them. "Go before the fighting reaches this floor. Go!"

As the formerly hypnotized humans dashed for the spiral staircase, the air rippled into a weird blur halfway between Rindasy and the refrigerator entrance to the pocket dimension.

Agent Glamour Esque, master of arcane arts, emerged from the blur, clapping politely. Presenting as a tall, handsome human male, he wore a slick ensemble that combined the layered look of the classic wizard robe with the latest styling in formal wear for combat zones, adding a little off-the-shoulder cape as a throwback. His skin was a glittery silver color, which looked good paired with his long, graying hair.

"That was extremely well done," said Glamour Esque in a smooth, friendly voice. "I've never seen such effortless conjuration. It took me fifty years before I could conjure so much as a small coin without bursting the blood vessels in my eyes."

Rindasy, sizing up zir new potential opponent, said, "You will need more than a small coin if you wish to face me." Ze scanned the lab quickly, attempting to determine if other threats loomed, but so far, only Glamour Esque caught zir attention.

"Yes, well, that was five hundred years ago," said Glamour Esque, conjuring a long, black stun baton into his right hand, and an ornate throwing axe into his other hand. "I did squeeze in a little practice since then."

Rindasy bowed zir head slightly, acknowledging Glamour Esque's evident skill.

"But you were probably conjuring toys out of thin air when you were a child," he said, taking a few steps farther into the room, testing his current truce with Rindasy.

"I was never a child," Rindasy replied, dropping down off the lab table onto the floor. "Shai-Manak are born fully formed. The first thing I conjured was a broadsword to cut off the head of my father."

"I see. Did you succeed?"

"No. He managed to conjure a bigger sword. We decided instead to become friends."

After a beat, Glamour Esque smiled, and Rindasy smiled as well, slightly pleased that the man understood zir attempt at humor.

"Rindasy, you had to have known from the moment you assumed Anjette's identity that Dimension Force would come for you. We have a brand image to uphold. If word got out that Anjette went rogue and set off an apoc weapon inside the Association . . . I mean, we could lose contracts over that. But! We are prepared to offer you amnesty, if you'll agree to hand over the apoc weapon to Dimension Force."

"I'm not interested in amnesty from the same villains who are attempting to exterminate my people," Rindasy said.

"Oh, the offer doesn't come from the Association. No, what I mean is that Dimension Force will ensure your safe passage on a jump ship headed off into the multiverse, destination of your choosing, as long as you never return to the Building. In exchange, we'll make sure the Association never gets its hands on that weapon."

"I see. What are my other options?"

"You could conjure a broadsword, I suppose, and try to cut my head off. Assuming you still remember how."

"Well, that was twelve hundred years ago," Rindasy said, instantly conjuring an enormous floating broadsword from the aethyr without breaking a sweat. It materialized in the air between them and tilted its tip toward Glamour Esque. "I did squeeze in some practice since then."

Rindasy abruptly lost zir focus on the sword as ze realized a burning sensation was spreading from the back of zir neck into the rest of zir body. It was a sensation that was all too familiar; ze'd experienced it once before, during training to become a spy. Ze reached behind zir head and found a tiny dart sticking out of zir neck—so small and sharp that it had penetrated zir skin without zir even noticing its impact. The dart had delivered a dose of a powerful paralytic, and Rindasy dropped to the floor, still dimly conscious but unable to perform even the simplest act of magic or move any part of zir body. The sword dissipated into immateriality.

Wynderia Gallas, master rogue and assassin, appeared from seemingly nowhere a few feet away from Rindasy's crumpled form. She stepped over zir, winked at Glamour Esque, and strolled past him.

"Just so we're clear," Glamour Esque said to her, "I had that under control."

"Sure thing, slick," she replied.

A series of much larger explosions rocked the floor above them, and the ceiling shook with the intensity of the blasts. The explosions were meant to cover Agent Steelplate's retreat as he stomped down the spiral staircase to the laboratory floor.

"Finished so soon?" Glamour Esque asked him.

"I destroyed the first team," Steelplate replied. "They sent a second team. While I was destroying that team, a third team arrived. It's getting tedious."

"I thought you enjoyed the heat of combat."

"I enjoy a challenge. They're not even sending actual special ops teams. They're treating this as a combat robotics experiment as far as I can tell."

"I'm sure they weren't expecting you."

"Yes, I'm not insulted, I simply don't feel like feeding their system any more real-time data about how I fight." Steelplate noticed Rindasy on the floor and asked, "I estimate the fourth team will be on-site and heading down those stairs in ninety seconds. Is this the target?"

Glamour Esque nodded. Steelplate pointed an arm at Rindasy. A small sprayer emerged from a panel in the armor around his forearm and sprayed zir down head to toe with a battlefield cryogenic mist.

"Control, we've secured the target," Steelplate said over his team's channel. "Which elevator should we take to get off this floor?"

"Left elevator, thirty seconds," Agent Grey replied from the team command center in the Vantage Point. "Down elevator in ninety seconds. Your call."

"Wynderia, what's your status?" Steelplate called out.

Inside the refrigerator, Wynderia was trying and failing to open up the shipping container. She shouted back, "I could've picked this lock, but now it's melted to slag! Are we a team or a bunch of frickin' amateurs?"

"We've got the target. We're getting out of here."

"Fleet's willing to kill to get their hands on something in this place, and I've got a pretty good hunch it's behind this door. We just need to get inside." Then abruptly, she said, "Are you kidding me?" and winked out of existence, moments before the door to the shipping container was blown outward with considerable force, causing the refrigerator that disguised the entrance to splinter into thick flying shards of metal. Glamour Esque waved a hand to deflect anything headed at Steelplate or himself.

Carissa floated out of the entrance and hovered nearby, keeping her eyes on the Agents. When she was satisfied that they were taking no hostile action toward her, she waved, signaling to Lorelei that it was time to join her out on the second floor proper. Lorelei emerged from the shipping container and quickly got away from the entrance.

Carissa glanced back into the shipping container, feeling serenity finally emanating from the colonies. Then she floated away to get some distance and used one of her new talents, pyrokinesis, to set off columns of flame inside the terrariums that swiftly devoured the colonies. The container's fire suppression system went off in a valiant effort to contain the blaze, but the damage was done. No one on-site would be harvesting live fungus samples, which were almost instantly consumed by the fires. There might be spore prints hiding somewhere, but she'd have to trust that Lorelei planned to stay on top of this until the end.

Assuming they survived, of course.

The Agents recognized Lorelei. Whenever Parliament wanted to send Dimension Force on a special assignment, Lorelei weighed in on the legality of the mission.

"Agents, what are you doing here?" she demanded.

"I assume you mean, what *else* are we doing here, besides protecting you from Fleet and Shai-Manak spies?" Glamour Esque said.

"What are you talking about?"

Suddenly, a flurry of tiny beads exploded in a controlled burst out of several recessed barrels in Steelplate's back. The beads ran headlong into a small fleet of drones that Fleet had launched down the spiral staircase, and a host of tiny explosions at the far end of the lab took out the entire drone wave. Many beads survived and proceeded up the stairs, where further explosions ensued, this time accompanied by human screams.

Steelplate smiled. "*Now* they're sending people. All of you— get moving to an elevator. I'll cover your escape. Don't wait for me." He turned and trundled off toward the spiral staircase, launching close-quarters rockets that could fly themselves up the staircase and choose targets as a way of announcing his arrival and terrifying them in the process.

"Madam Solicitor, the individual you thought was Agent Anjette was actually a Shai-Manak spy," Glamour Esque explained. "We came here to ensure your safety and to apprehend the spy. So far, so good, it seems. Now tell me, why is that Security officer levitating?"

Lorelei ignored his question and began distracting him with a series of her own questions about her relative safety, about why Dimension Force hadn't signaled to her team they'd be converging here, anything to keep his eyes off Carissa. But he was sharp, and the question remained in his mind even if he wasn't able to wedge the topic into their discussion.

Meanwhile, Carissa's mind was completely afire with new powers and new potential. She saw Steelplate holding his own at the top of the spiral staircase, which he might be able to do indefinitely. Fleet was slowing down in their approach, mostly trying to prevent him from getting onto the third floor but not really trying to take him out of commission. Then she saw why: technicians were almost finished assembling a much larger battlefield teleport pad in the auditorium. They'd ripped out most of the seats to make room for it, and they were expecting to bring through a wave of mechanoid soldiers to deal with Steelplate.

Carissa's mind was flooded with options as she attempted to process the waves of information that clairvoyance provided her along with the realization that she could feel each one of her new talents buried deeply in her mind. She could visualize combining these talents to unlock new talents no one had ever imagined.

Since her original talent only operated within line of sight, she was unprepared for how incredible it felt to realize that she could extend her reach throughout the entire facility. Clairvoyance operated almost without her needing to activate or refresh it, and that gave her a form of remote targeting. She decided to flex a little bit and brought a tremendous wave of pure force slamming down onto the battlefield teleport pad in the auditorium, smashing and shattering it to pieces and grinding core components into fine-grained sand. Jirian's team had labeled this talent *force blast*, but the Brilliant had always called it *the invisible hammer*.

Then she tapped into a talent her brother had possessed, telekinesis, and turned her attention to the teleport pad in the green room that kept feeding Fleet teams onto the third floor. With amazing precision and little conscious effort, she explosively disassembled it into its component parts, twisting and crushing them into a hailstorm of tiny metal fragments. Several critical components exploded before succumbing to this treatment, and the green room was temporarily immersed in white flames until the fire suppression system kicked in and smothered the fire. Behind her on the second floor, the pocket dimension winked out of existence, taking every last trace of its contents along with it into nothingness.

This only took seconds of clock time, and neither Lorelei nor Glamour Esque even realized yet that she was operating at such scale.

She focused her mind on the cryogenically frozen individual on the floor a few feet away from Glamour Esque. Using a talent called *energetic healing,* she quickly diagnosed the individual as suffering from extreme cold, obviously, but also from poison. Neither the poison nor the cryo treatment were designed to inflict actual injury; they were short-term effects that might wear off on their own, but Carissa preferred the idea of healing this individual herself.

As an experiment, she reached out with her new telepathy talent, which was one of the more common talents possessed by the Brilliant. It manifested as the ability to communicate messages into someone else's mind from a considerable distance away, and it was a one-way communication only.

She projected the message, *I'm using psionic talents to neutralize the poison in your system and melt away the cryo spray. We need to take out the wizard and dash for an elevator. We're not taking Lorelei, but she already knows that. I was told you're Shai-Manak. Well, I'm wearing a Security uniform as a disguise, but I'm actually the last survivor of the Brilliant. If we help each other escape now, we can work out how to take down the Association later.*

As she finished, she realized Glamour Esque had taken a few steps closer to her and was snapping his fingers to try to get her attention.

"Aha, you did hear me. Excellent," he said as she turned her gaze toward him. "Did you learn how to levitate here in this lab? You must have. It's fun, isn't it? I used to levitate all the time, because why take the stairs, but then I got my first portal spell, and once you have a portal, that's definitely the new thing at that point. Anyway, my colleagues back at base have been trying to confirm your identity while you were in a trance there, and, well, you probably know this already, but you're completely invisible to surveillance, which is highly unusual and extremely illegal."

Carissa glanced at Lorelei, who shook her head.

Glamour Esque noticed the sideways look and said, "Oh, we discovered that on our own. It was Agent Steelplate—he couldn't find you in his targeting systems, which, I guess the first thing he does when he meets someone new is he immediately targets them, you know, just as a best practice. Anyway—"

"Let me stop you right there," Carissa said to the wizard. "I need you to do something for me. If Fleet somehow manages to get past Steelplate, the only thing left that they care about in this facility is Lorelei, because she knows every evil thing that happened in this lab, and when she testifies in Parliament, they'll believe her. So please, if Fleet somehow gets a shot at her, could you do everything in your power to keep her alive?"

He seemed startled by the urgency in her voice, but he said, "I will. But you're making it sound an awful lot like you don't intend to be here much longer."

"It's true. Fleet doesn't know about me, and they *can't* know about me."

"Interesting. I was thinking we could make a stand here together, and that would make it possible for me to put in a good word for you after we've taken you into custody."

Carissa laughed almost involuntarily. Glamour Esque smiled, although he was quite serious.

"Sorry, I'm not trying to be rude," she said. "I just need to be super clear—the Association is *never* getting its hands on me."

"Yeah, that's a common misconception," he said, "but we're not the same as the Association—"

"No, I get it, you're not the Association; you're just the Association's rent-a-cops. You're still cops. You're not taking us anywhere."

"'Us'?"

"I expect I'll be departing as well," said the Shai-Manak, upright and steady on zir feet.

That was enough of a cue for Carissa. She deployed her original talent, the one she knew best: mind control, on a single subject, within line of sight.

"*Agent Glamour Esque, you are forbidden from taking any action that would impede the Shai-Manak spy and me as we leave this floor and then leave Association territory. Do you understand these instructions?*"

"I understand," the wizard said without hesitation. "Go now, before Steelplate runs out of Fleet officers to obliterate."

Carissa glanced at Lorelei and said, "Next time I cook?"

"Don't wait another hundred years," Lorelei replied.

Carissa launched herself toward the elevator in midair, and Rindasy quickly followed suit, not changing form but simply using magic to keep up with her flight. It was a clear straight shot across an empty floor to the Left elevator, which was waiting for evacuees. They landed side by side, and the doors began to slide shut.

Carissa quickly stuck her hand in between the doors to prevent them from closing.

"Hold that open!" she shouted. Rindasy obeyed without understanding why. "Can't reboot it while it's moving," Carissa explained. Using telekinesis, Carissa ripped a small decorative metal plate off the back wall, revealing a hidden maintenance control panel with an ancient-looking keypad and a tiny display screen. She began typing, and the elevator went dark; when the lights came back up, she shouted, "Local override, please acknowledge!"

"Confirmed!" said the blandly cheerful voice of a cloudlet.

"Disable traffic control module, load floor index from cache, disallow passenger calls, de-register public nodes, but do *not* block incoming peer requests on the back channel—shit, what am I missing?"

"You must specify an emergency profile."

"Just use the guest profile! Why do you even have to ask me that?"

"Okay. Would you like me to save these preferences as a theme?"

"No, *purge* these prefs the minute I get off this elevator!"

"Confirmed! Where are we headed today?"

"Going up," replied Carissa, "as far as we can go."

As Rindasy released the elevator doors and they began to slide shut, a single loud shot rang out. Carissa felt the projectile pierce the light protection of her Security uniform like a punch to the chest from a scalding hammer. She gripped the nearest handrail but almost immediately began to slide to the floor.

In the distance, Carissa saw the kneeling form of the assassin Wynderia Gallas, who was still aiming her firearm as though she might fire again when the elevator doors finally slid shut.

SEASON THREE

EPISODE 3.01

The Shai-Manak knew the day they'd all feared and anticipated was marching closer and closer. They'd fully expected the Association would find their floor and send an invasion force someday. They established elaborate defensive spellcraft around the elevator banks, and alarms were triggered almost immediately when Association surveillance dust arrived on their floor. The dust was swiftly incinerated, but the mere fact of the Association physically scouting their floor was disconcerting. Andasir's crimes in exposing two elevator banks to outside surveillance were such that rumors swirled about possible execution as punishment.

Now the Association could jump warships straight onto their floor, just as they'd jumped a shuttle onto the Wild Mega floor. Shai-Manak flying patrols had knocked plenty of individual warships out of the sky in Building airspace, but the bulk of the Fleet was always patrolling the multiverse somewhere. Undoubtedly, they could bring enough ships back to overwhelm the Shai-Manak's defenses.

They knew Rindasy hadn't used the pearl because the eleven sorcerers who'd infused it with their magic were still alive. That likely meant the Association's psionic weapons program had not been neutralized, which made the threat of an invasion all the more dangerous. They were prepared to deploy another pearl. They'd identified a good candidate for implantation, and they'd gotten the cost down to merely ten sorcerers' lives instead of eleven. They could put the new pearl-carrier onto the roof of an elevator as it descended below the border, primed to detonate it on an Association floor. Then they'd threaten Parliament with the prospect of dozens more pearls to come. Perhaps that would slow or halt an invasion.

Then Allegory Paradox sent a message to the Radiant Council

via the cloudlets, who offered several tiers of encrypted messaging to select Building inhabitants for a reasonable subscription fee. In the message, Serene Nova offered a truce and suggested peace talks should be held immediately if the Shai-Manak agreed. She would release their ambassador, Gresij, to participate in these talks. Serene Nova herself would represent the Association.

Taking Gresij hostage was the mistake that had sparked hostilities to begin with. The symbolism was obvious.

.   .   .

The summit took place one day after the destruction of Jirian Echo's facility, in a pleasantly bland virtual environment on the Wild Massive cloud.

There'd been little opportunity for Kalavir to brief Gresij before the summit, so Kalavir would take the lead in negotiations, and Gresij would offer what insight ze could when appropriate.

Serene Nova brought Lorelei Rivers to the summit to observe on the Association side of the table. Allegory Paradox, whose stake in these matters was amorphous, acted as a neutral moderator.

"I understand you have an apoc weapon capable of erasing an entire floor from existence," Serene Nova said as an icebreaker.

Kalavir nodded slightly in acknowledgment, then said, "Congratulations on your new psionic weapons program. I understand once the flaws are smoothed over, you'll be capable of overpowering our magic."

Serene Nova said, "And congratulations to you as well. Impressive spycraft managing to capture a Dimension Force Agent and infiltrate the Association using her identity."

Kalavir replied, "Equally impressive, I would say, was that Agent's escape from underneath the heart of our capital."

Serene Nova said, "I presume since all our floors remain intact that your apoc weapon is still loose somewhere in our territory."

That seemed a tacit acknowledgment that Rindasy had not been caught or killed.

"Of course, we have only your word that the weapon behaves

as we've heard it does," Serene Nova continued. "I'm curious how you conducted testing on such a weapon."

"If you're truly curious," Kalavir replied, "we can arrange a demonstration of the weapon's capabilities."

"The goal here is to avoid violence," Allegory interjected.

"I'm not suggesting violence," Kalavir said. "Just property damage."

"Can we agree that neither party is likely to admit to a significant tactical disadvantage in this forum?" Allegory said. "Indeed, that the entire point of this forum is that your mutual destruction would best be avoided?"

Serene Nova said, "As you wish. Kalavir, we've reconsidered your application for membership to the Association. On a vote of seven to two in favor, Parliament approved the application two days ago, subject to the standard conditions, which I assume you're well familiar with—all the stipulations regarding shared security, resource allocation and economic integration, resettlement agreements, knowledge sharing and cultural exchange, extension of the teleport network, and so on—as well as a few additional conditions inserted specifically as a result of our conflict, which we can enumerate for you now. I assume you're at least interested in hearing these?"

Kalavir seemed too surprised to respond, but Gresij nodded and said, "Yes, we're at least interested."

Serene Nova turned the floor over to Lorelei, who read from a tablet.

"First, Shai-Manak must agree to withdraw from floor 49,500," she began. "Next, both parties must commit to mutual inspection regarding apoc and psionic weapons. Shai-Manak must agree to disclose apoc weapon design to the Association and provide guarantees that no weapons of this class are deployed, subject to regular audit. The Association agrees to disclose psionic research and confirm that no weapons of this class are in use and that the psionic research program is effectively terminated, subject to regular audit."

Lorelei glanced up from her tablet, looking to gauge response so far, but neither Kalavir nor Gresij gave up a reaction.

"Your original application indicated an expectation of consideration for a seat in Parliament," she continued. "This expectation must be withdrawn. However, the Association is prepared to expand its military affairs council to include Shai-Manak representation alongside Fleet, Security, and the Prime Minister."

"You're proposing to enlist the Shai-Manak in your military?" Kalavir said.

"We're soliciting your advice on matters of security," Serene Nova said. "Service in our military branches is voluntary."

"Last, a reminder that the nonintervention amendments do apply to cultures beyond the fifty thousand original Association floors," Lorelei said. "This prohibits upward exploration of the Building for a period of a thousand years, with four hundred and twelve of these years remaining, but in your case, downward exploration between your floor and floor 50,000 is also prohibited. You'll be expected to cease any such exploration upon signing the treaty. You'll receive specifications for handling 'first contact' situations in case you're unilaterally approached by residents of an uncataloged floor."

"I imagine you'll need time to consider these stipulations," Serene Nova said. "That is, if you're even still interested in joining the Association at all, which I understand may no longer be appealing to you. We could limit this to a mere cease-fire if you wish, a truce that enables you to go about your business on your floor with no further interaction with the Association."

"Yes, we'll have some soul-searching to do, I imagine," said Kalavir. "One sticking point, though. The sorcerer who impersonated Anjette—the one who carries the apoc weapon—is off the grid and out of contact, with instructions never to return to our floor. We have no way of remotely disabling the weapon while it's in zir possession."

"I wondered about that," said Serene Nova. "As it turns out, your sorcerer was last seen in the company of a surviving Brilliant. The Brilliant was injured and if your sorcerer is protecting her, that's a problem. More to the point, if you sign the treaty, and your sorcerer attacks us with the help of a surviving Brilliant, that will be a big problem."

"What was your sorcerer's target?" Lorelei asked. "Is it still at risk?"

"Ze was instructed to eliminate your psionic research program," Kalavir said.

Lorelei glanced at Serene Nova, unwilling to say more without approval.

Serene Nova said, "That program has already been terminated."

"Without a legitimate target and with zir cover blown, Rindasy should not pose a threat to the Association," Kalavir said.

"The fact that Rindasy might be aiding a Brilliant makes zir an existential threat to us," Serene Nova replied. "You should know Dimension Force has been dispatched to find both of them."

"They're going to search the entire Building, are they?" Gresij asked.

"Gresij, this Brilliant acquired twelve new powers before escaping us, in addition to whatever powers she possessed to begin with," Serene Nova replied. "We know one of those powers was rapid healing. If she's still alive, she undoubtedly holds a grudge—the same grudge Rindasy might be holding. So yes, we're going to search the entire Building for both of them. Perhaps as a show of good faith, you might contribute resources to the search. Do you have any magical method to locate one of your own who has gone to ground?"

"If Rindasy uses strong enough magic, it would be detectable to us," Kalavir replied. "We can spare enforcers to join your search party."

"Can these enforcers destroy the apoc weapon?"

"The weapon is bound to Rindasy now. Ze alone possesses the passchant that detonates it. The only way to be sure ze will never use it is to end zir life. Our enforcers are capable of that task."

"The weapon becomes inert if Rindasy is killed?" Serene Nova asked.

"We would not have this weapon fall into enemy hands if ze were killed in the field," Kalavir replied. "It dissipates upon zir death for that reason."

"Presumably the Brilliant fugitive is headed for a similar fate as Rindasy?" Gresij asked.

Serene Nova nodded and said, "Dimension Force has been sent to destroy her."

. . .

The day prior to the summit with the Shai-Manak, in the afternoon after Jirian Echo's lab was destroyed, Lorelei arrived at the Prime Minister's office and requested time on her calendar. She'd received and ignored orders from Security to report to them for questioning; Serene Nova would be displeased if Security got a debriefing before she did. She planned to resign after she gave Serene Nova her full story, going all the way back to Minneapolis.

Sure, she had shut down an illegal weapons program, exposing massive corruption and multiple treaty violations on the part of Jirian Echo and, by extension, his patron, Admiral Slab.

But she herself had violated a Parliamentary order by not turning Carissa over to Security—or killing her outright—and allowing her to impersonate Security was an additional offense. By extension, she was responsible for Carissa banishing Jirian from this plane of existence, robbing Parliament of the right to decide what to do with Jirian's unique skill set.

Her resignation would at least deflect criticism away from Serene Nova regarding how the incident was handled. She had a good working relationship with Serene Nova, but she never forgot that Serene Nova was essentially a weird alien-demigod who might simply summon a flaming mystical axe out of thin air and cut her head off instead of listening to her tedious confession of guilt.

Half an hour after her arrival, she was ushered into Serene Nova's spacious corner office. The room was decked out with luxurious and comfortable white furniture and featured no executive desk to draw your attention. A small table was the only concession to the idea that business even needed to occur in this room. The room seemed to shimmer, as though a nearly invisible layer of silver was draped over everything. The white and silver were almost overshadowed by the orange sky outside the windows, but Serene Nova kept them sufficiently tinted to keep the colors in balance.

Serene Nova sat on a lounger near one of the windows and invited Lorelei to sit in the chair next to hers.

"If you're here to resign, just save it," Serene Nova said before Lorelei could say a word.

"Actually," Lorelei began.

"You don't get to mount that kind of operation—successfully, I might add—and then just walk off the job."

"But," Lorelei said.

"Look—the Admiral is halfway across the multiverse right now, not responding to my attempts to reach him. He knows he's exposed, and he knows he has to answer for it . . . either by testifying to Parliament, or by going rogue and taking some chunk of Fleet with him, no doubt."

Lorelei was horrified to imagine Fleet turning against the Association, all because she'd tried to do the right thing on behalf of Carissa's people.

"So I'm not sending any signals that I'm weak by throwing you to the wolves," Serene Nova continued, "just because you bent the rules to pull off your operation. You're staying put. And you should, by the way. This government operates without a conscience most of the time. It's good that you remind us of that on a semiregular basis."

"Thank you," Lorelei managed to say.

"You're welcome. But one major question remains that I can't deduce from Security's report. Who was that woman you were with?"

Lorelei was prepared for this question and saw no reason to avoid it.

"She was a survivor of the fall of the Brilliant," Lorelei said. "She escaped the floor before the attack." After a pause, she added, "I helped her escape."

Serene Nova allowed an eyebrow to raise in surprise.

"In my defense, I was quite young, and it was a stressful assignment—"

"I don't care about that. What I'm concerned about is what this woman's been doing with herself for the last hundred-odd years. And how did she know to show up on your doorstep on the eve before your raid? Is she precognitive? I thought we never found precognitive abilities among the Brilliant, but if she's precognitive, she'll always be a step ahead of us."

"You want to catch her," Lorelei realized—out loud, unfortunately.

"Of course I want to catch her!" Serene Nova exclaimed. "That woman marched into the Association with falsified credentials and made her way directly into a top-secret weapons facility, where she wreaked havoc on one of our test labs and destroyed all traces of Jirian's research. Now I'm to understand she's got every psionic ability at her disposal that Jirian had extracted, plus her own. Do you honestly think I can let that cannon roam loose in the Building?"

"The new talents will likely wear off."

"That's what happens when normal humans take a catalyst," Serene Nova replied. "We have no evidence they'll wear off in a Brilliant once she understands how they operate."

Lorelei tried a new approach. She said, "Carissa won't use them against us unless we move against her first. All she wants is to find somewhere safe and quiet to live out her life. She's a good person who's lost everything. The least we could do is leave her be."

"Wake up, Lorelei. She moved against us when she only had *one* psionic power, so don't tell me she's going to retire to a resort floor and pretend she doesn't hate us. Now more than ever she must hate us beyond words."

"We deserve it," Lorelei said flatly.

"No, Jirian deserved it, and she took care of him. Admiral Slab deserves it, and I will deal with him. But Carissa won't be satisfied that easily. We can't just wait patiently for her next terrorist attack. Don't try to protect her, Lorelei. Let her protect herself. Tell me how she found you."

"What will you do with her when you catch her?" Lorelei asked. "Put her in stasis like her brother?"

"No, we're not risking personnel trying to get her into a stasis pod." That was all the answer Lorelei was going to get.

Lorelei knew she was out of luck here. Nothing good would come from withholding information now, not for her, not for her family.

And still she resisted revealing what little she knew.

Serene Nova said, "I'm impressed by your loyalty. A little hurt that you're more loyal to her than me, but you haven't known me as long, I suppose."

Serene Nova's eyes began to glow hot, yellow, and merciless, piercing Lorelei's soul like an insect's stinger diving deep under her skin.

"You can tell me now and preserve our good working relationship," Serene Nova said, her voice suddenly vibrating with barely contained anger, "or I can dig through your memories for the truth, and we'll both just have to hope your mind survives intact."

"When she showed up outside my house," Lorelei blurted out, unable to disguise the terror in her voice, "she already knew that the Association had taken Brilliant survivors as prisoners. She even knew that her brother was one of them. And she knew that I could help her find them. When I asked her how she knew all this, she said, 'A baby magic-user told me.' And she said, 'She's been right about other things.'"

The glow in Serene Nova's eyes dissipated, and the terror Lorelei felt was quickly replaced by shame. Her only slight consolation was believing that Carissa would never hold this one moment of treachery against her if it somehow led to Carissa's capture.

"Thank you, Lorelei. I understand how difficult that was, I truly do. I'm a monster, but I'm not without compassion. Unfortunately, history is marching on all around us, and we must keep the pace."

· · ·

The next day, after Kalavir and Gresij disconnected from the virtual meeting hall when the summit was over, Serene Nova turned to Allegory Paradox and said, "I wonder if you have a moment to chat?"

"Of course I do," Allegory replied.

"I don't suppose you have any resources on your creative brain trust who might match the description 'baby magic-user,' do you?" Serene Nova asked.

Allegory said, "What a strange question. I have several apprentices and interns who'd meet that description. Wild Massive employs quite a few magic-users of varying skills."

"Do you recognize this woman?" Serene Nova said, abruptly changing the subject.

A 3D image of Carissa appeared in the air above the conference table. She looked noticeably younger in the photo, which had been retrieved from diplomatic footage captured during the Brilliant's application process back in Minneapolis. The "do not surveil" flag on her fake ID blocked their systems from recording her at all during her recent visit to the Association.

"I saw that woman yesterday in the Super park," Allegory said. "In the company of a Shai-Manak deserter and one of my narrative designers."

"Tell me about your narrative designer."

Allegory said carefully, "She's a bit of a visionary like me, actually. But she's just getting started. Her skill is quite limited."

Serene Nova smiled at Lorelei and said, "I think we have our baby magic-user."

Lorelei's heart cratered into the floor. But her face remained impassive.

"What's this narrative designer's name?" asked Serene Nova.

"Her name is Tabitha Will," said Allegory. "And I wouldn't think of her as a baby magic-user. I'd think of her as a baby Muse, if I were you."

"I'll keep that warning in mind," Serene Nova replied. "When can I meet Tabitha Will?"

Allegory shrugged and said, "You'll have to ask our Sentient Resources department if they'll make her available. If you think she's involved in activity you consider criminal, a reminder that Wild Massive doesn't extradite its employees."

"Allegory, it's likely Tabitha Will used her 'limited skill' to steer a surviving Brilliant into committing a terrorist act against the Association. You can either make Tabitha available to me for questioning yourself and we can do this quietly, or I'll skip your Sentient Resources department and ask your board of directors to make her available."

"Fine, you don't have to threaten me with a rebuke from the board for interrupting their lives of leisure with this business. I'll arrange for you to talk to her. But I want your word that you'll keep her name out of your reports and off the record."

Serene Nova nodded and said, "She's not the target, Allegory. She'll be fine."

Yes, they're talking about me. No, I'm not oblivious.

That day, in the hours before the summit, I arrived early for work, summoned by Allegory for an overdue private conversation before the rest of the creative brain trust arrived.

"Am I interrupting?" I asked as I materialized in the virtual staff room.

"Not at all," Allegory replied from in front of the whiteboards, where she was sliding index cards around between a couple of rows. "Just doing a little experimentation here."

The convention on our team was to wear avatars in staff meetings that closely resembled our actual physical appearance. Save your creative juice for the narrative, et cetera. My one usual cheat was to float above the floor so that I didn't have to stare up at Allegory like she was a giant alien looming over me. The side effect of making easier eye contact was a little more confidence when interacting with her one on one, which I knew I'd probably need during this conversation.

I floated over to her from my assigned seat at the big conference room table—my "spawn point" when arriving for work—to see if I could glean anything interesting by reading the whiteboard over her shoulder. But she was working so far ahead of me in the story line that I didn't even recognize half the characters.

"I imagine we both have questions for each other about that business with the Shai-Manak defector the other day," she said, keeping her eyes on the columns of index cards in front of her. "Would you like to go first?"

I said, "Why'd you turn Andasir over to those enforcers? I mean, why were you even there?"

Allegory nodded and said, "I cultivated a relationship with the Shai-Manak prior to beginning preproduction on their arc.

They traced the defector to the Super park on their own, but asked me for a favor when they realized an extraction would be complicated."

"Yeah, but—the defector was trying to stop a Shai-Manak spy from hitting the Association with an apocalypse-class weapon," I said.

"The Association can protect its own borders, I'm sure. My turn. Why were *you* escorting Andasir through backstage in the first place?"

"I *thought* I was helping zir escape, but apparently, I was just turning zir over to you so that you could turn zir over to the enforcers, which seems a little convoluted, but what do I know?"

"Tabitha—*why* were you helping zir escape?"

"It was just . . . a hunch that it was the right thing to do. I knew Andasir and Carissa would be in the Super park. They emerged as mysterious new characters in my book, and I just . . . assumed I needed to help them. I guess I'm not sure why I assumed that. I don't work from an outline, you know."

You'd think, of course, that a member of the *Storm and Desire* creative brain trust, with its multidecade planning approach and its whiteboards that could drill down to individual minutes of story from any character's POV, would use the same planning skills on her own personal work, but no—I was just making shit up and getting tiny little thrills out of seeing what happened.

This was the first time I'd gotten a hit about the future and gotten up out of my chair to get involved in the action, though. I was tacitly admitting that much to Allegory, who'd been following my progress with the book in our occasional one-on-ones. I wouldn't let her read the book, of course, because gah no way, but also because, forget it no fucking way.

"Fair enough," she said. "As far as Wild Massive is concerned, however, you were assisting me. You found Andasir in the park while I was meeting the enforcers at the gate, you led zir through backstage to protect our guests, and you delivered zir to me at my request. Can you live with that?"

I said, "Sure," but I wasn't sure. I mean, yes, I was glad to have executive protection in theory, but why was she lying to protect me in the first place? I hadn't done anything wrong. Anyone with a manager badge could escort people backstage. Someone with a fancier badge could tell us to turn around and get lost, obviously, but no one had paid any attention to us.

"As for your other friend," Allegory said, "we're fortunate that the enforcers weren't interested to know how Andasir bought a ticket under a false name to get into the park. That made it simple to exclude her from my summary of events, and the matter is closed as far as Wild Massive is concerned."

"Oh," I said. "I don't think it's closed at all, though. Like, I know you're very focused on the next arc now, but some of us are still working on the current arc. And I don't think it's as locked as everyone thinks it is."

"Tabitha," Allegory said patiently, "that arc has been locked for a very long time."

"Plot twist—the woman I was with yesterday at the elevator was a Brilliant. A survivor. I pointed her at the Association, and off she went because there might be other survivors. Her brother might be alive. You see where I'm going with this. It's not locked; it's not even over yet."

"I see. And what else do you know about her?"

"I got a few major hits last night. I know the Association is about to start actively hunting for her. They're planning to kill her on the spot when they find her. I know she's not alone— she'll be traveling with the Shai-Manak spy who has the apoc weapon. And apparently, I'm supposed to volunteer to help the Association and the Shai-Manak track them down."

Her lack of surprise was unnerving, as usual.

"Sounds like this is shaping up to be a clever bridge between the Brilliant arc and the Shai-Manak arc," she said.

Apparently, Allegory wasn't picking up my general mood about this, so I said, "Obviously, I'm not going to help the Association find them."

"I thought you said that this was a 'hit.' Am I misunderstanding how you use that term?"

"It *is* a hit, but I think for once, I saw something that I need to *avoid*."

"Nonsense," she said, turning back to the whiteboard. She summoned up a fresh deck of index cards and slowly began adding ideas and names to them as she spoke. "Your 'hit' is limited in scope. It's not telling you *why* you should help the Association."

"I can't help them kill Carissa!" I protested.

"Tabitha, be precise. You said you'd help them *track* her. Is it *track* or *kill* her?"

I hesitated, then said, "Track her, but—"

"Imagine you track her to a place where they *can't* kill her," she said. "Or imagine you track her but somehow warn her at the same time, so she's ready for them. Be creative with the limited information you've got to work with. And give Carissa a little credit—she undoubtedly knows they're coming for her, and I suspect she knows her way around parts of the Building the Association has never seen."

She swiped the whiteboard, shoving aside the episodes she'd been studying and bringing up the current arc in a holistic view.

"We still have time to introduce Carissa and the spy into the current arc," she said. "In fact, we could squeeze them into the main cast. And why would we do that?"

I had no idea.

"This hunt you're describing for Carissa and the spy . . . it would make sense for the Association and the Shai-Manak to coordinate their search efforts. I suspect that will be one of the outcomes of today's peace conference."

"Peace conference?" I said, flummoxed by the thought.

"Today at noon, hosted by Wild Massive," she confirmed. "I'm the moderator. Something happened yesterday that moved Parliament to offer a truce. Seems likely Carissa and the spy were involved, don't you agree? Anyway, the peace conference is why I'm here early this morning, trying to work out alternatives for the final arc. Because in real life, it might be satisfying for two enemies to fight for fifty years and then get bored and call a truce. In *Storm and Desire*, we need a much more compelling reason for the Association and the Shai-Manak to join forces. Here's what I came up with."

Now she swiped to get the final arc back into view. She peeled an index card off the board and handed it to me. It read: "A common enemy."

It made a sickening kind of sense.

I said, "And you *want* that to be Carissa? I mean, I get it, everyone loves a good fugitives-on-the-run story, but doesn't Carissa deserve better than being actively chased by the Association for the rest of her life?"

And I swear, Allegory Paradox practically jumped up and down as she said, "No, no, no. Look, chasing Carissa and the spy is just the *hook* into *finding* the common enemy. It isn't them at all. There's something else they should *all* be afraid of—the fugitives, the Association, the Shai-Manak, Dimension Force— all of them. Because look, where do you think the fugitives will go to hide from their pursuers?"

"I don't know," I said. "Up, I guess."

"*Yes.* As far up as you can go."

She peeled off another index card and handed it to me. It was a chilling gesture. It said, "*The chasm.*"

"Okay, I'll bite," I said. "How does a giant, mysterious hole in the Building become everyone's enemy?"

"I believe something lives in that abyss, Tabitha. Something intelligent that's been watching for a long time."

"Watching *Storm and Desire*?"

"Well, that, too, if it has taste, but more specifically, I meant watching the rise of civilization inside this Building. And I don't think it's impressed."

"How do you know that?"

She took the index cards back from me and carefully restored them to their locations.

"Your book shows you a day into the future," she said, "but as you gain more experience, you'll see farther and for longer stretches. Your predictions will become more frequent and more accurate. Eventually, you'll realize that you're not simply predicting the future with your book. You're *shaping* it—pieces of it, anyway."

She paused and studied me for a moment. This was one of those moments where you knew there'd be a test later, so comprehension was important. Some days with her it was riddles and, well, allegory—other days, she would straight up seem to recite from the instruction manual directly.

"There must be easier ways to shape the future," I said, only half-jokingly.

She sighed deeply. "With proper tools, yes, but mine are gone. Fortunately, we're not attempting anything so ambitious as shaping the sum totality of all future events. We're merely priming specific near-term event sequences to adjust their outcomes."

"Yeah, but *how* are we doing that? Why does reality care about what happens in my book?"

"It cares what happens in *your* book because you acquired a valid set of credentials," she said, "when you used your capture glass. As far as reality is concerned, you became a Muse that day."

Oh. That was a little mind-blowing to hear. She'd barely danced around this topic with me before and now she was dropping it like a bomb into my self-image. I'd always guessed that I'd been dosed with a blast of Muse energy from within the capture glass, like being hit with radiation, and then I experienced a mutation that gave me limited wild divination as a trait; the jury was out as to whether that was a favorable mutation or not. Didn't sound like she was implying that at all.

"How do you just . . . *become* a Muse?" I half whispered. Seriously—instead of a mutation, had I experienced a transformation? And was it a physical transformation or a metaphysical one or what?

"Tabitha, 'Muse' is a role, not a species," she said, her veneer of patience strained by having to explain basic concepts in the middle of a complex story-planning session. "It's a role that comes with privileges. Your environment—existence, I mean—pays attention to your thoughts now, listening for instructions, which can eventually work, but only in a meandering and vague fashion. Normally, we use a set of profoundly intricate tools for translating thoughts into precise instructions that reality will obey in a specified time frame."

"Like how the rides department does changeovers?" I asked. In the old days, when it was time to retire an aging ride and replace it with something new, robots would come in and decommission it, recycling parts and all that. Nowadays, the rides were made of industrial nanoswarms, meaning you could email a new design to the ride and it could reconfigure itself in place, right down to the molecule.

"It's similar, yes," she said brightly. "The difference is . . . rides are made of programmable matter. Reality is more like . . . *suggestible* matter. And *crafting* suggestions is an art form—one that I'm exceedingly good at, although to be fair, it's still slow going without my tools."

Her tools had vanished back to the mother ship when the other Muses all departed for parts unknown. The most she'd revealed about that topic is that the tools likely weren't stolen from her out of malice. They'd probably been recalled by some project manager trying to wrap things up, who didn't realize that Allegory still had legit work to do inside the Building. We'd never actually drilled down into how she used the tools, though. I'd asked a couple of times before, but she'd said it wouldn't make sense to me, not yet.

So instead of asking her outright one more time, I tried a roundabout approach. "Why can't you manufacture replacement tools? Or I mean, why can't you have the Association do it for you?"

"What do you think," she said, making it clear that her patience with me was now approaching epic levels, "I've been doing for the last two hundred years?"

"Uh, you mean besides *Storm and Desire*?" I asked.

"No, I don't mean 'besides' *Storm and Desire* at all. *Storm and Desire*, Tabitha, *is* a replacement tool set."

"Huh?"

"What do you mean, 'huh'? Did you think the only tools at our disposal were *physical* tools, like forklifts or hammers or something?"

"I thought industrial printers or robots maybe—"

She couldn't completely stifle a laugh at my expense, and my cheeks burned—but it was worth the embarrassment to get some real answers here.

"I use *Storm and Desire* to predict and ultimately shape a targeted slice of the future." She waved dramatically at the many whiteboards behind her and said, "Just like what you do with your book, but I've developed a window of six or seven months to work with instead of twenty-four hours. Even with that much lead time, I'm constantly wrong about things or surprised when things happen. I've only got line of sight along a very slender thread, which you might call the 'plot' of *Storm and Desire,* and yet there are countless other variables in play that my mind can't even conceptualize, let alone try to track on a whiteboard.

"Still, I do have an amazing whiteboard, with an entire creative brain trust focused on maximizing its potential, and as the series unfolds, those index cards on the whiteboard are sending signals, are making *suggestions* for how reality might want to configure itself ahead of us if it were so inclined. That's all I can do, by the way—just make suggestions, I don't *control* anything. The entire series acts like a sort of compiler, translating my suggestions into ethereal mathematics that describe potential *expressions* of those suggestions as real events in time and space—but only if they're *convincing* enough. And after decades of trial and error, I'm finally seeing signs that my suggestions are starting to be implemented. Not just that—I'm seeing *improvements* to my suggestions, signs that true collaboration might be unfolding."

"Hold up," I finally interrupted, my mind buzzing with questions. "You're telling me that everything inside and outside this Building is the result of Muses making *suggestions* to reality?"

"Are you not paying attention?" she snapped, her voice rising in volume and pitch. "This is what a single Muse, compressed into a limited-resolution bio-avatar, cut off from her peers and subordinates, lacking any of the kit she'd depended on, can hack together as a prototype communication interface to the underlying mysteries, using nothing more than the materials at hand and her sheer ingenuity. It's like you're trapped on a deserted island, and you call for help by telepathically convincing grains of sand on the beach to assemble themselves one by one into a functioning interdimensional transmitter. Trust me, a full complement of experienced Muses with the right gear makes *demands* of reality, not suggestions."

I'd never seen her this agitated before. Her corporate gray skin shifted toward a molten gold sheen as she worked to contain her ire. I knew she wasn't truly mad at me, but the real targets of her enmity weren't here to shout at.

"What 'gear,' though?" I protested. "What did they take from you if you don't need physical tools?"

"They took *all* the epic tales, Tabitha. All the grand sagas we used to generate truth and forge this place . . . they're all gone, consigned to civilization's distant memory. The only remaining traces of those sagas are now called *myths*. And the mythological era of history is *over*."

She fell silent, and we were both quiet for a few moments. She'd just revealed as much to me in one sitting as I'd managed to glean over the course of our entire working relationship, and although I had a thousand questions, I didn't want to interrupt her flow.

Finally, she said, "Let's talk about you for a moment. Will you help the Association find Carissa?"

That was a good question. I barely knew Carissa, sure, but the Association owed her more than it could ever pay, even if it somehow wanted to. So why should I pave the way for her death at their hands? I felt betrayed by my own book—by myself, really—for throwing that idea out in the first place.

But I'd also been wrong about my "successes" many times in the past. I was already drifting away from caring whether this one was a "hit" or not.

I said, "She deserves to be left alone. If anything, I want to help her *escape* from the Association."

"And *I* want to flush out whatever's lurking in the chasm. I didn't have a great plan for how to get there, but now it's becoming clear. Carissa's on the whiteboard now. She's managed to catch the attention of everyone else in play. They're going to hunt her down whether you help them or not, Tabitha, but if you *do* help them, you'll see the whole operation, and that will help you nudge her to safety, do you see?"

"Into the chasm? How is that safe?"

"I'm not sure. I expected to have a lot more time to work that out."

"Then why do you need to steer everyone there so badly? In all the previous arcs, there's been *zero* foreshadowing that the chasm would be important, I'm not sure it's even mentioned, and you want the whole story to culminate there?"

"No, Tabitha, not there."

She fell silent, waiting to see if I'd deduce what her real target was. And all at once, it was transparent to me.

She wanted to reach the top floor.

And she wanted the Association and the Shai-Manak and Dimension Force—and now Carissa—to clear out the chasm for her so that she could cross it.

Maybe she believed that the top floor was the only place she'd get answers about why the other Muses left her on the wrong side when they tore it open in the first place.

And then I imagined her working alone at the whiteboard, moving index cards around, trying to solve the problem of how to aim the story in that direction. Out of nowhere, I suddenly got the inspiration to write about Carissa and Andasir, to wedge them into a book that wasn't about them at all. It was too convenient.

"Allegory," I said quietly, "am *I* on the whiteboard?"

She almost looked hurt by the question. She said, "You mean, am I the one who really arranged to have you and Carissa meet?"

I nodded.

"I did not. A Muse's destiny is their own to shape. We don't interfere with each other's trajectories, and I haven't interfered with yours—except in the obvious manner of being your boss who tells you what to do. But when the Shai-Manak attacked Wild Mega . . . we're reaching the point where the story being told by *Storm and Desire* will become indistinguishable from the story of the people *telling* the story of *Storm and Desire*. Wild Massive itself is on the whiteboard now. You and I can get our hands on the narrative from *inside* of it. But for that to play out the right way . . ."

"You need me to help them find Carissa and the spy," I finished her sentence for her.

"It would be advantageous if you were the one directing their pursuit," she agreed.

I said nothing for a long while. I didn't want to disappoint Allegory. I didn't know why I cared so much about Carissa's fate in the first place. But I also didn't know why Allegory had waited for years to bring me into her confidence the way she had today. Today was different because she wanted something from me. What did I want most from her?

"Whose credentials do I have?" I finally worked up the courage to ask. "Whose memory is stored in my capture glass? Do you know—can you tell without experiencing the memory yourself?"

She leaned back slowly in her chair, keeping her eye on me, perhaps revising her opinion of me on the fly.

"I wondered if you'd ever get around to asking me that, Tabitha. Your gift—your infusion of Muse energy—is recognizably descendent from a specific Muse. I knew this Muse quite well, in fact." She withdrew a pendant on a thin rope necklace from underneath her shirt. I recognized it instantly.

It was a capture glass.

"After the summit, come to my office at corporate. You can wear this capture glass for a time and visit with your Muse—at least my favorite memory of her." Then she added, "Assuming the summit goes smoothly, of course; otherwise, I might be too upset to host you."

How convenient. I mean, maybe she'd been carrying that capture glass around ever since she hired me so that she'd have it handy when I finally wised up and asked her about my origin story. But it was much more likely that she'd been planning for this specific moment, maybe not on the whiteboard but certainly through some foresight of her own. The implication was clear—I could help her *ensure* the summit went smoothly by offering my services to the Association. This wasn't coincidence—this was bribery.

You didn't get to be Chief Content Officer of Wild Massive, Muse or not, without having an excellent long game.

I said, "Okay, I'm in." Then I added, "What's my Muse's name?" I'd wanted to know that since I was fourteen years old and first experienced my grandmother's capture glass.

"Her name is Epiphany Foreshadow," Allegory said. "I think you're going to quite like her."

.   .   .

I watched the peace summit on a tablet. Certainly, that was a breach of some security protocol, but fuck it, they were on our servers. Maybe I should've been surprised that the Association already had a lead on finding me, but surprises were stacking up so quickly today that I barely felt the impact.

Allegory said, "Tabitha, could you please join us?"

That was my cue to dive into the virtual conference room and join the fun.

I'd never been in the presence of Serene Nova before—and even her virtual presence managed to radiate a hint of pseudo-divine menace. Lorelei sat next to her, a stone-cold expression on her face. Yeah, she probably wasn't destined to like me very much.

"Hello, Tabitha," said Serene Nova. "You know, I'm surprised we haven't met before today. I thought I knew all the remaining Muses in the Building."

"I'm new to the organization," I said. "Hoping for a long career, of course."

She nodded her approval, as though it mattered to me, and said, "I understand you've already acquired some skill."

"Yes," I said. "I might be able to help you find Carissa and the Shai-Manak spy."

Yeah, Lorelei definitely wanted to kill me, I could tell. It wasn't really her fault; Carissa shouldn't have mentioned a "baby magic-user" in the first place. Of course, none of us have any idea what we're doing half the time, so these things do happen.

"Using precognition?" she asked.

"I would call it *divination*," I replied. "It's much less precise or 'on demand' than how a psionic talent works. My medium for divination is writing, it's time-consuming to perform it, and my range is limited to roughly a day into the future. It's error-prone, though, so I do get false hits occasionally." Not recently, I decided not to admit. "I don't get complete context usually. I learn little details, or I get flashes of insight, or I see particular moments of action, and when any of these ring particularly true, then it's up to me to deduce what they mean."

Serene Nova was silent for a long moment as she pondered what I'd said.

"And what possessed you to send Carissa into the Association in the first place?" she asked, her voice hardening against me. I didn't care. She wasn't the boss of me.

"It seemed like the right thing to do," I said. I could tell she didn't seem super convinced, but some things are pretty clear to me in hindsight. I said, "The Shai-Manak's apoc weapon has a 'margin of error' of up to a thousand floors, give or take, and their spy was sent to destroy the psionic weapons program. We thought if Carissa could get there first, maybe the spy wouldn't need to use the apoc weapon." Then I added, "Is that what actually happened? I'm always looking for feedback."

The way she kept staring at me, I got the feeling she was trying to suss out my motives, determining if she could trust me, wrestling with the fact that there was one more weird variation on the rules (me) that she had to keep track of now, and so on.

Finally, she said, "Kalavir didn't tell me about the margin of error. I'm surprised ze didn't brag about it. All the more reason to catch Rindasy and Carissa and be done with this business."

I said, "Once a day until we find them, I can reach out with whatever information I pick up. I can't predict how long this process will take. But judging by recent accuracy, it's days, not weeks."

"And how does Wild Massive benefit for volunteering its services in such a fashion, I wonder?" she said, turning to Allegory Paradox.

"You said you wanted us to change the ending of the Brilliant arc," Allegory replied innocently.

"Not what I had in mind," Serene Nova said, almost growling.

"We do like to think outside the box," said Allegory.

EPISODE 3.03

The moment the elevator doors closed after Wynderia Gallas shot Carissa, as Carissa slid down the back wall of the elevator, in shock as blood began to pour out of the wound in her chest, the elevator leapt into motion.

"Oh, pardon me," the cloudlet said, "but I'm transferring this elevator to a different cloudlet now. Enjoy the rest of your trip!"

And then a different cloudlet said in a calm, measured voice, "Check her pockets. She usually keeps a pouch of first aid pills with her." This was Carissa's cloudlet friend, assuming control of the situation.

Sure enough, tucked into one of the pockets of the Security uniform, Carissa had stashed her tablet, which had automatically signaled its location to the cloudlet, and a pouch that was half full of first aid pills.

"How many?" Rindasy asked.

"Start with five," said the cloudlet.

Carefully, Rindasy pressed each of five pills into Carissa's mouth. Within minutes, miraculous acts of healing were underway. Rindasy couldn't tell if this was all due to the pills, or if Carissa was starting to access her psionic healing talent, too, now that she was beginning to stabilize after taking so much sudden damage and shock.

"Where should we take her?" Rindasy asked.

"Don't take me anywhere," Carissa said softly. "Let's just ride for a while."

Carissa drifted into a deep sleep, prompted by a narcotic effect of the pills.

Rindasy allowed zirself to relax and sit in a corner, keeping a helpless watch over Carissa until she seemed restored to full health. The Shai-Manak had no healing magic similar to first aid pills or psionic healing, perhaps because they rarely fell ill or suffered injury, so the specialization had never fully developed.

Finally, Carissa's eyes opened.

"Am I remembering correctly that I got shot and you saved my life?" she asked.

Rindasy nodded.

"Thank you," Carissa said. "You're the Shai-Manak spy with the apoc weapon, right?"

"How did you know that?"

"I met Andasir. Landed on my elevator, looking for you."

"Unbelievable," Rindasy said.

"Ze got busted by your people, though, when we were hanging out in a theme park."

"Enforcers, no doubt. They're ruthless in pursuit of prey."

"Really?" Carissa said. "Do they get a lot of opportunities to jump down an elevator shaft after prey?"

Rindasy allowed zirself a small laugh and said, "No, but their training is extensive nevertheless."

"Fair enough. Anyway, I'm Carissa."

"And you're a Brilliant, according to your telepathic message to me."

Carissa looked almost surprised, as though she'd forgotten that fact.

"Yes, I am," she said. "Currently jacked up on twelve new psionic talents, most of which may wear off in an hour." She struggled to sit up a little straighter and said, "But even if I lose my last talent, I'll always be Brilliant at heart." Rindasy must have looked surprised or suspicious or something, because Carissa felt the need to clarify, "I was there because I thought they might have Brilliant prisoners on-site."

"Did they?" ze asked.

"No." She paused and then said, "Not anymore."

"I discovered the Association might have designed a psionic weapons program," Rindasy said, "which I was sent to destroy. Instead, I was nearly taken captive. Thank you for rescuing me."

"My pleasure," Carissa said. "You'll be happy to know, they did have a psionic weapons program, which I destroyed in a fireball. You can take all the credit for it when you get back home."

Rindasy shook zir head and said, "I can't go back, not now."

"Suppose that makes sense," Carissa said. "We're both covered in surveillance dust right now. Cloudlet, how do we purge surveillance dust?"

"You don't 'purge' surveillance dust," the cloudlet replied. "You negotiate terms for its amicable departure. Fortunately, it's lazy about filing reports on time."

"I don't understand," Rindasy said.

"Surveillance dust is just a nosy breed of nanoswarm," Carissa said. "Sentient but very focused on a task. Elevators are supposedly black boxes where you can't get signal in or out, but once the doors open, it could burst all its stored data back to home base."

"I've heard rumors that surveillance dust cheats, actually," said the cloudlet. "No one outside Security can prove it, but they're rumored to communicate via entanglement, which would ignore the black box properties of the elevator."

"There must be some kind of upper limit on the distance, though, right?" Carissa asked.

"Sure, but imagine they're using every elevator in the Building as roving repeaters," the cloudlet replied. "Eventually, most elevators hit the teleport relay network, and the data crosses the finish line easily from there. Anyway, you've certainly not reached such an elaborate distance yet."

"So they might know exactly which elevator we're in?" Rindasy asked.

Carissa said, "Maybe. If they want to catch us, the best place to try is at the border."

"Don't fret," said the cloudlet. "There's much less scrutiny on elevators leaving the Association than there is on arrivals."

"Sorry," said Carissa, "but I will continue to fret."

. . .

Rindasy scoured the magical inventory ze carried in zir mind, wondering what might be of use to deter or confuse or disable the nanoswarms that were spying on their every move. Ze found it difficult imagining zir magic operating at such a small scale; zir training hadn't included anything tailored to this unique constraint. At best, ze knew spellcraft to prevent scrying *into* the elevator, which ze went ahead and put in place around the entire car. No sense letting some external scan confirm whatever reports the dust might be sending out.

"Interesting," said the cloudlet. "There's definitely a traffic bottleneck at the border. They're stopping cars for physical inspections in this elevator shaft only."

That was almost a relief to Rindasy. Ze found it considerably easier to prepare for the notion that their elevator might be stopped and forcibly invaded. Security would receive several nasty surprises in that case.

They'd been teleporting occasionally the entire trip, in order to dodge other elevators, but now they began teleporting more rapidly for a burst of several minutes, flitting through slowing traffic. Rindasy's anxiety spiked, but Carissa seemed to take the experience in stride. Eventually, the pace of the teleports slowed down considerably, and they resumed normal climbing speed.

"We're past the border now," the cloudlet announced.

"Fantastic," Carissa said, closing her eyes.

Then something heavy struck the bottom of the elevator.

"Oh, come *on*," said Carissa.

. . .

"We're experiencing drag in our speed," the cloudlet said. "Something has attached itself to us."

"How?" Carissa asked. "Didn't you see it coming?"

"Collision detection only looks for other elevator beacons."

"That seems like a really bad design."

"I'd be happy to drop you off near a suggestion box."

"Teleport away from it?" Carissa suggested.

"It's attached to the teleport pad beneath the car. We're not going to lose it that way."

"Hang on," Rindasy replied. It was a trick to fire off a combat spell at a target you couldn't see while you were hurtling upward at high speed, but Rindasy liked a challenge.

A loud *boom* went off underneath the elevator car, the boom of a shock wave ze'd released to shake loose any drone or device that had clamped itself onto the car, then another *boom* that must've been the drone or device exploding in response. The elevator began to pick up speed again.

"Nicely done," the cloudlet said. "The teleport pad is reading clear now."

"What do you think that was?" Rindasy asked.

"Facilities drone, maybe," Carissa said.

"I'm guessing bounty hunter," the cloudlet replied.

"Already?"

"We went rogue several minutes ago. Plenty of time for traffic control to auction off the job to an idle bot."

"Should we change cars?" Rindasy asked.

"Yeah, I think we should," Carissa said. "Cloudlet, take us to the nearest intersection, please."

"Estimated arrival time is ten minutes," the cloudlet replied.

"Perfect. Love it," said Carissa. Once again, she leaned her head back against the wall and closed her eyes.

Rindasy took a cue from Carissa and allowed zirself to relax at least slightly. Made sense to switch cars at an intersection, where you only had to cross through a lobby to get to another elevator bank.

"Do you have a destination in mind once we switch cars?" ze asked.

Carissa smiled and said, "I do, actually. I think we should try to find a spa that offers a nanodermabrasion treatment. Maybe they can scrub the dust off us. I'm grasping at straws here, but if it doesn't work, at least we'll be freshly exfoliated when the assassins come to murder us."

"What about your appearance?" Rindasy asked. "Would you like an alternative to your bloody Security uniform?"

"I wish I still had my mechanic's overalls, honestly, but they wouldn't fit underneath this uniform."

"I don't know what that would look like, unfortunately. But I could mend the damage, remove the bloodstain, and change the color and cut of the uniform, all with minor magic, if you like."

"That's all 'minor' magic?" Carissa said.

"Yes. We describe changes of this nature as the minor transformations," Rindasy said. "The most common major transformation, of course, is shapeshifting itself, but there are others."

"Well, sign me up for some minor transformations, then," Carissa said.

After some experimentation, Rindasy actually managed to approximate the look of her old tan overalls, although obviously without the years of distress, adding a slightly big brown jacket with many deep pockets to complete the overhaul away from the crisp cut of the Security uniform.

"How did you manage to befriend an individual cloudlet?"

"Until a couple of days ago, I lived in an elevator," Carissa said almost wistfully. "Tricked it out for personal travel. Took some adjustment, but I think cloudlet figured me out soon enough."

"Is that how you survived after escaping the Association?"

She sighed and said, "No, I did not immediately move into an elevator right after escaping genocide. I had a few adventures. Repaired elevators for a while. Ran with the Explorers Guild for a while."

"Really?" Rindasy said. "Were you with them when they came to our floor?"

"Nah, I was gone by then."

"I wish I had spent more time with them, honestly. I confess to a certain leisurely attitude in those days. The Guild taught us the ways of being good citizens of the Building. I don't think we took their warnings about the bad citizens of the Building seriously enough."

"If you can't go home, where do you think you'll go?"

"I don't know. It might be safest for me to leave the Building altogether, don't you think?"

Carissa shook her head and said, "Something like ninety-five percent of the jump-capable ships that come and go from the Building are Association-registered. Last thing you need is to have your identity discovered and you're on some claustrophobic tin can with stir-crazy crewmates who just found out there's a bounty on your head."

"You think it will come to that? More bounty hunters chasing us?"

"They'll be patient about it, but yeah. Or one of us will make a mistake without realizing it, and the Association's spies will swoop in and grab us."

"Surely they can't operate with complete impunity everywhere in the Building."

"Maybe, but we have no idea where they've got contacts or where they're lurking in the shadows really. I suppose you've got it a little easier because you can shapeshift. I don't imagine that'll throw off your own people, but it'll mean fewer anonymous tips informing the Association of your whereabouts."

"Shai-Manak can detect each other's magic. I will still need to be cautious." Ze laughed and said, "Life would be so drastically different had I accepted the Guild's invitation to continue exploring up the Building with them."

Carissa paused for a long moment, then said, "Did they just sort of casually mention you might someday think about maybe considering the idea of traveling with them? Or did they specifically offer you a formal invitation to join the Explorers Guild?"

"Nicholas Solitude invited me to join the Guild. I'd already accompanied them on three major expeditions and taken them on several small visits to outposts we wanted to show them. When they were leaving, I gave Nicholas an artifact that I'd crafted, a key that can open all locks, and in return, he gave me an invitation that I could accept at any time." The implications landed for zir, and ze said, "But I don't know how to find them."

"They monitor a network of dead drops," Carissa said. "I mean, they also have email. I can reach them for you."

"Would you join them as well? Are you already a member?"

"I think I'm considered 'inactive.' Better than being 'kicked out.' I left on shaky terms with Nicholas. But these are difficult circumstances, and it sounds like he might even be happy to hear from you."

"Approaching the intersection," the cloudlet announced. Carissa and Rindasy climbed to their feet and faced the doors.

The doors slid open, and they began to step into the lobby of the intersection. Carissa noticed what was happening before Rindasy. All three of the other elevators were open at that exact moment, with passengers about to disembark. Their own elevator's arrival meant that all four elevators had arrived at an intersection at the same time.

"Oh shit," Carissa said, pulling Rindasy back into the elevator. "Get us out of here, please."

"I'm sorry," the cloudlet replied. "This is a Building protocol I can't override."

Indeed, none of the elevators would allow their doors to close, leaving their passengers to wander into the intersection, stranded.

"What's happening?" Rindasy asked.

"If all four elevators arrive at an intersection at the same time," Carissa replied, "some kind of party supposedly breaks out. I've never seen it before."

Rindasy took a look around the lobby at the other passengers, as they were doing themselves. A group of four out of the Down elevator, looking like tourists, probably human; a pair of Erchoi lovers out of the Up elevator, arachnid limbs entwined romantically, on their way to or from a date, apparently; out of the Left elevator, three stark pillars of smoke wearing human-style corporate business attire, and a young human teenager by herself, wearing an oversize Wild Massive bomber jacket and blue jeans, riding the elevator with the smoke people but clearly traveling on her own.

Oh, and out of the Right elevator, of course, there was Rindasy, dressed like a fashionable Association citizen, and Carissa, whose obvious impatience with this situation seemed like it could boil over at any time and flood the lobby.

A panel in the ceiling slid open. Then a human woman in a black cocktail dress and a climbing harness rappelled down to the floor from the opening, landing neatly in high heels.

"Could we get everyone all the way outside the elevators, please?" she said. "Step into the lobby, please, all the way. I need you all fully inside the lobby, please."

Once the elevators were empty, their doors all slid shut simultaneously.

"Perfect. Thank you. Now before we get started, there are a few things you should know. If you were in a hurry to get somewhere and you thought cutting through this intersection would shave some time off your journey, I want you to know how wrong you were about that. Second, if you have any particular food allergies, or if you're afraid of heights, or if you're mired in the deep self-loathing that truth requires, please don't mention that to anyone tonight; we've got our own problems.

"Okay! I want you to think of the experience you're about to have not as a game you can win or as a puzzle you can solve but, instead, simply as a thing that can happen to you. Like most things that happen to most people most of the time, these things will seem arbitrary at first, then your minds will seek to assign meaning, then you'll suddenly see through to the underlying secrets of reality, then you'll imagine that you're a god, then you'll start a doomsday cult, then you'll die in a shoot-out with local law enforcement. Sorry, just a little inside joke there for you Earth floor people!

"No, but seriously, these things will seem arbitrary at first, and then you'll look a little closer, and they'll still be arbitrary, and what do you know, that's how it's gonna go here for an undisclosed amount of time. Now, are there any questions I can provide misleading answers for or simply dodge altogether?"

"Do you get paid for doing this?" the teenager asked.

"The tears of my enemies are all the reward I'll ever need. Okay, enjoy!"

With that, the woman was lifted back up into the ceiling, and the ceiling panel closed shut.

After a beat, all four elevator banks opened their doors.

The elevators were all decked out in completely different themes. One elevator had become a high-end cocktail bar. One elevator had become a small movie theater with a screen against the back wall and six theater seats. One elevator looked like a birthday party or wedding reception, with a tall, freestanding cake in a corner. And one elevator now had a three-piece live band crammed inside it, encouraging people to come dance.

The passengers began to disperse to the various attractions. Carissa froze in place, and Rindasy felt obligated to remain by her side for the moment.

"Are you feeling well?" Rindasy said.

"Yeah, sorry, I just . . . need another first aid pill, I think," Carissa said as she fished the pouch out of her pocket. "Sorry, I just feel exposed here."

Rindasy steered them to the movie theater attraction, where they sat in the back row of two. The teenager sat alone in the front row. A projectionist pulled a curtain across the doorway, and the lights in the elevator dimmed. Then the screen lit up with the main event: a glorious, old-fashioned, 2D film, with mono sound coming from a tinny speaker in the corner on the floor.

The film was in full color and was entitled *Window Washers of the Building!* It depicted, over the course of five surprisingly engaging minutes, the saga of the Window Washers Guild, whose thankless task was to make sure the Building's exterior remained spotless, a pillar of shine in a world besmirched by smudges.

Elaborate window-washing rigs departed from ground level

and rose up the side of the Building, carrying entire generations of window washers. These tireless souls endured countless lonely hours as they crawled their endless routes.

Sometimes two rigs would cross paths, close enough to lash themselves together for a festive singalong commemorating their unique way of life. Sometimes, in those brief, fleeting moments, love would come a-calling.

On rare occasions, tragedy would strike—a safety cable would fail or a clip wouldn't quite hold. By the end of the film, you truly understood the sacrifices these humble laborers were willing to make.

As the lights came up at the end of the film, the teenager said, "That's all bullshit, right?"

"Well, look at it this way," the projectionist said. "Some people think the outside of the Building is a myth, and we actually live inside a self-contained toroidal universe with no way out. I mean, I've never seen the outside of the Building with my own eyes, have you?"

"What kind of bullshit answer is that?" the teenager replied. "Also, they would make robots wash the freaking windows."

"Are you kidding? Robots are expensive. Now hush up. This is a double feature, and I'm starting the next one."

The next film was called *Fire Stairs of the Building!* Every floor of the Building, even those containing pocket dimensions, provided access to fire stairs if you knew how to spot the Exit sign embedded in the landscape. Once inside the fire stairs, you joined long caravans that trundled down the Building toward the ground floor.

It was no trivial choice to enter the fire stairs, because the fire doors locked behind you when you did. Generations of families lived and died on the fire stairs, never encountering another open fire door on their travels, never reaching the parking lot outside the Building.

Other caravans established trading posts, holding fire doors open for years and funneling supplies into the stairs, before

Facilities finally arrived to shut them down. Facilities devoted nearly all its energy toward other aspects of Building maintenance; activity on the fire stairs eluded its notice on a constant basis.

Apocryphal legends described an event that had happened once in the distant past and would happen again someday in the distant future, a mighty supernatural occurrence called *the Building-wide fire drill*. The elevators would stop running, and the entire population of the Building would take to the stairs, until the fire captains on every floor reported their people safe.

Until that drill, it was up to you to familiarize yourself with the location of every floor's fire stairs, in case disaster struck.

As the lights came up a second time, the teenager said, "Where do you *get* this bullshit?"

The defiant projectionist said, "Shut up, kid. That was my thesis film. Anyway, that's it, friends. You'll want to step out into the lobby for our final event."

▪   ▪   ▪

Suddenly, the entire intersection was raided by "Security." Not actual Security, mind you, since this intersection was nowhere near the Association, but parody "Security"—misfits who dropped down through the ceiling panels in the lobby, wearing uniforms that featured gaudy silver pinstripes and incorporated snazzy individualized flourishes, like gleaming silver boots or bright epaulets that lit up and flashed. One enterprising young person was carrying a fully functional laser rifle with a keytar grafted onto it.

For the next ten minutes, all the cast members joined together to perform a short musical entitled *It's Always Better to Not Ask Questions,* featuring the breakout hit "Curiosity Is Boring," and then without further ado, the original elevator passengers were herded into the center of the lobby, the cast members climbed into the elevators and waved goodbye, the elevator doors closed, and silence filled the lobby.

244 · SCOTTO MOORE

Seconds later, four pleasant *dings* signaled the readiness of each of the four elevators. Their doors opened, and the elevators were empty, returned to their original spotless states.

Since they'd all come to this intersection intending to switch elevators, no one wound up back in their original elevators. Carissa and Rindasy boarded the Up elevator. The doors closed.

"I hope you enjoyed that little diversion," Carissa's cloudlet said.

"It's what I imagine dying feels like," Carissa replied.

"Oh, there's no need to be dramatic."

. . .

The spa was called Enamor, and it contained several beautiful and relaxing microclimates to choose from. The elevator opened into a reception area, with an adjoining teahouse and restaurant that filled the air with savory aromas. A display screen near the entrance showed off amenities on a rolling loop—pools and soaking tubs, climbs and hikes, massages and pampering, and a long series of wellness treatments that looked alternately pleasing and deadly, all available within the facility.

Rindasy had no conception whatsoever of how this was supposed to work.

"My treat," Carissa said, noticing the apprehension on zir face. "C'mon, we'll talk about this when we get inside. This is a no-stress zone."

At the front desk, Carissa requested adjoining rooms for the two of them and wound up getting a split cabin in a forested area for the night.

Then the receptionist asked, "Have you visited Association floors recently?"

Carissa said, "How recently?"

The receptionist said, "We're just detecting a lot of surveillance dust on the two of you, which our privacy policies don't allow inside the spa. A lot of people who visit the Association don't even realize they're always covered in it."

"They waste surveillance dust even on boring people like me?" Carissa asked innocently.

"They surveil *everything*," the receptionist said, rolling her eyes. "They surveil, like, newborns in case their first words are seditious. Would you mind if we took care of it for you?"

Carissa said, "Why, no, I don't think we'd mind at all."

The receptionist led them to a narrow booth off to the side of her desk and said, "So I'll just ask each of you to step inside the detox chamber here, one at a time, and I'll flash irradiate you for a couple of seconds—it's like a little EMP for your body, which disrupts the cohesion of the swarms. After the procedure, we'll give you complimentary first aid pills, which you should take immediately to prevent sickness or death. People often like to shower afterward, just to take care of the layer of ash that remains on the skin."

Before leaving the lobby, Rindasy remembered one task ze wanted to complete. Ze pressed the button to summon an elevator back to the lobby. This time, it arrived almost instantly.

"Wait for me. This will only take a moment," ze said to Carissa. Ze stepped into the elevator and let the doors close.

"Hello there!" said the elevator's cloudlet. "What's in store for our brief but mutually beneficial association today?"

"Please deliver the following message to the Shai-Manak floor, without including its floor of origin," Rindasy replied. Ze began with the coded phrase that Sellia had instructed zir to use, to confirm the message originated with zir. "I first learned the dreamer's song when I was a child. The objective was met. The pearl was not required. I've eluded pursuit, and my health is good." Ze hesitated, then said, "It's been my honor to serve. So I must never sing the dreamer's song again."

"Your message is on its way," the cloudlet replied.

The doors opened, and Rindasy rejoined Carissa in the lobby.

"The cloudlets have an arrangement with my people," Rindasy explained. "They're delivering a message for me, without revealing my current location."

"Letting them know the lab got blown up?" Carissa asked.

"Indeed. It's not something the Association will likely publicize. But it changes the playing field for us significantly."

"Excellent," Carissa said. "You know, after a morning like that one, I think we deserve some serious relaxation, don't you?"

Rindasy hadn't allowed zirself to truly relax since ze began working in Sellia's intelligence org at the start of the conflict—fifty years ago.

"I think it's well overdue," Rindasy agreed.

"And then," Carissa continued, "once we've had food and a soak or whatever, we'll need to figure out a way for me to get some practice with these new talents."

"They haven't worn off?"

"They most certainly have not. I mean, they still might someday, who knows, but they haven't yet. I can easily visualize the 'triggers' to activate each one. Maybe if I take time to get familiar with them, I'll stand a better chance of keeping them."

Unspoken, of course, was the implication that Carissa certainly expected she'd need to use them again soon enough.

EPISODE 3.04

The day after Carissa and Rindasy escaped from the Association and made their way to Enamor, on the day of Serene Nova's summit with Kalavir and Gresij, after I'd volunteered my services to help find Carissa and Rindasy, I got in an elevator and made my way to Wild Massive corporate headquarters.

The vast majority of its workforce was deployed throughout seventy-five park locations in the Building, with middle management typically expected to be on-site, in dingy offices stuck in some backstage lot, in case their direct supervision was somehow needed on a problem of the day out in the park. When corporate needed to summon that tier of management together for rah-rah meetings, they used virtual environments.

But Wild Massive also maintained a single standard floor for its corporate headquarters. Sometimes business partners were skittish about connecting to Wild Massive's virtual accommodations; sometimes the C-suite just wanted true, actual face time with a direct report; sometimes it was easier to woo some superstar musician to commit to a concert tour of your properties by bringing them to corporate HQ, wowing them with the museum-quality artifacts on display from Wild Massive's impressive history, and then getting them properly drunk or high in person.

Allegory Paradox lived in her office at corporate HQ. I'd gleaned over time that she maintained two or three other vacation properties throughout the Building, but she preferred staying at HQ while officially working, because the CEO of Wild Massive liked to pop in for surprise informal chats with his team on a semiregular basis.

Apparently, these spontaneous little moments of brainstorming were crucial to the CEO's management style. He believed those "meetings in between the meetings" or whatever the fuck produced spontaneous insights that you couldn't otherwise capture when your minds were devoted to a specific agenda. To me, this sounded like bullshit bordering on harassment, but there was also zero chance I would ever be reporting to that dude, so whatever. Allegory seemed to think he was "fine" for the most part. Certainly, he never interfered with a single bullet point in her content strategies.

In the intervening time since I left the virtual meeting with Serene Nova, got on an elevator from the flagship to HQ, and arrived here in the lobby at corporate, the CEO of Wild Massive had wandered into Allegory's office for one of these informal chats. He'd left the door cracked open, so as I sat in some bland but undoubtedly next-level-expensive waiting room furniture, I could overhear his agitated monologue, which Allegory absorbed patiently.

"Lucy got video of it. She knows somebody in the back office up there, and they sent her video of it," the CEO said. "He's been doing test runs on it, and it might be open any day now! He's calling it the Catapult, and he's going to market this thing as the most ambitious stand-alone ride in Wild Massive history! How can he say that? That's what *we* were going to say about the Cannon when we open Wild Mega! What—no, they're not the same ride at all, the Cannon is like ten times more mega than the Catapult—twenty times, maybe—some multiple I can't remember. The point is, he may have originally designed the Catapult, but the Wild Mega team took that design, they ran with that design, they *improved* that design by making it the Cannon, and *that's* the design that got my approval, Allegory, not this rinky-dink Catapult up in the sticks.

"Anyway, I've got to shut this down somehow. I know this isn't your sphere since the Catapult's not tied to any media properties or ongoing narratives. But I need *something* to use as leverage to cut him off without angering the Board. So maybe just put your thinking cap on and keep your eyes open for any opportunities to sweep this ride up into your domain. I'm not suggesting we shut the thing down. I mean, I'm sure it's a great ride and we already paid for it, but a nice rebranding would be just the thing if we can justify it. Thanks, Allegory. I'd appreciate the extra effort, I really would."

After the monologue was over, they exchanged a few pleasantries, and then the CEO departed Allegory's office. He didn't seem to acknowledge me as he jetted past, heading down the hall to his own undoubtedly impressive corner office. Couldn't say for sure; I always made it a point to keep my eyes focused on my tablet when I was busy eavesdropping on corporate maneuvering.

"Come on in, Tabitha," Allegory said.

Allegory's corner office was duly impressive. As someone who grew up on an Earth floor, I had never quite adjusted to the orange sky outside the Building, which I tended to see only rarely since I almost never left the Super park. All the varied airships and spaceships sailing around in their elaborate patterns as they waited to land somewhere were quite dazzling to see, really; I found it hard to imagine I'd get any work done in this room, with such a mesmerizing sight right outside these windows.

Behind Allegory's desk, a narrow floor-to-ceiling bookcase was the only interruption to the wraparound windows of the office. She wasn't using it for books; an assortment of awards from throughout *Storm and Desire*'s run adorned most of the shelves, along with framed photos of herself with various cast members and directors from *Storm and Desire* as well. The surface of her desk was entirely devoid of tablets or knickknacks or coffee mugs; she didn't use this room for creative work at all.

"Don't get comfortable," she said. "We're going upstairs."

She stood up and slid the bookcase to one side, revealing a short staircase going up into an extradimensional living space. I knew she had one of these, but still . . . when I thought about how expensive and difficult it'd been to acquire my tiny little extradimensional safe, an entire extradimensional condo seemed outrageous by comparison. Probably a perk of her contract, since she was clearly such a revenue generator. Wild Massive probably just sent engineers from the rides division up here on a weekend to build this out.

At the top of the stairs, a short hallway opened up into a big, round room, with inset couches in a circle around the perimeter, cushions in the center of the circle, and wraparound screens designed to simulate windows, displaying a variety of scenes on a slow-cycling loop—beneath the waves of an ocean, on the surface of a dying star, above a city under attack by giant flower monsters, the usual.

To my surprise, several standing lamps had come from one of the high-end Wild Massive boutiques. They were fashioned after some of the classic animated characters from Wild Massive's ancient archive of properties, and were spread around the outside of the circle as though they were sentries standing watch: Greedy Maxwell Tardigrade; Lieutenant Pipsqueak Khan of the Children's Fleet; Her Eternal Brightness, Elderex Mischafana, Supremity of a Thousand Worlds, She Who Avenges Across the Planes; and of course, Helpless the Bunny ("It's so cute, it just can't help itself!").

"Make yourself comfortable in the pillow pit there," Allegory instructed.

I took my shoes off at the edge of the inset circle and stepped down into the pillow pit. It wasn't easy to get comfortable. I mean, physically it was, but my nerves were on high alert. I hadn't "replayed" my own capture glass since that first time when I was fourteen; it just hadn't seemed like an experience I needed to repeat. But I vividly remembered the rush of it, the overwhelming and jarring nature of it. Somehow my fourteen-year-old self had kept her calm. Who's to say it would be that easy this time around?

But Allegory sat next to me and said, "This'll be a breeze."

She slipped the thin rope necklace over her head, and then handed me her capture glass.

"No setup required?" I said.

"What, you mean 'previously on'? Nah, you'll figure it out."

I slipped the necklace over my head and lay back.

Barely had time for my head to reach the pillow when the flood of sensation began.

． ． ．

So right away, you get slapped into a new body that you have to figure out, with just moments to spare before you then have to figure out what the hell is happening with this body in this precise and unusual moment in time, what's the emotional context, or the professional context, or the ontological context, just hurry the fuck up and figure it out, because people are staring at you.

But after that brief and exhilarating and confusing sideways shift, you're flooded with "oh yeah" moments, like "Oh yeah, that's where my desk was," and "Oh yeah, I had just gotten my quarterly performance review," and "Oh yeah, we were still just *building* the Building at that point," and so on. It's like you're wearing two sets of clothes, because you're still you underneath, but you're clearly also inhabiting the persona of Allegory Paradox, and not as mere costume, either, but as fully realized an emulation as this perfectly captured slice of memory can deliver.

Yeah, it's all coming back to you now, locking into clarity as though you're twisting a literal focus knob on this recollection, in which a mere ten minutes ago you received probably the most excellent performance review of your career, and bless you, but you're the kind of person who never takes your own talent for granted and actually gets a little misty when someone takes the time to tell you, "Good job!" because you forget, you really do, that you're good at all this, because you *care* about it, and to this day you don't understand why some people couldn't get that part right.

On your desk in front of you: a stack of your preferred grid-lined notebooks, your half-empty coffee mug that says LET'S NOT INVENT MONDAYS on the side, and a quantum supercomputer in a Magic 8 Ball housing—a gag gift you received at an office party. You work at one of those sitting/standing/floating desks, in case for ergo reasons you want to hover near the ceiling. And the ceiling's pretty far up there, too, because you're in one of those enormous warehouse spaces where a chunk of it has been refinished and tailored to appeal to high-end creative agencies with tasteful aesthetics, while the rest of it is wide open for future development and thus is currently a deadly swirling morass of dark matter.

And juuuust as you're starting to settle into this weirdly comfortable environment, you hear shrieking, delighted, unapologetic laughter coming from an Architect's corner office at the far end of the space. Someone's in a good mood, and there's no question in your mind exactly who is responsible for such unremitting mirth.

Sounds like Epiphany Foreshadow is pleased with her performance review, too.

She sails out of her Architect's corner office almost like a cartoon character, as though there are swirling line-animated dust clouds kicking up behind her as she careens toward your desk, narrowly dodging obstacles along the way—leaping over the foosball table, snagging a doughnut from the break room counter, ignoring the powerfully seductive appeal of nonexistence, and landing casually next to your desk, her long curly hair flopping down on her shoulders a second or two after the rest of her has already settled into place. She takes off the giant-lensed tinted glasses she wears as an affect and flips her scarf back into place, before leaning casually against your desk to strike a leisurely pose.

She says, "Special projects."

And you're giddy for her, because that's exactly the assignment she wanted, and you say, "Well, aren't you the hotness."

She offers her fist for a fist bump, and for a brief, terrible moment, the veneer is yanked away, you're painfully reminded that these surface-layer interactions are all heavily draped in analogy solely so that you can understand even a fraction of what's happening, because this isn't your body at all, and you're not working for some hipster creative firm, and this memory isn't yours to begin with, and you're not equipped with any of the theoretical frameworks you need to even be here, and it's only some undocumented property of the capture glass that protects you from being pulverized into null here, but you provide the fist bump with perfect timing, and she says, "I am indeed the hotness." Epiphany leans in to whisper conspiratorially so that your coworkers—who are only pretending to ignore you, by the way—can't hear: "They're releasing ten floors to me as a home base or a workshop or whatever for launching 'special projects' that I'm not supposed to tell anybody about."

"What region?" you ask.

"I can't tell you," she replies in a little singsong voice, smiling innocently.

"Oh, I see how it is," you say. "Getting a head start on being insufferable about it, are you?"

"Could be true." Whispering even more conspiratorially: "They're not even assigning an Architect; they're just cutting me loose."

Well, *that's* certainly news. You're almost jealous, except you've been very fortunate with the designs you've had the privilege of executing. You always learn something fundamental, it seems, about the nature of creativity in the process, and you like to imagine your interpretation feeds back up the chain as well. The system was implemented to capture iterative learning at every level, and you're pleased that so many of your own minor innovations have become standard tools and approaches over time.

Besides, you're well aware that Epiphany excels in the one area that constantly plagues you: she is *fast* and has never met a deadline she didn't scream past at high speed while giggling loudly over the sound of computation whining under pressure. Time is definitely running short before phase one is scheduled to go live, and at this late date, if you want something done from start to finish with a personal touch, your best option might very well be taking the brilliance of Epiphany Foreshadow and cutting her loose without so much as a drawing on a scrap of napkin to guide her.

"Do you even have time?" you ask.

"I've been given a blessing to keep working past the phase one deadline," she replies. She nudges your arm gently and says, "I hear you'll still be working past the deadline, too."

Yes, but for you, it's perfectionism, attention to detail, unwillingness to compromise, that's forced you to plead for extensions on nearly every one of your active features.

Fortunately, your work is deeply admired, and the extensions were mere formalities; they'd let you stay on and keep working until the end of phase three if you wanted to, and frankly, you're half convinced you'd take them up on that opportunity if they offered it.

"See, that's what happens when you're the best at what you do," Epiphany says, and for a moment, you don't realize she's talking about you. "I swear, I can hardly imagine what shape this Building would've taken if even a quarter of the others had your commitment to excellence. I see so many shortcuts and slapped-together bullshit during weekly reviews, and I just want to erase half of it and start over. Like, you and me and a couple of robust algorithms, we could've handled most of this on our own!

"I want to say right now," she continues, "before I've so much as developed the slightest outline of the tiniest hint of the merest drop of my own original ideas, that I was given a very specific list of floors that I should study, floors where everything is flawless or do certain things extremely well, so that I can *riff* off those things in particular, and I swear, Allegory, two out of three of the floors on this list are yours! It's absurd how good you are!"

"Riff how?" you say. You're genuinely moved by what she's told you but have a hard time understanding why her involvement is required. "You mean . . . parody? Satire?"

"Here's the crux of it," she says, and she's managing to whisper even more softly than before. "They want me to sabotage a bunch of shit and see how it responds. Aesthetic penetration testing, exploit every plot hole, that kind of thing. Final exam time for a bunch of these people. You're going to skate through this stage, but it's going to trim some people from the roster for sure." She pauses, perhaps for dramatic effect, and then says, "Some of these people don't know how to make difficult narrative choices, they can't prioritize a compelling story over their own personal ethics, they don't know how to kill their darlings, and we can't just carry these people's lazy tropes off to the next big project. The work isn't going to get less demanding after this project's over."

"'Kill your darlings'?" you say.

"Yeah, I just made that up. I should spread that around, huh," she says.

You realize with a queasy feeling that you're desperate to change the subject.

"So you're going to be working on-site now, out of your new workshop," you say. "I'll never see you!"

"Hey, you can work on-site anytime you want," she replies. "On-site inspections are an important part of the job, I'm told."

And you realize, underneath this veneer of unparalleled creative excellence, that you are a *lonely* individual, whose choices have left you increasingly isolated, whose uncompromising critique of others' work has limited your collaborators even as you've demonstrated how unnecessary they'd be to your process . . . and Epiphany Foreshadow has stood by your side, just as you've supported many of her unconventional choices because they're unique and compelling, just like she herself is. If she goes, and you're forced to sit through weekly reviews without her calmly nudging you to be gentle with these fools . . .

"You're getting such a late start," I say. "How much time did they give you?"

"The rough schedule is, phase one launch happens per the current schedule, then I do a surprise soft launch of my stuff somewhere in the middle of phase one, and then based on how everything shakes out, they'll adjust phase two launch and let us know." She adds, "The launch party is still planned for the start of phase two, by the way. I know how much you're looking forward to that."

She's right, of course. Launch party for a project this size is a big deal. Heavy hitters show up, influencers and stars and the like. Shiny awards are presented; bonuses are discreetly tucked away in your purse; you get a little tipsy. On your last project, you were too junior to qualify for such recognition; this time around, you maybe have your hopes up a bit.

"Just keep your eyes on the prize, Allegory. Someday we will start our *own* damn agency, just you and me—got it?"

You've both dreamed about that for a long time—you would be the strategic narrative mastermind, and she would be the unpredictably inventive wild card, and sparks would fly when you teamed up to tackle endeavors even more improbable than this one.

But first . . .

"You're going to fuck up my stuff, aren't you," you say, finally starting to grasp what she's been going on about.

"There's going to be some truly epic fuckery, to be sure," she says, almost gleeful.

"And I'll be rolling off the project before your stuff even launches," you realize out loud.

"They'd let you of all people stay on, I'm sure, assuming you wanted to," she says, laughing a little, not-so-secretly hoping that you do want to.

It dawns on you that if you did stay on past your projected end date, and if you were actually on-site, you could attend to a thousand little details of fit and finish. That, in turn, would make it possible to respond to any challenges presented by Epiphany's assignment, and then you could tidy up and neatly roll off the project in time for the launch party.

"I'll ask about staying on," you finally say, curious to see first-hand what she'll throw your way.

Epiphany's eyes light up.

"I won't fuck your stuff up too much, I promise," she says with a smile. It's this particular smile of hers that locks this moment into your memory, making it the key by which the capture glass will eventually retrieve this entire conversation for safekeeping.

. . .

Just like that, it was over, and I was snapped back into my surroundings, lying in a pillow pit in Allegory's extradimensional condo.

Allegory noticed my eyes were open and said, "Now you've at least had a glimpse of Epiphany Foreshadow."

I took the necklace off and gave her back the capture glass.

"So but, where is she now?" I asked, trying to parse more than just the emotional content of the memory I'd just experienced. "Like, if you stayed behind to watch her 'soft launch' and whatever, when does it actually happen? Or did it happen already? How much did she fuck with your stuff? Can we go to her workshop? Does she know about me, and my mother, and my grandmother? Did you win any awards at the phase two launch party, or are we still in phase one? I have questions, obviously."

Allegory smiled sadly and said, "Technically, we are now in phase three. I don't know where Epiphany is. My last chance to see her would've been the phase two launch party, but unfortunately, I arrived late, and by then, they had already pulled the ladder up, so to speak."

"What do you mean?" I said.

"The top floor used to be connected to the Building, obviously," she replied. "At the phase two launch party, they staged a celebratory fireworks display, as it were, and severed the top floor entirely, introducing the chasm in its place as a final grandiose statement of some kind. Perhaps its meaning was explained in a presentation at the launch party. I can't be certain, as I wasn't able to attend."

I said, "Weren't you . . . supposed to roll off onto another project?"

She sighed and said, "Apparently, my services aren't needed on the next big thing."

The understatement in her voice when she said that was shocking to me. I couldn't reckon how someone so inherently creative could seem so defeated.

"They can't just . . . abandon you," I said.

"They can do *anything*," she snapped. "But I can make them *remember* me."

"You think they watch *Storm and Desire*?"

She shrugged, but I had a feeling she thought they were all avid viewers.

"Why'd you share this with me now?" I asked. "And please don't tell me 'kill your darlings' is supposed to mean I should turn over Carissa and Rindasy to the Association for execution."

"Tabitha, sometimes you literally *must* prioritize a compelling narrative over your personal ethics in a given moment," she suddenly insisted. "Not 'you' as in everyone in existence, but *you*—the narrative designer bursting with Muse energy you barely understand. And the reason that's true is that you're serving a greater end."

"I'm just really struggling with the notion that coming up with a slamming final arc for *Storm and Desire* is worth sacrificing their lives," I said. "I could be the best narrative designer in the world, but it wouldn't matter if I couldn't live with myself because my choices in life were abhorrent."

"Securing peace between two warring enemies is hardly abhorrent," Allegory replied.

"Why get this close to peace and then just let them kill two more people for the hell of it?" I protested.

"That's twice you've indicated they have to die, Tabitha," Allegory replied, "but you're the damn narrative designer! All you promised was to provide their location to Serene Nova. You didn't promise the location would be hospitable, you didn't promise they'd be defenseless, and you surely didn't promise they'd go along quietly. You still think you're simply glimpsing the future with your writing. In those moments when you're glimpsing it, Tabitha, you're also influencing it, shaping it ever so slightly.

"But if you're anything like Epiphany Foreshadow, you're actually capable of some truly epic fuckery. Now's the time for it, if you ask me."

Shortly after arriving at the spa, Carissa dropped a message in an electronic dead drop, which in this case meant recording an actual voice message indicating that she and Rindasy sought a meeting, encrypting it, and dropping it onto a little-used bulletin board to get scooped up by a bot that would screen it for likely authenticity and then fire it off to the Explorers Guild for further consideration. She did not expect Nicholas to respond; he probably wouldn't be the one picking up the message, and they might not even mention it to him. Not everyone knew of their feud, which they'd managed to keep quiet. She expected to receive a response via a similar but separate mechanism, either letting her know the current location of the Explorers Guild or else providing some explanation as to why this would be a bad time to catch up to them.

At its peak, the Explorers Guild could mount dozens of full expeditions at once, but since the conflict with the Shai-Manak, they'd dispersed to make themselves less of a clear target for Association spies looking to extract the location of the Shai-Manak home floor from them. As a result, Carissa couldn't be sure what shape the Guild would be in if they did manage to catch up to it.

To Carissa's surprise, she picked up a response within hours, a text message with a time and place: "Tomorrow evening, after the nightly parade, meet inside the Origins Museum, by the *Hapless History of Helpless* exhibit, at Wild Massive Prime." Coupon codes were attached to provide both Carissa and Rindasy with free passes good for a whole week.

. . .

According to popular accounts, Wild Massive was the brainchild of an illusionist who gained notoriety performing stage shows under the alias Harry Prismatic. After roaming the uppermost reaches of the Building long enough, he created a circuit by attracting other performers to follow him on various legs of his journeys, until eventually the touring caravan's popularity demanded a permanent presence, still operating today, colloquially known as Wild Massive Prime.

And while Wild Massive corporate would never be so boastful as to claim that Harry established the first amusement park in documented history, certainly anyone would agree that Harry's creation was the first to truly make a lasting impression.

Wild Massive Prime was a fierce fucking park.

For instance, if you wanted the most thrilling roller coaster experience in the Building, Wild Massive Prime still held eight of the top ten positions in *Rigget's Frequently Survivable Guide*. If you wanted an archetypal haunted house experience, Wild Massive Prime offered the Hall of Emptiness, which was so demented and unnatural that they took to positioning a hypnotist at the exit who could scrub the entire memory of the attraction from your mind as needed. The bumper cars were equipped with side-mounted shock cannons. The carousel horses seemed to be alive and were highly pissed off about the giant poles that had been rammed through their backs.

And Harry Prismatic pushed the limits of stagecraft and spellcraft in the amphitheater every afternoon, headlining his infamous Whirlwind Cavalcade of Suspended Disbelief. Harry curated an exceptional show, to be sure, attracting some of the top talents of the day to perform as his opening acts—acrobats and contortionists, musicians and dancers, inventors and escape artists, spellcasters and gunslingers, mathematicians and philosophers.

After graciously allowing his colleagues to dazzle and impress the crowd, Harry would suddenly appear alone on the amphitheater's enormous stage and begin his act.

Harry's show was called *The True History of the Multiverse* (it wasn't, but tell that to his ardent fans), and in the vernacular of the era, it was considered an absolute ass-kicker. The show sent you on a journey through the far reaches of time and space, as

Harry peeled back successive layers of the *tremendous mystery*, until finally you felt like you were staring straight into the eyes of the all-knowing essence of life itself. And the all-knowing essence of life would run you through the wringer for a bit, really take a good, hard look at you through the implacable lens of ineffability, and say to you, "Not bad. Keep it up." And you'd just absolutely break down into atoms of joy and relief. Then Harry would come out for a bow, and you'd remember the whole experience had been courtesy of Harry, weaving the grandest illusion you'd ever seen.

Harry leveraged the popularity of that show to finance a second and third park, sent out touring versions of the show to those parks, eventually adapted the show for film, and sent the film buzzing all around the upper floors. And so an empire was born.

As this empire expanded its physical footprint, making deals farther and farther down the Building for bigger and better parks, even landing prime real estate encompassing elevator locations, the original park began to fade in prominence. And when Harry finally retired from show business, the most distinguishing factor about Prime—the original version of his show, starring him— closed for good.

But Prime stayed in business, held together with grit and gusto by Harry's loyal crew of performers and stagehands and park attendants—as loyal to one another as they were to Harry. Now they were led by Harry's son, Roland, who had taken the reins as General Manager of the park well before Harry's retirement, to ensure a smooth handoff. The risky, adventurous nature of Prime was actively maintained, in contrast to the increasingly sophisticated layers of polish and artifice you saw as Wild Massive developed its style across the majority of its parks. You could still die on the Tilt-a-Whirl at Wild Massive Prime if you weren't careful.

With Harry transitioning into an absentee owner role, more interested in arcane studies than real estate deals and media tie-ins, corporate HQ solidified its leadership of the Wild Massive media empire, and Wild Massive's expansion accelerated. But because Harry himself had installed Roland as Prime's GM, and Harry had retained a majority stake in the company, Prime was essentially untouchable. Corporate couldn't stop Prime from using the Wild Massive logo, or calling itself Wild Massive, or claiming the hearts of patrons on the uppermost floors.

Corporate thus worked hard to keep Roland happy, due to a healthy fear of the damage he could do to the Wild Massive brand if he somehow went rogue. Roland would never embarrass his father like that, but corporate didn't need to know that, of course. Prime was pitched to Wild Massive fans as a different kind of adventure—strange and mysterious, favoring magic over technology, a sliver of a percentage point more dangerous than usual in a vague and nonthreatening way. As long as Roland's quarterly reports kept the execs sufficiently happy, they didn't ask questions about how Roland's park lived up to its brand reputation. That was all well and good. Corporate didn't need to know the secrets Roland was keeping.

.　.　.

As they boarded the elevator leaving the spa the next morning, Carissa's cloudlet said, "Hello, friends! What excitement do we have in store for us today?"

"Wild Massive Prime," Carissa replied.

"Goodness. Settle in for a long ride. Presumably this is your same companion from yesterday?"

"It's me," Rindasy confirmed. "Any word from home? I don't mind if Carissa hears the message."

"I first learned the dreamer's song when I was a child," began the cloudlet, using Sellia's code phrase. "Enforcers and Agents are hunting for you. They plan to terminate you so that the pearl cannot be used against the Association. I wasn't invited to their peace talks, so I had no chance to protest. Go as far away as you can. So I must never sing the dreamer's song again."

Rindasy absorbed the news in silence. Ze'd expected exile; ze hadn't expected this.

"Peace talks?" Carissa finally said. "Didn't see that coming."

"The psionic weapons program was meant to be the Association's big advantage over Shai-Manak magic," Rindasy replied. "Without it, they must've decided another fifty years of conflict wasn't worth it."

"And there's no way to defuse the weapon you're carrying?"

"Attempting to defuse or remove it will instead trigger it, or so I was told. A fail-safe measure in case I was captured so that the weapon couldn't be turned against us."

Carissa said, "You people are hard-core."

"Yes. I suppose if I truly cared about my people, I'd turn myself in, but at the moment, I'm feeling inclined to survive."

"Perfect. Me, too. Sure, they're out to kill us, but we've got passes to a theme park, so screw them."

"They're hunting *me,* Carissa. You could go your own way and be safe."

Carissa shook her head and said, "They're hunting me, too. Trust me. There's a standing order to kill me on sight. Blowing up their lab reminded everyone why that order exists, I'm sure. If you're up for it, we should stick together for a while longer."

Rindasy said, "I'm definitely up for it. They will have trouble facing the two of us together."

. ■ .

Harry Prismatic's travels among the uppermost floors of the Building gave him a solid familiarity with the available options when he scouted for land to place Wild Massive Prime. That far up the Building, so-called Earth floors were like sketches compared to the rich detail of Earth floors below. You got the feeling they were auditioning ideas for climate and culture before settling on templates that bore productive fruit. But they were all teeming with people, and Harry wasn't interested in having neighbors.

Instead, Harry wanted a floor that was hospitable to the humans who would make up the majority of his audiences, without having to answer to local authorities or obey local ordinances or the like. You could find occasional single climate floors that were devoid of intelligent life, but comfortable enough; the Explorers Guild frequently camped on these floors, and Harry knew of a few himself. He found a temperate flatland that seemed to endure only mild seasonal shifts, near enough to a river but not on the waterfront, and put a stake in the ground.

The most fateful decision Harry made was to situate the park a good distance away from the nearest elevator, instead of constructing the park around the elevator location. His thinking was that part of the adventure of coming to Wild Massive Prime was the anticipation that grew as you exited the elevator and saw its silhouette rising in the distance.

A small town called Prism City had grown up near the elevator, providing lodging and staples and transportation to the park and the like. Prime never built a luxury resort for its patrons, instead pouring all its available resources into park rides and attractions, so visiting patrons frequently stayed at resorts on nearby floors. But if you couldn't afford that kind of luxury, the homespun comforts of Prism City would suffice. And many of the cast members and workers chose to live there as well, while others lived behind the scenes at the park.

Carissa and Rindasy stepped out of the elevator into warm summer air under a sunny sky tinted slightly purple, and immediately hailed a flying rickshaw to take them to the front gates of Wild Massive Prime. It was nearing dusk, and the friendly attendant at the front gate told them they still had a couple of hours before the parade and the fireworks show began.

Rindasy had never been to a Wild Massive park before. As someone who frequently jumped out of the actual Building, the appeal of roller coasters was rather muted for zir, but ze enjoyed sampling some of the carnival food and playing a few of the games in the sprawling arcade pavilion. It was difficult to relax, wondering if they'd made some critical error in getting here that would enable enforcers or Agents to pick up their trail. Once they realized the parade was underway, they headed for the Origins

Museum, wanting to be ready and waiting for their contact as soon as it was over, without having to fight through crowds to get there.

The Origins Museum was a blend of obvious mythmaking ("Harry Prismatic wasn't born like you and me, rather he emerged from an eerie mist fully formed one Friday afternoon before breakfast," etc.) and actual museum, with several of Harry's costumes and favored props on display, as well as knick-knacks and minor artifacts from Wild Massive's earliest media productions. So much history was crammed into such a relatively compact space that *Storm and Desire* itself only warranted a small fraction of a single corner to display props and storyboards from the first arc of the series.

They passed a small theater where screenings of Harry's film occurred twice a day, in rotation with bizarre cartoons and obscure short films produced by Wild Massive over the course of many decades. This was definitely the stuff that corporate wanted to keep out of the public eye nowadays, content rich with brazen mystic symbolism or jarring and unlikely fetishes, featuring characters too inexplicable to parade around the park—surreal gods from lurid pantheons, jesters and clowns from profane dimensions. Occasionally, Harry himself would appear on screen, his mesmerizing gaze still potent even in this two-dimensional form, to perform one of his signature illusions, such as the Bleeding Smile or the Severed Conscience, and Rindasy could see even from these battered films that there was something unusual about his mastery of magic.

Eventually, they arrived at the exhibit they were looking for, *The Hapless History of Helpless,* dedicated to tracing the evolution of Wild Massive's beloved and iconic mascot, Helpless the Bunny. They waited at the entryway, where the only thing Rindasy could determine by glancing at the nearest edge of the exhibit was that Helpless the Bunny's original helplessness was due to a severe opium addiction. Helpless was meant to be a tragic figure in cautionary tales about the dangers of debauchery, apparently, but his creators couldn't help but make him adorable and sympathetic.

Suddenly, a flash of light nearby caught their attention.

Their contact from the Explorers Guild, Nicholas Solitude, had arrived out of thin air.

Nicholas was instantly recognizable primarily thanks to the uniform he'd chosen for himself a long time ago: a silver flight suit so battered that its sparkle was now fading, underneath a thin, black all-weather jacket with various patches sewn on indicating particular milestones with the Guild, and an unnecessary pair of goggles hanging around his neck. He wore a black hard-shell backpack that contained an artifact called *the spacetime machine*, which had been his means of transport to get here. His hair was long and untidy, his skin always a deep brown color, and he looked incredibly youthful despite his impressive age. He'd participated in the first human trials of longevity pills and was fortunate to receive the pill and not the placebo; the dose he received was sufficiently powerful that he wasn't expecting to need another one.

Before they could say anything, Nicholas said, "Shhhh, follow me," even though the museum was devoid of guests, and handed them each an employee badge. Then he led them to an emergency exit at the back of the museum and out into the backstage area of the park. Outside, several golf carts were parked in a clump, and he encouraged Carissa and Rindasy to climb into the nearest one as he took the driver's seat and powered up the vehicle.

"Where are we going?" Rindasy asked.

"To the tunnels!" Nicholas shouted excitedly.

They zipped along narrow paths until they reached the streets and back lots behind the scenes of the park. Here were the campers and trailers and giant canopied tents where those who lived on-site made their residence. A few small office buildings were the only concession to proper business functions.

Soon enough, they veered onto a winding pathway to a ramp leading into an underground cavern and cruised inside, stopping at the bottom to park next to several other golf carts, a few bicycles, a few scooters, and so on.

"This network of tunnels runs underneath the entire park," Nicholas explained, "and most of them are still in use for maintenance or hurrying cast members from place to place, but one or two old storerooms were set aside for the Explorers Guild to use whenever we're in the neighborhood."

They climbed up onto a small loading dock, then ducked into a smaller tunnel of reasonable height, with dim lighting and that distinct smell of moisture somehow trapped underground. Eventually, they peeled off that corridor into a short side hallway, arriving in a spacious, comfortable chamber. Tapestries hung from the ceiling all around, covering the cement walls, and the lighting was warm and welcoming. Several couches and coffee tables were the center of attention, followed by a small kitchenette set against the back wall.

"Underground hideout, sweet underground hideout," said Nicholas. "Restrooms, unfortunately, are a little farther down that hallway, but you can't quite have absolutely everything, can you?"

As Carissa and Rindasy found spots to get comfortable, Nicholas gently removed his spacetime machine backpack and hung it carefully on a pair of hooks on the wall.

"What's that humming?" Rindasy asked. Ze could feel tingling vibrations that made zir unexpectedly nervous.

"Oh, those are the thaum generators a few doors down," Nicholas replied. "Hang on. I can fix this." He pulled out a tablet, and after a few swipes, soothing music began to play, potentially enchanted for all Rindasy could tell; it was sufficient to cut some of the psychic load of the nearby generators, which supplied a steady stream of concentrated magical current to the park.

Nicholas sat down on one of the couches near the two of them.

"Thanks for meeting up with us," Carissa said to ward off an awkward silence that was threatening to take hold.

"Of course. I'm delighted to see both of you," Nicholas replied.

"Really?"

"Yes. I thought I might never see either one of you again."

"Why are we meeting here? No base camp right now?"

"Not like you're used to, no. Also I wasn't sure from your message how much privacy we'd need, so I decided this little hideaway would be prudent. I presume this is more than a social call, so let's conduct business first, and then we can see about catching up over dinner if you're hungry. What can the Guild do for you?"

Carissa glanced at Rindasy, signaling zir to go ahead.

"I'd like to accept your invitation to join the Explorers Guild, Nicholas," said Rindasy. When Nicholas remained silent, Rindasy said, "But I'll confess that I've turned to you because I'm no longer welcome among the Shai-Manak, and I have no other friends in the Building."

Now Nicholas evinced a reaction, asking in quiet amazement, "What happened?"

Nicholas had avoided news of the conflict between the Shai-Manak and the Association for some time, so there was much for Rindasy to explain on the way to divulging that ze carried a doomsday weapon inside of zir. Then it was Carissa's turn to explain why she had risked exposing herself to the Association after a century of carefully eluding their notice.

Nicholas was appalled and impressed in equal parts.

"And what would *you* like to happen here, Carissa?" he asked.

"I thought I might tag along for a while to help Rindasy settle in," she said, "while I figure out what's next for me." Then she quickly added, "Assuming you're okay with that."

"Inactive members don't need my permission to become active again. I'm not in charge, you remember—just a glorious figure-head and all that."

"I know, but I . . . said some mean things to you before I left, and I'd understand if you were uncomfortable with me reappearing like nothing happened."

"Ah. Carissa, I don't hold grudges. I literally don't hold them at all; I off-load them to a storage solution, along with a subset of painful memories and character flaws, and hope I've tagged them well enough to retrieve them someday if I need them. So far, I never have."

"You mean I can say that shit all over again and it'll be fresh to you? Nice."

"Let me turn that around, though. I do remember the substance of our disagreement, and while my feelings have gained nuance, they haven't changed dramatically. Will *you* be uncomfortable tagging along, knowing that I operate much the same today as I always have?"

"I'm prepared to be accommodating," she said. "I know we're dragging a lot of trouble in our wake, but the Guild always stays out of sight, and that's all we need for a little while until they all calm down. We could be useful, I'm sure. I acquired twelve new talents while I was in their lab. You need something levitated across the room or set on fire without matches, I'm your Brilliant."

"I've gained considerable experience as a tactical spellcaster since we last saw each other," Rindasy said. "If you happen to need the skills of a Shai-Manak sorcerer . . ."

"Friends, I appreciate your generosity," Nicholas said, "but before you commit to joining up, you should understand the Guild isn't what it used to be. Do you happen to know where you are? I don't mean here in this room or in this park. I mean, do you know what floor you're on?"

They had no idea. When you traveled in the Building, you got into an elevator and you told it your destination, and the cloudlets used their proprietary index of floors to take you there. All Carissa and Rindasy knew was they were quite far above the border. (By convention, if you asked the cloudlets how many floors there were in the Building, the dodgy rascals would say, "Too many!" and laugh.)

"You are currently seventy-two floors from the chasm," Nicholas said. "That's where we're headed, you see. It's the final adventure of the Explorers Guild. We're going into the chasm, friends, and if all goes according to plan, we're going across it."

After a long, bewildered pause, Carissa finally said, "Yeah, but why?"

"To see what's on the other side, Carissa. Why else?"

. . .

The park soon closed for the evening, and Nicholas drove them back through the boisterous backstage area where the cast and crew held their nightly wrap parties, into the now empty streets of Wild Massive Prime. Night crews were doing their sweep through the park to clean and restore order before tomorrow's crowds arrived.

He took them to the centerpiece attraction of the park, the Space Elevator, which relied on powerful magic to suspend an observation platform at a dazzling height above the ground. Cars shuttled guests up to the platform at high speed along an impressive bundle of cables. VIPs were still up there even though the park was closed. They boarded a car and rode silently up into the night sky.

As they climbed, the extent of the park became more apparent to them. Judging by the boundary of lights around the perimeter, the park seemed easily larger than Prism City off in the distance, though certainly perspective was difficult to gauge.

But against the dark night sky, on the horizon away from the park and the city, glimmers of bright color seemed to swirl among the clouds, as though they were glimpsing a beautiful mirage.

"It's like the northern lights," Carissa said, assuming Nicholas would understand the reference.

"We'll get a better look momentarily," Nicholas replied.

They stepped out onto the observation platform, a broad, two-story disc, where the upper floor was reserved for dining and cocktails, and around the rim of the lower floor was proper unobstructed observation. An array of mounted telescopes was available, coin-operated of course. Rindasy used a cantrip to produce a set of coins for them to use.

"Careful, don't flood the local economy with magic nickels," Nicholas said.

"They disappear after you spend them, so I don't think that's an issue," Rindasy replied.

And sure enough, the telescopes did provide a much better look at the supernatural phenomenon on the horizon. Rindasy's magical senses became fully engaged as ze studied it, observing the contours of the distortions and the relative "distance" across which they peered.

Carissa tried again to describe it.

"It's like Niagara Falls, except for colors instead of water," she said.

"You're seeing the chasm," Nicholas said. "Emanations from it, anyway. Its depths aren't visible from this perspective."

"How is it visible from seventy-two floors away?" Rindasy said.

"I don't know," Nicholas said. "But when you're physically standing on the edge of the chasm, you can look behind you into the sky and peer straight across a hundred floors all at once."

"That must be an illusion or a mirage," Rindasy said. "Otherwise, you're describing a naturally occurring interdimensional tunnel or something, and I can't imagine that's what I'm looking at."

"Who can say?" Nicholas replied. "The chasm is the principal remaining mystery on the Guild's agenda. We're planning a proper expedition into the chasm, and we plan to survive to file an official report of our findings. After that, we intend to disband for good."

"I see," Carissa said. "So we got here just in time to go on one last irresponsible jaunt with you, is that what you're saying?"

"Something like that, yes. Certainly a Brilliant and a Shai-Manak would be very handy companions on the journey."

"Do you just ride the elevators up seventy-two floors to get there?" Rindasy asked.

"The cloudlets refuse to risk taking cars all the way there," Nicholas said. "They'll only go fifty or sixty floors up from here, depending on how brave the individual cloudlet in question happens to be."

"So how did you get to the chasm's edge?" Rindasy replied. "Did you find a way to climb up the elevator shafts? Or did you charter an interdimensional transport to ferry you the distance?"

Nicholas shook his head and said, "We took the fire stairs."

"Those are real?" Carissa said. "I've never once seen a fire door."

"Oh, they're quite real. Most people don't know to look for them, and many are unmapped, just like many of the elevators are unmapped. People have long derided Harry Prismatic's decision to build his first park at a remove from the nearest elevator, but few understood the brilliance of building it around a fire door. There's a fire door a hundred feet away from us."

"What's so brilliant about having access to a fire door?" Carissa said. "I mean, sure, in the event the entire floor is blanketed in a firestorm, you can exit single file down an infinity of stairs, congrats, but otherwise, what's it good for?"

"Carissa, there are dozens of cultures here in the upper regions alone where fascist regimes control access to the elevators for entire floors. Those populations don't benefit from access to the Building's knowledge and resources, never get a chance to appeal to the Association or anyone else for support. Meanwhile, the regimes flagrantly import high technology to keep their strangleholds on power. We use the fire stairs to smuggle supplies and weaponry to some of these places where the elevators aren't safe to use."

"How do you get the fire doors open?" Rindasy asked.

"The Key," Nicholas said. "I'm its usual caretaker, but we remember it as having been a gift to the Guild at large. When someone identifies a door that needs opening, I make sure it's available."

"Since when is the Guild involved in freedom fighting?" Carissa asked.

"Like I said, the Guild's not what it used to be. We splintered along a couple of different ideological lines regarding what the future of the Guild should even be. Amicable, to be sure, but sad nevertheless. One faction is now dedicated to running weapons and supplies up and down the fire stairs and supplying caravans that are heading to lower regions. The tunnels under the park are a convenient staging ground and rallying point. By mutual agreement, this faction no longer calls itself the Explorers Guild."

"Does this faction include you?" Rindasy asked.

"I keep my eye on them, but no, I'm more tactically involved in the other faction." He paused, for the first time in this conversation seeming to hesitate, before finally admitting, "Our ambitions are slightly more grandiose. We're going to explore the chasm by going straight through it and then file our report from the top floor itself."

Rindasy didn't know what to say. Ze was suddenly reminded of early Shai-Manak myths, which told of mountains in the clouds where the world-dragons finally arrived and settled, after scouring the galaxy looking for a place to cultivate life. Searching for the top floor felt like the reverse of those myths, like attempting to ascend to the peaks of those mountains in order to propel yourself out into the galaxy. Easy to dismiss on one level, but with the amount of magic that circulated in disparate pockets and pools in this Building, it was difficult to ever rule anything completely out.

"Another significant portion of the Guild simply drifted off, deciding neither of these missions suited their personal ambitions," Nicholas continued. A bit uneasily, he admitted, "To be fair, lives were lost during our first approach to the chasm."

"What happened?" Carissa asked, her eyes suddenly locked on him in disbelief.

"The chasm is populated," Nicholas replied, "and its inhabitants are not receptive to friendly diplomatic overtures."

Carissa remained silent, biting down on the acerbic remark she wanted to make, remembering she'd promised to be accommodating.

"I recognize that look, Carissa," Nicholas said. "But I can't scout ahead on this expedition. The spacetime machine refuses to function when I try to study the chasm. My suspicion is that, like the elevators, it refuses to risk itself within a certain range of the chasm's effects."

"You're saying the spacetime machine is sentient?" Rindasy asked.

"No, I simply mean that it obeys underlying principles that aren't always apparent."

"The principles of its operator, meanwhile, are plainly apparent," Carissa said.

Nicholas managed a laugh at his own expense.

"The Shai-Manak certainly viewed Nicholas as a principled person," Rindasy said.

"I know. I'm trying not to be catty," Carissa replied. "We're all principled here, we just . . . don't share all the same ones. If I owned a spacetime machine, let's just say I'd have different strategies for making use of it."

"Of course you would. But expecting the outcomes of those strategies to be predictable and reliable is wishful thinking. Sometimes the satisfaction of knowing you tried your best to change something is outweighed by the sheer fact that you *failed* when you tried. The outcome is just as bad as it was before you took action, but now you've accepted a measure of responsibility for it, so it's actually worse for you."

Carissa smiled as she turned to Rindasy and said, "This is where we always deadlock, because Nicholas always assumes I'm going to fail."

Nicholas looked away from Carissa and Rindasy, staring out into the darkness of the night sky as he seemed to gather the energy to continue.

"The spacetime machine is a one-off, a prototype that bends so many rules of life in the Building all at once that it's obvious why its inventors abandoned the project," he said. "I made rules for myself to survive as its caretaker. For instance, I absolutely refuse to use the spacetime machine to travel to tomorrow. Tomorrow's off-limits. I can travel to next week, I can travel to the end of time itself, but whatever today I'm currently experiencing, I can bloody well wait for its tomorrow to arrive naturally. Life is wasted if you always know what happens next.

"And for a long while every single time the Guild put together plans for an expedition, I was asked to skip forward in time and scout the outcome. But that's no way to experience your own personal timeline, skipping all the work, the trails forged, the lessons learned, the camaraderie that comes from shared failures and adventures—all of that evaporates if you witness the ending of an expedition before it ever gets off the ground. It's as disappointing as if you only ever experienced a book by first reading the final chapter. You'd stop reading books after a short while, I suspect."

"Except in this case, reading the last chapter saves people's lives," Carissa interrupted, "and giving up books altogether means letting people die. *Those* are the stakes."

Rindasy finally understood the nature of their disagreement. People lost their lives on Guild expeditions. Nicholas could scout ahead and try to avert the outcome, warn the individuals to steer clear, change the future in some fashion. And Nicholas didn't want to.

"Finally, I said to the Guild, 'Look, if you want spoilers for every expedition that I'm a part of, then the bylines on the reports will always be mine because I'll always get there first.'" He chuckled. "They stopped asking me."

He fell silent for a moment, as though all of that had spilled out of him unexpectedly and had cost him something to share.

"But yes, when we began considering an expedition to the chasm," he finally continued, "I wanted us to have every advantage. I decided to use the spacetime machine to slowly scout ahead of the first expedition. I thought I'd leap forward a few days ahead of our real position each day and then report back, allowing us time to adjust our tactics as we blazed a trail. Unfortunately, for inexplicable reasons, the spacetime machine refuses to leap anywhere near the chasm."

"So when you filed your report from the edge of the chasm," Carissa said, "you'd just climbed up the fire stairs until you reached it?"

"Exactly," Nicholas said.

"What did you see?" Rindasy asked.

"We were forced to turn back," Nicholas replied. "We have no idea what we're facing, really."

As if on cue, the vision of the chasm in the distance lit up with several sharp bright streaks, as though fireworks were being let off.

"There they go," Nicholas said. "They send out nightly flying 'patrols,' for lack of a better term, which harass floors that border the 'interdimensional tunnel.'"

"So they've got their own ships?" Carissa asked.

"I'm not sure," Nicholas said. "One of many questions we hope to answer as we explore. I'm sure they'll turn their attention to the park eventually. The floors closest to the chasm have emptied out, which is . . . worrying, since we saw no signs of mass evacuation."

"What do you call the chasm inhabitants?" Rindasy asked.

"They're called the Maladies," Nicholas replied. "I'm not sure how we learned that name, but that's what everyone calls them. If you live this close to the chasm, you've heard of the Maladies."

Carissa said, "This seems more and more like an absolute, total shit show, Nicholas. The chasm sounds like a freaky hell pit, and you plan on going straight through it?"

"There is of course another option," said a genial male voice from the steps behind them.

They turned toward the stairs leading up to the nightclub a floor above, to see a tall man with dark brown skin and an impressive mustache descending, wearing a red smoking jacket and a silver cravat over a Wild Massive T-shirt, and a top hat on top of a probably bald head.

"You don't have to go *through* the chasm, as I keep telling Nicholas," said the man. "You can instead go *over* it."

Nicholas graciously introduced the man as Roland Pierson, a.k.a. Roland Prismatic, General Manager of Wild Massive Prime. Having lived his entire life "practically within eyesight" of the chasm, as he put it, he'd developed a proper appreciation for the challenges involved in thinking about the chasm, approaching the chasm, negotiating a personal peace with the chasm, yada yada. As he spoke, Rindasy couldn't decide if he was a charismatic huckster, which would not be out of place here, or if he'd truly found some hook for understanding the chasm that others had missed for eons.

"If you could go 'over' it," Carissa said, "someone would have done it already."

"Perhaps someone *has* done it already," Roland replied. "Just because no one has ever returned doesn't mean their voyages weren't successful."

Every few hundred years, it seemed, an enthusiast adventurer chartered or purchased a jump-capable ship, loaded it with supplies, and set out to find the top floor. Surely flying a spaceship straight up the side of the Building or jumping repeatedly thousands of floors at a time would allow them to bypass the chasm altogether, they'd argue, and then they'd have a press conference and they'd depart from a hangar amid whatever level of ceremony they could afford, and off they'd go, only to vanish from the pages of history.

Maybe finding the top floor was easy, but getting back was impossible for some reason.

"But I hear you," Roland continued. "No sense making a fabulous discovery if you can't return home for the parades and adulation."

"So what do you mean, go 'over' it?" Carissa pressed him.

"As it happens, I will unveil my solution within mere days," he responded. "If you look down in that direction, see that large warehouse-like structure occupying the center of the park, behind that cordon of fences? We've been building in stealth mode for quite some time. Soon that structure and those fences will come down, and we'll have a grand opening ceremony for the Catapult, our first new attraction of the season. If you're still visiting, you're welcome to be among my personal guests. Oh! And on that note, you're welcome to join us upstairs for a cocktail before you retire tonight, if you'd like."

"Thank you, Roland. That sounds delightful," Nicholas said.

Roland nodded, bowed slightly, and wandered back upstairs.

"Seriously?" Carissa said after Roland was safely out of earshot.

"His father invented Wild Massive itself," replied Nicholas. "I wouldn't write off his son just yet. We don't know what Harry taught Roland, exactly."

"And where is Harry?" Rindasy asked.

"Shrouded in mystery somewhere, no doubt just the way he prefers it."

"Lucky him," said Carissa. "I'd prefer it, too, but reality is conspiring against me lately."

"Hard to say. It brought you here, on the cusp of the final grand adventure of the Explorers Guild. If you're interested, that is."

"Where's the Guild now?" Rindasy asked.

"We have an outpost five floors below the chasm. Around twenty people have gathered there. We're expecting a few more in the next day or two. I expect you'll both see some familiar faces."

"So we have at least a day or two to ponder our options," Rindasy said.

"Yes, and we won't leave right away even after we're all assembled. We're being thorough about our precautions and planning. Why don't you spend tomorrow enjoying the amusement park, and we can touch base at the end of the day? I assure you there'll be no hard feelings if you opt for a less perilous path forward for yourselves."

But Rindasy had the feeling all paths forward were perilous, no matter which path ze chose.

. . .

That night, right around the time Carissa and Rindasy first connected with Nicholas in the Origins Museum, I was well into scribbling away at my writing. I had a lot of catching up to do just to get current with where they'd been, let alone deduce where they might be within the next twenty-four hours.

By the time Carissa and Rindasy were likely mingling with Roland and VIPs in the nightclub atop the Space Elevator, I had deduced, or invented, or some blend of both, two things of note, extracted from the raw draft I'd generated.

I wrote an email explaining my findings to Allegory.

Allegory,

Finished drafting for the day. A rough outing, but they all are on some level, eh.

Please share the following information with Serene Nova, regarding the location of Carissa and Rindasy.

At some point during daylight hours tomorrow, the two of them will occupy the front seats of a roller coaster car as it leaves the station. The Space Elevator is visible in the distance behind them as the car sets into motion, which pinpoints the park as Wild Massive Prime.

I'm sure this will be obvious as you put plans into motion, but I feel obliged to call out that if they're riding a roller coaster, then the park will be open to the public when you find them. Prime may be a small park by corporate standards, but they're still admitting an average of twenty thousand guests a day.

Additionally—this bit is just for you, not Serene Nova—they've built a ride called the Catapult at Wild Massive Prime. It goes into service within days. I believe its hidden purpose is to propel select passengers across the chasm to the top floor. It doesn't work for that purpose, not yet, anyway. But still I thought you would want to know.

Tabitha

That was me, obeying the letter of my mentor Allegory's request, while preparing to circumvent the spirit of it. I could feel the literal "correctness" of the divination, even as I felt a loophole opening up, big enough for me to squeeze through it.

I cobbled together a few fresh notebooks and a box of pens, some protein bars, a water bottle, my tablet, a change of clothes, my park badge and park name tag, and stashed them all in a backpack. I changed into a Wild Massive T-shirt and jeans, and I put on my Wild Massive bomber jacket to complete the fangirl look. My full manuscript and my capture glass were stored in my extradimensional safe, accessible anywhere I went. I realized I didn't know if I was coming back to the resort, but I didn't quite have the guts to check out at the front desk.

I made my way to the elevator on foot since the shuttle train was no longer running. Heavy security was always stationed there at night in case anyone tried to get into the park after it had closed. They had no reason to prevent me from leaving, however.

Allegory would know something was up when I didn't show up for work tomorrow. I'd done exactly what I said I was going to do: I'd found the fugitives for Serene Nova. My services had been precisely rendered. Allegory's needs were met: a powerful coalition would soon be aimed straight up the Building, so close to the chasm that you could see it in the sky. No doubt Allegory had a parallel plan for shoving everyone over the edge of it.

And now I was a literal wild card on the whiteboard, heavily enmeshed in the circumstances but surprisingly free to act, and my own agenda was rapidly forming. I knew too much to let them play me like that and then just discard me. It was good that

Allegory hadn't already stopped me; it either meant she approved or else she wasn't paying close enough attention to me to notice.

I made small talk with one of the guards until the elevator arrived with a pleasant *ding*, and then I climbed aboard.

"Greetings!" said the elevator's cloudlet after the doors had closed. "To what singular destination is your entire life's journey leading you toward at this exact moment?"

"Prism City," I said.

SEASON FOUR

Explorers Guild Report: The Chasm's Edge
By Nicholas Solitude

As I dictate this, I am physically in sight of the chasm. It's simply a big canyon when you get right down to it, except it's also simultaneously somehow inverted, so just as it descends like a horrible gash in the landscape, it also rises up and swallows what should be the sky, spraying its unnatural multihued glow in all directions, until you start to imagine the object that you see blotting out the actual sun is the silhouette of the ever-distant top floor, never in reach.

To get to the chasm, you stroll through the main street of the last small town on this floor within walking distance of it. The sky is raging with tormented colors and howling wind. The street takes you a few kilometers beyond city limits before abruptly terminating at an enormous crevice that seems entirely out of place in this otherwise sleepy farmland territory. It's as though an epic sinkhole has somehow swallowed an inconceivable chunk of the terrain in front of you.

Without daring to peer directly over the edge, you can still see far enough into the chasm to detect giant rifts in the canyon's walls where the orange sky outside the Building is clearly visible.

Most of the others in our expedition turned back well before this point, hiking back the way we'd come as an increasing sense of dread overcame them. This was no ordinary expedition, we all understood that, so turning around brought with it no judgment; they'd wait for us at a predetermined rendezvous for a time, before departing the floor altogether and leaving us to our fate.

Only three of us managed to complete the trek to the chasm's edge—myself, Derald, and Janszen. We arrived at a lookout that prior inhabitants of the floor had constructed, as though this was a mere topological anomaly that served as a great tourist attraction.

Our mission at this point was only to take a few scientific and thau-maturgic measurements from this proximity and then retreat. Without the full team, this was clearly not the time to attempt to physically enter the chasm ourselves.

While Derald and Janszen unpacked their respective sensor kits, my task was to use the onboard instrumentation of the spacetime machine to scout for potential landing zones inside the chasm. To my dismay and disappointment, I received an error message I'd never seen before: "Insufficient certainty to perform travel operations."

The machine offers a "certainty rating" to guide your decision-making as you request spacetime jumps. I've only stretched it to what I believed were its limits on a few occasions. Even then, the certainty rating simply dropped from "certain" to "almost certain." But it still performed the jump in those cases. "Insufficient cer-tainty" meant the machine was dead in the water, and not simply for jumps into or beyond the chasm; we were surrounded by so much uncertainty that I couldn't even use the machine to jump back to the elevator or to our camp five floors below. I had always believed "cer-tainty" was primarily a temporal rating, but this thing no longer felt confident making a jump ten feet behind me even without traveling in time at all.

I shouted to Derald and Janszen the news that the machine was not providing useful data, and received no response, so I looked up, and was shocked to see they had both climbed to the other side of the safety railing to set up their instruments.

Somehow this had drawn the attention of an observer from the chasm.

I caught sight of it just as it finished climbing over the rim of the chasm, into the few feet of rock and dust between the chasm and the instrumentation that Derald and Janszen had deployed on a pair of tripods. I felt like I was watching a psychedelic cartoon version of an angel of death appear before us, tall and skeletal and shrouded in a cloak, but in truth the thing was deeply mesmerizing with swirling color patterns that defied the boundaries of its cloak; colors seemed to wisp from its cloak like steam rising off the surface of a hot spring. I couldn't get its face to come into focus in my line of sight, as though its features were only suggestions from a little-used template and not meant to provide identification or a means of expression.

Derald and Janszen each collapsed to their knees before it, frozen in fear. I was a good thirty feet away still, whereas they were directly in front of it, so close it could reach out with surreal arms and touch their foreheads if it chose to.

Now I watched as a platform of rock floated to the edge of the chasm, and Derald and Janszen were lured onto it by the beckoning figure floating before them, and without a word, all three of them rapidly descended out of sight. I'd been terrified the entire time and hadn't managed to emit so much as a single word of warning. I did not rush to the edge of the cliff to see the rest of their descent. As soon as I was capable, I fled, leaving them to their fate.

Per custom whenever we must abandon an expedition without our full party safely accounted for, we regret to formally report into the public record that Derald and Janszen are now numbered among the lost members of the Guild.

. . .

Agent Grey summoned the Agents of Dimension Force to the Vantage Point to review a time-sensitive mission request. They gathered in the small auditorium that functioned as their briefing room. Grey had not prepared slides.

"Serene Nova has received intelligence indicating the terrorists who escaped Jirian Echo's lab will both be at Wild Massive Prime in the morning," she told the assembled Agents. "She has formally asked Dimension Force to eliminate them. The assignment is off the books—the rest of Parliament will not be informed."

Wynderia Gallas sighed in disappointment. This was the team's first confirmation that Carissa had survived Wynderia's bullet.

"That sounds like cop shit to me," said Agent Whisper, elite technologist, a former computing supervillain who joined the

Agents because the ethical constraints of being good made certain classes of computational problems *slightly* more interesting for him than pursuing evil.

"The two of them together might be physically unstoppable," the wizard Glamour Esque said quietly. "That makes it *our* shit by definition."

"It's impractical to mount a Security operation that far above the border," Grey explained, "and Serene Nova doesn't want Fleet anywhere near these two. If the Admiral gets his hands on Carissa, he could restart his illegal psionic weapons program. If he gets his hands on Rindasy, he'd have control of an apoc weapon that has already infiltrated the Association once and gotten away with it."

"The psionic weapons weren't intended for fighting the Shai-Manak," Anjette realized out loud. "The Admiral planned to use them for a coup attempt."

"The Admiral and unknown collaborators," Agent Grey said, "if we want to be properly conspiratorial about an unproven hypothesis. Under the circumstances, I'm not surprised Serene Nova reached out to Dimension Force to handle this particular loose end. Coup or not, the Admiral's quest for firepower has taken an ugly turn."

"I studied the apoc weapon," said Glamour Esque, "during the brief window that Rindasy was in our custody. They've harnessed or simulated a sliver of the algorithmic creation logic that populated many regions of the Building. Releasing that sliver on a floor today would overwrite even a full-blown civilization with a fresh, clean slate of local existence. It'd be no more than an empty floor in need of a tenant. No magic in the Association is even remotely comparable."

"The weapon will disarm itself when Rindasy is eliminated," Agent Grey said.

"And if we fail, the bomb goes off?" Whisper asked.

"If we fail and Rindasy sets the bomb off, the bomb goes off," Agent Grey corrected him.

"Neat, so once ze realizes we're coming to kill zir, ze can pre-emptively vaporize an entire floor, including zirself, just to show us who's boss?"

"Ze doesn't need to vaporize a floor to show us who's boss," Anjette said. "The Shai-Manak already showed us who's boss a couple of times now, and it's them."

"The fugitives may not even realize we're coming for them," Wynderia said. "They're not being very careful if we already know a time and place to intercept them. Maybe they're getting cocky after thinking they escaped without any consequences."

"Don't mistake actual confidence for overconfidence," said Steelplate. It was a rare occasion when he took the floor. "I've been running simulations on my targeting computer since we left Ji-rian Echo's lab. In a straight up battle royale, Dimension Force versus the fugitives, we lose every time."

"The Shai-Manak who helped me escape said that the weapon has a 'margin of error' of a thousand floors," Anjette said. "We can't afford to lose."

That got everyone's attention.

"Fair enough," said Whisper. "I agree that this is our shit by definition."

Agent Pivotal Moment stood up at the back of the briefing theater and said, "Here's a question for you. What if we don't do this mission? Like, at all."

No one had seen him arrive; it was possible he hadn't arrived until just then.

Agent Grey was an expert at maintaining a neutral demeanor in the face of all manner of Parliamentary idiocy, but was un-accustomed to apparent rank insubordination, and her wither-ing glare betrayed her impatience with Pivotal Moment's stance. Technically, he was not being insubordinate; all the Agents were peers, reporting to Muses in the grand org chart, taking direction from Agent Grey only by convention. Nevertheless, her irritation was clear.

"We're doing the mission," said Agent Grey.

290 · SCOTTO MOORE

"I mean, let's be clear, *I'm* not doing the mission," said Pivotal Moment.

The other Agents were dead silent, as if mentally calculating the notion that they could simply refuse to accept a mission, as if this had never once in their varied tenures crossed any of their minds before.

And Pivotal Moment was a thought leader among the assembled crew. He had their sympathies, across the board.

Pivotal Moment's sphere of influence was negotiation and diplomacy—*applied pacifism,* as he liked to say. He also possessed a weird but helpful knack for "being in the right place at the right time" to nudge tense situations in a positive direction. He didn't tend to physically exist until his specific perspective or skills were needed, and once he felt his incarnation had served its purpose, he typically withdrew to rejoin the indeterminate smear of consciousness outside the perceptual realm called the Moments.

When the Brilliant in Minneapolis made first contact with the Association, Pivotal Moment took an interest and became the principal liaison between the Brilliant and the Association. He saw how precarious the Brilliant's position was within their shitty Earth floor and nudged them to consider resettling within the Association. Entire floors awaited where they could've found peace if not precisely happiness (because seriously, who promised "happiness" to anyone with a straight face in this reality?).

And when the Association decided to move military forces onto their shitty Earth floor, Pivotal Moment was almost omnipresent, in close communication with all sides of the conflict, attempting to prevent hostilities from reaching a peak. He became especially close with Kellin, leader of the Brilliant collective, well aware of what Kellin could unleash, equally aware of what the Association could dish out in retaliation, wanting nothing more than to deliver the peace he'd promised all of Kellin's people.

That was his mistake, of course. As a professional maxim, you didn't promise what you couldn't deliver (see above re: "happiness"), and just because you'd had a perfect track record on delivering "peace" *so far* in this reality didn't mean you couldn't eventually fail someday, and fail spectacularly at that.

So when the Association stabbed the Brilliant by launching annihilation strikes that obliterated most of their continent, Pivotal Moment was searching the local haunts of the Brilliant in downtown Minneapolis to warn anyone who might listen when the strikes hit, having spectacularly failed at the only thing he was theoretically good at. Every aspect of his being told him he should be anywhere but here, that this was the definition of the wrong place at the wrong time, and he could easily banish himself from this situation with no trace and no penalty. Instead, he was incinerated along with the Brilliant, and ironically, he could feel the pain of it now in every pore of his new incarnation, as fresh as if it was happening to him right. this. moment.

To make it ever so slightly worse, Agent Grey had knowingly lied to the Association when she told them her team had cleared the floor. Agent Grey knew Pivotal Moment had ignored her order to evacuate, but she refused to let one of her Agents lash himself to some bulldozer or chain-link fence or whatever in a futile and embarrassing attempt to stop a massive military operation, especially an Agent who reincarnated whenever the moment called for it.

"This is an all-hands mission," Agent Grey said curtly.

"Fascinating," Pivotal Moment said. "Does that mean our three incorporeal comrades will be joining the mission?"

Precedent was that the three incorporeal Agents did not, in fact, join all-hands missions, as Pivotal Moment well knew. Agent ClearMind was a sentient mathematical formulation who patrolled irrational and imaginary topologies. Agent Nihil Eon was an antibeing who monitored designated non-sentience dimensions for signs of nascent life and extinguished what it found. And Agent Sublime Promise of a Devious Puzzle (Delighting You, Exciting You) patrolled vividly surreal realms and improbable dimensions for inscrutable unreasons that resist easy description here.

"They will not, as per usual," Agent Grey said curtly.

Pivotal Moment nodded. You could argue that he himself was primarily an incorporeal Agent as well, given that he didn't exist until he did. To date, he'd instead aligned with the corporeal Agents as a preference for the purpose of being specifically useful.

"Well, I've clearly returned to this reality for a reason," said Pivotal Moment, "but I'm absolutely positive it's not to help you track down and murder these two fugitives. I'd have thought, Agent Grey, that you'd refuse this mission, that you'd instead choose to shield Carissa from the Association instead of letting them carry their genocide to its final conclusion. I'd have thought saving her life might assuage your conscience for your role in destroying the Brilliant, but perhaps the rumors are true, that you have no conscience, that you're a golem who merely simulates self-awareness."

"Agent, you're dismissed," said Agent Grey curtly.

"Point of order," replied Pivotal Moment, biting into his own measure of curtness with unexpected relish, "*no one* dismisses me once I've incarnated, not until the moment *literally* calls for it." Then, just to be clear, he added, "*I'll* be the Moment who literally calls for it, if that wasn't obvious." With a sudden winning smile, he further added, "But I'll surely get the hell out of *this* joint." He sauntered out of the briefing room and out of the Vantage Point altogether.

"Anyone else have any pressing existential concerns about this mission?" Grey said to the remaining Agents. The team would be Agent Grey as field commander, Anjette, Steelplate, Whisper, Glamour Esque, the Moods, and Wynderia Gallas, supported by enforcers to be provided by the Shai-Manak. If any censure was to come to Pivotal Moment for refusing the mission, Grey would handle it when the mission was over.

"Nah," said Wynderia. "I'm looking forward to a little rematch myself."

Eerie giggling from the back of the room indicated the Moods had been paying attention to the proceedings. They were currently wispy humanoids from the waist up, glowing balls of light from the waist down, hovering a foot above the floor, and their eyes were the anti-color of an unquenchable void they always sought to fill.

"Got an appetite for these two, for sure," one of them said. "But Steelplate's computer says we lose."

"Guess we die doing what we love the most," the other one said, "sneaking into theme parks without buying passes."

"This won't be a battle royale," Steelplate said. "They'll be on unfamiliar ground, they won't be expecting us, they don't know our tactics or weaknesses, and my model didn't factor Shai-Manak sorcerers on our side. We have experience operating as a unit; they barely know each other, and the Brilliant barely knows her own power set. All things considered . . . we might not die."

"What are the ground rules?" Anjette asked. "Do we eliminate them on-site if we can, or do we need to get them out of the park first?"

"They're too dangerous for extraction," Agent Grey replied. "Take them down on-site."

.   .   .

After Andasir played such a significant role in helping Anjette escape from the Shai-Manak floor, ze fully expected the resulting punishment to be severe. Ze was already accused of treason, jeopardizing a mission that was meant to save their floor from invasion by a more powerful force, blowing open one of the elevator banks in the process. Helping Anjette escape—and blowing open another elevator bank—definitely put zir in line for even more charges.

The situation was unprecedented, really. The Shai-Manak had always operated in lockstep throughout the conflict.

Except, Andasir reminded zirself, for Gresij.

Gresij ignored the will of the Radiant Council in order to descend to the nearest Association outpost and announce the existence of the Shai-Manak, claiming the role of ambassador for

zirself. Whether you agreed with Gresij's motives or simply blamed
zir for the outcome, the fact was that Gresij pursued diplomacy
with the Association, at great personal cost, intending to deflect the
violence that would come if the Shai-Manak unilaterally surprise
attacked the Association.

That's what most of the Shai-Manak were agitating for. They
blamed the Association for the humiliating fact that they'd been
trapped on this floor for most of history. They resented the Association for needing to break windows if they wanted to get
out of the Building, instead of having free access to the lobby.
They craved the Association's vast technological prowess. They
hated the Association for audaciously claiming the right to gov-
ern Building resources such as the elevators.

Mostly, though, they were sick of war games among tiny rival
bands of Shai-Manak, and were ready for the real deal.

Gresij was sickened by this appetite and acted accordingly.

Andasir felt like ze had acted in accordance with Gresij's example when ze attempted to stop Rindasy from departing on zir
deadly mission. It was not an argument that Kalavir and Sellia
found convincing, but it was something to hold on to while they
decided what to do with zir.

And in the end, it was Gresij, newly released from the Association's clutches, who visited Andasir in zir holding cell, with
an offering.

Kalavir intended to send a squadron of eight enforcers along
with the Agents to hunt Rindasy. Since Andasir had proven so
intent on stopping Rindasy and had also proven craftier than
expected in the process, would Andasir join this squadron as a
diplomatic resource, guiding these enforcers as need be? Several
of them hadn't left the Shai-Manak floor before; none of them
could be counted on to respect the Agents outright.

"And the intent is to kill Rindasy at the end of this hunt?"
Andasir asked.

"That is the requirement for peace," Gresij replied.

"Why can't we simply trust Rindasy not to use the pearl?" Andasir continued. "Ze has no remaining motivation to do so. Why is zir word not sufficient as a guarantee?"

"Trust is a quality not readily available in their leadership," Gresij replied. "We sacrifice Rindasy in order to prevent further sacrifices of larger magnitude, and then we join the Association."

"Two days ago, we sent the pearl to devastate their territory, and now we're joining them, just like that?"

"Just like that. Here I am before you now, a sign that peace has nearly arrived—except for this last crucial matter that stands in the way, which I'm asking you to help resolve on my behalf. Will you go?"

Gresij had clearly arranged this to give Andasir a chance to rejoin Shai-Manak life with distinction. And yet, the only thing that raced through Andasir's mind was how to help Rindasy *escape*. Fate was being particularly capricious in how it toyed with Andasir's loyalties, ze thought ruefully.

But Rindasy didn't deserve this dishonorable death, not after ze'd risked so much already, not at the hands of zir own people. There was no way Andasir could stand by and allow it to happen. Peace would have to arrive another way.

"Yes, I'll go," Andasir said, mentally preparing to betray zir people yet again.

■　■　■

Gresij led Andasir into the council chamber, where Kalavir and Sellia held court with Agent Grey and Agent Anjette. The eight enforcers assigned to the mission were on hand as well. A small argument of sorts seemed to be in process.

"Gresij, perhaps you could help us resolve a minor issue," Kalavir began.

"Let Agent Grey run the mission," Gresij said, anticipating the debate. "But, Agent Grey, I would ask that you consider the advice of my protégé, Andasir, as you deploy our enforcers."

Anjette murmured something to Agent Grey, who nodded and said, "Agreed. We'll return in a ship in less than an hour to pick up your squad and take them with us to the site."

"Kalavir, are we to accept this subjugation without a challenge?" one of the enforcers said. This was Elsethe, one of the two enforcers who'd pursued Andasir to the Super park and brought zir back.

"That will not be necessary," Gresij said, a warning tone in zir voice.

"I don't report to the diplomatic corps," Elsethe replied.

"We should not expect these Agents to follow the archaic customs of our past," Gresij continued.

"I, for one, would like to hear about this challenge," Anjette piped up.

"I'm sure you would," Elsethe said, "and you'd have just as much luck with it as the last time you faced us."

"Last time, it was a hundred to one," Anjette replied. "Pretty sure if it's just the eight of you, I've got this covered."

The squad snickered quietly, impressed among themselves at least at her bravado.

"Anyway, you wouldn't be challenging me, of course," continued Anjette. "You'd be challenging her." She nodded at Agent Grey, who remained impassive.

"My apologies, Agent Grey. We're in unprecedented territory here," Kalavir said.

"Is this challenge some form of one-on-one combat, to determine right to lead?" Agent Grey said.

"More or less," Elsethe said.

"I decline your challenge, on the grounds that I'd prefer eight of you on the mission instead of seven."

That remark certainly got everyone's attention.

"Or perhaps you'd simply prefer the indignity of begging for your life," Agent Grey continued, her tone as even and flat as it ever had been. "I suppose I'd consider that option, in the spirit of cooperation."

The silence that followed was impressive and hostile. Grey didn't care; she was on a tight schedule.

"Send your ship," Sellia said, tired already of the posturing. Ze turned to the enforcers and said, "Stand down from this nonsense. Whether you report to the diplomatic corps or the intelligence service or the military, you *answer* to the Radiant Council, and we've spoken."

Andasir watched the entire exchange in silence, finding it hard to believe that ze would soon be navigating the politics of this mission while trying to get Rindasy to safety.

But taking a ship with interdimensional jump capabilities on the mission was promising, because the options for getting Rindasy to safety might include stealing the ship and leaving the Building altogether.

EPISODE 4.02

I stepped out of the elevator in Prism City just as daylight began to break.

They experienced thirty-hour days here, which Harry had thought was fantastic because it meant they could convince families to stay in the park longer than many places could allow.

Even so, I'd arrived early. It was hours before the park would open. I didn't see any taxis or town cars. If I waited long enough, I could catch a train to the park, but service wasn't running yet.

I managed to find an early-morning café in one of the hotels on Main Street, which got me wondering whether I should get a room here for the night, if I was staying here longer than that, had I truly given up my old life and wandered off into the upper reaches never to return . . . I decided to delay answering those questions, ordered a coffee to go, and began walking to the park.

Along the way, I saw two individuals dressed like tourists prop open the elevator doors in the center of town by clamping a thick metal bar into place. As long as the doors were propped open, no other elevators could stop in Prism City. I sped up before one of them could make eye contact with me.

Had to be Security.

Fuck, I must have arrived in the elevator just ahead of them. If I had lingered even fifteen minutes longer in my suite back at the resort, I wouldn't have been able to get into Prism City at all.

They were assuming that my divination would come true regardless of anything else that might happen on the floor today. If you took that view, then barricading Prism City's elevator before the park even opened couldn't possibly prevent Carissa and Rindasy from taking the roller coaster ride that I'd predicted. And for *that* to be true, then Carissa and Rindasy must already *be* on this floor somewhere.

Just as I reached the edge of town on foot, a little flying rickshaw pulled up beside me and dropped to the street.

The driver said, "Hey there. It's not really safe to walk to the park. Want a ride?"

I did, in fact, want a ride. I asked as I climbed in, "Why is it dangerous?" Looked to me like any number of state highways in the Midwest, surrounded by plains or farmland or whatever, heading on a straight line from point A to point B.

The driver was humanoid, wearing a battered brown flight suit, with a leather helmet and goggles. Ze pulled up zir goggles and gave me a serious stare. Ze said, "They tried to build a 'magical wildlife preserve' as a secondary park once. Beasts of legend and myth, like that. *Tried* being the operational word." Ze flipped zir goggles back down and said, "We shouldn't see anything out of the ordinary. The beasts don't tend to hassle traffic going back and forth. But I'm not too sure how their attitudes might change if they saw a lone individual out for a stroll right at breakfast time."

.   .   .

It took fifteen minutes to get to the park. Towering roller coasters and free fall towers rose above enormous walls painted with gorgeous murals. Prime had seen its share of battles, though. They went to no trouble to hide the turrets atop the walls, for instance, where heavy machine guns seemed to be mounted. As you approached from the highway, you could be sure you were in someone's crosshairs the entire way.

A trip to Wild Massive Prime was considered a pilgrimage among longtime employees of the company. You didn't admit it to your executive bosses or whatever, you kept it on the down low, because HQ wasn't exactly proud of Prime anymore. But among the rank and file, you'd hear whispers about the fabled park that didn't adhere to brand standards. Their T-shirts could say whatever the fuck they wanted.

I'd never gone, because it truly seemed irrelevant to my day job on the creative brain trust. After all, Prime was always excluded from media tie-ins during their initial run in the big parks. But somehow the team here negotiated to cherry-pick those rides when they had outlived their tenure out in the main park system and steadily crammed as many of them into Prime as possible over the years, as though this place was a second-run movie theater that had four hundred available screens or something. You couldn't get away with migrating something as incredibly complex and expensive as the *Storm and Desire: Rise of the Brilliant* experience, but there were many smaller attractions that packed up and traveled quite nicely and were presented here as a kind of immersive, interactive pop culture museum.

I asked the driver to drop me off at the employee entrance, which required us to circle nearly three-quarters of the way around the perimeter of the park to a gate staffed by public safety officers. We wound up in a long but fast-moving line of rickshaws and scooters and rovers and banged-up buggy carriages. The line moved fast because at least eighteen public safety officers were checking IDs at the gate.

I paid the driver with a few swipes from my tablet and jumped out of the rickshaw.

"Good morning," I said as I handed my ID to the first public safety officer who reached me.

The officer scanned my ID with a hand scanner, and we waited an uncomfortably long time for a result to return. Finally, it beeped, and the officer did a double take, realizing what ze had in zir hand: a corporate badge, not a local badge at all.

"You picked a heck of a day for a site visit," the officer said. Ze turned and shouted to someone else to bring a golf cart over for me to use to get around the park.

"Why, what's going on?" I asked.

"Park-wide fire drill today."

The officer pointed me in the direction of the GM's office and sent me on my way.

.   .   .

I threaded my way slowly through the park's backstage area, a much less refined and more chaotic sprawl than what you saw at the Super park or probably any other park monitored closely by corporate. The folks who lived on-site seemed to be mostly show performers, who were always a tight-knit crew in any park, but here they seemed to live and breathe the park life. They might not have their first shows until later in the day, but their tents and trailers were already starting to rev up.

I passed by the cafeteria, where shift workers, performers, and managers alike congregated for morning eats before the park opened. I felt a pang of loneliness observing the camaraderie here, remembering the friends I'd left behind at the Super park after migrating to corporate for my day job. You didn't stay in touch with folks who knew you were suddenly making an astronomical salary while they were still scrambling for hours; the disparity was too much for a typical casual friendship to survive. But I didn't make friends on the creative brain trust, either, because they all sensed that Allegory was grooming me for a larger role than any of them could expect. That's what I told myself, anyway, as I got used to the not-so-subtle disdain they slid my way. I didn't have time to feel sorry for myself given how often I was asked to rewrite their shit.

I zipped up to a small office building, where the GM and other park managers held court when they weren't walking the premises. Inside, it had the atmosphere of an automotive repair shop that had been converted into cubicles and offices.

"Can I help you?" the receptionist asked.

"I'm here to see the General Manager," I said, putting on my finest corporate smile. "I don't have an appointment, but I was hoping he might have a slot on his calendar to chat."

The receptionist laughed, snorted really, and said, "He doesn't keep a 'calendar,' so no, he doesn't have any slots on it."

"I see. Is he in the park today?" Then I added, "I'm visiting from corporate."

"Yeah, no, I got that part," ze said. "He's here somewhere. What's your name?"

"Tabitha Will."

Ze pulled out a walkie-talkie and said, "GM, you got a visitor at the front desk. Tabitha Will from corporate. You busy?"

We waited quite a while, and then the receptionist repeated the call. Finally, a male voice: "On my way."

I sat down in one of the two chairs across from the reception desk, looked around the waiting area, studied the framed photos on the walls of old print magazine covers featuring Harry or some new attraction he'd launched at the park. Wild Massive had truly been one of a kind, once. It was just an observation, mind you; I wasn't feeling sentimental about the good old days before I'd been born.

But I did feel a tiny regret that I had missed the era of Harry Prismatic. It took several hundred people to produce something as epic and fantastic as *Storm and Desire*; by all accounts, Harry surpassed what our team could do, all by himself.

Half an hour later, Roland Prismatic, general manager of Wild Massive Prime, appeared in the office. He wore what appeared to be a battered red smoking jacket over a Wild Massive T-shirt and jeans, and a top hat for good measure. I couldn't tell if he'd just woken up or hadn't gone to sleep yet.

"Tabitha Will?" he said to me, and I nodded. "Didn't realize we were due for an inspection." He waved for me to follow him, and we stepped into a small conference room and closed the door.

"I'm not here for an inspection," I said. "I'm here because . . . I wanted to warn you . . ." And then I just froze, realizing how ludicrous everything I wanted to say actually was. His gaze was unrelenting; he simply waited patiently for me to speak. "You'll have a couple of guests in the park today who are wanted by the Association. I believe the Association will attempt to apprehend them while they're here. Or kill them. I guess that's the other option."

He looked at me even more closely, without a hint of expression. Then he performed a small feat of sleight of hand, producing a cigarette between two fingers and swiftly putting it to his lips.

Then just as quickly, he snatched it from his lips with an irritated look and made it disappear.

"Keep forgetting that I quit," he explained. "Tabitha, this park is hardly Association jurisdiction."

"I realize that. They've barricaded open the elevator in Prism City all the same and stationed people there to make sure it remains barricaded."

That seemed to maybe get his attention. I might possibly have seen the slightest hint of an eyebrow raise. I got the feeling he was frequently a very gregarious and outgoing man who was currently enjoying making his visitor from corporate squirm a bit.

"How do you know who blocked open the elevator?" he asked politely.

Well, this was awkward.

"Gut feeling," I said.

"I admire someone who trusts their instincts, don't get me wrong," he said, "but it could be routine maintenance by the Elevator Guild, don't you think?"

"Even so," I said, "my warning stands. At some point today, the Association will try to apprehend two of your guests by any means necessary."

He leaned back in his chair, studying me, perhaps looking for signs that I was trying to fool him with some elaborate con. His stare was disconcerting.

"That's a very serious statement," he finally said. "I do, despite all appearances and publicity to the contrary, treat the safety of my guests with the utmost concern and gravity. Can you tell me, though, these two guests, these fugitives from the Association, are they dangerous?"

I considered that question carefully. "They're capable of defending themselves," I finally said.

He shifted nervously in his seat and said, "What I mean is, will they endanger *other* guests, or my staff here, as they presumably attempt to elude capture?"

And I realized—I was giving them both the benefit of the doubt, that they'd do the right thing when pressed into a corner and innocent people's lives were at stake. But honestly, I had no idea what they'd do or what they were planning.

"I don't know."

"I'm simply wondering why you came here to warn me about the Association," he said, "instead of warning me about these two fugitives."

"Because fuck the Association," I said impulsively.

He actually smiled and said, "I do see your point."

"I came to warn you about this situation because . . . I don't think these fugitives deserve what's coming."

"I'm sure you understand how that's not my problem whatsoever."

"So if the Association shows up here and asks to search the park, will you cooperate?"

"Some reason I shouldn't? You're corporate; don't you people have a nice cozy relationship with the Association thanks to your popular entertainments? Shouldn't Wild Massive work to preserve that relationship, for the sake of the exciting stories we tell as a company?"

He was fucking with me, I was sure of it, but I couldn't figure out his angle in the slightest.

"Out of curiosity," he said, "how'd you get involved in the first place? How'd you come to know these fugitives are heading here, let alone that their enemies are hot on their trail?"

I sighed and said, "I've been tangled up in their lives for a few days now. I can perform limited divinations, and I spotted them here—in this park, I mean—in my most recent divination. My boss shared that information with the Association. And now I'm here, hoping to undo the mess I've made and maybe save their lives by giving them, or you, or anyone who could use it, a proper warning of the shit that's about to land on this park."

"Who did you say you work for at corporate?" Roland asked.

"Oh. I work for Allegory Paradox."

Roland whistled through his teeth.

"She know you're here?"

I shook my head.

"I think I'm getting a clearer picture. She saw potential in you, in your supernatural skill, she took you under her wing, and then when things got serious, she pressured you to help her find these fugitives. And after you went through with it, you didn't like how it made you feel."

He was right, but I didn't say anything.

"Most people just learn how to live with that feeling. Sounds like you took the next elevator out of corporate and came here to try to literally prevent the future from happening, betraying Allegory in the process. Sound about right?"

"I mean, for all I know, I'm just doing what she expects me to do."

Roland snorted and said, "She's good at her job, Tabitha, she's not omnipotent. You are hardly the first person to fall under the sway of her expert manipulation. That's all it is, plain old-fashioned manipulation of the most basic sort."

"It's not basic at all," I said, instinctively defending her before realizing I was accepting his core point.

He smiled and said, "Fair enough. No one knows the full extent of her grift, but in the meantime, she's making tall towers of cash for all the right people at corporate, so I suspect it's too late to stop her." He paused, then said, "But you do get a gold star for trying to slow her down a little."

I wondered if he realized she was a Muse and if that realization would change his opinion of her at all. I wondered if he'd believe me if I told him. Hell, I wondered why I even believed *her*. Maybe it was just turtles all the way down. I impatiently snapped myself out of the infinite regress and focused on the situation at hand.

"To answer a previous question of yours," Roland said, "when they show up and request to search my park, I do *not* intend to cooperate. Now if you'll excuse me, I have many preparations to attend to."

And with that, he threw the door open and strode out into the din and controlled chaos of the larger office beyond.

The receptionist came to boot me out of the conference room because some managers needed it, so I drifted out of the office altogether. From the sidewalk in front of the office, paths led off in several directions into their backstage regions. I hadn't been to a new park in so long, I'd forgotten the dizzying sensation of feeling both perfectly at home and completely alienated within the same environment. Like, I could get *lost* on these paths. They had more sprawl here than I was used to because they weren't constrained by an existing city when they set up shop.

I had no way of knowing if Roland had taken me seriously, no way of knowing if he'd pass on my warning to Carissa and Rindasy. I also had no way of finding them, because it hadn't occurred to me to ask Roland if he knew where they were. Maybe they were on a VIP list and eating an exclusive breakfast at the top of the Space Elevator, or maybe they'd snuck in and were hiding in a fun house or under a roller coaster until the park opened.

Gradually, I allowed myself to admit that the best option was to find a quiet place to write and hope that I picked up some clues via divination. I wasn't accustomed to writing with a goal in mind. I never imagined that was possible. I mean, shoot, if I could sit down with a goal and pick up actionable clues, then I'd win all the lotteries and solve all the crossword puzzles and all that. God, I'd be insufferable. I'd be drowning in wealth, but I'd be insufferable.

Anyway, that didn't seem like the spirit of the ability as I experienced it. To be fair, I wasn't looking for specific clues, like "What are the exact coordinates of Carissa and Rindasy?

Show me on an oversize illustrated tourist map of Wild Massive Prime." I just wanted to give my book one more chance to give me any clues at all about how today would unfold.

At corporate HQ, they reserved desks for visiting execs to use when they came to visit. Maybe they had a similar arrangement back at the GM's office building. As I turned to head back, a sudden flash of light startled me, and when the spots began to fade, Nicholas Solitude stood on the landing in front of the office doors.

A light round of applause surfaced from the nearby trailers and camps. I mean, sure, his entrance was snazzy.

Nicholas smiled and waved, then came down the steps to join me on the sidewalk.

I'd never met him, but I recognized him all the same. He wore a VIP visitor's badge clipped to his jacket that confirmed his identity. And he, similarly, consulted the corporate badge clipped to my own jacket.

"Tabitha," he said, "my name is Nicholas Solitude. Do you have any additional appointments this morning, or could I persuade you to join me for coffee and a conversation?"

I shook my head and said, "You did not just travel through space and potentially time just to offer me coffee."

"Well, also conversation. Topics would be discussed. And the coffee will be good."

I didn't want to sound hysterical or whatever, but his breezy tone was jarring against the backdrop of knowing the park was in serious danger. I did say, "This park is going to be invaded or attacked or something today, did you know that?" Then I realized who I was talking to and said, "Of course you knew that. You probably even know what happens and that's why you're so casual right now."

"No, I don't know the outcome of whatever might take place today. I'm suggesting we have coffee in my bunker in the tunnels under the park, though, which is likely the safest place to be in the event the park is invaded or attacked."

308 · SCOTTO MOORE

"Sorry, you seem to think I should trust you because you're a famous person, but I'm not going to your murder bunker where no one can hear me scream."

"Ah, I see my long history of not murdering people in a bunker hasn't circulated as widely as I'd hoped."

"Why are we having this conversation? What are you even doing here?"

"Yes, perhaps I should've led with this. Your grandmother Delia suggested that I reach out to you when the time was right."

The look on my face must've been something else, judging by his startled reaction. I was frozen in shock just hearing her name out of the blue like that.

"She couldn't say when or what the circumstances would be, but she planted the seed with me, anyway. When I learned you'd arrived in the park, I had just enough time to consider what you might need or want, and I've come up with two suggestions. Which I'd love to discuss over coffee—in my murder bunker."

I nodded, accepting his offer.

"Excellent," he said. "The spacetime machine only allows one passenger, so we'll need to steal a golf cart."

"I'm from corporate. They gave me a golf cart to use while I'm here."

"I see. Well, in that case, let's try to exceed the posted speed limit just a tad to preserve a sense of adventure."

.   .   .

Storm and Desire wasn't the only show ever produced by Wild Massive. I mean, they weren't all runaway successes like *Storm and Desire* was, but some pretty good stuff came out over the years.

One show I watched obsessively when I was a kid was called *Solitude Chronicles*. It depicted the adventures of young Nicholas Solitude during his apprenticeship in the Archives. He'd eventually become Master Archivist and hold the position for quite some time, but the show imagined that his Junior Archivist days were spent having adventures.

Because, see, the Archives were real, housing a collection of trophies, technologies, and artifacts collected (stolen) during the Association's exploration of its floors of the Building. But they also held a set of much older artifacts that supposedly survived from the mythological era prior to the formation of Parliament. You could see the original catalog of the bottom fifty thousand floors that formed the basis of the Association's territorial claim. You could see the actual treaty document itself, which was so charged with supernatural intent that you had to stand behind layers of warded plastishield because sometimes it would emit metaphysical lightning, like discharging static electricity, for reasons nobody understood.

And according to *Solitude Chronicles*, the Archives housed a one-of-a-kind spacetime machine. In the first episode, Nicholas is asked to transfer the spacetime machine to a different exhibit hall, and he sort of mishandles it, and it bonds to him. It's got these nanotendrils that slide into his nervous system, enabling him to pilot by sheer thought—although the spacetime machine is persnickety, and it's got "error correction" in case it doesn't agree with Nicholas about their precise destination.

So Nicholas in the show uses the spacetime machine to manipulate the course of history in the Association's favor, usually while saving countless lives by correcting vicious "anomalies," and then in the end, he always brings a new piece of (stolen) treasure back to the Archives and they all marvel at the wonders of this here Building, and that's the show, just Nicholas traveling through spacetime on a never-ending quest to catalog (steal) the amazing things reality has to offer.

Nicholas was played by heartthrob Cody Charles, and I admit to having more than one little heart in my notebooks back then with *Cody + Lily* written in them. He was such a rugged but charming hero that you just waved off how he trampled all over the fates of newly explored floors to ensure they became better citizens of the Association or better able to protect themselves from the big ugly menace of the season that always lurked in the background.

I don't know who came up with this show, but unlike *Storm and Desire,* only an infinitesimal percentage of *Solitude Chronicles* was based on facts. Nicholas was never a Junior Archivist. In his youth, he was an outspoken radical who hated the Association's iron grip on anything it could reach. You can't get any of his books or treatises from that period because the Association likes to disappear people who get caught distributing them. He jumped the queue of more experienced archivists to become Master Archivist, and most people assume that once he had the keys to the entire Archives, it was easy for him to steal the spacetime machine.

But if you ever happen to be doing a school report on anything and everything that heartthrob Cody Charles has ever done in his life, your diligent research might dig up a few stray interviews that Nicholas gave after he left the Archives. And in one of these interviews, he admitted he already possessed the spacetime machine when he asked for the Master Archivist job, and they said yes because "the spacetime machine could be used for good or evil, and they were hoping to use it for evil"—if they could get on his good side.

In one interview, when asked where he got the spacetime machine, he said, "Someday when I'm done using it, I go back in time and give it to myself." Which doesn't make sense for like eight reasons, but the interviewer doesn't clue in that it's a joke. There's only one other surviving interview from that period in which the interviewer asks him that question, and he just says he got it in a thrift store, cheap.

History never revealed his reasons for becoming Master Archivist, nor what prompted him to quit after a long tenure. He goes missing for a few hundred years, and then turns up in the Explorers Guild, writing popular reports from far above the border about the wonders they come across, the challenges they face, alla that. The reports were so good that Wild Massive tried to make a musical series called *Explore!* based on the adventures of Nicholas with the Guild. But Cody Charles got sucked into a weird cult, and recasting him tested like shit, so they shelved it.

We didn't speak as we zipped along the paths through back-stage. We emerged onto a road that passed behind the concert auditorium and terminated at a ramp that led down to underground tunnels where supply trucks could unload and so on. We arrived at a hidden bunker occupied by the Explorers Guild, where I could relax on a couch while Nicholas made coffee and attempted the feat of chatting amiably with me.

"Delia was a memorable character in camp and on our expeditions," he said. "We were friendly toward each other and perhaps even became friends for a time. She had a surprising combination of skills, which you may not have known about. She was an experienced geologist. She could repair lasers without voiding the warranties. Hard to 'sell' her on anything. Best you could do is lay out options and walk away, if that makes sense. She kept to—"

"Is she still alive?" I blurted out. "I mean, are you in the future right now, *your* future, and when you go back to your present day, she'll be alive?"

He brought me my coffee and sat down opposite me on a different couch.

"This is my present day," he told me. "You'd be surprised how much time I actually spend in the present day for someone traveling with a spacetime machine."

"Okay, so but what specifically did she tell you about me?"

"Well . . . she told me about your divinations, for starters."

"But she didn't *know* about them! She was gone before I started having them!"

"Tabitha, you were perhaps too young to notice, but Delia had her own methods for isolating strands of the future and weaving them together in surprising ways. Like I said earlier, she could plant seeds that flowered over long windows of time. I only knew her long enough to see evidence of it a few times, but if her stories were to be believed, she was quite a gardener in her day."

I suppose it made sense that she could "isolate strands of the future" or whatever. We both used the same capture glass, so we both probably got blasted with the same Muse influence. But she was a lot older when it happened to her, and we wound up with different ways to express the changes that happened to us. I got to see the future in short, immediate bursts; maybe she saw it more like an unfolding tapestry that she could occasionally interpret or influence.

I was guessing about all this, of course, because she never bothered explaining it to me. Nicholas was right; I hadn't noticed anything unusual about her. I tried to imagine the foresight required to "plant a seed" that would result in Nicholas Solitude crossing paths with me nearly a decade after her death to offer me coffee and advice, and my mind just filled up with static for a couple of seconds before I dropped that train of thought.

"Now can you tell me what brought you here today?" he asked.

"I saw two fugitives from the Association, riding a roller coaster in this park, during daylight hours today. I know their names. I've even met one of them. That was yesterday's divination about today. I handed that information over to my boss and, through her, to Parliament. I happen to know that Parliament and the Shai-Manak want these two fugitives dead, and now they have a location for them: here in this park, at some point during daylight hours.

"And I would love to say that I was under duress or that I was pressured to hand over that information. Or that I was manipulated, like Roland said, by a master manipulator who doesn't just plant seeds, she engineers tectonic shifts. How do you resist that when you're the golden child who's learning how to *do* that? And the answer is, you have a fucking spine and a moral code and you walk out *before* you give Parliament the information, not immediately after. I wasn't under duress; I just didn't feel like arguing or whatever.

"Anyway, what brought me here was that I decided to exploit a loophole. I told Parliament where the fugitives would be. I never promised Parliament a clean, lazy, unobstructed shot at them. I came here to try to find them and warn them. These two could fight back. Or they could flee deeper into the Building where the Association will never look.

"And then if Parliament or my boss try to coerce me into tracking them down a second time, I think by then I'll have developed enough of a spine and a moral code to say no."

Nicholas sat quietly and sipped his coffee for a few moments after I was done with my rant. I maybe didn't need to tell him all that. I was just . . . searching for forgiveness that I wouldn't get from anybody but Carissa and Rindasy, and I especially didn't expect it from them. And then I worried that I trusted Nicholas so quickly just because he claimed he knew my grandmother. I mean, he'd been the Master Archivist once upon a time, a high-powered role in the Association, maybe he still had ties with them, and why did I just remember that now instead of *before* confessing I was here to fuck them over?

"Well," he said finally, after the silence had gone past awkward into some new territory that felt almost punitive, like he wasn't quite convinced by my performance and could I take it again but with a little more fervor. "How do you plan to find these fugitives to deliver your warning?"

"Oh, I've reached the end of my plan." He probably got asked this next question a lot, but I had to ask: "Can you skip ahead to the future a little bit and see how it turns out? Wouldn't that give Roland better information to work with than what I told him?"

"Whenever you're about to suggest that I travel to the future to find a solution," he said, "assume I've already been to the future and we're now implementing that very solution."

Yes, Nicholas Solitude, renowned spacetime traveler, that was a smooth, well-rehearsed answer. I hadn't seen *Solitude Chronicles* since I was a kid, but I would not be surprised to learn that he'd cribbed that line from the show.

"Convenient," I said.

"Traveling to the future is full of unexpected risk, Tabitha. Whereas your skill, your ability to peer into the future while sitting safely in the present, is rich with potential. And Delia grew to where she *influenced* the future from her safe perch in the present."

I nodded and said, "My boss is trying to teach me how to 'nudge' the future with my writing."

"Ah, so you're already thinking along those lines. Yes, you're no mere oracle, at least you won't be when your skill is fully developed. Well, here are my two suggestions for you. You can take either or both, or you can reject them outright, and I'll have kept my word to Delia. The first suggestion is what I would call an 'iterative' step for you. I'd have you undertake a series of writing exercises."

"I'm sorry—what?"

"Observational exercises. My hypothesis is that if you hone and enhance your descriptive techniques for depicting the present moment, if you strengthen and deepen your articulation of the *now* . . . you might gain deeper influence over the *future* scenes you write."

"I see. And where are you getting these exercises from?"

My voice must've been dripping with skepticism, because he said, very crisply, "My dear, I have written seven hundred twenty-four novels and one thousand twenty-two scholarly texts in my time, not to mention thousands upon thousands of treatises, research papers, and Guild reports. I'm perfectly capable of fashioning exercises based on my own expertise. Now these exercises will all use a specific question as your prompt, and by the end, you should derive the answer to that exact question—and no other—via your writing. This would be an iterative step toward a much more purposeful process."

"Uhhh . . . I mean, sure, I'm game to try that. Maybe when this is all over, you know, if they don't nuke the park or whatever, I can try these—"

"No, you're missing the point. You *have* a specific question you need answered. Where are the fugitives? I'm proposing using these exercises to find them."

"What? How fast do you think I write? Even if I cranked out pages from now until whenever they nuke the park—"

"You can take your time, Tabitha. I will loan you the space-time machine. Spend as much time as you like on these exercises until you're satisfied you know where the fugitives are."

"And traveling to the past isn't risky like traveling to the future?"

"Traveling to the past is much safer, my dear, because it's already happened, and nothing you can do will unhappen it."

My mind was starting to hurt. I didn't want to offend him with this next question, but I needed to know the answer: "But if I can go back in time, can't I go back to a spot where I know one of the fugitives actually was and warn her then?"

"You can, if you prefer. That would fall under the category of rejecting the first suggestion. You'd deprive yourself of a valuable training opportunity in favor of getting straight to the fugitives, and for all I know, that's the right thing to do. But it's not exactly in the spirit of what Delia had in mind for this moment."

Damn. He sure knew how to play that card with me.

"What's the second suggestion?" I asked warily.

"This one's more dramatic. Delia mentioned you were just an adolescent when she gave you her capture glass and you wore it for the first time."

"The *only* time," I said.

"Yes, I figured as much. But, Tabitha, capture glasses are meant to be worn more than once."

EPISODE 4.03

The previous night, the night before Tabitha's arrival at the park, the night before Nicholas met Tabitha for the first time, after gazing out at the beautiful, inexplicable menace of the chasm through ancient coin-operated telescopes, Nicholas convinced Carissa and Rindasy to join him for a bite to eat and some potentially interesting people-watching upstairs, where Roland had invited them to close out their evening.

The restaurant on the second floor of the Space Elevator was a weird but welcoming scene, like stumbling into a wedding reception after the married couple had split and the families had gone home, and it was just their rowdy friends left to finish off the booze and harass the DJ. The décor seemed to Carissa like some avant-garde designer had been hired to create an "alien cocktail bar in outer space" set for a retro sci-fi B movie, but at the last minute, someone had shouted, "Make sure it also feels like we're in a circus!" The resulting mishmash of thematic touches was pleasantly disorienting.

There were two general sections: an extremely well-appointed bar, surrounded by a small cloud of standing cocktail tables where people could mingle, nibble appetizers, and gawk; and a proper restaurant that served a strange variety of cuisines, said to be Harry's favorite dishes from the many disparate floors he visited in his days as a young touring magician. Neither Carissa nor Rindasy drank alcohol or used intoxicants, but getting a good meal sounded appealing, and Carissa wanted a chance to observe Roland in his element. They grabbed a small table for themselves, tucked away from the rest of the patrons.

Roland held court at the center of a grand and opulent high-backed booth, in the company of a large group that appeared to be comprised of his good friends. Several cast members from the big afternoon magic show were here as well, mingling with Roland's friends, acting as minor in-park celebrities for the night.

They were all dressed up to varying degrees beyond what you'd expect to see from people who'd spent the day wandering the streets of a theme park. Carissa got the feeling Roland was one of those people who genuinely wanted everyone to just "have fun" and "get along," and she was reasonably cool with that as an operating philosophy of life.

Then, to Carissa's immense surprise, she realized that pop star Jaxxer Kwee was currently maintaining a secondary island of influence in the restaurant, at a similarly sprawling booth across the room from Roland's. She learned from one of the servers that Jaxxer's tour had stopped at the park for a scheduled show earlier that night.

Jaxxer Kwee originally built her career by riding the elevators around to cherry-pick the best songwriters from multiple Earth floors, recruiting them to write and produce her debut album, *The Sun Isn't Real and the Moon Wants to Kill Me*. It was hard enough being a star on one Earth; Jaxxer's original goal was to be a star on as many of them as possible. As she'd attest in later interviews, something she didn't realize was that the more Earth floors you saw, the more radicalized you became, and her music pivoted hard toward inciting rebellion. After falling out of favor with a number of tour promoters as a result, she and her band primarily toured other floors of the Building now, giving Earth floors a wide berth.

Carissa was a fan of Jaxxer Kwee's music, although she rarely listened to it anymore. It had been a balm to eventually find music she recognized out in the Building after fleeing Minneapolis with no possessions to her name. But now so far from home, with no intention to return, that same music brought her enormous spikes of sadness.

She'd tried to visit a few different Earths to see if she could be happy in some other Minneapolis, only to reach the disturbing conclusion that she'd been living in the "lite" version of American fascism compared to what you got elsewhere, and the more American fascism there was in a given Earth floor, the more the whole floor was poisoned overall by its effects. You could definitely do better if you were willing to explore the Building a little bit. Fuck, you could do better just by living in an elevator with a cloudlet as your best friend.

Now here she was on the verge of tears as she remembered seeing Jaxxer Kwee play live for the first and only time. She'd used her talent at the door to get in, because she was still underage—risking her brother's ire if he ever found out his little sister had snuck out into the world by herself. Then Carissa was front and center, pressed against the stage, watching Jaxxer attack all the songs off her first record like she might never get a chance to play them ever again. Carissa's experience at that concert was borderline spiritual, felt like the very first time she understood the raw urgency of life and the hunger underneath every moment.

And now, there was Jaxxer Kwee, inexplicably crossing paths with Carissa a hundred and some years later, and it wasn't weird at all. Jaxxer was performing another concert in the park tomorrow night, and Carissa might be able to see it.

She realized she hadn't had something to look forward to in so long that she didn't remember what proper anticipation even felt like. Oh sure, she'd deliberately lived an ascetic lifestyle for many years and had been perfectly satisfied with it as recently as a couple of days ago, no question about that; but that's what made this moment all the more surreal.

Carissa's light reverie was interrupted by a sharp beep that came from the wristwatch Nicholas was wearing. He checked its display screen.

"Interesting," he said after contemplating what he saw for a few minutes. "Another instance of the spacetime machine is nearby."

"There's more than one?" Rindasy asked.

"No, but now and again, I cross temporal paths with myself. The spacetime machine has a handshake protocol for these events, which alerts me so that I can avoid running into myself in the same physical location."

"Why? What happens if you meet yourself?"

"I don't know. I keep avoiding it. If it's me from the future, I don't want to inadvertently learn more about my fate than I already know. If it's me from the past, I don't want him to see how far adrift I've strayed from the ideals of my youth." He finally looked up at them and said, "It's very close."

"How close?" Carissa asked.

"I don't have sufficient resolution on this watch to pinpoint it. According to this, it's right on top of us, so . . . somewhere in the Space Elevator is my guess." He began slipping off the backpack so that he could view the situation on the better display built into the spacetime machine.

At the same time, Carissa decided to try her new talent, clairvoyance, extending her awareness throughout the entirety of the Space Elevator, looking for another Nicholas Solitude. With the amount of distraction in the dining room, she was barely able to concentrate and peer out to the perimeter. The din of laughter and noisy conversation around her caused momentary static blips in her psychic field of view, causing her to almost miss what she was looking for—or rather, what she didn't realize she was looking for until she spotted it.

"You've gotta be kidding me," she said, dropping out of her light trance state.

Almost simultaneously, Nicholas said, "That's unusual."

"You're not the pilot of the other one," she told him.

"No, it seems not. The other spacetime machine is currently using a guest profile for travel. Restricted function access, limited window of travel, remote recall enabled . . . it's legitimate, signed with my key. The only thing missing is the identity of the guest pilot; those fields were all ignored."

"I know who it is," Carissa said, standing up. "Let me check this out. If I need help, I'll signal you." She made her way to the stairway to the observation deck and disappeared.

.   .   .

The eerie spectacle of the chasm, smeared across the night sky near the horizon, was unavoidably seductive to look at, capturing her attention as she came down the stairs. The overhead lights were dimmed on the side of the deck facing the chasm, probably to enhance the view, allowing the distant glow to take center stage. She realized it'd be trivial to use her talents to blow out the glass in front of her and lift off into the night sky toward the chasm, to get an even closer look. But she hadn't lost her senses. Not yet, she thought to herself grimly. She'd find a way to be satisfied with the view from a distance.

She casually strolled toward the coin-operated telescopes facing the chasm, which were mostly unoccupied except for the one at the far end. At the last telescope, an individual wearing Wild Massive schwag and a backpack-mounted spacetime machine looked out at the chasm, oblivious to Carissa's approach.

"Don't suppose you have a spare nickel," Carissa said.

Tabitha looked up from her telescope to see Carissa and for a moment was genuinely delighted.

"Oh good," said Tabitha.

"What are you doing here?"

"Sure, yeah, let's just dive right into it. Wait, is Rindasy with you?"

Carissa said nothing.

Tabitha sighed. "Okay, first, you recognize this?" She pivoted to show off the spacetime machine under a dim overhead light.

Carissa nodded and said, "Fancy. Where'd you get it?"

"Thrift store," Tabitha joked. "Just kidding. Nicholas Solitude loaned it to me. You know Nicholas, right? Because you traveled with the Guild?"

"Three separate stints, yeah. Never heard of him loaning out his precious baby, though."

"Well, he configured some constraints into it so I don't just run off with it. It was for a good cause, though. I was trying to find you, and it worked!" Then she had a realization and said, "Is Nicholas here? Is he upstairs in the restaurant?"

Carissa nodded.

Tabitha nodded back, smiling as though she'd solved a riddle, and said, "This must be old hat to him, but I'm experiencing my first temporal strange loop, and it's a little exhilarating. But that's not the point of why I'm here. I came here because I wanted to warn you that the Association and the Shai-Manak are working together now to find you and Rindasy."

"I know."

"Oh. You do?"

"A former colleague of Rindasy's already warned us. Some kind of peace conference, only they won't sign anything until Rindasy and I are dead. Sound about right?"

"Yeah, it does, only I think my warning is worse than that."

"Worse than that *how*?"

"Well, you remember my boss, Allegory Paradox, yeah?"

Carissa nodded, immediately disliking the direction this was heading.

"Yeah, so she and the Prime Minister happen to be tight. And she wanted me to help them find you, which I originally resisted, but then she got me high on capture glass energy and I saw a glimpse of the full narrative vision that's driving her, and it was so *convincing* that I just . . . I caved, Carissa, I gave them what they wanted."

The air around the two of them seemed to suddenly crackle with a tiny jolt of static electricity, and the lights in their vicinity dimmed just for a moment. Tabitha understood before Carissa did that Carissa herself was the cause of those effects.

Carissa said, "What did you give them, Tabitha?"

"A divination. I saw a clear picture of you and Rindasy riding in the front car of a roller coaster, during daylight tomorrow in this park."

If Carissa felt betrayed, she gave no indication, and the wild psychic energy she'd inadvertently released a moment ago was now under her control. It didn't surprise her to hear that Tabitha was weaker-willed than Allegory Paradox. Tabitha had lived a weird life, sure, but she hadn't lived in *fear* for much of it. She did the math, and the way she figured it, Tabitha had earned considerable credit with her for reconnecting her with Lorelei. And then she'd burned all of it by giving up her location to the Association.

Now they were back to square one, two people who barely knew each other and had no reason to trust each other. Except Tabitha had come here to warn her that the Association was headed this way while there was still time to do something. That was probably not without risk to her.

Not as much risk as Carissa was now facing, of course. She wanted to punch Tabitha through the window behind her with a psychic fist.

She chose instead to stay calm and said, "Thanks for the heads-up. Now get the fuck out of here."

After only a moment's hesitation, Tabitha vanished in a flash of light.

. . .

Carissa returned to her table with Rindasy and Nicholas and explained the situation.

"I don't suppose you have any idea why you loan your space-time machine to her," Carissa said, imagining the answer would be no.

"Some idea, perhaps," said Nicholas. "I was able to grab the log from her spacetime machine. She's made several trips, but the machine's current constraints only allow her to travel within the past week, and they prohibit her from visiting the future beyond her trip's point of origin. Which is here in the park, tomorrow. When she's ready to return the machine to me, it's configured to bring her back here moments after she originally left."

"So she might be *here* when the trouble starts?" Rindasy said.

"It does seem unwise. But leave that aside for a moment. Bigger picture—if she's been telling Carissa the truth about her divination skill, and the window of her future perception is only a day . . . you could stay a day ahead of her for the rest of your lives if you were careful, but as long as she continues feeding them information, they'd always be right behind you."

"Nah, we're not doing that," Carissa said. "Absolutely not."

"What did you have in mind as an alternative?" Rindasy asked.

"We stay right here," Carissa replied, "and when they get here, we kill every fucking one of them."

That sentiment obviously caught Nicholas off guard. Rindasy, to zir credit, looked thoughtful as ze considered the idea.

"So . . . doing murders and violence is your . . . hmm," said Nicholas.

"I suppose I would settle for scaring the shit out of them," Carissa admitted.

"You mean to fight them—in the park?" Nicholas asked, incredulous at that idea, too. "Think of all the guests you'd endanger."

"I would endanger zero guests, Nicholas," Carissa replied. "She said it wouldn't happen before daylight. Plenty of time to clear the park of any late-night employees and keep anyone from showing up for work tomorrow."

"I see, so you simply plan to use the park as your battleground," Nicholas said.

"Exactly. I mean, if Wild Massive is going to sic their baby magic-user on us, it's only fair that they suffer some extraordinary property damage as a side effect."

They were surprised to learn that Roland Prismatic had quietly drifted close enough to their table to overhear their discussion—a skill cultivated in the interest of keeping the park safe. Naturally, he had other ideas.

"Did it ever occur to you that you could simply leave the park and take your trouble with you?" he asked them. "They'll show up, I'll turn up my palms, and with a melodramatic smile, I'll say, 'We're so sorry, but they fled from you fascist scumbags hours ago.' Did that thought cross your unsympathetic minds, or was it all just 'let's blow up some roller coasters, it'll be fun' as far as the strategic thinking was concerned?"

"They'll search your park whether you tell them that or not," said Carissa. "They have no reason to trust you."

"They will absolutely not search this park without my consent," Roland replied.

"Uh . . . yes, they will. They don't care about your consent, and unless you have a standing army waiting in the wings, it won't even be hard for them."

"Oh, listen to you. Now you're a military genius? Now you understand proper tactics for resisting a siege?" He finished the last of his cocktail and signaled for a server to bring him another one. "I don't mean to be dismissive—"

"Yes, you do," said Carissa.

"Oh, now you're also a *mind reader*?" he protested.

"Well, yes, but I'm not doing it right now."

"Enough! I've heard enough. There are attractions in this park that are older than I am, do you understand me? Irreplaceable artifacts of a historical era that is lost to us. My father's era. You will not engage in combat inside this park. And they will not pursue you inside this park, either, by the way. They won't get past the gates, nor will they come over the walls. We don't survive here solely by the good graces of our neighbors on nearby floors. We can defend ourselves here, have done so many times before, and are prepared to do so again." He paused for dramatic effect, then said, "Let the bastards come. This is our floor."

Roland's powerful showman's voice had inadvertently silenced the dining room. The VIP guests at every table in sight of Roland and Carissa were now paying rapt attention to their discussion.

From several tables away, Jaxxer Kwee interrupted the silence. She asked, "Sorry, but which bastards are you talking about?"

Roland glanced around at the assembled VIPs in the dining

room, a mix of familiar and new faces, and decided to address the whole room.

"Show of hands, please," he said, "how many people here tonight are card-carrying citizens of the United Association of Interdimensional Travelers?"

Every last bit of ambient conversation in the dining room stopped abruptly. The servers stopped moving on their intricate paths to and from the kitchen. Diners slowly swiveled in their seats to get a better view of the whole scene.

No one raised their hands.

"Tonight, friends," Roland continued, "we're harboring two fugitives from the Association. Someone has betrayed their location, and as a result, we will almost certainly receive an unannounced visit from the Association tomorrow."

The implications to everyone were immediately clear. You couldn't really imagine a favorable or positive outcome from receiving any attention at all from the Association, let alone so far outside their jurisdiction.

"But Wild Massive is not a signatory to their treaty, nor do we share extradition, and here at Wild Massive Prime, we do not allow thugs, hooligans, and terrorists to make demands and expect us to simply bow to their wishes. Since my father's day, this park has defended itself against bandits, pirates, militias, angry mobs, and outright villains. I have no doubt we'll rise to the occasion the next time an existential threat rears its head our direction. Which will probably be tomorrow.

"Now the small print on your passes clearly states that the price of admission to Wild Massive Prime does not include a guarantee that you'll enjoy or even survive the experience. Nevertheless, I will personally waive our 'no refund' policy for each of you if you choose to gather your belongings and evacuate the floor tonight. Daisy at the front desk will arrange your credit."

As Roland turned back to Carissa, the dining room rapidly filled up with the anxious chatter of the patrons.

"Nice speech. You're a natural," said Carissa. "Just so we're clear on what you're signing up for . . . the best-case scenario is that they send an extraction team to grab us or kill us. The go-to extraction team for Parliament will be Dimension Force."

"The Shai-Manak will send a team of enforcers as well," Rindasy said. "We're somewhat fortunate in that the best of our people are currently occupying floor 49,500. But we mustn't take any enforcer for granted."

"Worst-case scenario," Carissa continued, "they send Fleet to bomb the park into oblivion. For reference, they bombed half a continent once to kill a tribe of fifty people, so your park is a speck of dust in scale when it comes to killing two people."

"You assume I'd ever allow a bomb to go off in the vicinity of my park," Roland said.

"Probably won't be a single bomb, I can tell you that much," she replied.

"Yes, I acknowledge your ever-increasing escalation of the threat we face. Last I heard, our distant compatriots the Shai-Manak were proving Fleet's susceptibility to magic, and magic is something we happen to have pouring out of the park's thaum generators. Now I'd like to know exactly why they want the two of you. I'm presuming it's a terrible injustice that I can use to motivate my people, and if it isn't, you'll pardon me if I manufacture an injustice to use on your behalf. But first, I need to summon our people to prepare for an invasion."

"Thank you, Roland," said Nicholas.

Roland smiled grimly and said, "We have a term among the veterans here for our response to a day like tomorrow. We call it a *park-wide fire drill,* my friends, and as far as I'm concerned, the drill has officially begun."

. . .

Roland swiftly established the dining room of the Space Elevator as the command center for the fire drill. He liked the symbolic advantage of sitting atop the highest point in the park, overlooking all of Prime and Prism City and the surrounding environment. Several tables were commandeered, and diners were moved elsewhere in the restaurant. When Carissa, Rindasy, and Nicholas were asked to move, Rindasy split off to hover near the center of activity, eavesdropping on the proceedings and waiting for an opening to chat with Roland about how ze could support the park's magical line of defense.

Carissa and Nicholas retreated to the bar and watched the situation unfold in front of them. Roland's core staff began to arrive and the place took on a frenetic quality as they broke into teams to ramp up activity throughout the park.

"If I didn't know you better," Nicholas said, "I'd suspect you used your talent to convince Roland to protect you. This is a fairly incredible response to your dilemma."

"He's itching for a fight, you can tell," Carissa replied.

"Perhaps. All those conflicts he mentioned—the pirates, the bandits, and so on—happened on his father's watch."

"So he wants to prove himself by beating back the Association? Instead of just kicking us out of his park?"

"This park is a target now, whether you're here tomorrow or not. Roland needs to prove that he can keep the park safe. Prime isn't like the other parks. There are people living on-site who were with Harry when he scouted this floor and decided to stay. Whole generations of families have been raised here. He'll evacuate as many people as he can, but there's a crew called *the fire brigade* that trains to defend the park, and they'll be taking orders from Roland in the face of a real threat for the first time tomorrow."

They fell silent for a moment, listening to Roland's booming voice as it carried across the room. He was calling contacts on neighboring floors, activating an informal network of potential reinforcements. There were hotels on nearby floors that catered to guests of the park, and if nothing else, he hoped they could at least keep those guests on their respective floors tomorrow until they got word that it was safe. He was not getting many responses, but it was the middle of the night on those floors as well, so maybe he'd hear something as dawn approached.

Roland suddenly called out, "Nicholas, you busy? Got a favor to ask you."

Nicholas left Carissa at the bar and quickly fell into a discussion with Roland and one of his assistants. Rindasy was heavy in discussion with a pair of engineer-looking types in battered work clothes. She sat alone for several minutes, wondering if she should offer her talents to help in some way.

She realized that a woman from Jaxxer Kwee's table had been circulating around the dining room and was now headed toward her. The woman wore a Jaxxer tour T-shirt but had acquired the Prime edition of the Wild Massive bomber jacket, featuring the original feral design of Helpless the Bunny instead of his slick, modern look. A couple of passes—one for the park, one for the tour—dangled from a lanyard around her neck.

"Hi," the woman said as she approached. "I'm the tour manager for Jaxxer. We're just—"

"You're her sister, right?" Carissa said. "Bezzany, did I get that right?"

"Uh, yeah! Are you a fan?"

"I snuck into a club when I was a kid to see her on her first tour."

"That was like a hundred years ago," Bezzany said, clearly impressed. "So what'd you think of the show tonight?"

"Well, funny story, I didn't know she was playing here tonight, so I was probably wandering around in a museum while the show was happening."

"Oh no!"

"I thought I'd stay and see tomorrow's show, but that's assuming the park is still standing."

"Well, we've already canceled tomorrow's show," Bezzany said. "That's actually the reason I came over to chat. The tour came in three jump ships, and if we leave our gear behind, we can pretty much give everyone in this dining room a ride, so I'm coordinating an evacuation plan. We're leaving in less than an hour, probably. Would you like to join us?"

Carissa realized, or admitted to herself, that underneath her bravado, she would absolutely love to get on one of those ships and get the hell out of here. But she had way too much of Kellin's voice running through her mind, echoes of the speeches he used to give before a fight that psyched everybody up while threatening brutal punishment if you were a coward. He never had to deliver on the promise of punishment, because the Brilliant never seemed to feel scared with Kellin around.

Even with most of their individual talents all coiled up inside her, she wasn't ready to face a fight like this without Kellin around.

"I'm staying, actually," she said. "I'm one of the reasons this is all going down."

"Ohhh . . . are you one of the fugitives?"

Carissa nodded and said, "I need to stay here and punch the Association in the face as hard as possible."

"If you don't mind me asking . . . why is the Association after you?"

"Because I had the audacity to survive the last couple of times they tried to kill me." Then she added, "I don't know if you ever heard about this, but I'm from the Earth floor they nuked."

Bezzany's face seemed to heat up with sudden rage. "I did hear about that. Found out when we tried to book the same clubs for a tour the next year. You couldn't route messages to that floor anymore, the elevators wouldn't stop there anymore . . ."

"Well, the elevator stops probably didn't exist anymore."

"But there's always an elevator in Asia on an Earth floor, and that one stopped responding, and I mean people had no idea what happened to North America, and everyone else was terrified it was going to happen to them, too, so people desperately wanted off the floor. The only people who got out were the people rich enough to own their own jump ships. I'm talking hundreds of people, not even thousands."

"What happened to everyone else?"

330 · SCOTTO MOORE

"That's what I'm saying—who knows? What do you imagine happens to an ecosphere when a continent gets nuked? These rich people managed to smuggle out footage from the floor, but it wasn't signed with Association keys so no one believed it was real, and then it started disappearing from the network anyway, and if you reuploaded it, you got a nice, friendly visit from Security. Jaxxer started talking about it a lot on her next tour, and we were worried people were going to think she was a conspiracy weirdo, but then they revoked her citizenship and said if she ever came back, she'd be detained indefinitely. So we're not welcome on Association floors anymore." Then Bezzany sighed heavily and said, "Their citizens have no idea any of this ever happened."

Carissa didn't know what to say. She was a little ashamed that she hadn't spent a single passing moment wondering about the fates of the rest of the people on that floor. Not because she had no sense of compassion but because she understood how absolutely powerless she was in the face of the grinding machinery of the Association.

Bezzany reached into her jacket pocket and retrieved a reflective pass like one of the ones hanging from her lanyard. She offered it to Carissa.

Carissa took the pass and studied it for a moment. It was heavier than she'd expected. On one side was a raised, refractive tour logo; the edges were adorned with tiny, embedded light sources. There was no writing anywhere on it.

"What is this?" she asked.

"That's a VIP backstage pass, good for every show on the tour. Wait, not VIP—it's the tier above VIP, it's for god-tier fans."

"No, I mean, physically, what is this object I'm holding?"

"Oh, it's a little steel plate laminated in plastic and then embossed with a diamond layer. Jaxxer likes the design because it's 'mega rock star.' But you can also run software on the diamond layer, which is how we authenticate the pass. It's really difficult to counterfeit all that right now, at least in the places we visit. So look. Hold on to that, and when you're done punching the Association, come see a show, okay?"

EPISODE 4.04

I materialized in the Explorers Guild bunker beneath Wild Massive Prime approximately five minutes local time after I'd departed. Five-minutes-ago me was heading off with cautious enthusiasm and heightened curiosity; present-moment me was returning with Carissa's voice still ringing fresh in my ears telling me to "get the fuck out of here."

Nicholas was sitting at a desk in the corner, waiting for me. I'd returned according to the schedule we set before I left. When he saw me, he stood and said, "Welcome back," handing me a water bottle because he knew I'd be parched. He helped me slip the spacetime machine off my shoulders, and then he took it and hung it on a pair of hooks on the wall near the desk.

I wandered to one of the comfy couches and collapsed. I was surprisingly exhausted, given the amount of time I'd spent staring at blank pages and hoping to find the inspiration to fill them.

Nicholas sat nearby and said, "Did you find the fugitives? Or do you need more time? I could give you another week with the machine."

"Look, I actually took the liberty of spending six weeks on this, Nicholas," I admitted.

His eyes narrowed and he said, "I thought I had it locked for only one specific week of travel."

"Right, and I experienced that specific week six times, in different locations," I said. "Little loophole there in case you loan out the machine again. I almost gave up. Like somewhere around week three, I lost faith for a stretch, but then in week four I regained some hope, and then week five was just demoralizing, but then week six, also demoralizing, except right on the last day, when I realized with a jolt that I would locate Carissa today if I could finish the chapter I was on.

"It took me six straight weeks of alternating between your exercises and my book. With a specific question in mind, writing got so much harder. It's like the more detailed and specific the writing gets, the harder it is for divination to find any space to express itself. I'm not going to have six weeks every time I need an answer for something, anyway, and I bet if I want to know something more complex than the current spacetime coordinates of a person, six weeks will hardly be enough. I mean, I bet this is the continuum that my boss is on. She's been fully focused on *Storm and Desire* for two hundred years.

"But you were right, Nicholas. I wanted to know the current spacetime coordinates of a person, and by wrenching my book into a new section of the bookstore, so to speak, I did finally get the answer."

He perked up at that analogy and said, "What section?"

"I'd always parked my book firmly under fairy tales and mythology, and that's still the core of it. But now it's trending into memoir as well."

"Fascinating," Nicholas said, "and marvelous. Well done."

I took another big swig of water, then asked, "Are you off to rejoin the rest of the Guild now? You know, the Association blocked open the elevator in Prism City, so you might be one of the few people that can get off the floor before they bring the hammer down."

"We're not quite finished here. Did you happen to devote a sliver of your past six weeks to considering my second suggestion?"

"Yes, Nicholas, I thought about it constantly. Whenever I suffered from writer's block, or impostor syndrome, or insomnia, or anxiety, or total boredom—none of which are mutually exclusive states, mind you—I thought to myself, maybe I should've opted for suggestion number two."

"Yet you resisted the temptation," he said, "in favor of methodically climbing your way to a new technical understanding of your skill. Admirable and, more importantly, successful. I think it's a strong position from which to undertake further exploration of your capture glass."

"You mean, right now?"

"Yes. In a real sense, our time is running short, Tabitha. Once our business is concluded, I do plan to leave this floor and rejoin the Explorers Guild. We happen to be planning our final expedition. We're going into the chasm, and hopefully charting a course across it to the top floor."

That caught me off guard. For some reason, I had accepted Allegory's insistence that someday she'd reach the top floor. I didn't realize other seemingly intelligent and rational people also thought they could get there somehow as well.

I said, "My boss thinks the chasm is inhabited."

"It certainly is."

"And she thinks . . ." I dwindled off, remembering the scope of the vision she'd described to me. And then a sharp inspiration hit, and I said, "She thinks that setting up a big fight here today will draw them out. And when the fighting's over and the chasm is safe to cross . . . she thinks she'll be able to reach the top floor uncontested."

I hadn't really crystallized it in my mind like that before, but it resonated strongly as the truth. It had the vibe I got when I realized I'd just written a divination and hadn't noticed it in the moment. But this wasn't divination; this was just me assembling all the pieces I'd learned into a coherent story and seeing it for what it was: expert manipulation, tectonic shifts.

Nicholas said, "In my experience, only crackpots seriously try to reach the top floor, and we never hear from them again. I rather expected to be the only exception to that rule, but I suspect your boss is not a crackpot."

"She's a Muse," I said.

Nicholas said, "I know who she is. Look, if you want to help everyone involved—if you want to help Allegory in her quest to reach the top floor, if you want to help the Explorers Guild find a path for Allegory through the chasm, if you want to help Carissa and Rindasy survive whatever's headed here to the park today, one thing we could all use is a good solid understanding of what truly lurks in the chasm.

"And you were young when you first used the capture glass. Now you're more in command of yourself as a person, and your skill has begun to develop. You might see things in that experience now that you were simply incapable of comprehending when you were younger. The worst-case scenario is that you discover nothing, and we're all left to find out for ourselves, which is the current situation regardless. But a capture glass is a Muse's tool, and in your hands, it could be the instrument we need to navigate safely through the upcoming storm of events."

I said, "Or—hear me out—the worst case is that I *damage* my ability somehow. But I'm just going to replay the same static memory I experienced when I was fourteen. I don't buy that being a few years older is going to dramatically change how I experience that memory."

Nicholas gave me a strange look, then said, "Delia must've placed the capture glass into its training mode for your first experience. Wise, no doubt, but most capture glasses have additional modes that range in degree of interactivity, not to mention a 'write' mode that can replace the memories stored on the glass. Any of the interactive modes might be vehicles for asking questions and receiving timely responses."

"She never told me any of that," I said.

"Who knows what she was thinking? Why didn't she teach you how to use its full feature set? Who knows what *else* is even stored on it?"

"*She* does," I said abruptly. Then I said, "Can I borrow the spacetime machine one more time? I think before I expose myself to any more Muse radiation from the capture glass, Grandma Dee needs to answer a few questions for me, and those questions are all 'What the fuck?'"

.   .   .

I traveled back in time nine years, but instead of simply appearing in front of Grandma Dee with a flash and surprising her half to death, I arrived in a secluded nook backstage at the Super park, a little haven where I used to sneak off to smoke cigarettes with a friend on breaks. Here I put my bomber jacket on over the spacetime machine to try to disguise it. I thought it was best if I approached Grandma Dee—and the Explorers Guild—via the elevator, instead of popping onto their floor via spacetime machine, to avoid any questions about why I had the machine in my possession in the first place. This nook was a cozy, familiar spot near an elevator where I could start that journey.

Of course, it didn't hurt that I knew I had a pack of cigarettes hidden back here in an old-timey mailbox that no one used anymore. After a few quick puffs for confidence, I got in line for the elevator. Today was a slow day at the park apparently, as I only had to wait forty-five minutes to get on. Then I was on my way to the floor where Nicholas told me the Explorers Guild would be camped. It was a "nature floor" where humans hadn't settled yet, except for the eighty or so temporary residents of the Guild's campsite. The Building contained many unpopulated floors like this, making it possible for the Explorers Guild to stay out of any one particular culture's backyard for too long.

Flags marked a path from the elevator along the short hike to the clearing where they'd established camp, on the rim of an impressive natural canyon. The weather was nice, the air was clear—I felt like I'd stepped into a gift shop postcard.

The perimeter of the camp wasn't bounded by any physical structure, but the path from the elevator did culminate at a checkpoint of sorts, where I used a passphrase that Nicholas had provided, which designated me as a guest of a Guild member. I didn't have to specify which member.

With eighty people stationed here for up to a couple of months before moving on, the atmosphere felt a bit like a small festival. Scattered throughout the tent village were larger structures, such as geodesic domes, scaffolded towers, and tall multiroom tents with canopied openings for social gatherings. One of these structures housed a communal kitchen, another a repair shop for tinkering with adventuring gear.

And one structure, a wide, raised canopy with no side walls, was a teahouse, with cushions for seating, tapestries hanging from the ceiling to gently subdivide the interior, infused with the light scent of incense. This is where Grandma Dee was known to volunteer much of her time in camp when not engaged in tactical activities supporting expeditions, and Nicholas suspected she'd likely be there, or someone taking a shift there would know where her personal tent was located.

I drifted up to the edge of the teahouse, not in a rush now that I was here, and scanned the small crowd of fifteen or twenty people who were seated throughout the interior. Many of the individuals here were of nonhuman races, none of which I could identify, and no one inside the structure paid me any attention whatsoever. A table at one end of the room featured an array of self-regulating kettles and pots with water at different temperatures to accompany a variety of teas that were neatly displayed, and a rinsing station was set up nearby for mugs and cups. It wasn't completely self-service; a young man making conversation at one end of the table seemed knowledgeable enough to answer questions and was having a nice discussion about the origins of some of the more exotic blends on offer, collected on various expeditions.

I didn't see Grandma Dee, so I decided to wait for the young man's conversation to end, so that I could ask him for directions to her tent. I sat on an empty cushion near him, just underneath the edge of the canopy, but still in the shade. I hadn't meant to distract him, but he noticed me and excused himself from his chat to come over to greet me.

"Welcome," he said, a warm smile on his face. "You must be Delia's granddaughter. She wanted me to tell you that she might be late to join you, but just stay put, and she'll be here soon. Would you like a quick tour of our tea selection? Or I can just bring you something if you know what you might like."

"Surprise me," I managed to say, and he wandered back to the table.

Naturally, if she had a skill anything like mine, it made sense that she might expect me here today. I should have seen that coming, like literally. Here I thought that I had the upper hand because I'd had a little time to prepare for this visit, but she might've been thinking about it for months before I ever considered this possible.

The last time Grandma Dee had seen me would've been around three years ago in her timeline. I wondered if she'd even recognize me. I imagined the Wild Massive jacket I was wearing might give me away.

I thought I heard her laugh coming from the opposite side of the tent, out on the path leading here. Sure enough, there she was, standing in an intersection of paths, chatting amiably with someone, a genial smile on her face, looking much more "alive" than the last time I saw her. She'd always been trim, but now she seemed a little built, too, like she'd taken up mountain climbing and gotten really good at it. She used to wear boring midwestern housewife attire, which I now recognized was an urban disguise, but here, apparently in her element, she looked like one of those movie adventurers who stole artifacts out of temples. I hadn't realized she had an affinity for outdoorsy activity—which, let's be clear, you didn't get a lot of adventure camping in Des Moines.

An array of emotions hit me, from sadness to rage, all the unprocessed trauma I'd held on to in the absence of therapeutic care seemed to come rushing over me, and I could feel my cheeks flush and my eyes starting to water. I wanted to be calm, and civil, and polite, I wanted to impress her even though she didn't deserve that much respect from me, I did *not* want to admit to her that she'd managed to do any damage when she left me.

But if signs were to be believed, I wasn't going to have that luxury.

Then, with a sudden shock of recognition, I realized who she was talking to.

I wasn't the only visitor in camp today.

Allegory Paradox stood there chatting with Grandma Dee, and she too looked pretty much exactly like she had the last time I saw her.

Before I had a chance to process this information and decide what to do—hide under the tea table or dash off into the forest?—they hugged, and then Allegory headed down the path back to the elevator. Grandma Dee, in turn, came into the teahouse tent, scanning the crowd for me. I managed to put my hand up, and she spotted me. She threaded her way carefully toward me, without stopping to chitchat with anyone along the way.

Yep, this wasn't going to be awkward, not at all.

■   ■   ■

I was caught between competing impulses as she approached. I'd never been a "hugger" per se, but I desperately wanted to hug her—well, I wanted the comfort that would be required to be willing to hug her, anyway, which was absent.

But if she knew via her own method of divination that I was going to be here today, had she seen anything further? Did she know her next expedition was also going to be her last?

She sat down smoothly on a cushion opposite mine, a sweet, genuine smile on her face, and said, "Lily. Look at you." Then she added, "I see there's been a growth spurt."

I nodded and said, "Multivitamins. They work."

She laughed at my admittedly childish attempt to defuse the tension.

The young man from the tea table brought two mugs of tea, and quietly departed.

I had so many questions that I didn't really know where to start. She seemed willing to patiently wait me out, just looking at me and sipping her tea until I said something to break the ice.

"Nice floor you got here," I said.

She raised an eyebrow, but was game for a little small talk.

"We call floors like this 'biome dimensions,'" she replied.

"Seeded with life up to a point—plants, microbes, insects, whatever—and then left alone."

"What's the point?" I asked. "Why make a bunch of 'empty' ecosystems and then just scatter them about randomly throughout the Building?"

"One answer is that like so many things, it comes down to *practice, practice, practice*. You think it's easy getting all *this* to function as a cohesive ecosystem? Takes a few tries to master the evolutionary techniques. Some of those tries were probably sufficiently interesting that they decided to leave them be, instead of writing over them. A place like this—capitalist scavengers would call this floor 'unexploited.' A better way to think of it is like a wilderness reserve or a national park. It warrants its own floor because it's pretty, and it's better off if no one ever shows up and starts strip-mining it."

"So the Building is just the result of . . . Muses learning the rules of reality?" I asked.

"The Building isn't where they learned rules," Grandma Dee replied. "The Building is where they learned *style*."

"But these floors are . . . simulations of worlds out in the multiverse, right?" I said. "Every floor is a simulation environment, churning out modeling data so they can build better shit somewhere else."

"They care about more than *data*," she said. "If they were purely data-driven, they wouldn't call themselves Muses. They report to Architects, yes, but do you know who the Architects report to? The Architects report to Artists. We're not living in a simulation, as though some alternate, 'realer' version of reality awaits the results of what happens here. We're living in a *pastiche*—a pure celebration of artistic ingenuity and variety. Everything here is as 'real' as it gets, and you won't find anything truly like it anywhere else you go." She sighed and said, "But I imagine you're here for a slightly less whimsical conversation than this one, am I correct?"

I nodded, although I hadn't found any of the preceding conversation whimsical in the slightest.

"Then tell me, Lily, why did you come to me today of all days, wearing Nicholas Solitude's spacetime machine under your jacket, no less?" she asked.

"You don't already know?"

"I have my suspicions."

I thought I had come here to ask questions about the capture glass, but she was so blithe about me being here that I almost wondered if I should just turn around and leave. That would be a pure panic response. Alternately, I could pin her under the spotlight of "why did you leave me?" angst and drama, but if she didn't care to bring it up, maybe I didn't, either.

I said, "I've developed a rudimentary skill for divination, using writing as the medium. I don't really have a lot of control over this skill yet. I'm writing a book, and sometimes when I reread what I've written, I realize I've left little clues about my own future in the text. And then most of the time, my gut feeling about these clues is wrong, but lately, I've been getting it right more and more often . . ."

She asked, "What's your book about?"

I said, "Oh, it's sort of . . ."

And then to my surprise, I choked up a little, caught off guard by some stray emotion buried deep inside me that must've been eavesdropping on this conversation. She was patient and sipped tea until I regained my composure and could answer her question.

"Usually when people ask me about my book, I tell them I'm writing an alternate history of the Building using fairy-tale idioms. That sounds more professional than admitting I'm writing fan fiction spawned from my grandmother's bedtime stories to me about her adventures. I started writing them down right after you left. I wanted to—I *needed* to capture everything you told me about your life in the Building. I didn't want to go through the dull pain of realizing years from now that I'd forgotten them all. When I ran out of stories about you getting into trouble, I started inventing *new* stories about you getting into trouble, and that led to new characters and new situations and new floors . . ."

"Let me guess," she said as I trailed off. "Some of these new characters weren't make-believe after all."

I nodded, relieved she'd made that leap on her own so I didn't have to convince her.

"I can't be one hundred percent certain, but I think I picked up this weird little talent after I wore the capture glass that first time, like I must've gotten so overdosed with aesthetic mojo during the experience that now my book drops hints about the future in tiny increments. Does that make sense?"

"It makes enough sense," she replied.

"Right. So—I've reached a point in my life where having better control of this skill would be super useful. Nicholas suggested using the capture glass to see if that might kick things into high gear. Like, if the capture glass triggered or awakened the skill in me in the first place, maybe using it now would trigger an upgrade. It sounded like wishful thinking to me, but then he told me he thinks I've only experienced 'training mode'—pure playback, zero interactivity—but there might be interactive levels I can access.

"He was ready to start experimenting, but I was like . . . what if I break it somehow, or what if I accidently overwrite the existing memory with a new memory while I'm trying to figure out how it works? Or worse, what *other* undocumented features are there and what if I accidentally trigger one of those?

"I just . . . don't know what I don't know.

"Nicholas knows capture glasses in general, but . . . I figured if anyone could help me understand *this* capture glass—our family's capture glass—I was hoping it would be you."

She eyed me closely for a long time, gauging my true motivation, probably wondering if I was secretly laying a trap for her in which she'd say the wrong thing, or fail to provide the exact piece of data I was seeking, and when she didn't, I'd stand up and scream, "BUT YOU *LEFT* ME WHEN I WAS JUST A *CHILD*!" in front of her entire Guild. But I wasn't going to do that. I met her gaze without hesitation, though, silently demanding information from her because she owed me, and she knew it.

"How many times have you used it?" she asked.

"Just once," I said.

She nodded approvingly and said, "I had it for three hundred years and I used it seven times." She laughed. "Nicholas probably used every capture glass in the Archives at least once, maybe more than that, so he's certainly an expert on the technology. But you're right to be cautious. His experience is limited in one fundamental way. I suspect none of the capture glasses in the Archives contain the memory of a Muse."

"Why do you think that?" I asked.

"Because if Nicholas had experienced even a single Muse's memory, even one time—then just like you, he'd have been *changed* by it," she replied. "But if you take away his spacetime machine, Nicholas is as normal a human being as they come. So he doesn't know the fire you might be playing with if you start exploring the features of your capture glass. It's no simple thing to rouse a trapped sliver of Epiphany Foreshadow's awareness and then pretend that *you're* the one in charge of the subsequent exchange."

We were silent for a moment, while our respective teas were graciously refilled.

She looked thoughtful as she sipped hers. I hoped she wasn't going to ask to see the book, because no, not even Grandma Dee got to see the book.

"Well, I was right," she finally said. "Allegory Paradox is going to *love* having you on the creative brain trust."

I was confused for a moment, then said, "She *does*. I'm, like, her favorite."

"I'm happy I got the chance to put in a good word for you," she replied.

"What are you talking about?"

Even as it came out of my mouth, I knew that was a silly question.

She knew I applied for a job at Wild Massive the same way she knew I was coming here for tea today. She was infused with

Muse energy, she'd used the capture glass seven times to deepen her exposure to it instead of one, and she'd had three hundred years of practice with manipulating outcomes instead of nine.

She might possess more hooks into the actual narrative of reality than I could envision on my best day.

Did that mean she knew she was fated to die on her next expedition?

"I've kept tabs on you, just a little, over the years," she replied, and I finally started to hear a twinge of regret in her voice. It wasn't particularly rewarding to hear, I wasn't interested in seeing her suffer, but it was . . . reassuring to me that she did feel a little regret all the same. It softened my memory of being abandoned to at least imagine that she'd doubted herself when she was doing it or had second thoughts about it after the fact.

"How'd you meet Allegory?" I asked.

"Oh, let's see," she replied, "I think it was the fourth time I used the capture glass where I managed to really get myself into serious ontological trouble, and Allegory spotted me flailing, and she saved me. She likes to call me *the anomaly* as if that encapsulates the whole episode. Anyway, we got to be friends. You know, she's used to having peers, assistants, construction crews, back office staff, the works, and now she's just . . . Everyone she worked with is gone." She became unexpectedly bitter on Allegory's behalf and said, "For some inexplicable and inexcusable reason, they left behind the shining star of their entire operation."

She took another long sip of her tea, as if she needed to steel herself to continue further down this conversational path.

"Your capture glass has three distinct memory suites. You've experienced the original passive memory, and I suggest you experience it again before moving on to the next one, because the next one is interactive. You can ask questions and usually get answers, as long as the real, external Epiphany Foreshadow knew the answers. This is as far as I decided to go."

"What questions did you ask?"

Grandma Dee hesitated, sighed deeply, and said, "I know what it's like to have someone walk away clean. I wanted to know all kinds of things. The capture glass was . . . cruel, but informative."

Oh. That sounded non-fun.

"But my questions were the wrong kind of questions. The device had to scrape my surface thoughts, maybe deeper, to figure out how to answer me. You might have more straightforward questions."

"Oh. Well, the main thing—"

"Please don't tell me. I have a feeling you'll just make me worry about you."

I bit down on the urge to say, "Not for long," and kept my mouth shut.

"The third suite apparently opens direct, real-time communication with Epiphany," she said. "I've never used it. Never had the courage to attract a Muse's attention, and never had questions pressing enough to justify doing it."

"Isn't Epiphany gone with everyone else, though?" I asked.

"The whole point of these devices," Grandma Dee answered slowly, "is to facilitate the flow of visionary information from— wherever it comes from—to workers operating in the Building as it was going up. So for all I know, it's still active, like a hotline."

Oh, I was already itching to try out the hotline.

We spent maybe twenty minutes reviewing the mnemonic devices you needed to know to navigate between the three memory suites on the capture glass. Getting into the third suite was by far the most difficult. There was no danger of accidentally wandering into that suite. You needed to work for it.

"Now listen to me," she said when we were finally through with our training session. "If you've got questions that require a Muse to answer a call from an ancient capture glass, you should take that as a sign that you are getting too deep in . . . well, in whatever business motivated you to come visit me."

"I'm already in too deep," I said. "When a character I'd been writing about turned out to be a real person in the real Building, I suspected that I'd crossed a line."

"You should expect that your divination skill will fail you in direct proportion to how much you personally are a mover and shaker now instead of just an observer."

"That doesn't make sense. I'd have thought it would be the opposite."

She shook her head adamantly.

"Years ago, Allegory invited me to sit in the back of the room while the creative brain trust was breaking episodes of her show," she said. "I assume you still use the big whiteboard, with all of the index cards, yes?"

"Of course."

"You're used to being in that room, manipulating index cards, shuffling them around. Now imagine that your name is *on* one of those index cards, and guess what—you can't manipulate your *own* index card. At that point, you'll be a proper participant instead of a mere seer, so *central* to the story you were telling that you can no longer nudge it or manipulate it from a safe and pleasant distance."

Huh. Maybe that explained why it was so easy for me to find Carissa and Rindasy the night I handed off that information to Allegory, but so damnably difficult to locate Carissa when it was *my* agenda at stake.

She said, "Even Allegory Paradox, with her extraordinary ability to influence the 'big picture' of reality's future history, comes up empty when she tries to focus on exactly what happens to *her*. She has no idea. That blind spot is probably a fail-safe in the design of the holistic system."

"To prevent pure omniscience," I said as the implications unfolded in my mind.

"Or to preserve the illusion of free will." She allowed herself a small, quiet laugh, and said, "Welcome to the big leagues."

If that was true for Allegory, it was true for Grandma Dee. She must have no idea that she was fated to die on a Guild expedition in the immediate future.

"Can I use the capture glass here?" I asked.

She shook her head and said, "This camp isn't quite safe enough for flaunting magical artifacts."

"I suppose that makes sense," I said. "It's not every day you get to see actual physical treasure from the mythological era."

"As long as even one Muse still inhabits the Building," she replied, "the mythological era isn't over. History hasn't been written yet. It's barely even been experienced."

"Oh. Nicholas said the past can't be unwritten, so I assumed it was locked."

"It's locked to Nicholas, I'm sure, or rather, the spacetime machine is smarter than it looks when it comes to minimizing its impact on the timeline. But when a Muse needs to fix a problem in the present, sometimes the most efficient method is to adjust the past."

Interesting. In the writer's room, Allegory was almost allergic to the notion of retconning any aspect of the show, despite producing so many episodes that no one could possibly remember every last detail from a couple of hundred years ago or whatever.

I finished my tea, and realized either the caffeine had made me jittery, or I was just anxious to use the capture glass, because I was very fidgety in my seat for a few moments. But I waited, holding open a gap where I stopped asking questions, because she knew there was one question I hadn't asked. I didn't want her to think I was obsessed or anything, so I wasn't prepared to prompt her, either.

"It's so good to see you, Lily," she finally said.

"I'm Tabitha now," I said. "Tabitha Will."

"Tabitha Will," she repeated, committing it to memory. "It rings true."

And that was it. I couldn't say I was disappointed, exactly, because I hadn't expected much.

We walked back to the elevator together in silence, and I pushed the button. I didn't have long to wait.

As the door opened, she hugged me tightly, and I hugged her back.

She said, "I can't apologize to you, Tabitha, because I don't ever want you to forgive me."

I got into the elevator, watched her turn around and head back to camp before I finally allowed the door to close.

"Hello there, passenger!" the bright voice of a cloudlet rang out. "Where can I deliver you on this fine whatever day of the week it is on the floor of your choosing?"

"Don't worry about me," I said. "I'll get my own ride."

I activated the spacetime machine and vanished from the elevator, content to leave the past where it belonged: firmly in the past.

SEASON FIVE

EPISODE 5.01

It was twelve in the evening when Carissa and Rindasy met up with Nicholas at the Origins Museum. By the time the park closed at thirteen in the evening, the three of them were on the observation deck of the Space Elevator, having arrived in time to witness several sharp, bright streaks of color escape from the chasm, as though fireworks were being ignited or rockets were launching themselves upward, and disappear into the distance.

"Those streaks, those are the Maladies," said Nicholas, his somber tone making it clear they were something to be feared.

By fourteen in the evening, the three of them were in the middle of a late-night dinner at the Space Elevator restaurant, when Carissa received a visit from Tabitha, warning her that the Association would be headed here soon.

The time was almost exactly fifteen in the evening, otherwise known as midnight, when Roland announced the park-wide fire drill, and word immediately began to spread. Roland asked Nicholas if he'd be willing and able to call in a favor on the park's behalf, and Nicholas left the floor immediately to see what he could arrange.

Prism City needed to be empty by no later than six in the morning.

Roland wouldn't admit it to anyone else, but he questioned his own judgment for agreeing to this confrontation. No matter which way the wind blew, in the end, today would be a day that people got hurt. You couldn't live long in the upper reaches of the Building without a measure of risk, obviously, and the denizens of Wild Massive Prime were an incredibly hardy and experienced crew by any measure.

But the Association had earned its reputation for cruelty.

He did not lack self-awareness about his personal stake in this situation. Someday, when the dust settled, if the walls of this place were still standing, he'd get around to adding a small exhibit to the Origins Museum in honor of Nadia Pierson, whose contributions to Harry Prismatic's success—as his stage assistant, then his business manager, then his romantic partner—were everywhere he looked. He would be unsparing in detailing the Association's role in her eventual fate and Harry's subsequent withdrawal from civilization as a result.

In the practical execution of a park-wide fire drill, if things were going well, Roland was required to do nothing but wait and try to contain his own apprehension. While things were going well, he wouldn't hear news for hours unless he started poking his nose into the machinery of the operation.

If things began to go poorly, however, the bad shit would immediately roll straight uphill to him to address.

· · ·

Around one in the morning, a tall woman stepped out of the elevator, wearing the battered overalls of a member of the park's Ride Maintenance Department, streaked with an unlikely amount of grease that was more ornamental than realistic. Ideally, no one would even see this disguise, but she liked to be prepared for surprise outcomes. When it became apparent to her that no one in Prism City was paying the slightest attention to the elevator at that moment, she took a confident step onto the floor, and then promptly vanished into the scenery.

Agent Wynderia Gallas, master rogue and assassin, had arrived.

She'd arrived five hours ahead of the rest of Dimension Force, in fact, to see if the fugitives could be neutralized without the need for the rest of the mission team. Barring that, she'd fall back to infiltration, surveillance, and sabotage.

In other words, the usual.

· · ·

Around two in the morning, Roland got a call on his park radio: "GM, this is gate. You got eyes on the front porch?"

Roland glanced out the nearest window. The "front porch" in park parlance was the pavilion outside the front gate where the line to get in each morning culminated, and Roland could see the edge of it from where he stood.

But more importantly, half a mile beyond it, he could see three ancient shuttles had landed in plain view of the park. For reasons beyond his technical comprehension, their hulls were venting steam or smoke or noxious gas into the air in large clouds that shimmered in a variety of colors whenever they drifted into the path of a park spotlight. The current generation of jump drives used conceptual components for negotiating transit instead of physical ones, which eliminated the unsightly venting issue. The old jump drives still worked, though, most of the time, just like the shuttles' passengers.

That right there would be a small wave of Massive Irregulars answering his call, in this, the park's hour of need.

"That's Leticia's crew," Roland radioed back. "When their ships cool off, run some visitor's badges out."

"They don't get VIP badges?" the gate asked.

"Uh, no," Roland said. "We do want them to leave when this is over."

■   ■   ■

Rindasy sat quietly at zir table, carefully observing Roland and his team, pondering zir next move.

Carissa had pulled a couple of chairs together and had managed to fall asleep, an impressive feat amid the steady din of activity all around. Nicholas had left the floor to ask for help evacuating Prism City from someone called the Pirate King. *Pirate* wasn't an occupation in use on the Shai-Manak floor, nor was its nearest equivalent, *thief.* But out in the multiverse at large, thieves and pirates could attain legendary status, or be romanticized in popular entertainment, or in this case, become monarchs of a criminal empire without suffering any reputational penalties, it seemed.

It nagged at zir that Roland had decided not to deploy zir anywhere throughout his web of defenses. It was a squandered opportunity to use zir considerable arsenal of spells to protect the park. But in Roland's mind, the park benefited most from keeping Rindasy and Carissa off the board as long as possible. No sense letting their opponents focus their efforts on Rindasy after detecting zir presence in the middle of a fight. Better to keep them wary of the entirety of the park's defenses.

As a result, Rindasy felt alienated from all the heroic activity happening tonight. Clearly, the people running this park had something they were itching to prove, and Rindasy and Carissa must've presented a cause to rally around. But if Rindasy were to slip out of this restaurant and find zir way to Prism City, ze could jump in the elevator and escape this floor altogether and no one would be the wiser. Their arrival as fugitives had set things in motion here, but now Rindasy and Carissa were sidelined and useless. It made no sense.

So when Roland decided he needed to head down to the front gate and greet the Irregulars who had just arrived, Rindasy decided ze needed to greet the Irregulars as well. Ze followed him down the stairs to the observation deck, and to Roland's surprise and slight irritation, ze boarded the elevator going down to the park with him.

"Something I can do for you?" Roland said as the elevator began its rapid, vertiginous descent.

"Your thaum generators are leaking badly. I can take care of that if you'll let me."

"Thaum generators are highly sophisticated and deeply improbable pieces of gear. I can't just allow 'Fugitive B' to go poking around inside them with a wrench and a dowsing rod."

"Fugitive B is a Shai-Manak sorcerer, Roland."

"And that means . . . what, exactly? You feel empowered to practice magic without taking a certificate program first?"

"It means I'm more fluent with magic than anyone in this park," Rindasy said.

Roland almost chuckled, but caught himself and said, politely, "Is that so?"

"It is, yes. Shai-Manak don't learn magic—we *are* magic."

"Well, it sounds like you'd be perfect for the main-stage variety show," Roland replied. "Especially . . . I mean, do you sing?"

"I can manifest multiple independent singing voices, actually."

"Perfect, you can be your own backup singers. Let's chat about your day rate when this is over. Now if you'll excuse me . . ."

The elevator arrived at ground level, and Roland practically bounded out ahead of Rindasy, but ze caught up quickly enough.

"You're risking everything you have here to protect us, and I want to do my part," Rindasy said.

"Aha, you think we're doing all this for you?"

"Aren't you?"

"Listen, you are not the first fugitives from the Association to wind up behind our walls," Roland said. "If we let them get a taste for extending their filthy tendrils into this park whenever they want to ruin someone's life, we'll never see the end of it."

"Then let me help," Rindasy said.

"We don't have time for a maintenance pass on the generators."

"*You* don't have time, I agree," Rindasy said. "But I'm a Shai-Manak sorcerer, Roland."

He stopped, faced zir with a slightly exasperated look, and said, "Okay, let's hear it. What are you proposing here?"

"I can heal the crystals in the focus regulators," Rindasy said.

Roland said, "You can't heal focus crystals. They have to be replaced."

"*You* can't heal them," Rindasy said. "But it's minor transformation magic for me. I don't even have to take the generators out of service."

Roland's skepticism gave way to a flicker of hope. They'd been losing auctions on new focus crystals for his aging generators for two years now. "What do you need to make this happen?" he asked.

"Physical proximity to the generators," Rindasy replied. "Or proximity to a substation, or even just proximity to a ride that pulls thaums from the grid."

Roland led zir on a route through the park that weaved behind the scenes and then out into the public streets and back again several times, until they arrived at a giant construction site, illuminated by powerfully bright lights on tall poles. An armada of bots was steadily tearing down the temporary warehouse-style privacy housing around a shiny new roller coaster. The roof was already gone, and the walls were being peeled away from scaffolding in orderly strips, revealing most of the ride beneath.

Rindasy wasn't overly familiar with roller coasters beyond what ze'd seen walking around the park earlier, so the layout of the track was inscrutable to zir as more than just an intricate steel sculpture of sorts. Two tall hills stood out, though, and one of the hills seemed to still be missing a chunk of track at its peak.

Rindasy followed Roland through the controlled chaos of the site to a stairway up to a boarding platform, where several shiny, colored ride cars awaited their turn to be sent out on the rails.

Rindasy's eyes were drawn to a steel podium on the platform, which featured a few simple ride controls—green button for go, red button for stop, that sort of thing. Immediately, ze could sense the substation components inside the podium. This was perfectly sufficient as an access point for Rindasy to inject arcane instructions into the grid and then monitor their progress as the focus crystals regenerated and the grid began to recover. Ze set to work.

· · ·

Once Rindasy initiated the healing process, ze took a step back and studied the roller coaster again, attempting to make sense of what ze saw.

"This is the Catapult," Roland said, immediately noticing Rindasy's curiosity and smoothly beginning a spiel. "You get launched out of the station here, and up that first big hill. As you float over the peak, you get yourself a little of what we call *air time* as you're lifted out of your seat just a bit until you're pressed against the lap bar, and then you plummet down the other side. It's steep enough, but really, we're just lulling you at this point. 'Eh,' you'll say ten seconds into this course, 'I've seen taller hills with steeper slopes right here in this very park,' and you'd be right.

"And then we jerk you through an ascending helix that takes you back up as high as the first hill, but it's slow and you're getting impatient, and we only give you one inversion as a reward, one weak little loop on your way back down to ground level after all the time you burned in that spiral, and you're practically tapping your toe with impatience by this point.

"But see, that first big hill and that steadily ascending spiral, those are both *opportunities* for you to start to appreciate the main feature of this attraction. Because we're giving you repeated viewings of the *unfinished track* at the top of that *much bigger* hill over there. The steadily ascending spiral takes you past that *much bigger* hill seven complete times, giving you plenty of chances to contemplate mortality at your steadily ascending leisure.

"Because that's not actually a proper hill at all, do you see that? It goes up, but it doesn't come down like a proper hill should. Why, goodness me, did someone simply *forget* to lay track coming down the other side of it? No, Rindasy, we did not forget to do anything of the sort.

"So you come out of that gentle loop over there and it seems like you're just going to glide back into the station, but surprise! Before you reach the platform, you switch tracks and you're shunted over to *that* platform—which, as you can see, is a *drop* platform, meaning we *drop* your car down a level and into position for a *second* launch.

"You have time to emit the tiniest of shrieks as our good friend, magnetism, *propels* you straight up that *very big* and *very incomplete* hill. You clearly see the tracks ahead of you are literally pointing straight up into the sky, because that's where you're headed, Rindasy—straight up into the sky at high velocity. And I mean, talk about air time, this is the *real deal*, this is *soaring* through the literal air, clear across the park.

"The only thing in the vicinity that's higher off the ground than you in that moment is the Space Elevator.

"And then, you reach the peak of your parabolic journey and begin your compelling descent back toward the ground, as we now introduce you to the thrill of pure, unfettered free fall. This time, they hear you shrieking all the way in Prism City as you plummet toward what appears to be a giant bull's-eye painted on a cement slab outside the walls of the park, which is decorated with the scattered wreckage of a half dozen cars that attempted this perilous journey before you and were pulverized on impact.

"But instead of crashing headlong into pavement, you descend *through* the bull's-eye in the blink of an eye and feel an unexpected but not uncomfortable jolt as your car reacquires a position on actual steel track. Finally—*finally*, you feel the soothing presence of an actual braking mechanism slowing you down, slowing you down, slowing you down, and then before you quite realize exactly what's just happened to your poor central nervous system, you glide gently back into this very boarding station and come to a complete stop. A ride host releases your lap restraint, and you are free to exit the station down that little ramp right over there.

"Anyway, that all works. I've done seventy-eight test runs myself.

"But that's just the configuration we'll use for typical guests. For a certain caliber of VIP guests, those who've come to expect that little something *extra* from Wild Massive Prime, someday we'll offer to adjust the launch trajectory of the Catapult. Our eventual goal is to launch our VIPs *clear across the chasm*, to the very top floor of the Building itself. Naturally, we expect it to be a one-way trip, and no refunds will be given to those you leave behind. But think of the pinnacle of adventure you'll have when you reach the top floor! Unprecedented!"

He fell silent, finally, and waited patiently for Rindasy to say something. Ze chose zir words carefully.

"You would need more than your good friend magnetism to accomplish that adjusted trajectory," said Rindasy.

"Yes, I would need the additional capacity of three-quarters of one additional thaum generator, which is not in the budget for the foreseeable future," Roland replied, dropping his showman's spiel for the time being. "Right now, I can reliably launch cars *into* the chasm. But not *over* it."

Almost involuntarily, Rindasy's mind began to toy with the question of how to squeeze that capacity out of the existing grid somehow. Maybe if Roland was willing to yank other attractions out of rotation for a time . . .

Roland said, "Where are you headed after this, Rindasy? What's your grand plan?"

The question caught Rindasy off guard, but ze managed to stammer, "Joining the Explorers Guild, I guess. That was Carissa's idea, anyway."

"Well, let me propose a counteroffer," Roland said. "Maybe you might like to stay and help us rethink our grid configuration and teach our techs a few things about generator maintenance while you're at it. We'll give you your own trailer and a nice salary in Wild Massive scrip." He waved at the Catapult in all its glory. "I mean, this is the kind of shit we do for fun around here. The place grows on you. You don't have to answer now; just think about it while we're being invaded or bombarded or whatever happens today."

"Could I actually sing in one of your shows?" Rindasy asked.

Roland shrugged noncommittally and said, "I mean, you'd still have to audition."

Of all the things Rindasy expected from zir visit to Wild Massive Prime, acquiring additional options for the future was not on the list. Ze found zirself rather pleased by the notion of having a new choice to consider.

"What's the big deal about the top floor, anyway?" Rindasy eventually asked.

"You kidding me?" Roland sounded shocked. "The fabled executive suites of yore? Tell you this much, I've already got a waiting list a mile long for the VIP experience."

"Why are you rushing to open the ride today of all days?"

"In addition to being a fantastic roller coaster," Roland replied, "the Catapult can also function as a siege weapon. I figure we'll fill some cars with explosives and launch 'em at the parking lot if the Association shows up with tank divisions or something."

. . .

Carissa was startled awake by the sound of someone accidentally dropping a tray of glasses. As she looked around, for a brief moment she thought she was in Minneapolis, in the bar at Lorelei's hotel. She was both saddened and relieved to realize that she was mistaken.

Rindasy and Nicholas were both gone, and they were outside the range of her clairvoyance. She made mental notes to get Rindasy a tablet and to get the network address for the spacetime machine, so that they could all stay in better contact in the future. But for now, she was on her own.

She made her way down to the observation deck, which was much quieter, and gazed out over the park and beyond, all the way to Prism City, glowing brightly in the distance. Four or five giant resort hotels stood prominently in the skyline. Train tracks were lit up in a loop from the park to Prism City as well. Ordinarily, the train wouldn't start running until six in the morning, but they'd fired it up early to speed up evacuation. A steady line of vehicle headlights in the darkness lit up the main drag from the city to the relative safety of the park.

Roland expected Carissa and Rindasy to stay hidden in the Explorers Guild bunker during any confrontation today. Originally, she'd been very amenable to that idea. Now Kellin's voice in the back of her mind became more insistent, suggesting that she wouldn't truly feel that justice had been served unless she herself was out dealing her share of damage to the Association.

Which might be true, but she was far enough removed now to understand that Kellin's code of honor, admirable in some respects, was a form of rudimentary masculine preening that never motivated her.

No, she was perfectly content to let Roland do the punching today.

But sitting up here in this restaurant waiting impatiently for something to happen was going to aggravate her to no end. She wanted to be in position to do something in case Roland had somehow underestimated this situation, and although she hadn't had a chance to test the range of each of her talents, she had a feeling being this far off the ground and away from the park gates would be too far away to make an impact.

She scanned the skyline of the park, looking for someplace other than the Space Elevator to tuck herself away where she might have a solid view of the entire park while basically staying hidden. She didn't have a perfect view, since the nearer attractions often obstructed her view of those beyond, so she consulted a park map on her tablet to look for candidates.

The obvious choice was atop the high towers of Castle Tormento, the primary setting for a jewel of an old fantasy series called *Even My Demons Have Demons,* about a family of demons who escape from a hell dimension and try to live peaceful lives in the suburbs. What starts off as a gentle comedy of manners—in one early episode, young Missy Tormento wants to go to the prom, but she's nervous that she'll incinerate her human date—eventually evolves into a galactic war in which the Tormento family finds redemption by systematically assassinating God over and over until God finally agrees to stay dead for a while.

The attraction itself had been cutting-edge maybe thirty years ago, with variations running throughout the Wild Massive network of parks. But when the show eventually came to an end, Roland began scooping up each version of the attraction, combining them into one preposterous behemoth of a ride that required eighteen minutes to complete. As a result, Castle Tormento at

Wild Massive Prime featured no fewer than a dozen towers of varying heights.

She walked the distance to Castle Tormento, surprised to see considerable activity on every street along the way. The windows and doors on all the shops were being boarded up, street carts were being wheeled out of public areas, entrances to rides and backstage areas were being sealed off with temporary fencing and chains.

Roland had assured her that there'd be no fighting inside the park walls, but clearly, he felt he couldn't guarantee that.

As she arrived at Castle Tormento, she took a deep breath, levitated at a moderate speed to the top of the highest tower, and then landed gently on a wooden platform hidden behind the tower façade. She had no idea when dawn was due to arrive, but this would be a fine place for watching it.

.　.　.

As the earliest hints of sunlight appeared, Rindasy took to the sky above the park in the form of a small flying lizard and patrolled in search of Carissa. The search was quick. Carissa had fallen asleep atop her chosen tower, tucked in a corner leaning against a low safety railing. Even though ze landed as quietly as possible on the roof, zir mere presence was sufficient to awaken her. Ze quickly transformed into the human form that she'd recognize, and she smiled.

"Would you like company, or shall I go?" Rindasy asked.

"You should stay. You got here just in time for sunrise," she replied.

Rindasy surveyed their location. At the front of the tower, facing into the park streets, a flimsy-looking half wall was the extent of any cover from being seen. On the other side, facing into the backstage area, safety railings enclosed the perimeter. But as far as places to see the sunrise, this was a great choice. And the view of the park in every direction was surprisingly good.

"What did you get up to while I was zonked out?" she asked as ze sat down nearby.

"I assisted with some repairs on the park's thaum generators, reclaiming some badly needed capacity on the park's grid."

"Seems like a weird time for repairs."

"There's no time like the present to ensure that you have enough energy to fire the weapons you're planning to use."

"So everything works now?"

"I don't know. They're trying to load test my repairs at the moment."

"And where'd you learn to repair a thaum generator?"

Rindasy smiled and said, "I studied thaum generators to learn how to destroy them without destroying myself in the process. I'm a saboteur on occasion these days." Then ze added, "Roland's gear is hardly cutting-edge, but it should perform well as long as none of the substations or generators themselves take direct hits."

"I thought that gear was all in the tunnels."

"Most of it is, except the generator at the auditorium normally dedicated to stage shows, and they can't power every park defense at once without it. They are learning, under pressure, the cost of ignoring difficult maintenance work. I could've done more troubleshooting for them, but they didn't exactly enjoy having me poke around their operations."

"Probably embarrassed to have an actual wizard judging the quality of all the hacks they used to keep their grid propped up."

"Ah, well, they needn't have worried. Among our people, I'm considered a sorcerer and artisan, but not quite diligent enough to be a wizard."

"I'm sure the park engineers care about that distinction."

Rindasy laughed and said, "Fair enough. And to be honest, I needn't be a wizard to pass judgment on their many hacks."

Carissa stood up to stretch her muscles and take another look at the activity in the streets, which had dwindled almost to nothing. They must have completed the "fire drill" portion of the proceedings, and now the volunteer fire brigade and their helpers were resigned to wait until something happened that required a response.

"I don't know about you," she said, "but I don't plan to hide in the tunnels today. I thought I'd stay right here and watch whatever goes down. I couldn't let all this just . . . happen . . . without at least witnessing it."

"That does sound preferable to hiding in the Guild bunker," Rindasy said.

"It's pretty much the opposite of a smart move, right? Just sitting here watching it all go down around us? A single drone on a flyover could spot us."

"I can obscure our position from drones and dust and the like, if that's what you're worried about."

"That's one of the things I'm worried about, yeah. But also like, if *anything* goes down out here where we can see it, anything that threatens people's lives . . . do you think you could just sit here and let them risk their lives on our behalf without doing something to help them?"

"They're not defending us," Rindasy pointed out. "They're defending the home that they treasure."

"Which we're putting at risk by being here. I mean, sure, defending your home is noble and all that, but I'm going to be upset if people die trying to protect a bunch of roller coasters." She laughed a bit cynically and said, "Of course, I've never been given the option to fight the Association and decided, 'sure, let's fucking *go* for it!' I'm used to running for an elevator."

Rindasy hesitated for a moment before admitting, "The Shai-Manak would have died down to a person defending our home if the Association had invaded us."

"Why would you do that?" Carissa said, her voice sharp. "The Brilliant fought down to a person. Not recommended." Then she added, "You can make a home *anywhere*." That sounded trite to her as she said it, yet she couldn't shake the truth of it.

"Believe me, the notion of evacuating our floor has been considered more than once. But we never developed our own jump drive. We have no ships of our own to simply carry us away, sight unseen. An evacuation would require us to enlist enough ships to carry a thousand people, as well as all the artifacts and such that we consider important enough to keep. Who do you imagine we could trust to take that job without mentioning a word of it to anyone? Our current answer to that question is 'no one.'"

"You can't buy ships?" Carissa asked. "Through a third party?"

Rindasy shook zir head and said, "Buying even a single jump-capable ship without using Association currency for the transaction is quite challenging. The unique resources we have to offer for trade are magic artifacts that we handcraft ourselves. Our military prohibits export of any artifacts of appreciable power, fearing they will be used against us or reverse engineered by the Association. We could craft artifacts with much less magical potency, but demand for these trinkets would not be equal to the cost of a single ship."

Carissa's mind raced through the options she could envision to get around these constraints, as though the Shai-Manak hadn't already put their best minds to work and come up short. She couldn't think of anyone who'd be willing to put themselves in between the Association and its current enemy of choice.

"Okay, but why couldn't you evacuate using the elevators?" she asked.

"We discussed that option with the cloudlets. They shielded the location of our current floor under the auspices of their own first contact protocols. We'll not receive that protection again, and in fact, some of the cloudlets are loyal to the Association and are eager for that protection to drop. As an absolute long shot, we tried to develop our own teleport relay network so that the cloudlets needn't be complicit in our evacuation, but that project is a long way from success.

"More importantly . . . we've lived peacefully on that floor for eons. We live in harmony with an ecosystem that has rewarded us with incredible power to shape our environment and ourselves.

The bones of our ancestors infuse the literal foundations of our temples and academies, Carissa. When the Explorers Guild camped on our floor for a time, we learned that some of our sacred spaces are too potent to allow tourists to visit, for their own safety, but for us, they are sources of sustenance. We cannot simply pack these sacred spaces into parcels for shipment to some mundane floor. And some theorize that our magic would necessarily wane as we drifted farther from its source. We would wane as an entire culture in that event."

Rindasy had maintained eye contact with Carissa as ze spoke, but now ze turned away, as though ze was embarrassed to face her.

"The course we charted for ourselves was sound," ze said. "The Shai-Manak now sit as equals for peace talks with the Association, and the only thing these two old foes need to properly seal the promise of a glorious future together is the blood of two fugitives." A bitter laugh escaped zir, and ze said, "If the Radiant Council had simply *asked* me to sacrifice myself for this cause, I would be dead already. Instead, they *hunt* me. The Association's brutality is swiftly becoming our own."

"For what it's worth," Carissa said, "I greatly prefer that you're not dead."

"The circumstances are appealing to me as well."

Carissa gestured toward the park streets and said, "So you think these people are fighting for the park the way you were prepared to fight for your floor? They've got some kind of absurd theme park nationalism going here?"

"That's the sense I got when I worked side by side with Roland and his engineers. Which brings us back to the original question at hand. If the park's defenses turn out to be insufficient against today's threats, and lives are truly at stake, should we fight, or should we run?"

"If we run, we'll spend the rest of our lives wondering what we could've done if we'd been here to help," she said. "I know that for a fact, Rindasy. I know that feeling so well, it's like the crucible of my fucking personality. If the time comes . . . I plan to fight."

"Just so you understand," Rindasy replied, "if the time comes, I plan to fight right alongside you."

.   .   .

The evacuation of Prism City was extremely efficient. By the time Tabitha emerged from the elevator at five in the morning, the residents were essentially gone, and they'd shut down the train. The animatronics that operated the shops and restaurants had gone into standby without guests to attend to.

But Tabitha did interact with a couple of animatronics, when she ordered a coffee at a small café, and when she got picked up by a rickshaw driver, who fed her an entertaining line about the dangerous wildlife along the route to the park. Some junior narrative designer at the start of their career must've written all the dialogue spoken by the animatronics on this floor, and it was convincing enough to fool Tabitha.

And when she saw what she assumed were undercover Security officers barricading the elevator doors, she was actually seeing Wild Massive public safety staff locking it down. They'd allowed the elevator to continue arriving on this floor up until the last moments of the evacuation, to give personnel living on other floors every chance to get here for the fire drill, but now it was truly time to lock it down, before stray guests began to appear. Tabitha had managed to time her arrival on the floor perfectly.

Around half past five in the morning, Roland's team in the command center learned the evacuation was complete, with sign off from an array of responsible parties that the elevators, the front gate, the employee entrance, and the train station were all barricaded, and that no one had been forgotten outside the perimeter.

Roland ordered that the automated defenses be put into high alert, at their highest sensitivity rating. Average sensitivity was good enough to discourage the typical miscreant from sneaking into the park without a pass, but this move would really step it up a notch on the lethality side of things.

He was asked to give an inspirational speech to the loyal but maybe not entirely fearless crew collected out in the park right this minute, ready for action but hoping not to see it. Roland was not known as a speechifier, and he was somewhat distracted still by operational details, but his assistants all thought he should say something before it was too late. This was one of those moments, they thought, that could become an integral part of the Wild Massive Prime legend, and they assured him he'd regret it someday if he passed up the opportunity. They patched his radio into the park-wide announcement system, and the whole command center fell silent so that they too could be inspired.

He cleared his throat and said into his radio, "Listen up, everyone. This is your GM speaking." He paused for a long while, for what could only be dramatic effect, it seemed, before finally collecting his thoughts enough to continue. "Don't get killed today. I mean it."

And so, the legend of Wild Massive Prime grew ever so slightly.

Nicholas arrived in a flash of light nearby. Roland could tell he'd failed just by looking at his forlorn expression.

"No dice?" Roland asked.

Nicholas shook his head sadly and said, "The Pirate King sends his regards and best wishes, but in the end, he declined to send shuttles."

"I thought you had this locked up," Roland said. "What changed his tune?"

"Rumors are circulating in elite circles about this situation," Nicholas replied. "A steady flow of wagers is underway, facilitated by the Pirate King's betting exchanges. He can't be seen taking a side without risking credibility, unfortunately."

"His credibility is more important than the lives of our

guests?" Roland said through gritted teeth. "And how did these rumors start circulating?"

When it became clear that Nicholas was unable or unwilling to answer on behalf of the Pirate King, Roland sighed. At least they'd gotten those people into the tunnels.

"Out of curiosity," he said, "did he tell you the odds?"

"No, he pointedly did not, and he reminded me I'm barred from utilizing his gambling operations. Something about how the spacetime machine gives me an unfair advantage."

Roland's radio squawked loudly, startling both of them.

Then his receptionist from the front office said over the radio, "GM, you got a visitor at the front desk. Tabitha Will from corporate. You busy?"

Nicholas looked unsurprised. He said, "Looks like I got here just in time to meet her."

"Who is she?" Roland asked.

"She's the person who warned us that the Association had located the fugitives and would be heading here today."

"And how did she happen to know that the fugitives were here?" Roland asked.

"Apparently, she can see the future," Nicholas said with a distressingly straight face. "Just a little bit at a time, anyway."

Roland felt the sudden sharp start of a headache, but it was probably psychosomatic. "So why is she here?" he asked.

"I have no idea in the world," Nicholas replied.

Roland pondered the situation for a long moment, prompting his receptionist to repeat the question. Finally, he told his receptionist, "On my way."

■　　■　　■

At six in the morning, the hour that the trains normally began running from Prism City to the park so that folks could stake out a place in line before the park opened, the Agents of Dimension Force arrived on the floor in their sleek silver Squadship, a jump-capable fight-and-rescue craft with enough carrying capacity for all the Agents participating in this mission, as well as Andasir and the eight enforcers they'd picked up from the Shai-Manak floor.

The Squadship was practically a showroom prototype for several sophisticated forms of defense and resistance against physical and magical attacks, tech that was frequently too expensive or impractical in some fashion to roll out to Fleet at scale, but well inside Dimension Force's formal budget for one of its key assets. A few items in the Squadship's arsenal of weapons ranked higher up the immorality scale than Dimension Force was generally known for, but those weapons were easy to exclude from the vehicle's specs on the team's marketing website.

Anjette set the Squadship down on the crumbling pavement of what was once intended to be an enormous overflow lot for jump-capable ships, before Harry cut deals with better-equipped facilities on nearby floors to handle traffic control, parking enforcement, and the like. They were approximately two kilometers from the front gate.

Agent Whisper set to work infiltrating the park's network, using a combination of illegal tech implanted in his skull and an old handheld video game he'd modified as a control interface for additional tasks.

"Heads up," he announced. "They've been scanning employee badges in all night. Way beyond the minimal graveyard security staff we were expecting."

"Suboptimal," Anjette said. "So much for our early-morning advantage."

"And they took their ticketing system down in the middle of the night," Whisper continued. "Until it comes back, they're not selling tickets, they're not scanning passes, no one's getting in the front gate." He shot Agent Grey a look and said, "It's almost as though they knew we were coming."

"If they knew that, why wouldn't they evacuate?" Anjette asked.

"Beats me," Whisper said. "I never understood show people."

"If they're keeping civilians out of our way, they're doing us a favor," Agent Grey replied.

"The park employees are civilians as well," Andasir interjected. "They're not our targets."

"These people showed up in the middle of the night to defend the park. They're not civilians. They must think we're an invasion force from another floor."

"Yes, technically that's correct," Andasir pointed out.

"Does that mean we can shoot them?" Steelplate asked.

"To be determined," Grey said. "Surveil the floor."

. . .

Fifteen minutes later, Whisper provided the team a quick overview of his findings. He'd blanketed the area with surveillance dust, but the swarms were promptly incinerated by an invisible protective dome around the park, extending from the top of the Space Elevator all the way down to ground level. He sent microdrones to study this protective dome more closely.

It wasn't a physical barrier; in theory, they could easily just lob grenades over the walls or shoot missiles at roller coasters if they were so inclined. Of course, the park would absolutely shoot back.

The Agents had good, clean visuals of the artillery mounted on the walls: an aging but intimidating series of military attack platforms mounted approximately every twenty feet, all the way around the entire park. Their armored housings were designed to look like little medieval towers, with festive Wild Massive flags mounted on top. Peeking out through large portholes on the front of each one were the tips of devastator-class automated omnidirectional laser cannons.

You could fire these as nonlethal long-distance stun guns, essentially, or you could fire them via beam-splitters in wild sustained bursts that rained annihilation on everything in range, or you could utilize a variety of tactical attack patterns that were less purely destructive but still thoroughly lethal. And you could sit back and sip a martini while targeting AI did all the work, or if you were feeling especially vindictive, you could push the red button yourself to remotely fire the cannons at your enemies.

For reference, Agent Steelplate had a streamlined model of this weapon grafted into his left arm, pulling power from a nuclear battery installed in his chest.

It was an ostentatious display, meant to dissuade the park's likely opponents from trying to enter without a day pass, and it posed a stark contrast to the whimsical nature of the environment behind the walls. It wasn't the most modern, cutting-edge military gear you could get; the park couldn't afford that stuff, and anyway, the older stuff was instantly recognizable to a certain class of scoundrel, which was a desirable attribute in this situation.

Meanwhile, the other key asset to the park's defense in plain view of Whisper's microdrones was the Space Elevator. The park wanted you to see the array of cannon mounts all around the periphery of its twelve-thousand-tonne observation platform. These were used to launch fireworks every night after the parade, impressive supplements to the primary fireworks that were launched from the ground. No one doubted that the platform could launch more than simply fireworks.

Although the cannons on the walls were capable of antiaircraft duties if necessary, the Space Elevator featured a properly dedicated antiaircraft system, designed to pick off any vessel that jumped onto the floor and into park airspace without registering with the park's traffic control system first, capable of intercepting missiles and other projectiles in flight from any direction. Given the necessity to prevent debris from showering down onto the park, the weapons on the platform were disintegration-based with a broad swath.

If they did happen to get inside the park despite these deterrents, Whisper's reading of the human resources network told him that roughly 250 public safety officers were authorized to carry lethal weaponry on their person at any time inside the park. The checkout system for the park's armory was steadily ticking away even as Whisper watched; the park staff was definitely preparing for a confrontation.

After this briefing, Whisper turned over the floor to Agent Glamour Esque, combat wizard extraordinaire, who had performed a similar analysis of the park's magical defenses.

The signature of Harry Prismatic's magic was quite unique, and no academic study had yet unraveled its inner workings. So for instance, you could detect the presence of an elaborate system of ethereal trip wires that surrounded the park, but couldn't determine what might trigger them. You could admire the dense network of curses embedded into the walls themselves, but could only guess at what horrors would be unleashed if you managed to set off one of these curses by damaging the walls too badly. You could observe with your mind's eye how the streets inside the park hummed as though spellcraft was baked into the pavement, but couldn't begin to fathom what might happen if you found yourself walking those streets when such spellcraft was activated.

Harry was primarily famous as an illusionist, however, and all these detectable traces of heavily engineered magical defenses might be misdirection.

Additionally, there were too many magical hotspots inside the park to count, too many rides and attractions that relied on magic to accomplish some or all of their effects. If you wound up roaming around inside the park, he might recommend you avoid the Hall of Maniacal Mirrors, and steer clear of the Inverted Hyper Ferris Wheel, and by all means, do not ride the Strobe Machine, a roller coaster that gave you the sensation of winking in and out of existence every few seconds for the entire duration of the ride. There was simply no telling how any of these pools of magic could be weaponized in a surprising manner.

The amphitheater and a couple of smaller stages were bathed in residual magic from performances, leading to the conclusion that the park might count a sizable number of capable magic-users among its cast members.

And no one knew exactly how much magic Roland Prismatic had learned from Harry.

When Glamour Esque finished his briefing, Agent Grey took

the floor once again, taking the opportunity to remind everyone just how dangerous their actual targets were as well. The enforcers were not familiar yet with Carissa as an opponent, so Grey rapidly got them up to speed.

Carissa had acquired twelve new psionic talents during her visit to Jirian's lab, which was only a few days ago, so she hadn't necessarily had much time to practice using them. But she'd demonstrated near-instant proficiency with skills like pyrokinesis and levitation in the lab. She might also now be proficient in telekinesis, telepathy, clairvoyance, astral projection, energetic healing, energetic draining, weather control, force walls, and two categories that Jirian had labeled "psychic storms" (an area effect) and "psychic blasts" (akin to a punch).

That was all in addition to her base talent, short-range mind control.

It was quite possible all her new talents had worn off by now. It was equally possible that as a psionic herself, she'd actually added these new talents to her permanent skill set.

Then it was Andasir's turn to review Rindasy's skill set with the Agents. Ze'd attempted to prepare for this moment. They were all familiar with the baseline Shai-Manak arsenal: shapeshifting, heavy resistance to both physical and magical attacks, regenerative healing on the off chance they did take damage, capable of detecting any magic used in their environment, a myriad of powerful attack spells at their disposal.

But Andasir was expected to provide additional intelligence specific to Rindasy's unique skills and potential weaknesses. Dimension Force would have no way to evaluate the accuracy of anything he said, but the eight enforcers might very well see through any attempts at deception here.

This was it, then, the moment ze once again betrayed zir own people and, for good measure, betrayed Dimension Force at the same time.

Ze spoke at length about Rindasy's skills, slowly cranking zir description away from the truth as ze went on. Be wary of engaging

Rindasy in aerial combat; Rindasy has single-handedly faced Fleet warships without suffering so much as a scratch. Rindasy is exceptionally skilled at rapid shapeshifting and has a master spy's knack for disguise; anyone you encounter inside that park might actually be Rindasy, so proceed with extreme caution. Rindasy was a perfect receptacle for the pearl because ze'd completely abandoned zir moral compass in service of an almost psychotic desire to bring down the Association; ze will show no one mercy today.

Et cetera.

If Dimension Force was impressed, intimidated, or bored by Andasir's recitation, ze couldn't say for sure. But that was mere preamble.

"Rindasy does, however, have one key weakness," ze said, taking on a somber tone. "It's the actual reason I've been sent on this mission. Just prior to our first contact with the Association, Rindasy and I reached a culmination point in our long history together as a romantic partnership. We committed to performing a consecration ritual known as the Binding of the Spheres."

That got a murmur out of the band of enforcers, which helped convince Dimension Force to pay closer attention. Binding of the Spheres was so potent that it was rarely used in modern times, but it played a significant role in historical lore.

"The ritual takes three months to complete, at the end of which time each participant in the ritual holds an inviolable claim of dominion over the other. The ritual raises and collects a pool of magic that either participant may draw from to issue compulsory suggestions that the other must obey to their utmost ability, on pain of extreme distress until the suggestion is followed. Suggestions of this nature are rarely ever offered, because of the mutuality of effect; each party is equally capable of proposing them and so they rarely choose to, instead striving to attain a life of pure cooperation."

"And that's like a romance thing for your people?" Whisper asked.

"More than romance is required for the ritual to succeed."

The only skeptic among the group was the wizard, Glamour

Esque, who asked, "What happens when one of you wants a divorce?"

Andasir shrugged and said, "I'll let you know the day any Shai-Manak ever expresses such a desire."

"Nice," Glamour Esque replied. "You're saying divorce is so alien to you that you have no idea what would happen if someone wanted to try Unbinding the Spheres?"

"We have never perceived a need to develop an Unbinding ritual—"

"Yes, thank you, once again the Shai-Manak demonstrate their utter moral superiority over all aspects of Association life, blah blah until the last blah in the universe has been spoken. I get it. And I see where you're going by telling us this lusty tale of deadly passive-aggression, but why don't you spell it out for us so we're all on the same page?"

"You will spare yourselves considerable struggle if you can pinpoint Rindasy's location and summon me there. I can then suggest that ze surrender and deactivate the pearl."

"No promises," said Agent Grey, "but we'll take that under advisement."

It was now half past six in the morning.

First milestone on the tactical plan, listed as optional: attempt a peaceful extraction by requesting that the park turn over the fugitives. Since the park already knew a hostile opponent was incoming, Grey and Steelplate agreed this option was worth a try.

To be maximally persuasive, Grey would make this request herself, in person, at the front gate of the park.

One of her nicknames was "the Commanding Word," after all.

·   ·   ·

At seven in the morning, an hour prior to when the park would ordinarily open for guests, Whisper released a few sacrificial drones to find out the range at which the automated defense platform would try to kill you. Right around one kilometer out from the walls, you started getting a laser show.

Agent Grey walked the distance from the Squadship to just outside the triggering range of the defense platform, facing the front gates in the distance, secure in the knowledge that she was being monitored closely by park surveillance. It was an affectation, coming here in person, but she enjoyed the symbolism of a lone Agent staring down their entire apparatus and then almost cheekily making a demand.

"My name is Agent Grey," she began, raising her voice slightly but not shouting, letting it echo across the empty parking lot as best it could. "I'm here to retrieve two fugitives who are wanted by the Association. Send them out to me, and we'll take our leave. I'll give you five minutes to comply."

Then she stood silently and waited. So far, she had simply made a demand. She had yet to issue a *command*.

.   .   .

Agent Grey's message was relayed up to the command center, played back so the whole room could hear it.

Roland declined to respond in any fashion. He had a pretty good feeling the two fugitives had ignored his request to hide in the tunnels, so he probably had no way of turning them over to Agent Grey even if he wanted to.

But as it happened, he didn't really want to.

.   .   .

One of the many seemingly unlikely attributes of the Building was the complete saturation of Building Modern, as it was called, as the default language of record.

Out in the multiverse, languages proliferated across and within cultures.

They evolved, cross-pollinated, drifted across generations and regions, mutated and spawned slang, arose via pure invention and spilled out of computers fully formed, and so on.

In the Building, language was heavily restricted to Building Modern. You might think, *Fuck that, I'm going off to school on some planet far away to learn a different language,* and it might even stick, but then you'd come back to the Building to visit your family on spring break and, *surprise,* you'd find that Building Modern was the only language you could remember.

Certainly the designers allowed Building Modern to evolve naturally over long periods of time. In fact, as colloquial variations established themselves in a given region, they were then pushed out through a queue, which silently distributed them to the Building's inhabitants. That had been one of the selling points of Building Modern in the pitch: "You're always on the latest version of Building Modern!"

The descriptor *Modern* pointed to the existence of an earlier variation, which was now referred to as Building Archaic. Written documents from the mythological era had survived, which provided a window into how Building Archaic had been used.

Academics of the modern era referred to Building Archaic as a "command language," a language that encoded status information about the speaker along with the meaning of the speaker's message, and moreover, enforced obedience to the message's intent along lines of status.

Naturally, Building Modern could accomplish a diluted version of that effect. If your boss sent you an email and said she wanted something done in the next ten minutes, you'd likely do it. That's Building Modern working its little bit of magic. But you wouldn't be *forced* to do it, which was the critical distinction about Building Archaic that made it much more compelling and effective when used to accomplish something like, to use an entirely random example, the construction of an impossibly tall, philosophically ridiculous Building in the center of reality.

Building Archaic could be also used for far less noble goals, of course.

Building Archaic was retired from popular usage prior to the end of the mythological era, its ethical dilemmas and potential for abuses fully researched and debated to the satisfaction of the design team, who gave Building Archaic a big thumbs-down during its final design review.

Building Modern would subsequently be implemented as the common language of the Building, becoming one of the Elements of Design Unity that governed how the Building worked. Projects in the Building always began with an approved template that gave you a set of common attributes for free: specs for mandatory gravitational effects, acceptable ranges for breathable atmosphere and survivable climates, inherent language proficiency in self-aware populations, and so on. Consistency of experience from floor to floor was a guiding principle, if not a rigid requirement. The designers wanted residents to largely feel comfortable traveling up and down the Building.

Exceptions to these elements were approved on a case-by-case basis, such as the introduction of subversive and dangerous floors that added to the Building's mystique and aura of adventure. Certain heavily modified templates pushed this exploration to its extremes and even became popular for a while, until their flaws became deeply apparent and their further implementation prohibited (see the controversial implementation of Earth floors).

By default, however, the vast majority of floors shared these holistic Elements of Design Unity, allowing the monumental achievement of the Building to stand tall as a contrast and complement to the chaotic creative maelstrom of the multiverse at large.

Agent Grey was fluent in Building Archaic.

And if you lived in the Building, you understood Building Archaic perfectly, whether you could speak it or not, whether you'd ever even heard it or not. The implementation of Building Modern was dependent upon this inherited library, in fact.

From a status and rank perspective, Muses outranked Agent Grey. The other Agents were her peers, and the ministers of Parliament enjoyed status beyond Grey's influence.

These parties would all be immune if Agent Grey attempted to command them with Building Archaic.

Any other living being in the Building, however, would almost certainly be susceptible.

At the five-minute mark, Agent Grey repeated her request, this time somewhat more forcefully.

. . .

The entire park trembled down to its foundation as the nearly deafening sound of a thousand shrieking trumpets rang out.

If you were in the tunnels, you heard it only as a muffled, distant roar with no clear intent behind it.

If you were in the command center, you heard it as a sudden howling windstorm far below you, its meaning elusive to you that far up in the sky.

But if you were anywhere in the park itself, you couldn't escape the sound of that cacophonous voice as it invaded your mind and hijacked your free will. You involuntarily decoded the instructions in the message, understood them to come from a source that could not be denied, and immediately began to execute these instructions to the best of your ability.

Every person in the park began searching for Carissa and Rindasy.

Even if you'd arrived with no prior knowledge whatsoever that the park was even harboring two fugitives named Carissa and Rindasy, somehow now you knew, and somehow now you desperately wanted to find them. You abandoned whatever makeshift station you occupied, compelled to satisfy the voice.

And the voice was ceaseless.

It rang out without interruption for minute after minute after minute, each successive repetition of its core command a reprimand for not fulfilling the command sooner. You worked with frantic desperation, self-organizing with others into teams and squads according to knowledge of the park's twists and turns. You and everyone around you flooded into the streets, looking high and low for anyone inside the walls who didn't carry an official employee badge.

Up in the command center, Roland's team started to panic. They could see the resulting chaos in the park on video surveillance and fortunately were clever enough to avoid patching in live sound as well. And they could see from surveillance that this sonic attack was all coming from a single individual, a kilometer away, with her mouth open to an unnatural degree, and enormous, inexplicable, gleaming feathered wings rising from her back, billowing to help in some way with shaping the sound that was unfolding.

"Would someone please shoot her?" Roland barked.

Across the room, the Director of Public Safety acquired manual control of the lasers and began firing at Agent Grey.

.   .   .

Agent Grey anticipated the attack, her unnatural reflexes providing her enough warning to fold her extended wings all around herself. The lasers singed her silver wings but did not penetrate them.

And still, her voice was ceaseless.

It was a kind of meditation for her, in fact, to allow the steadily unfolding intricacies of Building Archaic to stack upon themselves, providing increasingly intense waves of urgency to the recipients of the message.

Perhaps she'd lost the slightest hint of volume as a result of folding her wings around herself, it was true.

But as long as the park employees could still hear her at all, they were in thrall to her voice.

.   .   .

Building Archaic had flaws, of course. You couldn't easily instruct someone to do potential harm to themselves. Your target could conceivably resist an instruction like that, capable of weighing the purely psychic pain of disobeying the command versus the immediate physical damage to their person that might come from carrying out the command and deciding nah.

It wasn't difficult to extrapolate that Agent Grey intended harm to come to Carissa and Rindasy in the long run, giving the two of them an opportunity to resist her command.

But although their reactions were delayed almost a minute by this struggle to resist, they eventually succumbed to the inexorable pull to descend from the tower and hand themselves over to the mobs that were prowling the streets of the park below.

Of course, no one recognized them.

They began shouting to get the mob's attention. "We're the fugitives!" and the like.

They couldn't be heard over the sound of the voice from outside the walls and did not receive the response they desired. Surely the fugitives wouldn't simply be walking around in the streets, the employees must've thought; surely they'll have to be dragged out of some obscure hiding place.

When it became clear that no one was going to take them into custody, they decided to go to the source of the voice of their own accord. They took flight, united in their desire to obey.

.   .   .

They didn't get far.

A new soundscape suddenly rose up throughout the park, blaring at top volume over banks of loudspeakers mounted on poles on every street corner.

Ordinarily, these speakers provided gentle background music throughout the day or played soundtracks during the parade. But during emergencies, the system could be utilized for other broadcasts as necessary.

Soon the sound of Agent Grey's voice was entirely frequency-bombed by the sound of the theme song to the classic live-action kids' show *Helpless the Bunny's Strip Mall*.

The show provided a modern take on the iconic character, surrounding him with an ensemble of wacky neighboring shopkeepers and talking consumer goods as he attempted to make a living as a Pilates instructor. Although the show was advertised as a kids' show, older audiences found its offbeat humor and its implicit critique of rampant commodification's degrading effect on the working class and the poor to be appealing as well.

Suddenly, the mob's own voices rang out in multipart harmony, singing along with the diabolically catchy theme song. Naturally, if you were employed by Wild Massive, you knew this song forward and backward.

Agent Grey's hold over the denizens of the park was lost.

Carissa and Rindasy came to their senses and quickly reevaluated their situation. It wasn't super clear to either of them exactly what was happening, but their decision to watch this morning's proceedings from atop Castle Tormento now seemed, in retrospect, exceedingly foolish.

They began making their way on foot through the crowded streets to the tunnels.

. . .

Agent Grey fell silent for a moment, recognizing what had happened inside the park.

They could keep that music playing on a loop for the rest of the day.

Clever. But they'd made her angry.

Oh, she could get closer, go inside the park herself, compete directly with the sound of the PA system. But she couldn't be sure her voice would be heard even then, and regardless, she wanted to stay outside the perimeter of the park in case more destructive options needed to be deployed; no sense wandering into the potential blast radius just yet.

"Commence extraction," she ordered her team.

"Are we allowed to shoot these people?" Steelplate's voice came back in her ear. He wasn't hungry to shoot people; he just literally wanted to know the answer.

"Please wait for them to shoot first," Agent Grey replied.

If they needed to get indiscriminate with violence at some point after all, her other nickname was "the Cleansing Fire."

■   ■   ■

Steelplate and Anjette approached the front gate on foot, passing Agent Grey along the way. Grey had chosen to stay in the field to watch the proceedings for the time being. As usual, Anjette carried no weaponry, and as usual, Steelplate was fully armed with his complete arsenal of doom.

Steelplate's rare organic components were currently fully encased in thaumaturgically resistant armor plating, rated to withstand volleys from most sub-apoc weapon classes. Anjette was already indestructible and resistant to magic. The lasers the park deployed against them might eventually punch a hole in Steelplate's armor, but not before the two of them punched a hole in the front gate.

Abruptly the lasers stopped firing.

Whisper shouted in their ears, "Front gate, you have incoming!"

"Incoming *what*?" Anjette asked.

"Incoming, uh, flying robot!" Whisper replied.

■   ■   ■

The folks in the command center watched Steelplate and Anjette's steady ground approach to the front gate with a certain amount of incredulity, wondering what the catch was that they were sending two people into the direct line of fire of the automated defenses.

This was the moment that Leticia's Irregulars had been waiting for.

In the employee parking lot on the other side of the park, the three aging shuttles that had delivered a small handful of Irregulars to the scene seemed to jerk to life in impossible fashion, as though some powerful magnetic force was twisting them like puzzle cubes and then smashing them together into a new configuration.

Where once three aging shuttles were parked, now stood a towering robotic sentinel. Its arms culminated in enormous electrically charged wrecking balls, and it spat plasma as a test that melted through the pavement below it and kept going deep into the ground. It swiftly took flight toward the front gate, remotely piloted by a team of Irregulars in the command center.

"That's pretty snazzy," Roland said to Leticia. "What do you call that thing?"

"Its name is Hammertron Alpha," Leticia replied proudly. "My kid's idea."

"Interesting," Roland said. "Can you make it dance?"

. . .

Hammertron Alpha emerged from behind the visual distortion of the protective dome in midleap and landed with an enormous *whump*, destroying the pavement underneath it on impact. It stood twelve meters tall with a footprint almost as wide, and it took mighty swings at Steelplate from a considerable distance away.

Steelplate was surprisingly dexterous for a cyborg ogre, leaping backward to avoid the sizzling wrecking ball appendage aimed at his head. With relish, Steelplate considered those swipes at his head a permission slip to start firing at the thing.

To determine what would be most effective against Hammertron Alpha, Steelplate's onboard targeting automation activated in a "spray" mode in which it rapid cycled through all its available weapon classes in the earliest stages of an encounter as a test, then selected the one that would produce the most damage in the shortest time to use for the rest of the encounter. For a moment, Steelplate looked like fireworks were going off from every part of his armored body.

To Steelplate's delight, the targeting system chose his singularity rifle as its preferred weapon for the combat.

In auto-fire mode with a singularity rifle, you could group your shots to the point where the fabric of reality tore open temporarily and your target was slurped out of existence. It was absurdly cruel to use this weapon against organic targets, but he noticed that his targeting system was also busy trying to jam the robot's remote piloting receiver, meaning no live pilot was aboard.

At pretty much the same time that Steelplate released his first volley, Hammertron Alpha fired a hundred tiny rockets that exploded against Steelplate's chest and knocked him onto his back. Only a couple of his singularity rounds managed to land against Hammertron Alpha as a result. The shots weren't lucky enough to knock the robot out of commission in one go. The robot was also surprisingly mobile itself, rocketing forward and preparing a mighty overhead smash of one of its wrecking balls toward Steelplate's prone body.

Anjette leapt in front of Steelplate and caught the wrecking ball on its downswing.

The crunching and straining of robotic gears grinding against her strength was its own satisfying reward, but moments later, Anjette wrenched the arm completely off and hurled it into the distance. She just barely managed to spot its other arm coming toward her on a wide swing and ducked and rolled underneath it.

From his back, Steelplate fired off a full barrage directly into the center of Hammertron Alpha, and as the bursts went off, he watched the entire giant robot crumple in successive sections, until it was no more than the tiniest possible sliver of matter, and then it winked out completely.

Then he stood and switched to a concussive grenade launcher, which blew the barrier off the front gate of the park.

The volume of shrieking curseware that escaped into the air as the barrier was breached was truly impressive. If you were the average gatecrasher and you invoked this amount of curseware, you would suddenly regret being alive in a hundred diabolical ways. But the curses were ineffective against these targets. Steelplate's thaumaturgical shielding held fast, and Anjette brushed off the effects of the curses without noticing them.

Moments later, Steelplate and Anjette strolled into the park.

. . .

Roland saw the crestfallen look on Leticia's face and wanted to think of something consoling to say, but he was already distracted by a new threat.

The train from Prism City was coming toward the park.

It was moving faster than he'd ever seen it move, giving the impression of turning red with heat as it approached, although clearly that was some kind of comical illusion. Steam rose as though the entire train was literally sizzling, also clearly ridiculous. In fact, he could almost make out a spherical wall of superheated air preceding the front of the train, which, come on now.

But it was clearly headed straight for the park at an unprecedented speed. Should've braked automatically, but somebody must've disabled the safety sensors on the track.

Not only that, but the train was specifically excluded from the targeting parameters of the automated defense platform, because never in a zillion years did you want those lasers going off by accident and incinerating a trainful of guests. Those lasers couldn't physically fire on the train even under manual control.

He jumped on the radio and shouted, "Clear the train station!"

The train station was barricaded similarly to the front gate, with thick metal plating tied into the curseware that was running throughout the walls. The Agents had been smart to target physical weak spots like the front gate and the train station.

Roland hadn't been smart enough to prepare additional defensive surprises in those specific locations.

Well, you live and learn, he thought. *Assuming you do in fact live,* he added to himself.

. . .

The train pulverized the steel plating blocking its way and careened without slowing all the way through the train station, until it smashed headlong into the backstop.

The backstop did its job admirably. The train car in front was

388 · SCOTTO MOORE

completely smashed in between the backstop and the several cars trailing behind it. These cars buckled and flipped upward and spun and ultimately ripped the entire train into unwieldy pieces before finally the whole ensemble came to a halt in its new form as a flaming pile of wreckage.

Following closely behind the train, four Shai-Manak enforcers in flying forms entered the train station. The enforcers shifted into their hulking humanoid lizard forms.

Moments later, Agent Glamour Esque floated into the station as well.

■ ■ ■

Meanwhile, two balls of glowing colored light, blue and purple, sailed toward the park at such speed that they appeared to observers in the command center as thin, wispy threads in the sky.

The Moods were headed for the park, unhindered by the defensive lasers, which passed harmlessly through them. They were going over the walls, not through them, so the curseware baked into the walls wasn't triggered.

But first, these two energetic vampires flew directly at the protective drape of magical energy that surrounded the park and stopped to feast. And once they were fully suffused with this energy, they tore open a temporary opening in the dome, just wide enough for four Shai-Manak enforcers in flying form to sail into the airspace over the park.

The Moods followed through after them.

■ ■ ■

Just as the Agents made their initial assault on the park, Tabitha reappeared once again in the Explorers Guild bunker, only a few minutes after she'd left. She was surprisingly good at navigation with the machine.

Nicholas helped her disengage from the spacetime machine, catching it as it slid off her shoulders and hanging it up in its customary position on wall hooks. From there, he could scroll through the machine's logs on its little display to verify that the machine had traveled to the intended destination and returned safely. Diagnostics turned up green.

He turned back to Tabitha, who was lying down now on one of the couches. She had a broken look on her face—the look of someone who'd just seen a ghost, perhaps. He brought her a water bottle, which she accepted without enthusiasm.

"Thank you for loaning me your spacetime machine," she finally managed to say. "Twice, even. And for the writing exercises. And just . . . for being here." She made eye contact with him and said, "I think you're off the hook now, as far as your commitment to Grandma Dee is concerned."

"Strange loop complete," he said, satisfied.

"Did anything happen while I was gone?"

"Dimension Force arrived a few minutes ago."

"Oh," she said, her exhaustion swept aside by adrenaline. "I thought Carissa and Rindasy were supposed to be here with you."

"I thought so, too."

"You're not going to stick around for this, are you? You could catch up with the rest of the Guild."

"Yes, although I was hoping to take our fugitive friends with me when I go. For now, I'm content to stay in case there's anything else I can possibly do to help."

Tabitha recited the incantation that provided access to her extradimensional safe, and withdrew the capture glass on its thin silver necklace. She felt her heart rate increase just at the sight of it.

"You told me you don't like traveling to the future," she said, letting the capture glass rest in her open palm, where it gave off a soft multihued glow. "If I had to guess, I'd say it's because for you, the future can't be unwritten any easier than the past. You're only ever a witness. The future has already accounted for your visits, and there's nothing you can do if you witness something you desperately wish you could change. All you can do is return to the present and then wait until that agonizing moment arrives right on schedule. Or eventually, you could flee into the past for good and never meet that future moment again. Am I close?"

"At last, I feel seen," he said quietly.

"The Muses weren't witnesses."

"No, unequivocally not."

"But they left some of their tools behind," she said, rotating the capture glass so that it caught reflections of the overhead light. "Do you think we should use them? Or put them carefully back where we found them?"

He hesitated a moment to consider the subtext of her questions, then said, "There are artifacts in the Archives that we do not list in any accessible catalog of our collection, because the estimable Archivists of old believed they were too dangerous for any mortal to wield. Without proper catalog entries, we don't even remember what some of those artifacts do or represent." He nodded toward the capture glass and said, "Your artifact, however, is a family heirloom. It's your legacy, and if I'm not mistaken, you've just received proper instruction for using it. I think it would be a lost opportunity for you to set it aside or leave it in a safe. What outcome are you searching for?"

"Allegory can't see into the chasm because her own future is tied up in it somehow. Maybe I can light a path for her."

"You're still loyal to the person who threw you into this mess?"

"I got myself into this mess when I got in the elevator to come to this park. Either she manipulated me into having a conscience about what I did, or I actually have one, and either way . . . she keeps a creative brain trust around her because she can't see the details the way we can, just like we never see the huge shifts in the story that she instigates. So look, I'm here, I'm her protégé, I've got an artifact that might help us understand the road ahead . . . so how would you feel if I used the capture glass right here and now?"

He said, "Well, one thing is true about this situation . . . As a leading expert in the field, I can safely say that there is literally no time like the present."

. . .

In a sudden flash, your consciousness is both expanded beyond belief and crushed into the tiniest sliver of its potential as you transition from human to human-as-Muse.

Now, you're Epiphany Foreshadow.

You're sitting at a desk, you're an unassuming low-level resource at an agency so powerful it defies even your comprehension, and you're—what the fuck is happening here—you're copyediting marketing collateral? In a fucking cubicle? Is the capture glass even working correctly? You scan your surroundings with increasing concern—where is the high-ceilinged loft with the brick walls where it's an open office plan and everyone's drinking espresso or whatever?

But no, you're an apprentice, barely above intern, and you're nowhere near the home office; this is regional.

Except.

You're also spitting out proposals. Pitches. They've got an "employee suggestion" email address you can send ideas to, and you email that fucker twice a day.

Ambitious. Inventive. Unorthodox. Slightly insouciant about it, like you're *supposed* to be copyediting marketing collateral, certainly they expect you to do *something,* but look, the fuck you're just going to let these ideas of yours rush past without taking note, and anyway you get to take a lunch and you can spend that time how you want, dammit.

These are no mere half-formed sketches, either. Upgrades to mythologies and belief systems; artifact families to compensate for flawed engineering decisions earlier in the project; ergonomic office chairs for the cubicle farm floors—nothing escapes your consideration. You've developed your ideas in detail, you've done the research you can do without a team at your disposal, you're knowledgeable enough to make informed suggestions about implementation, and you're passionate about the big engineering issues and the tiniest little fit and finish items, it's all part of the grand package of each pitch, each little mini-presentation you craft and fire off into the aethyr, where presumably somebody is considering them for at least a split second or two.

You start to develop themes, like you'll submit a whole string of suggestions to that email address that are fine on their own, but when you see them stacked or collected, you realize how deep the vision goes. You're fast, too—these ideas seem to come to you fully formed, almost as fast as you can document them.

And sure, you're offering some sly critique along the way, little digs here and there at actual approved initiatives, but it can't be helped, some of these people are a little bit—mmm, shall we say *lazy* with their thinking, to be generous, or let's say *derivative* if we want to be mean about it.

After all, did they set up an apprenticeship program because they wanted an injection of fresh blood and new ideas, or did they just need more freaking copy editors for marketing collateral?

Months go by. You're relentless. Maybe it's your imagination, but are your coworkers avoiding you, giving you that weird side-eye like they know something about you that you yourself haven't figured out yet? Endless marketing shit to deal with, websites to update, socials to manage, but you're figuring out exactly how they message what they're building, the lingo they use is the first line of creation, and you see the opportunities staring at you. Your pitches to the suggestion box aren't vanity pitches designed to glorify your name, they're fucking keyword-optimized for maximum impact in search.

You don't eat lunches with everyone else. You eat lunches alone, at your desk.

Because fuck these clueless fucks.

Someday it's gonna be different. *Real* different.

. . .

News spreads fast: an Architect from the home office is coming to visit. Like, tomorrow.

Not one of these junior architect pricks you see parading around your office like they're influencers or some shit. The Architects at the home office call the shots. Carve out firmaments. Set the wheels of history in motion. Harness elemental forces. Create style guides.

Short notice, hasn't put any meetings on anyone's calendar, just a drive-by visit apparently, which is unheard of.

Your supervisor is unusually cruel to you.

"I know exactly what you're thinking"—which, no, they fucking don't—"and if you say one word out of turn for the duration of the Architect's visit, you'll be bounced so far out of this place, you'll be counting grains of sand for the rest of eternity"—which, no, you fucking won't—"because you think I haven't noticed all your little 'suggestions'? Well, guess what? Suggestions from this office are reviewed and must be approved before they go to the home office, and who do you think sits on that review committee, hmm? Do you understand me?"

What?

You might possibly be capable of murder.

Your supervisor continues, "You think so *highly* of yourself"—which, hell yes, you do—"that it hasn't occurred to you that there are those in this organization who have *paid their dues* and you have the *audacity* to suggest *improvements* to their designs"—which, fuck yes, you do—"it's frankly outrageous and will be noted in your next performance review, so you will keep your mouth *shut* and keep out of the way while the Architect is here. Do you understand me? Do you?"

You're captivated by all that fear in their eyes. That's appealing to look at, now isn't it? But you nod your assent. Time and place.

First thing the next morning, you are at your desk before anyone else even thinks to climb out of bed for the day, diligently assembling new FAQs, swapping creative elements on landing pages, analyzing A/B tests and promoting the winning campaigns, updating terms and conditions of the latest offers, liking and reposting blurbs from your paid influencers, inserting the latest revisions into the master deck for the upcoming review, mentally slitting your throat over and over, when the Architect arrives.

And peruses the empty desks all across the floor with a bit of light disdain, before realizing that *you're* here.

The Architect strolls in your direction, perhaps thinking you'll sub in for the missing receptionist and point out which office they can use for the day.

Instead, the Architect sidles up to your desk, cosmically smooth, impressively benign and gentle, and yet sharp as a razor, and says, "You're Epiphany Foreshadow, aren't you?"

You nod.

"Let's find a conference room. We have much to discuss."

You smile and say, "Of course."

The conference room you choose is the fishbowl in the center of the floor.

For the next three hours, the Architect grills you about every aspect of every suggestion you ever sent to that email address. Unbeknownst to your supervisor, blind cc's were going up to the home office the whole time, because they just don't trust regional politics when it comes to recognizing creative genius.

And you chose the fishbowl so that every one of your so-called coworkers gets to see you and the Architect having a long, intricate, enjoyable, provocative conversation about the core fundamentals of this agency's approach and how they might be due for a refresh in the form of your library of suggestions, and there's your supervisor strolling in and *wow* the way their face just lights up with pure antipathy as they realize what's happening in the fishbowl is deeply satisfying, but look, you're too busy to gloat just this exact second. That day will come, yea verily, that day will come.

Finally, the Architect says, "I'd like you to come work for me at the home office."

This is it—*this is the moment you remember most from the first time you wore this capture glass*—the moment you've literally hoped for since you were practically a child—*the moment that transformed you in ways you still don't understand*—and you're practically vibrating with excitement—*and if it hits you again as hard as it did the last time, who knows what you'll be at the end of this experience*—as the Architect starts to explain what responsibilities you might pick up in your first days on the job—*which was kind of the point, sure, but you've also grown into a version of yourself that you're really rather happy with*—and you're nodding along because the potential of it all is so unreal—*but you realize you can't simply disconnect from this experience now, not when she's so close to getting what she wants, it would be cruel*—and finally, you're actually humbled by the opportunity you're receiving, and it seems daunting and challenging and how could you possibly be ready for this—*so you get yourself ready for this, because you realize you don't know how to interrupt this before it runs its course even if you wanted to*—and you say, "I'm totally in."

And then the metaphor of this entire experience starts to break down because metaphor is only sufficient up to a point for translation purposes, and the Architect opens their mouth wider than should technically be possible, and like a dragon spitting fire, they unleash a barrage of pure creative energy that flat out fucking

destroys you

and reconstitutes you from atomic particles of ingenuity itself.

You've been promoted to Muse, full-time position, endless hours, unimaginable benefits.

And you see it now, you see how you missed so many different hooks and handles and levers and knobs, you see how the underlying tapestry constantly unfolds according to millions of steady micro-adjustments to the original instruction set, you see how you yourself could start making greater contributions to the flow of micro-adjustments and then anticipate the results with greater and greater fidelity until you're no longer simply divining the future but outright creating aspects of it, along with the untold others who contribute to this tapestry at the same time, and you're unbelievably awed by what you see and what you've learned, hoping beyond hope that you can remember everything you've absorbed here, until something new happens, something you absolutely do not remember from the first time you wore this capture glass.

It's the suddenly thundering voice of Epiphany Foreshadow herself, filling every corner of your awareness, saying:

"AH, *THERE* YOU ARE. I THINK IT'S TIME WE MEET IN PERSON. I'LL SEND SOMEONE TO FETCH YOU."

Suddenly, you're no longer in control of your actions. Epiphany Foreshadow is driving you now, issuing her own steady micro-instructions about you and your fate that you are compelled to obey. Not this captured memory of Epiphany, you realize without a shadow of a doubt—instead, it's the contemporaneous Epiphany, wherever she might be, who has taken an interest in your immediate future, guiding you along a predetermined track and you're along for the ride, and you can see that big, terrifying hill in front of you, but it's too late to turn around and head back to the station.

You realize you're standing now, moving toward the door of the bunker, shouldn't be possible, but the capture glass is no longer in play-back mode. You were yanked out of static playback right into the inter-active suite, the hotline straight to a Muse, only it hadn't occurred to you that the capture glass also accepted incoming calls. Now Epiphany's steering you through the situation. Nicholas tries to intercept you, and you're shocked by your immediate, vicious response. You step over him, unlock the bunker door, and head into the tunnels.

You may be a central character, a crucial thread in the underly-ing tapestry, but wearing a capture glass doesn't actually make you a Muse.

. . .

Carissa and Rindasy were not sufficiently familiar with the park to make rapid progress on the streets or backstage paths toward the tunnels. Carissa tried to use her clairvoyance to stretch her mind out and deduce a clear path, but there was far too much psychic noise in the park for her to concentrate on anything specific. Instead, she nearly lost herself to an overwhelming torrent of panicked, heightened emotional and sensory information coming from all corners of the environment. Maybe someday she'd be skilled enough with that talent to find her way through a situation like this one, but not today.

Instead, they flew over the park at low altitude, hoping to avoid surveillance, moving quicker than they would've on the ground but certainly not at top speed, looking for landmarks that would help them find the path to the tunnels.

Rindasy was the first to understand that they were now being actively pursued. Ze felt the four enforcers shapeshifting from something small into something more menacing. And ze could only detect that particular act of magic from close range. Ze didn't dare look back.

Ze shouted to Carissa, "They've found us!"

The two of them sped up dramatically, outpacing the four enforcers who were now in pursuit. Flying at top speed was taxing to Carissa's concentration, leaving her vulnerable and without her other talents easily accessible. Rindasy too found it hard to imagine casting any spell that would be effective on a Shai-Manak enforcer while pushing zir speed to its limit.

The enforcers caught up, flanking them and tailing them, threatening to crash into them and knock them out of the sky, following them closely toward the center of the park, a town square facsimile with a clock tower and rows of quaint little shops and hot dog stands and a little stage where crooners sang the hits of yesteryear. The parade marched proudly right through this town square each night to celebrate the literal fact that it'd been another joyous and delightful day here in maybe not the biggest Wild Massive park but certainly the *best* Wild Massive park and anyone who didn't agree with that assessment was a corporate tool.

And right smack-dab in the middle of all that artificially wholesome wholesomeness was a swirling miasma of colored light, a gorgeous display like a prism undergoing a constant transition from liquid to solid and back to liquid again while rainbows were shot through the center of the whole thing.

Rindasy realized the enforcers were *herding* them toward this display of light. And by then, it was too late to resist.

The Moods had captured both Rindasy and Carissa in their seductive grip.

.   .   .

The nature of the Moods' embrace was that you desperately wanted to succumb, even as your life force was drained right the fuck out of you.

As Carissa and Rindasy landed gently in front of the swirling miasma lure presented by the Moods, Carissa thought she could help the situation by opening up a telepathic link between her and the Moods. She thought this new channel would give the Moods enhanced access to the essential stuff they were trying to drain from her.

This opened up a terribly weird feedback loop, in which she felt the essential spark they'd drained from her reflected right back at her through the telepathic link, mixed in with all *their* essential spark, and Rindasy's essential spark, mixed in with the pooled energy of the giant magical dome around the park that they'd gorged on before coming here. All that spark practically spilled, overflowing, into the telepathic link, and not only did she get her own essential spark "back" but she got it back *amplified* by, like, mega.

Importantly, she abruptly got *control* of herself back.

There was a split second when the Moods fully and absolutely realized what was happening, caught a glimpse of Carissa's intention, and hurriedly tried to sever the link connecting the three of them together. But before they could disengage, Carissa utilized all the excess spark she'd accumulated to launch a tremendous psychic storm across the telepathic link.

In an instant, the Moods were psionically pulverized by an

energetic torrent, hit so hard that every last sliver or fragment of consciousness that held them together as souls with minds was scattered to the far reaches of existence, never to find union as beings of intent again.

The physical manifestation of this event was a sudden explosion of light, as though a small supernova occurred right there in the town square, comprised of every possible color both real and imaginary, devoid of heat but painfully bright in an existential way, as though the light laid bare every particle of doubt and meanness and regret and pettiness and selfish angst you'd ever carried around, shining an overpowered spotlight on your fundamental flaws as a person.

The explosion of light seemed to avoid Carissa, but Rindasy caught the full brunt of the blast and collapsed in a brief moment of agony before passing out altogether.

The four enforcers who'd been circling the plaza, under instruction to let the Moods work first, were blown out of the sky, crashing into nearby shops or hitting the street hard, unconscious just like Rindasy.

Carissa reached out with her mind and provided a dose of energetic healing that got Rindasy back on zir feet.

Behind Carissa, Rindasy spotted the other four enforcers, in hulking lizard form, sprinting through the plaza toward them, then shapeshifting in midair and at high speed into what most closely resembled nightmarish hornets, each about the size of a small car, with long, sharp stingers.

Rindasy recognized their attack formation and said calmly, "Get down."

Instinctively, Carissa dropped to the ground, giving Rindasy room to leap forward to meet the oncoming wedge of monsters. Ze transformed into a magical creature called a *flamewind*—imagine a cross between a tiny winged pony and a sloshing pool of molten lava—which infiltrated their formation and swept the hornets up in a tornado of magical fire that melted their current forms and hurled the slag of their bodies in all directions.

Rindasy resumed human form, landing deftly next to Carissa. "We need to get out of this plaza," ze said.

"Do we?" Carissa replied. "Cuz we're kinda kicking ass here."

"I don't even know which way we're headed anymore," Rindasy admitted.

"Oh shit," Carissa suddenly said, and Rindasy braced for some kind of impact.

But this time, Carissa wasn't referring to an incoming threat. Rindasy turned and saw a young human woman wearing a Wild Massive bomber jacket wandering slowly through the plaza toward them, seemingly oblivious to anything that had just happened. She seemed locked in a struggle, as though she desperately wanted to be free or at least to make eye contact with them, but was losing that battle altogether.

"Do you know that person?" Rindasy asked.

"Yeah," Carissa replied, bewildered by the sight. "That's Tabitha."

Tears streamed down Tabitha's face as she approached, but as she reached the exact center of the plaza, she stopped and turned her attention to the sky.

Impulsively, Carissa reached out to Tabitha telepathically.

The sudden connection was jolting, like grasping a live wire. Carissa's mind was filled with screeching rebellion at her attempt to probe deeper than Tabitha's surface thoughts. But she surprisingly heard Tabitha's actual voice quite clearly, Tabitha alone, shouting for help in some distant recess of her mind. She glimpsed the thing that now controlled Tabitha from across an improbable distance, not its physical form but a sliver of its psychic presence, and could tell the thing resented any attempts to expose its unfolding plans and schemes.

History was already in its grasp, but *this thing thought it could use Tabitha as an instrument to take control of the immediate future.* And as she gaped, she could practically see the wheels of history pivot ever so slightly, as though all of history was being micro-adjusted just barely, just enough, to engineer a mechanism for shaking Carissa loose from her invasive voyeurism at this exact moment.

Suddenly, a gunshot rang out, and a bullet struck Carissa in the chest, knocking her onto her back, severing the telepathic link with Tabitha and her controller.

Agent Wynderia Gallas, assassin and rogue, leapt down from the clock tower, just before Rindasy destroyed the entire thing with an enormous raging fireball.

While the debris from the clock tower was still raining down onto nearby shops, Rindasy's attention was forcibly yanked away toward a greater threat.

Someone in the vicinity was casting a potent spell with zir as the target.

Ze turned toward Carissa and almost instantly realized ze'd acted too late. As ze took a step toward Carissa, the distance between the two of them grew instead of shrinking, and as ze took another step, the distance grew even wider, until ze clearly understood that ze'd been enveloped in an illusion that was distorting zir perception of zir surroundings. Every direction ze looked, the environment seemed to somehow be steadily receding away from zir, until ze felt like a tiny molecule suspended in a smeared, abstract interpretation of reality.

. . .

Agent Glamour Esque inspected his work from a distance. He'd come prepared with a handcrafted illusion that no Shai-Manak had seen before, designed to be completely immersive as opposed to a common dazzle spell. The illusion had succeeded in immobilizing Rindasy. Satisfied that the illusion was firmly set in place, he conjured a sealed block of magical energy around Rindasy (and the fallen body of Carissa for good measure), a cage that would act as an additional line of defense in case Rindasy found a way to dispel the initial illusion.

Killing Rindasy would be Steelplate's problem to solve.

He floated to the ground near the cage to catch his breath. He saw Wynderia approaching from across the plaza and waved to acknowledge her.

"I've got both fugitives in custody," he announced. "Sorry, Andasir, it looks like we won't need your kinky 'binding ritual' magic. Steelplate, this cage will last another fifteen minutes."

"I'll be there in five," Steelplate replied.

Now, Glamour Esque turned his attention to the remaining individual in the town square. He didn't recognize this woman, but he clearly recognized the energetic signature of the capture glass dangling from a necklace she wore. The capture glass was acting as a conduit for some kind of remote signal that must have overwhelmed the woman in some way. Wynderia had stopped to talk to her, but she was unresponsive.

Finding a Muse artifact on the scene was a strange and unhappy escalation to the situation.

"Heads up, I've got a woman here under the hypnotic influence of a capture glass," Glamour Esque said as he headed toward the woman. "I don't remember covering this in the briefing."

After a brief silence, Agent Grey said, "Is she interfering with the mission?"

"She is not," Glamour Esque reported.

"Then she's not our problem," Grey said.

Glamour Esque bit down on a response. True, the woman wasn't interfering with the mission, but you didn't wander around in a hypnotic daze, openly brandishing a Muse artifact, on an average day in the life. He had a suspicion the woman was in trouble or was capable of making trouble, and that probably did make her the Agents' problem.

"Friends, we have new parties incoming," said Whisper.

The woman turned toward the horizon, her attention suddenly locked on something in the distance. It was difficult to discern against the bright morning sky, but soon enough, Glamour Esque and Wynderia had a good idea what she was looking at: four bright streaks like comets with exceptionally long tails were descending through the sky at the horizon, on a course that would take them into the chasm.

Then, a sudden course correction, and now the comets swooped in a low curve into a leisurely trajectory straight toward the park.

"I'm having trouble getting a reading on distance here," Whisper said, "because that mirage on the horizon is giving my instruments the runaround. Our bogeys could be a hundred miles away, or they could be just outside the parking lot."

Wynderia said, "I'm no magic-user, but I'm getting intensely unpleasant vibes from those things. We need to be somewhere not here, and fast."

In case anyone was confused about the intent of these incoming comets, they began to emit horrible, chilling howls and barks, trumpeting their imminent arrival.

"Can we shoot them?" Steelplate asked.

Agent Grey sighed and said, "Once the fugitives are eliminated, you can engage them at your discretion."

.   .   .

In the command center, the approach of the comets brought everything to a standstill.

Roland had lived his entire life in sight of the chasm. He'd always expected this day would come.

They were about to make first contact with the Maladies.

"All right, listen up," he announced to his comrades. "Get every laser on the wall aimed at those things and ready to fire. Arm every missile launcher and load every cannon we've got up here. The minute those things are in range, rotate the deck and fire until the guns are empty."

He turned to Leticia with a grim smile.

"Looks like you get to see a fireworks show after all," he said.

"Looks like this new parade's out to kill us, though," she replied.

"Well, some days are better than others."

The automated defense lasers began firing. Oh, how the

automated defense lasers began firing. Any laser with an unobstructed view of the Maladies fired in concert.

Still the Maladies approached.

Missiles and rockets sailed through the air. The observation
deck of the Space Elevator—a level below the command center—
began a steady rotation so that all the repurposed fireworks cannons could get clean shots off at the Maladies.

Roland couldn't afford the really good heat-seekers, but magic
had a way of flummoxing heat-seekers anyway, and they didn't
make magic-seekers, so you really just had to point your missile
launchers at a thing, and then hope the missiles' visual targeting
systems worked well enough to reach that thing for exploding purposes.

The culmination of this effort was the near-complete destruction of the outer hulls of what now appeared to be a strange design of single-passenger ships. They seemed to be sleek capsules
outfitted with thrusters that were spitting out those brightly colored comet tails, and they were getting dented by rockets and
scored by lasers and starting to generally deteriorate.

Then they passed right through the energy drape that descended from the Space Elevator down to the walls of the park.
The guns and lasers stopped firing, inhibited by fail-safes from
targeting anything inside the walls.

The magical energy in the drape was sufficient to finish the
job on these strange little ships. They burst apart in gorgeous explosions that showered the park below with debris. Colored fires
began to burn wherever the debris touched down, giving the fire
brigade a challenge they were qualified to handle.

But the individuals piloting those strange little ships were still
very much alive, wearing wingsuits or some bullshit that kept
them in the air. Maybe they were actual wings. It was hard for
Roland to tell because the park's surveillance fritzed out trying
to get a clear picture of these things. You could get a general
sense that they were extremely tall humanoids, giants maybe,
but you couldn't make out distinct features, or determine what

they were wearing, or whether they were carrying weapons, or whether they had fangs or claws. You couldn't really determine much about them except that they were made of ill intent, although to be fair, that was more just a gut feeling than a proper physical description.

They began circling above the park, sweeping back and forth on a hunt.

.　　.　　.

Glamour Esque quickly surmised they were hunting for the woman with the capture glass, which acted like a flashing beacon, giving away her position.

"Excuse me. Did you call for a ride?" he asked the woman.

She ignored him, kept her attention focused skyward as the aerial pattern narrowed toward her.

"Are they your friends?" he asked. "Can you even hear me? Is there a malevolent psychic force controlling your body while your mind is trapped in a tiny prison screaming to get out?"

The woman tilted her head toward him ever so slightly.

"We can help, you know. We're Dimension Force. We're frequently helpful, especially if you're not wanted by Parliament."

.　　.　　.

Public safety had a protocol for the unlikely event that an unwanted intruder somehow miraculously made it over the walls and into the park, where they might threaten the well-being of paying guests. They didn't answer to some outside municipal authority; they *were* the municipal authority, and they had wide latitude to shoot first and ask questions later. And they sourced their weapons from the same Pirate King who fed weapons to the Explorers Guild gunrunners. The good stuff, in other words.

But something about the absolutely bone-chilling howls these four Maladies emitted near continuously as they circled above the park put fear in the hearts of every member of public safety and every other armed employee. And anyway, Roland had ordered them not to get killed today. So the protocol did not play out. Those who could scurry to the tunnels to join their hidden compatriots made a break for it, but most hid in place, under counters, in storerooms, within machine shops, inside various attractions. Today was not a day to make a run for employee of the year.

The howling and shrieking of the Maladies reached a fevered peak as they arrived above the plaza.

One of them swooped down toward Tabitha and was soundly smacked across the plaza, where it crashed with a yelp into a corner ice cream shop that crumpled into debris all around it.

"You do that?" Wynderia asked.

"Uh-huh," Glamour Esque replied. "Invisible fist." Originally the spell was called Zudenklezen's Fingers of Five, but even Zudenklezen had admitted the name was pretentious.

The other three scattered, momentarily startled at the sight of one of their own taking such a blow, then let loose an angry cacophony of screams and hisses as they regrouped and prepared to dive.

"How many invisible fists you got?" Wynderia asked.

"Just the one, really."

The debris of the ice cream shop exploded outward as the giant wrenched itself to its feet and spotted the two of them. For a brief, shimmering moment, all four of the Maladies were keenly focused on Glamour Esque and Wynderia Gallas, their imminent attacks hanging suspended in a moment of pristine antipathy between intention and action.

The moment was savagely interrupted by a fusillade of rockets and pellet grenades from the far end of the plaza. Steelplate had arrived at full momentum. One of the flying Maladies took the brunt of the barrage as parts of it exploded into giant chunks while other parts were yanked out of existence via micro-singularities.

Meanwhile, a much faster figure arrived in the plaza at roughly the same time as the rockets and grenades. While the Malady in the ice cream shop's attention was on Glamour Esque and

Wynderia, Anjette crossed the distance in a blur, hurled herself through the air, and drove her fist through its skull completely down the height of its body until it nearly split apart and then dissipated in an ugly mist.

Almost in concert, the two surviving Maladies unleashed disturbingly potent breath weapons. The first blasted a wave of ill intent at Steelplate that melted his armor and reinforced skeleton into slag, causing his frame to buckle and then crumple into a heap. An autonomic system managed to fire off a single tiny drone that arced away from the battle like a flare, and then every munition or weapon he'd been carrying that could explode promptly *did* explode, showering bits of him and his armor in every direction.

The other attack targeted Glamour Esque and Wynderia. Or rather, targeted Glamour Esque, as he noted that Wynderia had chosen that moment to no longer be observable by the combatants on the field and was gone.

The breath attack enveloped him in a powerful stream of malevolence, which hissed and sizzled against multiple protective wards that cloaked him, protective spells that absorbed psychic damage in particular since he'd expected Carissa to be one of his primary threats. At this rate, the Malady's ill intent would burn through his entire suite of wards in just a few more seconds, but to compound the problem, this Malady was diving straight toward him with intent to pummel him with a very visible fist.

He summoned a large portal behind himself and sank backward through it, and the forward momentum of the Malady carried it through after him. The portal snapped shut and did not reopen.

The remaining Malady landed with a thunderous boom next to Tabitha. Anjette sprinted forward, but the Malady intercepted her with a powerful kick that launched her clear across the park and over the nearest section of wall.

Satisfied with the outcome, the Malady leapt into the air with Tabitha in its arms, forming a new flight capsule around the two of them by literally willing one into being—a minor prestidigitation for this thing, scooping up wreckage from previous capsules and instilling it with new purpose—and then rocketing off toward the chasm in the distance.

. . .

Carissa sat up slowly, dazed but certainly alive, inside the shimmering energetic cage that Glamour Esque had established.

She reached into the front pocket of her overalls and withdrew the diamond-encrusted backstage pass for Jaxxer Kwee's tour. A small hunk of metal that had once been a bullet fell off the pass and landed in Carissa's lap.

If I can't get backstage with this anymore, Carissa thought, *I'm gonna kill all living things.*

She stood up, careful not to brush the shimmering energetic cage, and turned her attention to Rindasy, who seemed paralyzed, standing motionless with zir eyes wide open, staring into the distance.

"You okay?" she asked.

Rindasy did not—could not—respond.

Carissa tried to apply a current of healing to Rindasy, to no effect. Whatever was affecting Rindasy couldn't be "cured" outright.

A flurry of sudden combat exploded in the plaza outside the cage, the action partially obscured both by the arcane energy of the cage and the sheer speed at which the combatants clashed. But the end result was easy enough to discern. Tabitha was gone.

Suddenly, the shimmering energetic cage briefly sizzled and then dissipated. Nicholas Solitude stood behind Carissa, wearing his spacetime machine, the side of his head caked with blood. In his hand was a small artifact, about the size of a remote control, with jewels in place of buttons. It was the Key of Rindasy, which opened any lock and broke any chains. Dispelling a cage was clearly within its purview.

"I would've arrived sooner," Nicholas said quietly to catch Carissa's attention, "but I was briefly out cold due to a head injury."

Now he turned his attention to Rindasy. Zir namesake key was useful for more than simply opening doors or defeating locks. As Rindasy had explained when ze first gifted the Key to the Guild, "It can dispel illusions that mislead you and illuminate the true path if you're lost."

Rindasy was lost deep in illusion, but as Nicholas pressed the artifact into zir hand, Rindasy steadily surfaced until ze could breathe real air once again.

"Thank you, Nicholas," Rindasy said. Then, noticing the blood on his face, ze said, "What happened to you?"

"Tabitha attacked me, I'm afraid," he replied. "She was using her capture glass to retrieve the memory of a Muse, and I think that the Muse in question got control of her instead. I tried to stop her from leaving, and she became violent. I think this Muse is potentially alive and present in the Building."

"In the chasm," Carissa concluded.

"That would be my guess," Nicholas said.

Carissa was torn. On the one hand, Tabitha had rained this entire mess down on all of them. But Tabitha was young and wrestling with a power she barely understood—Carissa could empathize with that feeling all too well. And now a potentially malignant force had control of Tabitha, which meant her ability to influence the future with her writing was at risk of being corrupted, which held unpredictable implications.

She turned to Rindasy and said, "I think we should rescue Tabitha."

"Does she mean something to you?" Rindasy asked. "She's worth risking your life?"

Carissa realized that Tabitha *did* mean something to her. If it wasn't for Tabitha, she'd have lived the rest of her life wondering what had happened to Lorelei and the rest of the Brilliant.

Besides, you always had to help people in this ridiculous place.

Carissa said, "We're the only hope she's got. Just us."

Rindasy nodded, suddenly alert to the challenge ahead. Ze tucked the Key of Rindasy away in a pocket.

Then ze turned to Carissa and said, "Follow me."

.   .   .

Rindasy and Carissa landed gently on the boarding platform for the hot new ride of the season: the Catapult.

But although multiple cars sat ready for action, Rindasy found that ze did not understand the controls to operate the ride. Carissa watched, torn between bemusement and frustration, because clearly Rindasy had a reason to believe this was a useful thing to try. It just wasn't working out the way ze intended.

"Looks like you folks need an operator," said a voice coming up the stairs.

The man approaching them wore a Wild Massive uniform and an unassuming smile as he approached the control podium.

"I just trained up on this baby, and let me tell you, this coaster's a beauty," he said, flipping a few switches until the sound of humming power filled the air. The nearest car jumped a little bit forward into a boarding position. "Have a seat."

"I want the VIP experience," Rindasy blurted out.

The man smiled knowingly and said, "Of course you do." He turned back to the controls, flipped a few more switches.

A section of track on the far side of the ride ratcheted itself into a new position. Rindasy leapt into the nearest car and waved impatiently for Carissa to join zir.

Carissa was unclear on exactly what bullshit was going on right about now, but she climbed into the car nevertheless, prepared to literally go along for the ride.

The man lowered their lap bars and latched them, locking the two of them into place.

"You realize this is a one-way trip, I hope?" the man asked.

"Understood," Rindasy replied.

"One-way trip *where*?" Carissa asked.

The man chuckled and said, "Straight into destiny, I imagine."

"Oh, fuck you with that folksy shit," Carissa said. "Who are you, anyway?"

The man tapped his name tag, which clearly read PIVOTAL MOMENT.

Carissa looked at him again, startled to see that name. Now she recognized him: the Agent who took an interest in the Brilliant, who lived downtown alongside the Brilliant for two months, who befriended Kellin and coached him on what to say to the diplomats, who acted as a "character witness" for them that the Association might respect. She thought he'd died with the rest of the Brilliant, but leave it to an Agent to execute a daring escape from certain doom.

"Nice work blowing up Jirian's lab," he said.

"You know they captured Kellin, right?"

"Yes, I did hear that. Apparently, he surrendered hours before the bombing."

He strolled back to the controls.

"What the fuck are you talking about?" she shouted. The idea of Kellin surrendering was laughable. "Who told you he surrendered?"

Pivotal Moment flipped a few switches and then pressed a big green button on the control console. The car lurched a little and then began smoothly accelerating.

As they rolled past the control podium, he shouted, "Don't forget to smile for your picture!"

The car rolled forward around a corner that would deliver them to the bottom of a tall hill. From there, the car would be magnetically propelled up and over that hill and into the full experience of the roller coaster.

Although they couldn't have known this, as they accelerated up the hill, they experienced the moment that Tabitha had foreseen in her book, the vision of Carissa and Rindasy riding a roller coaster in Wild Massive Prime.

This was the inaugural public voyage of the Catapult, as far as history would be concerned. They were the first people besides Roland to ride the course.

Their car completed the leisurely main run, then dropped down a vertical track into the launch position for the final stage of the attraction.

The car suddenly rocketed up an unbelievably steep hill, and then reached the end of that hill, and then left the comforting confines of actual track behind. The car sailed high above the park, higher than any of the tallest roller coasters the park had to offer, higher than anything the park had to offer except the Space Elevator itself. The car sailed unimpeded through the magical barrier drape, over the walls of the park, over the long expanse of empty parking lot, across the unexpectedly beautiful terrain of the rest of the floor, rolling plains leading to foothills leading to a gorgeous mountain range, and they seemed to be higher than that, heading for the tantalizing, colored haze on the horizon, the smear of surreality that signified the chasm's edge.

Carissa screamed louder than she ever had in her life.

SEASON SIX

EPISODE 6.01

The steel-and-fiberglass ride car was surprisingly aerodynamic, and it flew straight and true without any turbulence. A little windshield even popped up as they left the track so that their faces wouldn't be blown off.

The car accelerated as it sailed toward the chasm, as though miniature propulsion rockets kicked in to keep the car climbing upward instead of falling out of the sky. They weren't chemical rockets, though; the car was airborne thanks to a set of flight spells that kicked in shortly after leaving the track.

Rindasy realized there was no steering mechanism for the flight spells, which were operating according to predetermined navigational instructions. With enough time, and when ze wasn't struggling desperately not to panic, ze might be able to harness the flight spells, or supplant them with zir own, but not today. In the back of zir mind, ze found it ironic that leaping out of the Building itself was less stressful than this roller coaster ride was turning out to be.

Carissa stopped screaming after a few solid minutes, as she realized she was still alive and likely to stay that way for the time being. It seemed like it would only take another couple of minutes to reach the distinct smear of colors and light on the horizon that represented the shrouded opening to the chasm. Either it was much closer than they'd understood that night when they observed it from the Space Elevator, or they were moving astonishingly fast, or some magical factor was compressing the distance. It was exhilarating and frightening at the same time.

Moments later, they sailed into the colors and light.

For maybe thirty seconds, they were surrounded by a warm, colorful mist. Without sight of terrain below them, they began to feel as though they were floating stationary in the mist instead of hurtling through it at high speed.

Then they were suddenly through the mist, and they were thankful for their lap bars as the car lurched up and down and side to side, buffeted by the flight spells' attempts to understand which way to orient the car in the new environment that surrounded them.

Conceptually, the chasm was below the top floor, separating it from the rest of the Building, but it was simultaneously *between* the top floor and the Building, like a canyon that separated them, so you could see a vertical slice of the Building as though the exterior wall had been ripped off and the uppermost floors were exposed to the open air in a cross section, and those were the same floors where the chasm was visible in the sky, but when you looked down into the chasm from there, you didn't see down the length of the Building to the flat desert plain below, because you weren't over the ground at all, or at least, not *that* ground but clearly you were over *something* stable and solid because you could see a landscape below, like a volcanic rock bed but with towering pillars like stalagmites rising everywhere, and you could see an enormous palace made of glass and mirrors and crystal glittering at you in the distance, but which *direction* was the palace you couldn't say because was it up or was it yonder or below or what the fuck even. The sky outside the Building was the familiar shade of bright orange, but the sky in the chasm itself was dark, as though the top floor was up there somewhere, out of sight but still casting a massive shadow over the landscape, except what light source it could possibly be blocking you just didn't even know, and you saw the tops of the four elevator shafts plain as day, four lonely spires, as though they'd risen up past the boundaries of their floors in vain attempts to deliver their poor passengers to the top floor, only to be severed by an impossible sword and if those elevators hadn't stopped their ascent in time then holy hell they might have just flown off into the chasm, and the volcanic landscape was littered with the shattered wreckage of dozens of roller coaster cars just like this one, and it was starting to get very vertiginous and weird in this particular roller coaster car, that was the one thing you could absolutely say for certain.

Anyway, the flight spells gave up on any attempt to continue navigating, and their roller coaster car began to fall.

.   .   .

Moments before the roller coaster car crashed nose-first into the ground, Carissa caught the car in midair using telekinesis and held it there, a couple of meters away from becoming more shattered wreckage in the graveyard of roller coaster cars.

She was surprised by the strain of catching. It turned out to be *hard* to stop a heavy thing with significant momentum as it fell out of the sky while she herself was freaking the fuck out. Recognizing one of the limitations of this talent broke her concentration on it, and the car went ahead and fell the last couple of meters and crashed. But it crashed gently instead of catastrophically, which was good enough.

Rindasy used the Key to unlock the lap. Ze stood up immediately and climbed out, but Carissa remained in her seat. She wanted to be absolutely sure the car wasn't just going to start back up and leave without them. The air was silent at first, but soon enough, they could hear the tinkling sound of chimes coming from the palace in the distance, which somehow rose out of the ground at a forty-five-degree angle.

The ground between here and the palace was curved like the inside of a wheel, and if you looked in either direction along this wheel, forward or backward, you saw the same palace in the distance either way, which was disconcerting to say the least. The tall, smooth canyon walls that rose on either side of them seemed to be made of the same black glass that covered the exterior of the Building, but they were pockmarked with giant holes, through which they could see the sky outside the Building.

Carissa was sick of this place already. She slowly climbed out of the car and set foot on the volcanic rock surface. It was not as reassuring as she'd hoped.

"Are you all right?" Rindasy asked.

"Nope," she replied. "It was a bad idea to come here."

"You wanted to rescue Tabitha."

"Who's gonna rescue *us*?"

She took a long look around, as though any threats that might be in the vicinity would be clearly visible. The distance from here to the palace seemed devoid of life or threat. She could maybe locate Tabitha with clairvoyance if she was nearby, but if she was in the palace, they'd need to get a lot closer to confirm it.

"I'm surprised they haven't sent out a welcoming committee for us," she said.

"Apparently, they've gotten used to falling roller coaster cars by now," Rindasy replied. "Shall we go to find your friend?"

"She's not my friend," Carissa instantly corrected. "I barely know her. I'm not sure what I was thinking when I said we should do this."

Rindasy paused, then said, "We could leave the chasm, you know. Fly through one of those holes in the glass, down the side of the Building. I know places where we could get back inside safely."

As much as Carissa wanted nothing more than to spend the next six months riding an elevator alone, she wasn't ready to leave the chasm just yet.

"Nah," she said. "Do you have any spells to make us invisible or something?"

Rindasy smiled and said, "Pure invisibility is beyond my skill, but there are many ways to hide our approach."

EPISODE 6.02

When Tabitha came to her senses, she was alive. That much she could tell right away; she hadn't been sure for a bit there, when something else was in control of her mind, if she was suddenly just an apparition left floating in her own skull, some distant backseat driver who no longer maintained a permanent physical address in a human body.

But here she was, relaxing comfortably in a plush and elegant chair in an elaborate sitting room of some kind, with seven chandeliers above her head of different styles and sizes providing a warm glow to the room, and a teapot and two cups waiting on a small end table. A cozy chair opposite her was currently empty.

The room seemed to have no doors, but perhaps she simply didn't know where to look, given that all four walls were covered floor to ceiling with shards of broken mirrors and hunks of misshapen crystal. Somewhere a door might be lurking on one of those surfaces, but she didn't have the courage to stand up and hunt for it.

It wasn't even clear that the walls were solid, because on closer examination, it seemed like they rippled slightly every so often, as though a gentle breeze came through and all these mirrors and crystals were hanging on wires that weren't properly anchored to the floor. Reinforcing that image, the chandeliers above swayed ever so slightly as well.

The Malady who had carried her into the chasm was nowhere to be seen. She didn't remember being deposited here.

But then she remembered she'd been using her capture glass. She looked down and realized her capture glass was gone.

"Looking for this?" said Epiphany Foreshadow with perfect timing.

Tabitha looked up to see that the chair opposite her was now occupied, and its occupant was holding her capture glass, dangling it by the chain.

Epiphany Foreshadow didn't allow herself to be perceived too directly. Instead, she appeared as a constant shimmering silhouette that almost resolved into the form of an absurdly tall human woman without ever committing to specific features beyond that. Her choice of garb cycled slowly but continuously through various ensembles or costumes, transitioning from the gown of a queen into crisp equestrian riding apparel into comfortable fuzzy pajamas and on and on.

The effect was strangest where her face should be. It was a blur in which the position of the eyes remained relatively constant, but their shape, and the shape of all the features around them, and the color of her skin were all constantly up for grabs, subject to some whim or pattern that Tabitha couldn't detect. It was as though someone were flipping through the pages in a book of faces at a plastic surgeon's office and playing mix and match with potential options for a base template of a face.

This was not how Tabitha remembered Epiphany from her experience with Allegory's capture glass, but then again, that entire experience had been translated into a metaphor that her human mind was able to interpret. Sitting here now, she still felt as though her mind was being forced to do some translation of what she was seeing just to provide her with even this much of a visual impression of Epiphany.

"Your family's had my capture glass for many years," said Epiphany.

"I'm sorry," Tabitha said instinctively.

Suddenly, Epiphany was pouring tea, and the capture glass had vanished from her hand. Glancing up at Tabitha, she said, "Oh, you needn't apologize, Tabitha. You know how the saying goes: don't blame the children for the sins of every last person up the matrilineal line of a family stretching back to the literal dawn of time itself. Why, that would be unjust." She offered Tabitha tea and said, "Anyway, I wanted you all to have it. After all, how else would I have found you?"

Tabitha's hand trembled as she added sugar to her tea.

"Relax, Tabitha, please," said Epiphany in a soothing voice. "I know it was rude of me to bring you here in such a forceful manner, but I hope you at least appreciate the thrilling drama of the gesture."

"Where are we?" Tabitha ventured to ask.

"We're in my home," Epiphany replied. "I call it the Memory Palace. You know, memory is one of the principal tools we use to craft the narrative of history. A memory, after all, is just a story that we tell ourselves about our past, and stories are subject to revision. The future is more inevitable than the past, to be frank. You can block out your memories of the past, whereas the future is just going to keep happening to you. Anyway, drink your tea, and then I'll give you the tour."

Tabitha took a sip. The tea was flavored with cinnamon and apple, a blend she happened to love.

"I understand you're writing a book," Epiphany said with an overly friendly tone.

Tabitha nodded.

"Can I read it?" Epiphany asked.

Tabitha hesitated, then shook her head.

"Show me your book, Tabitha, or I'll kill you," said Epiphany.

Tabitha recited the incantation to open her safe, reached in, and pulled out a few notebooks, which she handed to Epiphany.

"Sorry about my handwriting," said Tabitha.

"Oh, it's lovely," said Epiphany, already reading the first page. "Give me a moment."

Epiphany read silently for several minutes, rapidly flipping through pages, occasionally muttering a *hmm* or an *aah* but mostly remaining silent and focused. When she reached the end, she set the notebooks down on the table. "But you haven't written anything about the chasm!" she exclaimed.

This was true, of course. Tabitha's book ended abruptly with her description of Carissa and Rindasy riding a roller coaster in Wild Massive Prime. She hadn't had a chance to write any further than that.

"You've barely said anything at all about *me*!" she exclaimed, waving at their surroundings. "Oh, but don't you have *guesses*? Haven't you brainstormed about me at all?"

Tabitha shook her head.

Epiphany seemed to relish that answer.

"Oh my goodness, Tabitha, we're going to have such fun together."

"I don't believe you," Tabitha managed to say.

"Yes, be a little rebellious while you can. Get it out of your system."

Reality seemed to blur in front of Tabitha for the merest of moments, and now a tray of cookies sat next to the teapot on the end table. Epiphany snagged one and then slid the tray toward Tabitha.

"I can imagine the generic questions you likely have," Epiphany said, "such as 'What am I doing here?' and 'What does any of this have to do with me?' Well, I believe it's customary for those occupying the position of nominal villain to get a monologue, so let's get that out of the way while you finish your tea, and then we can get on with your perfunctory attempt to stop me. Don't worry, I won't hold it against you. In fact, I'm curious to see what you come up with.

"First of all, I'm an enormous fan of *Storm and Desire*. I've been hooked ever since day one. It's Allegory's masterwork, you know. I mean, the ingenuity of using the format of long-form intermedia storytelling to literally engineer hooks into guiding and controlling the future is just . . . Give her all the prestigious awards, invent new ones even, is what I'm saying.

"I know you've had your part to play in it, it's a collaboration, but let's give Allegory credit here. She's done something that defies the spirit of the Architects' specifications without violating any specific precept or maxim and in so doing proves the specs were inadequate and misguided in the first place. And she's not doing it out of spite, which she'd have every right to do, if you asked me. She's doing it because she's a fountain of pure creativity, and she doesn't know how to do anything except be a genius, constantly at the top of her game, always pushing to improve and innovate.

"Anyway, the flip side of that coin is that while I love her work, I am also contractually obligated to fill the role of her nemesis.

"I was not excited about this assignment at first. My Architect said, 'Think of it as just another level of quality assurance. Look for the flaws, the rough edges, the scuff marks where her implementations are a little faulty, and give those a little push or a shove for us so that they just, you know, collapse. So that she can do better the next time.'

"I said, 'What do you mean, a push or a shove? You actually want her to fail?'

"They said, 'It's important for audit purposes to know if she *can* fail.'

"And I said, 'How does this help *my* career development?' Because I'm not a quality assurance resource, you understand. I had my own string of successes going. I cut my teeth designing innovative hell dimensions, you know, back when hell dimensions used to be artisanal, before they franchised the core concepts out to the Earth floors.

"But my Architect told me this assignment was coming straight from up top. They wanted creative stress testing of Allegory's work, and they wanted it done by the same Muse who introduced the philosophical concept of 'catastrophic failure modes' into the project glossary.

"Well, it's true you can flatter me on occasion.

"They thought I would have my hands full, because Allegory was so productive, her fingerprints are on practically everything now, so they gave me a full staff to work with, a team of talented Muses looking to climb, and we started strategizing. It would take me a month to describe to you all the various plans and schemes we prepared for the moment when we could leap into action.

"But the problem with this assignment was that Allegory Paradox didn't have any detectable flaws to speak of.

"She was ludicrously by the book, but somehow stylish at the same time.

"Can you imagine how infuriating it is to spend eons waiting around for even the tiniest of imperfections in any of a zillion projects she's juggling and realizing either I was incompetent for not spotting flaws in her work that I could exploit, or she was literally operating at the highest level of proficiency in the history of history?

"It really seemed hopeless. I admit I went through a very dark phase for a while there. Made some drastic changes to the team, developed some disturbing hobbies and addictions, that sort of thing.

"Allegory's projects became more and more conservative, as though she'd realized the hammer was yet to fall. Her aesthetic became sanitized and smooth—and boring, frankly. I think she's known all along that I'm still here in the Building, studying her every move. It's probably galling to her that they left someone here to *critique* her eons *after* the project end date.

"*Storm and Desire,* though . . . that's some audacious work right there. Openly positioning herself as an auteur of the future, without requiring any adjustments to the past to pull it off . . . maneuvering herself and you and Wild Massive into position as core pillars of the overall narrative, instead of simple behind-the-scenes technicians . . . it's impressive.

"But she did in fact make one major mistake.

"*Storm and Desire* needs a villain for its final arc, a proper villain who can top all the menaces and challenges that have come before, and she knows it. I don't think she understands what she's summoning, but I'll make it clear to her shortly. She's engineered herself into a position of influence in the storyline because she wants to defeat this villain *herself*, for reasons I don't understand, little realizing this is the opening I need to target *her*.

"She may be the best of the best when it comes to the pure act of creation, but she's completely outclassed when it comes to wreaking havoc and fucking things up.

"The thing I'm going to fuck up right proper is the final arc of her precious *Storm and Desire*. There'll never be peace between the Association and the Shai-Manak, because soon neither one of them will exist in a coherent fashion. In the ashes of their demise, I will reveal myself—villainous and victorious.

"Now, how about the tour?"

. . .

The walls and chandeliers of the room seemed to vibrate out of existence, and now they were standing on a wide spiral staircase in the center of a vast chamber that felt to Tabitha like being in an opulent grand hall in a museum. They were on a landing, positioned about halfway between the floor and an opening in the ceiling above to another level of the palace.

Around the room, the walls were covered with glowing pinpoints of light, each gently cycling through colors, joining with their neighbors in creating mesmerizing patterns of color that periodically washed across the walls like waves. This was the only source of light in the grand hall, but it was sufficient. The floor seemed to be tiled with crushed glass or crystal. And mounted haphazardly all over the walls were mirrors of various sizes, not in frames but rather affixed straight to the walls somehow. Large archways on either side of the hall led to identical chambers beyond this one.

They were quiet, reverential even, but Tabitha thought she could hear whispers and lamentations.

Epiphany was holding Tabitha's capture glass again. She said, "I've saved a place for this one."

"You could've just come and asked me for it," Tabitha said.

"You didn't have to hijack my mind and kidnap me out of the park."

"You haven't been part of Allegory's creative brain trust very long, have you," Epiphany replied. "I'm building my legend as a villain. Kidnapping you makes it *personal* for Allegory, which increases the dramatic stakes, you see?" She began walking down the stairs and added, "You should take notes; this is solid craft advice."

Tabitha followed her down the stairs and through the hall until Epiphany located a spot on the wall that was devoid of a pinpoint of light. She snapped the chain off and threw it away, and affixed Tabitha's capture glass to the wall in the empty position.

That's when Tabitha understood—the walls were entirely covered with individual capture glasses, thousands upon thousands of them. These colored lights represented stored memories.

She drifted slowly to the nearest mirror and dared to face it.

Her reflection in the mirror was obscured by an apparition pounding at the other side of the glass to get out.

Epiphany gently took her by the arm and steered her away.

"What was that?" Tabitha asked. "What did I just see?"

"Sweetheart, those are capture mirrors," Epiphany replied. "I have an array of memory capture artifacts at my disposal—capture wands, capture cloaks, capture 5D optical storage discs—but the capture mirrors and the capture glasses are among the most aesthetically appealing."

Epiphany led Tabitha to the next hall, where more capture glasses and capture mirrors were on display. This hall also functioned as a sculpture gallery. A dozen crystalline statues stood on mirrored pedestals throughout the hall. Most of them were humanoid, although she recognized representations of a couple of other species as well. The carvings were absolutely exquisite and minutely detailed.

"These statues are made from the same reminiscite crystal that we use to make capture glasses," Epiphany explained.

The statues refracted the glow of the surrounding capture glasses in such a fashion that Tabitha briefly thought she could see the statues moving ever so slightly, but it was probably a trick of the light.

A sudden horrible thought occurred to Tabitha, and she blurted out, "Is this what happened to your team of Muses?"

Epiphany seemed genuinely caught off guard, then laughed and said, "Of course not." She started off toward the next hall in the row, waving for Tabitha to join her, and said with a wink, "This is what happened to my neighbors, silly."

"What neighbors?" Tabitha asked. "The people who lived on the floors nearest the chasm?"

"Some of them, yes, the ones with the most fascinating memories to work with. Distilling a person down to their core memories and sculpting the resulting reminiscite into these forms is no easy task. Very few people are worth the trouble."

"Are they . . . alive?" Tabitha dared to ask.

"In a manner of speaking," Epiphany said. "In fact, now they're immortal."

"What happened to the other Muses on your team?"

"I decided to reorg them into new roles, to suit the team's new direction," Epiphany replied. "They're called Maladies now."

They arrived in the final hall of the museum tour, with fewer and larger individual crystals and mirrors on the walls. Several display cases, however, held a different type of exhibit altogether, as Epiphany began to explain with delight.

"And here we have my narrative artifact collection," she said proudly.

Tabitha slowly gazed around the room at the assorted jewelry and weaponry and clothing on display behind the glass cases, but there were no helpful plaques to provide metadata about the objects.

Epiphany pointed at a gold ring, a little bigger than a pinkie ring.

"This gorgeous little number, for instance, is a Plot Twist Ring," said Epiphany, grinning at the sight of it. "When you're wearing it, you can twist it on your finger, and it generates an immediate plot twist in the ongoing narrative. Isn't that clever?"

"What 'ongoing narrative'?" Tabitha asked.

Epiphany waved her hands around and said, "All of *this* is *your* ongoing narrative, Tabitha, a sliver of *the* ongoing narrative, which yes is just another way of saying 'life within the confines of a reality,' but the point is, this ring can give you or someone you designate a surprising *twist* on how life will unfold from that point forward."

Another piece of jewelry caught Epiphany's attention in the same case, a small emerald-and-gold brooch in the shape of a feather pen.

"This is the Quill of Coincidence," Epiphany said. "Once a day while wearing it, a surprising narrative coincidence occurs centered on the wearer. You don't get to specify what it will be or plan for when it will happen, of course. You know, we like to say that every story is allowed one big coincidence without alarming the audience. You used yours in your book, when that rogue shapeshifter miraculously happened to land on an elevator carrying the last surviving Brilliant in the Building. Can you imagine if anyone else had been in that elevator? We'd never have met!"

They moved on from that jewelry case to a mannequin that was outfitted with a leather doublet underneath a long cape. The doublet seemed to be striped with a thin metallic weave throughout its surface, as though someone had tried to physically infuse the leather with extremely fine chain mail.

"This is Plot Armor," Epiphany said, almost dismissively. "Keeps your narrative on the narrow path toward a happy ending. No harm befalls the wearer, et cetera. Reality hates this particular invention, though, so while you're wearing Plot Armor, you'll be fine, but every living thing down to the last microbe in your immediate environment is at a dramatically increased risk of a sudden and brutal death."

Finally, they arrived at what seemed to be the trophy piece of the collection, a beautiful silver pendant fashioned into a stylized metal gear, with a glowing jeweled eye in its center.

"This is called the Deus Ex Machina," Epiphany said softly, as though she might disturb it if she wasn't careful. "No one knows how it works or what it actually does. No one knows if it's ever even been used before. I stole this from an Artist. You ask me, ze should've used it instead of letting me get my hands on it."

"What am I doing here?" Tabitha suddenly asked. "What does any of this have to do with me?"

Epiphany said, "These are tools that Muses operating at peak levels can hope to utilize or even create. I wanted you to see these, Tabitha, and imagine what you could do with them. I respect that you've cut your teeth as an elite narrative designer on *Storm and Desire*, but please consider that you now have . . . alternative career opportunities than what you imagine for yourself at Wild Massive. With me."

Tabitha blinked at the implication. Was Epiphany seriously suggesting that she . . . what, become her apprentice? Aid Epiphany in this absurd quest to take down Allegory? And these artifacts were, like, a bribe to take the gig? After she'd been freaking kidnapped by Maladies and mind controlled by Epiphany herself, she was expected to suddenly trust Epiphany just like that?

But Tabitha could see how this was going to go if she said no to the offer. These specific four narrative artifacts would become the exact four artifacts that Epiphany would use to make her final moves against Allegory. You didn't systematically introduce a set of artifacts like these if you didn't intend for every last one of them to go off before you were done.

How could Tabitha even remotely hope to stop Epiphany from whatever she was planning, when Epiphany would forever be so much further ahead in understanding the narrative than she was?

She realized—she needed her book back.

She desperately needed to peer into the future for any kind of clue that she could use. She needed to sit down and *write*.

"I can tell you're thinking about how to screw me over," Epiphany said casually.

"No, I'm not," Tabitha said.

"Sure you are. Your whole face is scrunched up like you want to shoot lasers out of your eyes at me."

"Well, look, you're trying to destroy my mentor. It's just a lot to process."

"I hear you," said Epiphany. "Unfortunately, you have about thirty seconds to decide if you want a promotion to full Muse working as my assistant or if you want to waste what's left of your life on loyalty to your doomed mentor. Chop chop."

"What happens in thirty seconds?"

"Your friends show up and we all try to kill each other."

It hadn't even remotely occurred to Tabitha that anyone would come to rescue her.

Her notebooks were sitting on that damn end table, in a room she wouldn't be able to locate if she tried. Damn, damn, damn.

Epiphany took a step toward her and said, "Look at that creative mind of yours spinning. You've almost got smoke pouring out of your ears from the exertion."

A cacophony of wailing erupted from every corner of the museum. The Maladies had become agitated.

"Time's up," Epiphany said.

"I'll pass," Tabitha said.

"I don't think so," Epiphany said, and she grabbed Tabitha by the neck, lifted her off the floor, and carried her out through the gallery halls and up the spiral staircase to the level above. What Tabitha could see of it as her eyesight clouded with stars was that it reminded her of a medieval torture chamber, except all the torture devices were made of reminiscite crystal.

Tabitha blacked out before she could determine anything else.

EPISODE 6.03

Carissa and Rindasy flew slowly toward the Memory Palace, hugging the side of the canyon, masked by a black mist that shrouded them so that they would blend in with the canyon wall if someone was visually scanning the surroundings. Rindasy held a spell ready in case ze detected someone scrying on them magically as well, which would convince the person who spotted them that they were really just receiving a false alarm from their scrying attempt.

The exterior of the Memory Palace was not, as it happened, constructed with reminiscite crystals and fragments of mirrors. It was a patchwork structure, comprised of scrap material that had been salvaged from the Building and repositioned into this new and imposing silhouette. Steel girders and plates were strapped together with cable to provide flooring for the many levels of the palace. Similarly, long, jagged shards of black glass were affixed haphazardly into position on the palace exterior in an attempt to mimic the surface of the Building. The effect was like looking at the Building in a fun house mirror and seeing an ugly and weird distortion as a reflection.

As they approached, the Memory Palace seemed to adjust out of its skewed angle, slowly righting itself to their point of view.

They were nearly overwhelmed by the sight and smell of the moat that surrounded the Memory Palace. It was not filled with water but rather seemed to be a dumping ground for corpses. The moat overflowed primarily with human remains, but other species could be identified among the remains as well.

Carissa thought to try clairvoyance to see what she could glean about the events that led to what she was seeing and decided against it. Right now, on the verge of breaking into this palace to rescue Tabitha, she didn't need a potential psychic backlash.

Rindasy was willing to venture a guess, though.

"So many people went missing from the uppermost floors," ze said and left it at that.

A mix of terror and rage welled up in Carissa's throat, a scream that she didn't dare let loose.

Carissa signaled for a halt to their approach. She wanted the opportunity to rest a little before going any farther. She also had the steadily growing feeling that they were heading into a trap.

They stopped short of the moat, landing on the edge of a floor where a gleaming residential complex stood, now in a stage of advanced disrepair and completely deserted thanks to the chasm's looming presence.

"That horror show out there is meant to be a deterrent," Carissa said. "Are you feeling deterred?"

"Not currently," Rindasy said.

Carissa visually scanned the exterior of the palace for signs of doors or windows.

Nothing obvious struck her as a point of entry. As she studied the exterior of the structure, she became convinced that it wasn't meaningfully solid. She could see seams where light from within seemed to escape, and every so often, it looked to her like one of the slabs of black glass shifted a bit.

They were suddenly startled by a strange display. A column of comet streaks launched from what appeared to be the roof of the palace, rising in colorful bursts into the weird optical illusion of sky above them. Each of those comet streaks was a flying capsule containing a Malady pilot, or a larger shuttle containing multiple Maladies, and there were easily hundreds or more vehicles in the air by the time the display was fully underway.

"That doesn't seem good," Rindasy said.

"Good for us, maybe," Carissa replied.

In rapid succession, each of the comet streaks abruptly disappeared from the sky above the canyon. The entire column of Maladies simply rippled out of existence as each vehicle vanished with a small flash. Those Maladies must've been piloting jump-capable vessels, and they'd jumped off the floor to unknown destinations. They could be anywhere in the multiverse now.

"We need a plan," Rindasy said.

"Here's one. We rip the walls off and tear the place apart until we find Tabitha."

"Perhaps stealth would make for a better plan," Rindasy said. "We should pinpoint Tabitha's location inside that palace before we enter it. I have a tracking spell that might reveal if she's nearby."

Ze sat down on the edge of the outcropping and directed zir focus toward the palace, while also closing zir eyes and turning zir attention inward as well.

Carissa pondered her options. She'd known a kid back in Minneapolis who could use telepathy to converse with people all over the city, a far cry from the limited range of her mind control talent. She visualized Tabitha with as much detail as she could muster and attempted to project a short message: "It's Carissa. Are you okay?" She received no response. Tabitha might've been unable to respond, or her message might not have reached Tabitha at all.

A couple of minutes after Rindasy began the tracking spell, zir eyes snapped open. "We have little time to save her," Rindasy said as ze jumped to zir feet. "Your plan is best."

. . .

Carissa took the lead, focusing a psychic blast on the nearest wall of the palace, which sent hundreds of shards and slivers of black glass flying. The result was a jagged but inviting opening in the wall.

Then Rindasy took the lead, following the trail ze'd seen in zir tracking spell, through a rapidly unfolding fun house of capture mirrors and capture glasses, which covered every wall in sight. The various staircases were covered in crystal, the ceilings were covered in mirror and crystal chandeliers, the furniture even seemed to have crystal crawling all over it as though the crystals in this place were barnacles attaching themselves to ships in the ocean.

As Carissa's eyes swept her surroundings, she spotted a small stack of notebooks inexplicably sitting on a table. If they were Tabitha's notebooks, it was bad news to see them outside her safe. Carissa grabbed them, and the pair kept moving.

Eventually, they found a particularly large spiral staircase, and Rindasy signaled that this was the end of the trail. They stopped here, across the room from the staircase, not quite ready to proceed.

"I know you're down there!" shouted a woman's voice from the chamber at the top of the staircase. "Come any closer and I will drain Tabitha dry!"

Carissa didn't know what that meant, but she knew how to obey the letter of a request while flagrantly disregarding the spirit of it. With an immense telekinetic yank, she tore the spiral staircase out of its position and then ripped out the floor of the upper chamber for good measure, letting it all collapse into a heap of rubble.

The room's occupants fell into view, and Carissa telekinetically caught both of them before they hit the floor. Tabitha was strapped to an examination table, wearing a weird crystal helmet that glowed like a capture glass; she seemed to be unconscious.

The other person, undoubtedly the one who'd shouted at them, was wearing a similar crystal helmet, also glowing. This person was extremely conscious and rather irritated at the interruption. Aside from the helmet, this person's attire was steadily shifting among a variety of costumes—for a few moments a firefighter's uniform, then an elaborate wedding dress, a trapeze artist, and so on.

"If you sever my connection with Tabitha before this process is over, you'll kill her," growled Epiphany Foreshadow.

"Liar," said Carissa. She telekinetically yanked the helmet from Epiphany's head and hurled it to the floor, where it shattered and released a quick burst of billowing colored light into the air. Tabitha's helmet immediately dimmed.

"That's a neat trick," Epiphany said. "My turn."

Carissa wasn't sure how Epiphany triggered it, but suddenly, every capture glass and capture mirror in Epiphany's vast museum exploded at once.

.　　.　　.

First, Carissa experienced the buffeting of psychic shock waves hitting her from all sides, which derailed her focus on holding Epiphany and Tabitha in the air. Epiphany used the opportunity to somehow escape from her view, while Tabitha's table crashed heavily to the floor and toppled onto its side.

Next came the severe physical effects: thousands of glass slivers and shards filled the air, blasted outward from all directions. Carissa managed to throw up a force wall in a dome around herself, but she hadn't reacted quickly enough to avoid the pain of a hundred deep, slicing cuts.

Finally, an onslaught of memories that had lived inside the capture glasses washed over her, like a river escaping its banks or rushing over a dam and swallowing Carissa where she knelt. She became lost for a time, experiencing them as a towering simultaneous stack of memories, with little to cling to for a frame of reference. Each successive memory competed for her attention.

But without capture tech to mediate a playback experience, these memory bursts quickly faded, allowing Carissa to briefly clear her mind. She knew she'd carry flashes of them with her for a long time to come.

Meanwhile, the capture mirrors had contained more than just a single memory each. Snapshots of entire lives were stored within, and now they wandered free of their prisons, dissipating slowly without capture tech to preserve them. Thousands or more of these simulacra now focused their limited awareness and energy on her, ignoring Rindasy and Tabitha, drawn instead to the peculiar signature of Carissa's psionic talents.

They piled onto her psyche before she could summon the means to resist.

Between the memories from the capture glasses and these memory specters that now assailed her, she was starting to get a pretty good idea of what had happened to the people on the uppermost floors.

Epiphany Foreshadow siphoned collections of their best memories into capture glasses, or entire psyches into capture mirrors if she was particularly fond of certain individuals, and then discarded their physical shells when she was done.

They'd almost lost Tabitha the same way.

She mustered up as much stamina as she could, desperate to survive the onslaught, recognizing these memories weren't enemies.

These were desperate swimmers, clawing their way into a lifeboat.

She realized a psychic blast would scatter the last vestiges of these specters in all directions, freeing her from the frightened sadness that was all any of them really had left.

But instead, she chose to greet them with healing energy, attempting to quiet and soothe them before ultimately dispelling them. The torrent eventually slowed and finally dissipated. She realized she had no healing left to turn inward, even as she was surprised to find that her own original identity was still intact.

Carissa blacked out, which caused her to drop the force dome she'd established around herself. She collapsed onto a thick layer of broken glass, soaked in blood and memory.

EPISODE 6.04

Even in human form, Rindasy maintained an extremely tough and resilient exterior, too used to being shot at by warships in the air or Fleet officers on a hangar deck.

Consequently, the barrage of glass that assaulted zir from every side was largely blunted on impact.

Meanwhile, Carissa seemed to absorb almost the entirety of the psychic blowback from the explosive detonation of all the reminiscite crystal in the palace.

That gave Rindasy a clear view of Epiphany Foreshadow during the event. She landed nimbly in a crouch, and the costume she'd been wearing smoothly transitioned into a sleek, puncture-resistant spacesuit, complete with helmet, which protected her from the barrage of glass.

Epiphany turned and sprinted away, down the long series of galleries that led from the wreckage of the spiral staircase, disappearing into darkness.

And it was rapidly getting darker all around them as each fragment of crystal lost the glow that had previously illuminated the interior of the palace. Now they were mostly lit by the illusory sky above them, which resulted in a murky, shadowed dimness.

Rindasy was briefly tempted to chase Epiphany, but instead ze cast a spell that illuminated enough of the area to triage the situation.

Tabitha and Carissa were both unconscious, and both seemed likely to bleed out from countless cuts and wounds before ze could conceivably get them out of the chasm.

Then ze remembered—Carissa carried a pouch of first aid pills.

Ze found the pouch in one of the zippered pockets of her overalls. Twelve pills remained. It had taken five to save Carissa's life when she was shot in the chest on their way out of Jirian's lab.

Ze managed to force a couple of first aid pills in Carissa's mouth to stabilize her, then forced a couple in Tabitha's mouth as well. Carissa coughed, while Tabitha remained motionless. It was eerie how quickly the pills worked; you could see streams and rivulets of blood drying up as their cuts started to heal. Ze focused on getting Carissa upright, hoping Carissa could then use her own healing talent to pull Tabitha back from the brink.

After a few nerve-racking minutes, Carissa was on her feet, healing Tabitha with the last ounce of energy she seemed to possess.

"Can someone release these straps?" Tabitha managed to mumble.

Carissa tried to unlock the straps, but they were cinched tighter than she could handle in her current state, and she gave up in frustration.

Rindasy produced the Key and popped the straps off, catching Tabitha before she rolled off the fallen table onto the glass. They stood the table back up so that Tabitha could sit on it as she recovered.

Little remained of the structure of the Memory Palace. They still had solid floor underneath them. Pillars and beams still stood here and there. A few rooms remained intact at the periphery of the structure, but the walls in their vicinity had all been blown to pieces, and they could easily see straight into the canyon beyond.

Rindasy gave Carissa back the remaining first aid pills. There were three left in the pouch.

"Cool, that'll keep me alive another couple of hours at this rate," Carissa mumbled, only half joking.

"Thank you for saving me," Tabitha said. "Thank you for even being here."

Carissa and Rindasy each nodded an acknowledgment, but the moment was awkward. No one was sure what was supposed to happen next. Were they simply going to meander back to Wild Massive Prime and turn themselves over to the surviving Agents? Were they going to hit the elevators, in perpetual flight from those very Agents, to spend the rest of their extremely long lives as a trio of fugitives? Would they be better off going their separate ways and fleeing into disparate corners of the Building?

Suddenly, a solitary capsule launched itself from elsewhere in the remains of the palace, vaulting into the air with a streak and vanishing.

Tabitha watched the streak and sighed.

"I imagine that was Epiphany Foreshadow escaping," Tabitha said. "We need to find her, and then we need to kill the shit out of her."

"Why?" Carissa asked.

"She's a Muse gone bad, a mass murderer," Tabitha replied. "And now she's on the loose somewhere in the Building, and her army of Maladies is out there somewhere, too. We can't let her—"

"Yes, we can," Carissa said. "We got lucky once. No reason to think we'll get this lucky next time."

"Sure there is," Tabitha said. "Can you hand those to me?"

Carissa picked up the battered notebooks she'd dropped and gave them to Tabitha.

Tabitha opened her extradimensional safe to fish out a pen.

"Just now, I had my brain invaded by the Muse who gave me my divination skill in the first place," Tabitha explained patiently as she flipped open a notebook and began writing. "Those memory helmets created an open two-way channel between our minds, and there's no primary or secondary, you just *commingle* your minds and whichever mind is stronger gets *more* out of the experience."

"So what did *she* get out of the experience?" Rindasy asked.

"No clue," Tabitha said, "because you interrupted us, but I can certainly tell you what *I* got out of the experience, which is a powerful imprint of Epiphany herself, which I can *use* whether she officially promoted me to Muse or not."

She scrawled furiously in her notebook for a minute, then handed the notebook to Rindasy for examination.

"That's what I see happening within the next day or so," Tabitha said.

"Don't you have to embed your divination in an actual story?" Carissa asked.

"Until this imprint of Epiphany wears off," Tabitha said, "I'm not sure the old limits to my skill apply."

Rindasy read Tabitha's most recent page out loud. Instead of blocks of storytelling prose, Tabitha had hastily written three bullet points with salient information.

"'First, Epiphany Foreshadow goes to the Archives, to steal the original treaty,'" ze said.

"So what?" Carissa said. "Don't they have a web version?"

"Surely you've seen the pilot episode of *Storm and Desire*," Tabitha replied, "where we learn that the treaty is what holds the Association together. It's not just a document, it's an artifact. It encodes an immense power of intent."

"What can she do with it?" Rindasy asked.

"I don't know," Tabitha said. "Keep reading."

"'Next, Epiphany makes her way to the Parliament of Storm and Desire, which conveniently happens to be in session today,'" Rindasy continued. "'There she intends to murder the Prime Minister, Serene Nova.'" Rindasy looked up and asked, "Why?"

"She's trying to ruin the last arc of *Storm and Desire*," Tabitha explained. "The Association can't sign a peace agreement with the Shai-Manak if their Prime Minister, and probably every other minister, is dead. Not right away, at least. It'll be mayhem for a while, and she'll be right in the middle of it somehow."

Rindasy looked back down at the notebook and almost gasped out loud in shock at what ze saw.

Ze read aloud, "'Finally, Epiphany plans to annihilate the Shai-Manak altogether, by bombarding their home floor.'"

"Give me a break," Carissa said. "If the Association couldn't pick off even a single Shai-Manak sorcerer, how could she possibly pull that off?"

"I don't know," Tabitha admitted. "I came up with three bullet points, high level, no color, superfast, and that's all I've got for now." She smiled grimly and said, "But she told me she's expecting a 'perfunctory attempt to stop her,' and I don't want to disappoint her."

Carissa's exasperation nearly reached a peak.

She said, "*You?* You mean *us,* because what are *you* going to do? Why would I volunteer to save the life of the Prime Minister? Who cares if this Muse fucks up *Storm and Desire?*"

"Look, *Storm and Desire* is just a fancy way of saying 'reality' at this point," Tabitha said.

"The Shai-Manak are not a part of *Storm and Desire,*" Rindasy protested.

"Wrong," Tabitha replied. "We're in preproduction. You're on the whiteboard."

Rindasy took a deep breath and said, "Tabitha, I'm sure this all makes sense to you in your mind or in your book, but I don't understand. Why are you—or any of us—responsible for stopping this Muse? What made her choose this path in the first place? What else is she actually capable of?"

Tabitha sighed and said, "You want backstory. It's not a quick explanation."

"Then just put a stop to all this shit once and for all," said Carissa. "Write *The End* in your little book and let's be done with it."

"Oh, come on."

"No, *you* come on, Tabitha," Carissa snapped. "Rindasy and I are only in this mess because of you."

"You've only *survived* this mess because of me," Tabitha replied. "I didn't *manufacture* these circumstances. I just started *noticing* them, with enough advance warning to *survive* them."

And then her face clenched with sudden sharp bitterness, realizing that wasn't quite true. She'd moved her share of index cards up and down the whiteboard.

But it was definitely fair to say that if anyone had manufactured these circumstances, no doubt it was her mentor, Allegory Paradox.

Were they supposed to *warn* Allegory that her nemesis, Epiphany, was on the loose?

Were they just supposed to *handle* Epiphany so that Allegory never had to get directly involved?

Suddenly, a new sound caught their attention from far down the canyon, the sound of rockets and thrusters coming from a midsize cruiser or a small fighter craft.

Carissa steeled herself for a fight.

"I guess I wasn't finished destroying shit," she said.

"Wait," Rindasy said. "I don't think you should destroy this."

"Why's that?"

"If it's what I think it is," Rindasy replied, "I'm going to destroy it myself."

EPISODE 6.05

Agent Anjette lay motionless for quite a while in the deep crater where she'd landed in the Wild Massive Prime parking lot, eyes closed, pondering life's mysteries but with perhaps more attention than usual. The lack of chatter over the comms was unsettling, and she tried to put that out of her mind for the time being.

She opened her eyes just in time to see Carissa and Rindasy hurtle across the sky in a roller coaster car, and she realized there would always be another set of mysteries to ponder, so there was no sense in getting hung up on any of them in particular.

As she crawled out of the crater, she saw Agent Grey in the distance, standing motionless, staring at the park. Then without warning, reality rippled and flashed and swallowed Agent Grey whole.

That meant Parliament just summoned Agent Grey as its sergeant at arms for a session. It must've caught Grey completely off guard, for her to vanish without saying a word to the team. It was unusual to see it happen without warning like that, but then again, it was unusual for Grey to even be on a field assignment in the first place.

With Agent Grey out of pocket, Anjette was the senior Agent in the field.

She was potentially the *only* Agent in the field.

"This is Anjette," she said over comms. "Who's still standing?"

"This is Whisper," was the only response. "I guess I'm actually sitting. I'm, uh . . . sitting outside the Squadship, uh . . . I'm actually tied up with safety straps and couldn't really stand if I wanted to . . ."

"Whisper," she said, biting down her immediate frustration, "what's going on?"

"That Shai-Manak nerd . . . Andasir . . . is trying to steal the Squadship."

Instantly, Anjette broke into a sprint.

Fact was, the Squadship was designed so that literally anyone could figure out how to fly it. You just sat down at the controls, whether you were a wizard or an ogre or a vampiric ball of light, and you could fly the freaking Squadship, thanks to a design so intuitive that its invention was credited to "common sense" in the annals, so no doubt a Shai-Manak sorcerer could figure out how to fly it.

She heard the jets warming up. Somehow she found a way to increase her speed, cracking pavement underneath her feet as she bolted toward the Squadship. It was starting to taxi forward, dammit. Apparently, the sorcerer hadn't figured out vertical takeoff yet or noticed the big red jump button, but still.

Also hadn't figured out how to close the ramp, apparently.

She managed one more burst of speed, and then she leapt onto the ramp, grabbing hold of one of its support struts.

The Squadship shot forward with a jolt of acceleration and then lifted off, heading straight for the chasm. She clawed her way into the passenger hold and manually closed the ramp.

"What the hell are you doing?" she shouted at Andasir.

"You had your chance to murder them!" Andasir shouted back from the pilot's chair. "Now we're going to *rescue* them!"

Anjette climbed to her feet and began making her way toward the cockpit.

They were on a straight course toward the smear of light across the sky in the distance—toward the chasm's edge. Anjette realized she was still on mission, and this misguided sorcerer was actually taking her closer to her targets.

. . .

Soon an announcement came over the park intercom system for all to hear: "Folks, we are all clear. You are free to stand down, repeat, free to stand down."

Cheers rose from all corners of Wild Massive Prime.

Half an hour later, Allegory Paradox arrived in the employee parking lot at Wild Massive Prime in a corporate cargo ship. She made her way unescorted to the Space Elevator. As she ascended toward the observation platform, she saw the wreckage of the train station, the wreckage of Hammertron Alpha and the front gate, and the wreckage of the clock tower and the nearby shops.

She was pleased to confirm that the Catapult looked sharp amid the chaos of its surroundings. Oh, it was deceptively simple, even old-fashioned in its scenic design. You wouldn't want to mar this ride's surroundings with flashing lights and bold font choices.

But there was no mistaking the majesty of that section of track that pointed straight up toward the sky and then terminated in midair.

▪   ▪   ▪

Roland studied the delivery manifest for several minutes. Finally, he looked at Allegory and said, "What's the catch?"

They were in the middle of the command center as it slowly transformed back into a restaurant. Many of his lieutenants were silently observing their interaction. Allegory had rank on paper, but Roland was legacy, and Prime would always be *his* park, not hers, not corporate's.

"You requisitioned this, did you not?" Allegory replied.

"Yeah, I put in for this *years* ago," Roland said. "And corporate blew it off, just like every other capital expenditure request."

"Timing is everything," Allegory pointed out.

"So what, I repeat, is the catch?" he asked again.

"I go first," she said bluntly.

Roland was impressed. That was an arrangement he could get behind with no trouble.

He unclipped the radio from his belt and said, "Engineering, this is your GM. There's a cargo shuttle from corporate parked in the employee lot. Inside you will find one shiny new thaum

446 · SCOTTO MOORE

generator, still in the wrapper, ready for immediate installation. How fast can you drop that soldier into the grid? We have a VIP waiting."

"Couple of hours, tops," came back the response from engineering. Roland glanced at Allegory to see if that would be acceptable.

She smiled and said, "Perfect. I have one last matter to attend to, and then I'll return for the proper maiden voyage."

Rindasy couldn't decide whom ze was more irritated to see at that moment: Andasir or Anjette.

The last time Rindasy had seen Andasir was a disaster, in which Andasir attempted to physically restrain zir from departing on zir mission, blathering on about the pearl's so-called margin of error of a thousand floors. It was a rotten way for the two of them to part, with such ill-advised anger in what they both expected were their last moments together.

And the last time Rindasy had seen Anjette was just before that, in a cell below the temple, for a ritual that replicated Anjette's identity. The replica was fully integrated now, as expected, and as a result, Rindasy felt ze could easily predict Anjette's likely attitude toward zir.

Now here they both were, arriving together somehow, striding down the ramp of an impressively sleek fighter craft, crunching their way across a layer of shattered reminiscite crystal that was several inches deep, and trying to look nonchalant about keeping their balance.

"Are they trying to be threatening right now?" Carissa said in a low voice. "Because I'm not feeling it."

"Andasir won't fight us," Rindasy replied. "The Agent may try to punch us."

"My understanding is that she punches really hard," Carissa said.

"I don't plan to find out," Rindasy said.

"Uh, okay. Should I just watch, or maybe blow up their ship while you're busy not getting punched, or what?"

"Don't blow it up," Tabitha interrupted. "We should steal it."

"Rindasy, we're here to rescue you!" Andasir shouted as they closed the distance.

"No, we're not!" Anjette added quickly.

.   .   .

But then Anjette stopped in her tracks, looked away, and said, "This is Anjette," responding to a call over her comms.

She was silent for a long while.

Then she looked up and said, "This charming reunion will have to wait. I have a higher-priority assignment."

As Anjette turned to go, Tabitha said, "Someone just broke into the Archives, right?"

Anjette stopped in her tracks, turned back to Tabitha, and said, "That's right."

"Friendly tip," Tabitha offered, "she's a renegade Muse, and she's planning to assassinate Serene Nova during the emergency session of Parliament that's about to start."

Anjette crossed the distance to Tabitha so quickly that Rindasy practically thought she was a blur. Both Rindasy and Carissa foolishly tried to step in front of Anjette, and each received a body check that knocked them backward out of the way.

"I can warn the sergeant at arms to protect Serene Nova," said Anjette. "But if I sound the alarm and find out you're lying—"

"Stop wasting time," Tabitha said.

Anjette turned away from Tabitha and said, "Agent Grey, this is Anjette. You have an incoming assassination threat to the Prime Minister. Lock it down." Then she fixed her gaze on Tabitha again and said, "Where did you get such disturbing and useful intel?"

"She's a baby magic-user," Carissa said. "Get off her case already."

Anjette shot a glance at Carissa, seemed to make a conscious decision not to start a brawl, and then she spun on her heels and headed back the way she came.

As she passed Andasir, she said, "Get your own ride home."

Rindasy called after her, "I'll come with you."

Andasir seemed instantly confused. Ze said, "Rindasy, don't get involved in Association turmoil—"

"The Shai-Manak are next on Epiphany's hit list, Andasir.

Find a way home and warn the Council. What was the word you used, Tabitha?"

"The word is *bombarded*," Tabitha called out.

"Our floor's going to be bombarded, and you need to convince them to evacuate," Rindasy said. Ze quickly swept past the bewildered Andasir and jogged to catch up with Anjette.

As the two of them approached the Squadship, Anjette said, "Listen, if you think saving the Prime Minister's life will scratch your name off their hit list, you clearly don't understand the Association."

"I'm hunting the Muse," Rindasy replied. "I don't care about your Prime Minister."

"Perfect," said Anjette.

Anjette sat down in the pilot's chair and took the controls. Rindasy sat next to her in the copilot's chair.

Just before the ramp began to close, a loud thump came from the passenger hold behind them. Rindasy swiveled in zir seat and was pleased to see Carissa had swooped in to join them.

"I thought you were averse to saving the Prime Minister's life," Rindasy said, trying not to sound accusatory in any way.

Carissa shrugged and said, "The irony, though, of the last free Brilliant and a rogue Shai-Manak saving her life is just, mmmm, chef's kiss, am I right?"

"Minor suggestion, brag about it *after* you've pulled it off," said Anjette. "Whisper, are you still on comms?"

Whisper replied, "Uh, yeah, I'm actually, uh, still tied up in this parking lot—"

"Can you modify the defense net around the Inexplicable Hall so the Squadship can jump in?"

"Whoa, those are some strange words to put in a sentence together. Are you suggesting—"

"We don't have time to take the elevators, Whisper. Can you get us in?"

"Sure, probably, who knows, but look—jump coordinates have a margin of error, you understand?"

"No, Whisper, you literally can't make an error on these coordinates. I need pinpoint precision."

Whisper fell silent for a moment, then said, "Okay, I've updated the defense net with an exception to allow the Squadship through and incidentally filed charges of treason against the vendor because it was so easy to do, so congrats on getting some bystanders executed today. Stand by for jump coordinates. I just need to run my calculations past a couple of million supercomputing clusters to verify accuracy."

"How long will that take?" Anjette said.

"Dunno, I need to get them to stop laughing at me first."

"Whisper!"

"C'mon, you're trying to land a jump-capable war machine inside a tiny little fishbowl of a room without sucking every living thing inside it into your jump wake and blasting their atomized particles across the multiverse," Whisper explained. "It's nontrivial."

Agonizing seconds passed.

Then Whisper said, "Okay, betting pool on this is green, your nav deck is updated with my jump coordinates, the Squadship is ready with environmental fire suppression on landing, and you will be going in weapons hot, in case singularity missiles are the precise thing you need to solve today's problem. Happy hunting, Agent."

"Thank you, Whisper," said Anjette. "Cloudlet, you can jump anytime."

"It would be my distinct honor to attempt this theoretically possible jump," replied the Squadship's cloudlet.

Moments later, the Squadship disappeared from the canyon floor.

EPISODE 6.07

Summoning the Parliament of Storm and Desire into special session required serious convincing if you expected all nine ministers to be present, on time, alive, and informed when the session began.

Only one individual besides Serene Nova had the credibility to pull off requesting a special session.

This individual was known as the Auditor.

A peer of the Muses in the org chart, the Auditor's consciousness was housed in a two-ton block of computronium in the twenty-third subbasement of the Building. On a recurring basis throughout history, at intervals with no discernible pattern but typically hundreds of years apart at minimum, the computronium's operating system fed instructions to a random bioprinter on an Association floor, and shortly thereafter, the latest physical incarnation of the Auditor took up his duties.

Audits could last mere days or might last months on end, depending on what the Auditor found during that particular visit. Particularly unlucky divisions or individuals might find themselves under extended review for reasons the Auditor was not required to disclose.

The Auditor was frequently friendly in a formal way, often claimed to be "on your side" when asking difficult questions, and was never shy about providing praise or constructive feedback when warranted. Infrequently, the Auditor was required to suspend or terminate work on a project or program or disband an entire division due to quality, budgetary, or aesthetic concerns.

And on the rare occasions that outright corruption was detected, the Auditor was authorized to enact individualized punishment on the spot.

Although ministers of Parliament themselves were not subject to audit control, any of their subordinates could suffer these and other penalties at the Auditor's discretion—presumably the audit results could be reversed by those who imbued the Auditor with authority in the first place, but this had never been witnessed.

By convention, the Auditor's first appointment was always to announce his arrival to Parliament. Failure on the part of any minister to arrive in person for this inaugural meeting was a surefire way to spark a particular interest on the part of the Auditor in that minister's sphere.

Today, they were given a generous one hour to assemble.

By now, rumors had circulated among the ministers and their key staff about Fleet's attempt to neutralize an audit team in one of its Building facilities, about the rogue Security officer with a fake ID and a "do not surveil" flag on her profile, about the Shai-Manak spy who impersonated an Agent of Dimension Force. And as the minutes ticked down on the one-hour grace period the Auditor had granted before meeting with Parliament, another worrying rumor was added to the list: Cadence Array was missing, last seen fleeing the Building altogether, and was not expected to resurface to answer to the Auditor.

. . .

Agent Grey, sergeant at arms, arrived first to open up the Inexplicable Hall and verify that its defense net was operating within expected parameters.

Gunmetal Sally arrived next, with a pair of young apprentices by her side to answer any questions about Elevator Guild operations that might come up on short notice. Cryptex Halo, head of the Arcane Coalition, arrived with an adept in training. Echelon Macro, head of the Technocratic Coalition, brought a small cadre of android bodyguards along. The Blissform's silver bowl of water was wheeled into its booth by two young functionaries.

Engine of Creation, the planetary overmind that ruled a roving fleet of conscripted worlds, always sent a different pair of influential religious leaders from among its populations to act as ambassadors in Parliament on its behalf. They would have limited autonomy during the session—more limited than usual, that is.

Shiv Disturbia, head of the Loyal Opposition, arrived alone and sat brooding in his booth.

As predicted, Cadence Array did not respond to the Auditor's call.

With minutes to spare, the Admiral and his retinue entered the hall, each of them in full ceremonial garb for the occasion. They paraded single file down the aisle of the auditorium, and you could almost hear jingoistic theme music rising in the background. The Admiral occupied his normal booth along with a single advisor, and the retinue of additional Fleet personnel filled several rows of seats behind him like a cheering section.

Finally, Serene Nova arrived and assumed her customary position behind the bench. Ordinarily, Lorelei Rivers would assume her position nearby at this time, but Lorelei would not be appearing before Parliament today per Serene Nova's desire to keep her safely out of sight for the time being.

As the Prime Minister quickly scanned the room, no one could miss the unusual agitation on her face, and the room fell silent.

"No sign of the Auditor, I take it," Serene Nova said to Agent Grey, who shook her head. "As I suspected. Friends, the message we all received, subject line 'YOU'VE BECOME A DISAPPOINTMENT,' was *not* sent by the Auditor but was instead a cunning forgery."

"That's impossible!" exclaimed Echelon Macro.

Serene Nova's eyes burned with irritation. Echelon's Technocratic Coalition, somewhere down the line, was responsible for Parliamentary communication systems.

"No, Echelon," said Serene Nova, "it turns out that spoofing interlocking nested multitiered quantum digital signatures to literally just muck about with our email headers is still extremely possible."

"What led you to suspect it was a forgery?" asked Shiv Disturbia.

"Ordered an audit of all the bioprinter logs," Serene Nova replied. "You can usually spot the little fucker early that way."

"I don't like it," said Admiral Slab. "Whoever's done this has gathered all of us together at a time of their choosing. We're targets now—physical targets."

Serene Nova's gaze turned to Agent Grey for confirmation, only to find Grey fully engaged in conversation over her own comms. Grey said, "Understood. Mobilize the entire team—what's left of it, I mean." Then she looked up at Serene Nova and said, "*You're* the target."

Serene Nova practically laughed.

Agent Grey announced loudly, for the benefit of the ministers and the Security officers elsewhere on the floor monitoring via surveillance, "Attention! Initiating lockdown immediately! Stay where you are and prepare to produce valid identification."

"Oh, let me just spare you the trouble," said Shiv Disturbia, the brooding Loyal Opposition, rising from his seat. "It's me. I'm the assassin." He stood up, and for the first time, everyone in the room really appreciated how toweringly tall Shiv Disturbia actually was. "The real Shiv Disturbia's been dead for thirty years, and I've just been . . . coming to your little meetings all this time, what can I say."

The chill that fell over the room was pronounced.

"I get it," said Epiphany Foreshadow as the distinct features of Shiv's face began to slowly cycle through other possibilities, "you think you know the Loyal Opposition that you've never actually spoken to and who has no real political responsibilities, when suddenly, what do you know, you've been infiltrated at the highest level of your government by a malicious actor who's been voting this whole time, but hey, if it's any consolation, it's actually worse than that, because I'm one of the last surviving Muses left in the Building and I'm here to dismantle you fuckers bone by bone."

Serene Nova's eyes began to glow a fierce red, and she practically snarled, "Unless you're planning to bore me to death—

which might work, I admit—get on with it." Already she was starting to mutate into something more suitable for self-defense.

"Agent Grey, kill the Prime Minister," said Epiphany.

Without hesitation, Agent Grey emitted a horrific, wrenching screech from deep within herself, instantly summoning a powerful superheated column of flame into existence all around Serene Nova, which melted the Prime Minister into boiling mist in less than a heartbeat and demonstrated to the other ministers why Agent Grey had earned the nickname "the Cleansing Fire."

The Agents, after all, maintained only a dotted-line relationship to Parliament. But they reported directly to the Muses in the org chart, and Agent Grey was compelled to follow an order given by a superior.

Epiphany said to Agent Grey, "Well done. I wasn't sure that was going to work."

But within moments, they both understood their mistake. The thick, bloody mist that hung in the air above Serene Nova's chair began swirling into a small tornado, complete with tiny electrical flashes, and then that tornado expanded as a significant amount of metaphysically charged biomatter squeezed its way into the Inexplicable Hall from an impossible direction and began molding itself into a form that already inspired terror before it was even close to complete.

Only a sliver of Serene Nova's true presence had ever truly been present in the Building. Agent Grey's attack had merely trimmed the tip of Serene Nova's nose, so to speak, which only served to enrage the entity. Now the ministers and their assistants and bodyguards all understood that Serene Nova intended to make them *see* her and, more importantly, make them *fear* her.

You could detect only the merest traces of her original humanoid form pulling itself together now, emanating from a golden torso with perfect skin that glowed from the massive radiance welling up within it. Eight sets of golden wings steadily unfurled to a wingspan that formed a border around half the auditorium.

Her three heads—one hawk, one dragon, one her original hu-man head—raised their voices in harmony, singing death metal anthems as a clarion call to announce her arrival and demand the undivided attention of every mortal in the room. Six arms emerged from her sides, each wielding a mammoth, gleaming broadsword, capable of slicing through the spine of existence or stabbing its malignant heart.

Epiphany said to Agent Grey, "Kill her again, please."

Without hesitation, Agent Grey began to summon the cleans-ing fire down once again. This time, however, Serene Nova simply reached out with the tip of one of her golden wings and flicked Agent Grey powerfully across the back, launching her into the far wall of the auditorium before the cleansing fire had a chance to appear.

"*You ignorant fuckwits,*" said the three voices of Serene Nova. Then she took a giant step forward, climbed onto her desk, and faced her peers, her fellow ministers of the Parliament of Storm and Desire, in the full flower of her true form, with her six broadswords poised within easy striking distance of most of them. She registered the absence of Cadence Array as more than mere abstraction now, and two of her three heads and most of her swords angled toward the Admiral, who sat perfectly still in the face of the prowling menace now pondering what to do with him, or to him, as the case may be.

But that entire maneuver was a feint, because she knew full well who the real threat in this room was. It was Epiphany Fore-shadow on the other side of the floor, a Muse who had somehow escaped her notice all this time, who'd spent by her own admis-sion at least thirty years impersonating the Loyal Opposition, and all for what? She realized it didn't matter, because as a matter of personal policy, Serene Nova never trusted a Muse.

A moment of decision must've crossed her faces, an expression that must've signified to her audience that at least a subset of them were about to die, because some of them scrambled to escape, while others froze in terror awaiting a killing blow. The Admiral's cheering section seemed to become a wave of bodies attempting to position themselves between her swords and the Admiral's neck. As Serene Nova's muscles rippled and her entire body began to swing into motion, Epiphany Foreshadow stood her ground.

"DON'T MOVE OR THE TREATY GETS IT!" she bellowed for all to hear.

Serene Nova stopped in her tracks, before any of her broadswords had completed a downswing.

The actual treaty itself, freshly stolen from the Archives, was in Epiphany's right hand, which she raised high above her head. Every one of them could feel the accumulation of densely inscribed power radiating from those rolled-up scrolls, which collectively reified the Association itself into being. The signatures on that document were tangible evidence of the mythological entities who walked the floors of the Building before the Association was even so much as a stray thought on a slip of paper at the bottom of a suggestion box. Every living being in the room realized all at once that Epiphany meant to tear that treaty into pieces, and nearly all of them despaired.

That document, and everything that flowed from its idealistic vision out into the sprawling contours of reality, was the deliverable that Serene Nova had originally been hired to produce. Technically, she'd fulfilled her obligation to the Architect who hired her eons ago, but only now was she herself ready to move on to the next challenge.

"*Let me offer you all an unsolicited word of advice,*" said the three voices of Serene Nova, inaugural Prime Minister of the Parliament of Storm and Desire, elite executive management consultant. "*Next time you want to depose your Prime Minister, CALL A FUCKING ELECTION.*" And then for the benefit of the surveillance dust that archived every session of Parliament for posterity, she announced, "*I resign my position in Parliament effective immediately.*"

With no further preamble, her entire physical form collapsed back into swirling mist and then dissipated without a trace.

The Inexplicable Hall was silent for several unprecedented moments.

Then a huge section of amphitheater seating exploded into splintered pieces with a tremendous roar as it was forced to make way for the sudden, unexpected arrival of the Squadship in the Inexplicable Hall. The ministers and their assistants scattered to all corners of the room.

Seating platforms collapsed for several moments, while the crew inside the Squadship tried and failed to convince its cloudlet to fire on the person that sort of looked like Shiv Disturbia.

"Kill whatever comes out of that ship," Epiphany ordered Agent Grey, who was racing down the aisle to intercept this new threat. "Don't hurt the ship, though. I think I'm going to steal it."

The first person down the ramp was Agent Anjette, practically sauntering down a fragment of stairs that had somehow survived, eyes locked on her nominal superior officer.

Agent Grey knew this was a lost cause and still unleashed a towering cyclone of cleansing fire all around Anjette.

But Anjette remained as indestructible as ever, impervious to flame and devoid of pain receptors. However, she realized this powerful attack could just as easily be directed next at Rindasy and Carissa, who didn't share her immunity, and she couldn't allow that. Shame, because despite their many differences over the centuries, she almost liked Agent Grey.

Agent Grey saw what was coming and threw up her wings around herself for protection.

But Anjette punched Agent Grey so hard that time seemed to stop for a moment, creating a fleeting tableau of the two of them in which this was nothing more than a changing of the old guard for the new, a natural exchange of energy and responsibility, taking place with dignity and reflection and sentiment.

And then one of the last surviving remnants of the mythological era survived no longer, as Agent Grey's lifeless body collapsed in a heap near Epiphany's feet.

With Agent Grey's powers neutralized, Carissa and Rindasy could safely emerge from the Squadship.

Carissa intended to telepathically crush Epiphany under the psychic weight of the memories she was still practically drowning in from the explosion at the Memory Palace, dropping those memories on Epiphany in the form of the most blistering psychic storm she could muster.

Epiphany was slightly quicker to act. She gave the Plot Twist Ring a nice healthy spin on her ring finger.

As Carissa came down the stairs toward Epiphany, a voice from the sidelines said, "Carissa! My god, is that you?"

Carissa was startled to recognize that voice, so startled she almost shrieked like she was trapped in a nightmare.

A young man wearing a Fleet uniform emerged from hiding. It was Admiral Slab's personal assistant.

"Kellin?" Carissa whispered.

"Hey there, Cee," said her brother.

The room seemed to freeze for a few moments as Carissa and Kellin saw each other for the first time in a hundred years.

Kellin possessed four psionic talents: levitation, telekinesis, pyrokinesis, and telepathy. She'd heard his voice inside her mind so many times growing up—taunting her, keeping her company, training her, encouraging her, telling her to cheer the fuck up—that sometimes, now and again, she experienced her own thoughts in his voice.

But now she too could speak telepathically, and their conversation could happen almost as fast as they could think, while others around them still remained in something of a daze.

Did you enlist or what? she asked.

He replied, *It's a living.*

I only found out you were still alive three days ago! she exclaimed.

Same, he replied. *What are you doing here? This is a bad scene.*

Oh my god, you have no idea, she told him. *I need to murder that Muse before she does any more supremely horrible shit.*

In a few seconds, the Admiral's going to realize who you are, he replied, *and he's going to order me to kill you.*

Are you fucking kidding me? she almost shouted out loud.

Kill order on the Brilliant is still good, except for a tiny carve-out for active-duty Brilliant, he informed her. *Want to sign up?*

Are you a clone or some shit? she demanded. *No, I don't want to sign up.*

C'mon, genocide is really only a sliver of what we do.

Are you literally joking about—

Carissa, I was given the option to sign up, or go back into cold storage and eventually have my head removed and dissected for science when they finally got around to it. Which, by the way, is exactly what happened to Indira. So it's just you and me now, last of the Brilliant, and if you run from me, I'll be forced to come after you. If you join Fleet instead, I can protect you.

I'm looking for the telepathic vomit emoji, and I can't find it.

"Is that your bitch sister?" exclaimed Admiral Allon Slab from across the room. "KILL HER ALREADY!"

Instantly, the entire room exploded into a frenzy.

Kellin lifted Carissa telekinetically and hurled her at high speed toward the nearest wall. She caught herself in the air halfway there, spinning in flight to face him, and he rose into the air as well.

She was thoroughly disoriented by the situation. He'd drilled it into their heads so many times while she was growing up— you did *not* use your talents to commit violence against other Brilliant. If any outsider ever saw the slightest hint of infighting among the Brilliant, Kellin would be furious about it for days. She'd been proud of him for instilling such an ethos about how to live with these talents.

He'd been especially rigorous with her, making sure most Brilliant never even guessed what her talent was, let alone experienced it firsthand. Prejudice against a teenage girl with mind control, he said, would be difficult even for Kellin to handle if it spread to too many people.

But now she wondered for the first time if all that ingrained training was meant to keep the Brilliant from attacking *him* and deposing him along the way.

The eight outer doors to the Inexplicable Hall burst open, and dozens of heavily armed Security shock troops charged into the arena, demanding everyone drop to the ground.

It was not clear that Security had gotten the memo regarding the "tiny carve-out for active duty Brilliant," because they became extremely agitated at the sight of Carissa and Kellin levitating on opposite sides of the room. They immediately got an earful from the Admiral about focusing their fire on Carissa. Anjette tried to intervene, and she and the Admiral and the shock troops entered into a loud argument.

Kellin lifted an array of broken seats and shattered risers and hurled them at Carissa. She threw up a force wall in front of her that blocked the debris.

He was toying with her, and she couldn't bring herself to retaliate against him.

There had to be a better way out of this mess.

All she had to do was literally *tell him to back down*, but she knew deep down that if she used mind control on him, the moment she relaxed her control, he'd come at her with the full force of his fury and murder her outright.

Maybe you didn't hear, but I have thirteen talents now, she tried to warn him.

Oh, I heard about your upgrade, replied Kellin. *You've acquired Jirian's entire first-generation talent set. That's good. That'll make you an incredible asset.*

Shock troops began firing nonlethal energy blasts into the air at Carissa, but she blocked them with force and then blasted back with a psychic storm that caused half a dozen of the shock troops to drop in agony and the rest to back off significantly.

But you should know, Kellin continued as he drifted gently toward her, *I'm testing third-generation talents now. We call this one "solitary confinement."* The gleeful cruelty in his voice was incredibly jarring to her.

Suddenly, Carissa's entire sensorium became empty and silent, devoid of sensory data of any kind. She was instantly, cleanly detached from every physical aspect of reality as she understood it. Her conscious mind shrank to a pinpoint of fear in an endless, featureless void, unable to communicate outward in any fashion.

She was unable to hear her own thoughts.

She was unable to scream, trapped in an infinite moment of gasping for air from beneath a sheet of ice.

Then, the ice shattered, and she was back in her body again.

She was in pain—she'd fallen out of the air when Kellin's attack had hit her, and she'd landed brutally hard. Theoretically, she could heal herself if she could concentrate, but the pain overwhelmed her senses. She was unhappy to finally realize that she could be so powerful and yet so fragile at the same time, and frustrated to realize it was so difficult to access her healing talent when she wasn't already perfectly healthy.

An enormous arachnid creature with a dozen razor-sharp appendages and a ferocious set of teeth and fangs was now the star attraction in the Inexplicable Hall, taking weapons fire from the shock troops on all sides and mostly brushing it off. Occasionally, one of its appendages would get blown completely off, only to almost instantly regenerate, but the trunk of its body seemed impervious to their attacks.

The creature had speared Kellin from behind, plunging a talon clear through his back and out his chest. That's what had freed her from his attack. His eyes were lifeless.

She was used to thinking of him as dead, so this was just a visual confirmation as far as she was concerned. That's what she hurriedly convinced herself to stave off the incoming wave of shock and horror that was about to roll over her and drown her if she wasn't prepared for it. All the psionic talents in the world weren't going to give her another chance to see her brother ever again, and the only consolation was realizing that the Fleet had molded him into an irredeemably hateful bastard. It felt like she'd lost her brother multiple times in the past few days, but she was certain she didn't need to hear the cruelty in his voice ever again, so maybe it was a wash.

The creature flung Kellin's body aside.

Admiral Slab was apoplectic with rage, and Carissa was his clear target. He wrestled a rifle from one of the shock troops and stomped toward Carissa's crumpled form, imagining he was safely approaching the creature from behind its line of sight. The pain was still too intense for her to concentrate on using a talent for self-defense.

But the creature apparently had full range of vision in every direction, because it swung one of its appendages like a sword through the air and neatly decapitated the Admiral before he could get off a shot.

Then it swiftly shapeshifted into the most recent form Rindasy had worn. "Are you hurt?" ze asked.

"It's nothing that three first aid pills can't handle," Carissa replied.

Suddenly, a sonic whine filled the air, the unmistakable sound of the Squadship's jump drive warming up.

Epiphany Foreshadow occupied the pilot's seat.

"I need to go," Rindasy told Carissa.

"Don't get killed," she said, surprising both of them with her urgency.

Rindasy nodded even as ze transformed back into an arachnid creature, this time with the addition of wings, and propelled zirself through the air toward the Squadship, landing on the exterior of its cockpit and gripping tightly to the surface of the ship by plunging talons into the hull.

The Squadship jumped off the floor, its destination unknown.

The Squadship reappeared in the middle of a war zone.

Specifically, the Squadship reappeared in the airspace above Wild Mega, on floor 49,500, where ninety-nine Shai-Manak sorcerers had been instructed to hold their ground for ten days.

The Maladies were here in force. They seemed to have swarmed the floor by surprise, in numbers far beyond those of the Shai-Manak. Rindasy realized this must've been the destination for all those jump-capable capsules and shuttles that launched from the roof of the Memory Palace.

The four Maladies that Rindasy had seen at Wild Massive Prime were among the medium tier in terms of size and spectacle. Many truly giant Maladies roamed freely here. Several large fires were raging around the park, and the wreckage of toppled roller coasters had crushed shops and other rides.

Pockets of fighting were still ongoing, where cornered Shai-Manak had banded together to create intense collaborative spell attacks and defenses, but most of the floor was firmly occupied by Maladies.

Rindasy had never seen so many dead Shai-Manak scattered throughout a single location before.

Ze let loose zir grip on the cockpit and slid off the Squadship into the air. A nearby horde of Maladies recognized a new combatant in their midst and swarmed Rindasy, who instinctively managed to whirl and slash zir sharp appendages through several of them before firing off a concussive force spell that cleared the air around zir for a moment.

But the swarm redoubled its efforts to overwhelm zir; in fact, these Maladies must've somehow been obeying commands from Epiphany, because instead of killing zir, they drove zir hard into the ground, so hard that ze snapped most of zir appendages and tore zir wings. Ze was pinned down under what seemed like a colossal amount of weight coming from things that shimmered and refracted light as though they only half existed as material beings in the first place.

Before Rindasy understood what was happening, a net made of crystalline mesh was draped over zir, unnaturally flexible despite its clear origin as reminiscite, but impossible to shred or rip.

The mesh instantly flooded zir mind with a wave of harsh and confusing memory playback from unknown sources—either that, or it was yanking zir own memories to the foreground but in a painful, disorganized, unrecognizable barrage. Under such a smothering sensory assault, Rindasy couldn't concentrate on spellcraft, couldn't shapeshift, could barely stay conscious and aware of what was happening.

A pair of giant Maladies wrapped thick cord around Rindasy until ze was tightly bound inside the mesh net, and then ze was unceremoniously dragged through the streets of the park.

The Maladies seemed to be gathering around a central location, coming from all corners of the park with bundles of Shai-Manak prisoners like Rindasy, or Shai-Manak corpses in most cases, wrapped in reminiscite mesh. They began to pile these bundles, which came in a variety of shapes since the Shai-Manak fought in many different forms, inside the entrance to what was clearly intended to be a premier attraction when this new park opened.

According to the gaudy, sensationalist signage at the entrance, this roller coaster was called the Cannon.

Rindasy deduced by studying the visible sections of track that this roller coaster was intended to be Wild Mega's version of the Catapult, with a much more intense layout for the majority of the run, and then finishing off with a section of track that shot the ride car out of a chute into midair, destination unknown.

Given the ride's name was the Cannon, Rindasy began to think it might be no coincidence that Tabitha had emphasized the term *bombardment*.

The Cannon leveraged Roland Prismatic's Catapult design, expanding on it in several ways. After all, Wild Mega was plugged directly into the Association's thaum grid, providing an astronomical amount of juice for the park in general and for this featured ride in particular.

The basic guest experience was similar: after a gut-wrenching tour around an absurdly challenging track, your car is dropped into a launch tube and then electromagnetically fired into the air above Wild Mega—a park with a much bigger footprint than Prime.

Now add in a variety of in-flight menaces, curated from Wild Massive's library of popular media villains, forcing your car to engage in physics-defying midair course correction. Already you can see how this is a more exciting design than the Catapult.

And finally, after you've escaped your enemies, the car precipitously loses altitude, and you plummet into the artificial ocean that bounds an outer edge of the park. Here Wild Mega's design again significantly improves on Roland's, because your car converts to an underwater vehicle just prior to impact, and now you're touring a gorgeous aquatic landscape that ultimately delivers you to the center of Wild Mega's extensive water park neighborhood.

But the Cannon also has a VIP experience.

For an astronomical upsell price, you can specify one of the ten most popular Wild Massive parks elsewhere in the Building as your destination, and the Cannon's trajectory is adjusted to launch you there. The car in this case becomes a projectile that punches temporary rifts across the actual dimensional boundaries of the intervening floors. Within these rifts, you are incorporeal, captured in a state of thaumaturgical excitation as you rocket across realities.

This is not the instantaneous hop of a mere teleport, you see. You are instead accelerated supernaturally until you are functionally a smear of consciousness perceiving as many as thousands of floors at a time along your interdimensional route before you are abruptly slammed back into your physical form and the car makes a perfect landing on a receiving track at the destination park.

That was the design on paper, anyway.

Epiphany Foreshadow marched through the scene, greeting the Maladies by name as though they were all comrades. A few of the Maladies grabbed bundles from the pile of prisoners and corpses and followed her onto the boarding platform itself.

Rindasy felt the activation of the Cannon as it began drawing thaums. Ze thought ze must be delirious, hallucinating the sight of these Shai-Manak bundles loaded into roller coaster cars on the platform.

Abhorrent magic was unfolding here.

Epiphany stood briefly at the control podium for the ride, overriding its current instructions. The ride system absorbed her intent, welcoming the active sculpting of a Muse, and a million micro-adjustments to the programming and the physical components of the ride occurred within an instant. Then the chute section of track gently adjusted to a new angle.

Once she was satisfied the Cannon was primed as she wanted it, she moved to the edge of the platform, looking out over the Maladies who had gathered as though they were waiting in line for the ride. Before activating the ride, she had one other piece of ritual ceremony to attend to.

Now she once again held the treaty high above her head in her right hand. The Maladies fell eerily silent.

She uttered a short incantation, and her opposite hand became covered in magical blue flame.

"So begins the unraveling!" she shouted, and she touched the blue flame to the scrolls of the treaty, setting them alight. Then she raised the burning treaty like a torch for all to see. Weird and wispy smoke arose, letting loose hisses and murmurs and admonitions. The scrolls burned, but were slow to be consumed, seemingly resisting their fate with every fiber.

Suddenly, the floor was rocked with a powerful, thunderous,

cracking *boom*. The light flickered—not the lights of the park but the light of the sky in this pocket dimension. Every pane of glass on the floor shattered instantly, any coaster or contraption with the slightest wavering or fault to its construction collapsed in a heap, and the entire Building itself seemed to sway.

The Maladies wailed in sudden fear, and Rindasy realized ze was wailing along with them.

The cracking boom stretched out for minutes, blasting them with a horrible foreboding vibration, before the sound finally dwindled to a bearable level. The Cannon still stood tall and proud.

Epiphany thought that was a perfectly acceptable christening for the Cannon's maiden voyage.

One of the Shai-Manak corpses wrapped in mesh was loaded into the first available roller coaster car. Epiphany touched the flaming scrolls to the mesh, and the mesh ignited with a gorgeous refractory flame that would not easily be extinguished.

Then Epiphany turned to the control panel and smacked the big green button with gusto.

The flaming car dutifully twisted and looped its way through the course, before dropping into position as ammunition for the Cannon. And then with a sickening *whump,* the car was fired into the sky of the pocket dimension, streaking toward the horizon like a comet with a long, eerie tail of flame.

But instead of dropping down eventually toward the artificial ocean, it climbed ever higher and then violently tunneled its way across floor after floor after floor in succession, until it suddenly tore open a hole in the sky of its destination floor, and for a sickening moment, Rindasy saw home—saw the Shai-Manak civic temple in its clearing in the rain forest—and then ze watched as the roller coaster car landed like a bomb on top of the temple.

An absurdly intense magical explosion followed, sending chunks of the temple flying in every direction, even all the way back through the fading interdimensional tunnel, where they struck several Maladies dead on the spot.

Shai-Manak were resilient to all manner of physical damage, but ze could feel the impossibility of surviving a magical bomb like that. They would find no survivors in the ruins of the temple.

Epiphany had ninety-eight more bombs she could fire once they'd finished subduing the resistance at the periphery of the park. Already another body was loaded onto the next car, this one struggling just enough that Rindasy could tell ze was still alive.

Andasir had told zir the pearl had a margin of error of up to a thousand floors.

Perhaps that was meant as a caution against implanting the pearl in someone with lesser will.

But Rindasy was no baby magic-user. Ze was a 1,300-year-old master of sorcery and arcanum.

Ze would commit no error today. The weapon was intended to overwrite one floor only, and by the sheer force of Rindasy's will, only one floor would suffer its effect.

Ze whispered the passchant that only ze knew.

The pearl released an annihilating wave of algorithmic energy across the entirety of the floor, utilizing Rindasy as its focal point. To Rindasy, the experience of being in the center of its blast was like a discontinuity in zir awareness, as though several moments were simply edited out of the flow of consciousness as ze experienced it.

When zir awareness resumed, the mesh and cord that had restrained Rindasy were gone. Ze was free to sit up and take stock of the situation.

Wild Mega was gone.

Ze was no longer in a pocket dimension, because the reality emitters were gone. The tunnel in the sky that the Cannon had created was gone, because the sky itself was gone.

The Maladies were gone. The Shai-Manak were gone, their survivors sacrificed to bring about this moment.

The hangar door was gone. This floor was no longer an inviting target to raiding parties.

Instead, the floor was a standard floor, unfurnished, dimly lit, with exterior-facing windows wrapping all the way around it, tinted, letting in a gentle orange glow from the sky outside. Ze was sitting near the center of the floor in fact, on nondescript gray carpeting, and as ze looked around from where ze sat, ze could easily see all four elevator banks of the Building.

Unfortunately, ze was not alone on the floor.

Epiphany Foreshadow had also survived the detonation of the pearl. The burning treaty she'd held was gone. The Plot Armor she wore was still intact.

They locked eyes for a long moment.

Then Epiphany turned and dashed toward the nearest elevator.

Rindasy struggled to stand despite zir injuries. Zir appendages and wings were regenerating, but much too slowly to catch Epiphany before she reached an elevator. Ze could shapeshift, but the new form would include similar injuries until zir natural healing had concluded.

Ze opted instead for spellcraft, firing off a bolt of lightning from one of zir appendages at Epiphany. The lightning struck Epiphany in the back as she ran, and for a moment, a web of crackling electricity had her in its grasp.

But when the lightning dissipated, Epiphany was unharmed, and the Plot Armor she wore was *still* intact.

Epiphany laughed as she reached the elevator and pressed the button.

A pleasant *ding* immediately signified that one of the countless elevators in the Building's vast fleet had already arrived right here on this floor.

The doors opened, and Epiphany took a triumphant step forward, before suddenly freezing in the doorway, stunned to see a passenger she recognized waiting inside the elevator.

"How . . . is this *possible*?" Epiphany whispered.

"If I had to guess," said Allegory Paradox, "I'd point out that you're wearing the Quill of Coincidence."

Allegory grabbed Epiphany by the front of her Plot Armor,

yanked her into the car, and jabbed the Close Doors button. Moments later, they were gone.

Rindasy was deeply exposed here on this floor. Surely someone would come to investigate, since ze'd just destroyed Wild Mega in one fell swoop. Ze was left alone without so much as an Association ID to get zir through the checkpoints on the way out of Association territory.

The last time ze'd fled Association territory by elevator was with Carissa, and Carissa's friendly cloudlet had been willing to smash through the border checkpoint without stopping. A random cloudlet with no tie to Rindasy would undoubtedly refuse such a request.

Then zir attention landed on a feature you didn't usually get a chance to see on most floors of the Building.

Ze saw an Exit sign above an emergency exit to the fire stairs.

Ze could flee into the fire stairs, which were largely unmonitored and forgotten, and take zir chances traveling up five hundred floors or more to get beyond the border. Sure, the fire doors were always locked, preventing access onto Building floors from the stairwell, but ze was still carrying zir namesake artifact, the Key of Rindasy, which ze'd absorbed into zir body for safekeeping after taking an arachnid form that had no pockets for it.

Afraid that Security might arrive at any moment, ze hurriedly limped the distance to the door and escaped into the fire stairs.

EPISODE 6.09

"Greetings, new passenger!" said the elevator's cloudlet. "What destination did you have in mind on this perfectly average day where little of import has occurred anywhere in the Building?"

"She's with me," said Allegory. "Same destination."

"How delightfully unlikely," the cloudlet said. "I shall continue apace to the twenty-third subbasement."

"The fuck?" Epiphany said. Allegory had pinned her against an elevator wall with one hand, and Epiphany smacked that hand away.

"You've been so busy all morning that you missed the email we both received from the Auditor," said Allegory, graciously taking a step back. "An *actual* email from the *actual* Auditor, demanding our presence at our earliest convenience."

"You're the absolute worst liar in the Building," Epiphany said.

Allegory pulled a tablet out of her jacket pocket and handed it to Epiphany so she could read the email in question.

To: Allegory Paradox, Epiphany Foreshadow
From: The Auditor
Subject: Are you absolutely fucking kidding me

Get your insubordinate asses to the 23rd subbasement NOW. You've left me no choice. We're closing the books on this project TODAY. Really looking forward to hearing you both justify all your many deviations from spec.

"Insubordinate!" Epiphany exclaimed, tossing the tablet away. "Clearly, he hasn't bothered reading my creative brief."

"More of a destructive brief, isn't it?" Allegory said.

"Innovation was involved!" Epiphany snarled. "We deserve our end-of-project bonuses!"

"Let me lay it out for you," Allegory said. "You were assigned to find flaws in my work, which, congratulations, you've firmly accomplished that I'm imperfect, so I'm not getting a bonus. But you've proven to be so *eager* to find flaws that you've become bloodthirsty about it, so you're not getting a bonus, either."

"What are you talking about?"

"We'll be lucky if we get severance, Epiphany. Closing the books means they're done paying attention to this project. It means they're officially pivoting to the next project, and they don't need our skills for that one. I mean, what, you thought they'd submit your grand murder spree for a round of design awards?"

Epiphany smirked and said, "There's a thing called *context*."

"Anyway," Allegory said, "if the Auditor's not even bothering to bioprint himself a body, that implies he doesn't expect this audit to take long. Which itself implies the likely outcome is termination, for both of us."

Epiphany froze. Clearly, the double meaning of the word *termination* was intentional.

"No fucking way," said Epiphany.

Allegory looked away.

"Absolutely *not*," insisted Epiphany. "That is *not* how it ends."

"Wrong," Allegory said. "I can practically taste inevitability in the air. We're on an elevator ride to a foregone conclusion."

Epiphany fell silent for a moment, mind racing. Allegory was the narrative designer here, the expert in beginnings, middles, and in this case, endings. What if she was right, and this was summary judgment day for both of them, and their best efforts simply hadn't been sufficient?

Or what if this was a test, to see if they could find common ground right at the last minute, so they could go on to become a dream team that defied expectations? What if pitting them in opposition in the first place had been a ploy to see if they could overcome that very barrier to greatness and instead unleash a golden renaissance era of aesthetic beauty and kindness? It would be a new palette for her, sure, but she could get behind it if she had to.

"Maybe we just need to ask for an extension," Epiphany said.

"Epiphany, you *cracked the foundation of the Building* when you burned the treaty," Allegory told her. "Trust me—they're done investing in this project."

Epiphany jabbed the red Stop button, which brought their descent to a gentle halt. "So that's the end of your big master narrative, seriously?" asked Epiphany. "You're going to just prostrate yourself before some asshole who hasn't been involved in a single creative decision about this place? I mean, last I checked, they left *him* behind, too, and it's two against one if we decide to tell him he can fuck off with his condescending big-boy attitude."

"He's got just as much authority now as he ever had."

"He's only got the authority *we* give him, because *we're* the authorities now, in case you had your head encased in cement and didn't notice that the actual authorities are *gone*, Allegory. They're gone, and this whole . . . *everything* between us was just . . . manufactured to distract us—"

"I do not feel *distracted*, Epiphany! It's all I think about, constantly! I'm extremely ready to *not* think about it." She hesitated and then said, "It was cruel of them to leave us with hope to begin with. They never intended to come back for us. You must understand that by now."

Epiphany smiled and said, "You rose to the occasion, anyway. Did your best work in the face of staggering adversity and despite flagrant ignorance."

"My best work?"

"*Storm and Desire*. It's so good that I'm almost sorry I ruined it. Almost."

Allegory looked away.

"I'm not going with you to the Auditor," Epiphany said. She released the red Stop button from its depressed position and said, "Cloudlet, take us up, as far as you're willing to go."

The elevator gently accelerated into motion.

"What will you do?" Allegory asked. "He can mobilize the entire Building to hunt you down for insubordination, you realize. Everything in this Building—every person, every weapon, every ship, every spell, every floor, every elevator—it all becomes his to command during an audit. There's literally nowhere you can hide from him if he decides your tenure as a Muse is over."

"Then he should've ended my tenure just a little sooner," Epiphany replied, "because I haven't quite run out of surprises."

Epiphany reached underneath her doublet and pulled out a beautiful silver pendant in the shape of a stylized metal gear, with a glowing jeweled eye in its center, and let it hang down on a chain where Allegory could see it.

Allegory clearly recognized it. "Deus Ex Machina," she whispered.

The eye began to glow brighter in response to Epiphany's psychic command. Epiphany said, "See you on the other side." She closed her eyes.

The glowing jeweled eye in the center of the pendant slowly blinked. And then the glow of the pendant faded slowly and went out.

Epiphany opened her eyes, saw Allegory watching her closely from across the elevator, right where she'd been standing moments ago.

Allegory shrugged. "Let me guess, you didn't keep it on a charger."

Epiphany sighed as the demoralizing feeling of anticlimax flooded over her, and said, "You have to admit, if it had worked, it would have been spectacular."

The elevator began to decelerate, and the cloudlet announced, "Now arriving at your destination."

"Uh, I said as far up as you'll go," Epiphany reminded the cloudlet. "We've barely moved."

"On the contrary," the cloudlet replied, "we are arriving at the top floor."

The elevator came to a stop, and a pleasant *ding* indicated their journey was complete.

The doors opened.

Standing there waiting to greet them was the Architect who had promoted Epiphany to Muse, plucking her out of obscurity and drudgery, elevating her to the high echelons of project responsibility.

"Epiphany, so good to see you," the Architect said warmly. "You're just in time. Follow me."

Epiphany glanced at Allegory, who seemed stunned. "You coming?" she asked Allegory.

Allegory hesitated.

"She's not invited," said the Architect. "Just you, Epiphany."

For a brief moment, Epiphany felt inclined to protest. But she bit down on the impulse, stepping off the elevator without another glance at Allegory.

This wasn't Allegory's prize to claim, after all. The elevator doors slid shut behind her.

·　·　·

The Architect led Epiphany through the fabled halls of the top floor, past the unnaturally exquisite executive suites, before arriving at the opulent and spectacular executive boardroom.

Dozens of figures crowded the main floor of this room, circling the immense golden table that was its centerpiece. Seated around the table were several of the Artists and many of the Architects who had led this project from the beginning, with shiny golden binders of information on the table in front of each of them. Behind them, in a standing-room-only area, an additional array of directors and managers was gathered to observe the proceedings, and a balcony level around the perimeter of the room housed many of the midlevel and junior staff.

At the head of the table stood the Creative Director, and appearing via video conference was the agency's Chief Content Officer.

As soon as the Creative Director noticed Epiphany's arrival, she said, "Everyone, if you haven't met her, this is Epiphany Foreshadow." She started a polite round of applause, which was taken up by the entire room.

Epiphany froze in the doorway. Her Architect gently escorted her to a chair at the opposite end of the table from the Creative Director and indicated she should sit. She did not feel like sitting just yet.

"What's happening here?" she asked.

"We've reached a major project milestone," the Creative Director replied. "I'm of course referring to the bold moves you made today, Epiphany. I think I speak for all of us when I say that we had all—genuinely—*forgotten* about your brief."

Epiphany shot a questioning look at her Architect, who seemed chagrined and would not make eye contact.

"We've rectified that, of course, and now everyone here is quite familiar with the scope of work you were given. Certainly your . . . creative *spree*, if you will . . . has come at a complicated time, when we're in the midst of negotiating new project work with the client. So before we're formally called to explain and justify this late-breaking phase of quality assurance testing, I thought we could circle up as a team and try to align ourselves on the story we plan to tell.

"And I thought *you* could lead the discussion, Epiphany, since you've clearly found an interpretation of the original brief that is, shall we say, beyond what we ever could've reasonably expected."

All eyes in the room were locked on Epiphany now. She knew it without even bothering to visually confirm it. It was highly aggravating.

"Let's hear it in your own words, Epiphany," the Creative Director said. "How do you justify the vacuous brutality and aesthetic bankruptcy with which you've operated since your assignment began? We'd love for you to step us through your thought process here."

Actually, at least one person wasn't quite paying attention. The Chief Content Officer seemed to be scanning feeds on a tablet that must've been just off-screen, apparently bored by the proceedings in the conference room.

Frankly, Epiphany was rapidly getting bored herself.

"I'd be happy to," Epiphany replied. "In fact, I've prepared a slide deck."

This was true. She'd been fastidiously maintaining a slide deck that showcased her creative genius, because she'd anticipated a day like this would eventually come.

"Excellent," said the Creative Director, summoning her to the front of the room, where a wallscreen came to life. The Creative Director took a step to the side as Epiphany approached and located her slide deck on the network.

A title slide filled the screen, with stylish text that read, "FORESHADOWING: A Muse's Journey to Success."

"I know for many of you, this must seem like a strange journey into the past," Epiphany began as her presentation spooled up. "You waltzed away from this project eons ago, I realize. And some of you were simply never very bright to begin with. So we'll start with an overview of the original project goals, refreshing your memory about each of the original design tenets and aspirations, the narratives we told ourselves in those earliest days to motivate us toward new levels of excellence.

"Then we'll review the history of each phase of project ideation and development, with a keen eye on how small changes to the specifications along the way resulted in major faults that could be exploited down the road.

"We'll look at the implementation challenges faced by Muses on the ground in the thick of construction, examining the tools they were given to work with, and the tools they invented. To support my observations and hypotheses in that section, we'll take a necessary detour through the overall project budget on a line-by-line basis, calling out disparities and discrepancies that led to corners being cut and objectives being abandoned or, in some cases, even corrupted.

"We'll examine the psychological and metaphysical effects on

WILD MASSIVE · 479

the Building's inhabitants of the decision to sever the top floor from the rest of the Building. We'll explore how core members of this agency's own executive team were complicit in an attempt to sow despair instead of trust among the seed populace, during that critical window before we'd locked down the final inventory of ideologies in play.

"We'll study the career of Allegory Paradox in some detail, up to and including an episode-by-episode recap of her crowning achievement, the intermedia series *Storm and Desire,* and the unprecedented and unanticipated aesthetic effects she produced in her role as the finest narrative designer on the entire project.

"Finally, we'll closely inventory every step I took along the way as I carefully positioned myself to fulfill the mandate of my creative brief. You will find yourselves surprised and amazed at the level of preparation required to execute the events you witnessed today.

"Then we'll break, and come back for Q&A. Settle in, folks, because this slide deck has over eleven trillion slides, and we will be carefully reviewing each one."

In the stunned silence that followed, the Creative Director said, "Perhaps you could just . . . give us an executive summary."

"Perhaps I could kill every person in this room, but I'm not going to," Epiphany replied. Then she added, "Probably." And then she further added, "I'd definitely start with you, though, let's be clear."

The Creative Director's eyes widened. Clearly, Epiphany's reputation preceded her on some level, because the Creative Director didn't interrupt her again.

Epiphany advanced the deck to her first slide. "In the beginning," she said, "was the RFP . . ."

. . .

Allegory's experience was somewhat different.

Epiphany said, "See you on the other side." She closed her eyes.

The glowing jeweled eye in the center of the pendant slowly blinked.

A bright sheet of horrible purple lightning filled the elevator for the briefest of moments, striking the Deus Ex Machina and shattering it into pieces, and enveloping Epiphany in a vicious energetic web. A sound like thick ice on a frozen lake cracking in hundreds of places drowned out Epiphany's startled scream.

When the lightning and the cracking finally dissipated, Epiphany had been alchemically transformed from a living, breathing Muse who walked the Building with freedom into an immaculately carved statue of Epiphany that represented her with near-perfect fidelity.

The statue was made of pure reminiscite crystal.

Epiphany's psyche was captured inside it, fated to spend eternity in perpetual review of the consequences of her actions.

A little on the nose for Allegory's taste, but you didn't get to pick and choose your outcome when you dared to use the Deus Ex Machina.

Of course, Epiphany might not have used the Deus Ex Machina in the first place if she'd suspected Allegory had been mucking about with email headers, crafting a forgery of an email from the Auditor that fooled Epiphany. Perhaps Allegory was on shaky moral ground by deploying that tactic. It was admittedly a shady use of her root access.

But that didn't cloud Allegory's relief in the outcome, not in the slightest.

"Cloudlet," Allegory said, "I'd like to revise our destination."

"Certainly," the cloudlet replied. "Where in this absurdly fantastical Building would you like to visit next?"

"Take me to Wild Massive Prime, if you please. I believe I'm due a vacation."

EPILOGUE

In the end, there was no fanfare.

Ride engineers removed one of the front seats of a roller coaster car so that they could maneuver the statue of Epiphany Foreshadow into position next to Allegory Paradox in the front seat. They used a combination of straps and cables to secure the statue in place.

Roland Prismatic ratcheted Allegory's lap bar into place, making sure it was firmly locked. Then he made his way back to the controls.

Before the car left the station, I went to Allegory and said, "I've got a going away present for you."

I handed her the stack of notebooks containing the story I'd finally finished telling, the book that had played its little part in bringing about this moment in the first place.

It was always nice when you got to see a little hint of surprise on Allegory's face.

"Are you looking for critique?" she asked.

"Nah, just try to enjoy it," I said. "Trust me, I'm not planning a second draft."

"What's it called?"

"*Folk Tales of the Building,* I guess."

"I see. We'll consider that a placeholder." She clasped the notebooks to her chest.

I took a step back and signaled to Roland. He flipped a few switches, triggering the adjustment of the track into its proper VIP configuration. The ride pulled a more than adequate amount of juice now thanks to the additional thaum generator Allegory managed to procure, and testing had proven to Roland's satisfaction that the ride was ready for its first good and proper VIP voyage.

He gently pressed the big green button on the control panel.

Allegory and Epiphany slowly left the station, and we watched their car accelerate through the deceptively bland early section of the course, taking its time as though these passengers were but simple sightseers, and all the while I held my breath until the car reached the drop track and fell into position for the final maneuver.

Then the Catapult launched the car across the park, across the floor, across the chasm, on its one-way trip to the top floor and into legend. I never heard from Allegory Paradox again.

And so the mythological era of the Building's history finally drew to a close.

.　.　.

With Serene Nova gone, Allegory Paradox gone, and Wild Mega erased, tension between the Association and Wild Massive reached a peak, and in the end, Wild Massive decided to cancel *Storm and Desire*. For now, the fall of the Brilliant at the hands of the Association would remain a secret footnote in Association history, instead of becoming part of the pop cultural fabric of the times.

The crack in the foundation of the Building, caused by Epiphany's destruction of the treaty, ran up the Building almost one thousand floors, causing widespread destruction and natural disasters, and requiring heroic rescue and evacuation efforts. I was never privy to the forecasts that described likely milestones in the Building's future if the crack was left unaddressed. But the fact was, the original construction crews and their equipment were long gone, leaving the Association no good way to address the crack, so the forecasts regarding some distant future catastrophe weren't something I had an appetite to see.

I never glimpsed the future ever again the way I had while Allegory was mentoring me. My propensity for seeing and nudging the immediate future pretty much wore off when I was no longer in daily contact with a Muse and with my capture glass destroyed like all the others.

Getting to the top floor had always been Allegory's one true goal for as long as I knew her. She didn't expect anyone to be there waiting for her. She figured it'd be long deserted. But she believed that she'd been left behind not because of malice but simply by mistake. And she believed, for whatever reason, that the top floor of the Building was the only place in this reality where she could call for help with any credibility and have a shot at getting a response.

I hope she was right.

On that note, I hereby close the book on my recounting of this unlikely tale. As Helpless the Bunny would say, "I've done the bare minimum, kid. What else do you want?"

Don't worry, though—if anything particularly interesting happens in the Building as it enters a new era in history, I'll probably want to tell people about it, so make sure you're on my mailing list or whatever.

ACKNOWLEDGMENTS

This book draws inspiration from four prior creative projects:

In 2008, the mighty Annex Theatre in Seattle produced my debut full-length play, *interlace [falling star]*, which is set in the Building, and follows heroes from the benevolent Association as they try to help a mysterious stranger find the top floor before something terrible happens. At the expense of spoiling a play that'll never be witnessed again, I must inform you that they found the top floor and (surprise!) something terrible happened anyway. This was Annex taking a risk on a novice playwright and jump-starting my artistic life.

In 2015, director Kelly Kitchens asked me to write a one-act play for Seattle Public Theater's youth program. I delivered a play called *Dimension Force: a time travel escapade*. (I was going to call it *Dimension Squad*, but the students shot that down, saying "it doesn't sound awesome enough.") A number of characters in *Wild Massive* appeared first in *Dimension Force*, in which heroic Agents must retrieve a time machine that was seemingly stolen from the Association by a young psionic woman. Many story seeds were planted thanks to this production and the enthusiasm of its participants.

In 2016, artist Eddie DeHais and I developed a webcomic called *Storm and Desire*, about an explorer who finds the Building by locating the beacons, making her home world a candidate to join the Association. I created volumes of detailed world-building for that project, which I leaned on as raw material for building out this book. Ultimately, we couldn't do a webcomic justice while still maintaining any semblance of life in theatre. But working closely with Eddie for those months and years, studying and attempting an art form that was new to us as creators, was a major stepping-stone to this book, and was intrinsically insightful as well.

Finally, our low-budget sci-fi comedy web series *The Coffee Table* premiered its three seasons in 2013, 2015, and 2016. A family unit discovers their new coffee table is an ancient alien artifact, which accidentally launches them on an interdimensional journey. Tabitha is one of the leads, Pivotal Moment plays a—wait for it—pivotal role along the way, and embryonic versions of the Muses and Maladies are introduced. This is something you could still theoretically watch (the most common way people watch it, in fact, is theoretically).

Each of these projects had a powerful impact on my development as an artist and as a person. I want to thank all my collaborators and supporters on these projects, for your kindness and patience as I flailed around in various stages of bewildered inexperience trying to make art happen, and for dedicating meaningful slices of your lives to making art happen alongside me.

On to *Wild Massive*:

Thank you to my fearless beta readers for being generous with your time and critique: Mike Gilson, Susie Lindenbaum, Jen Moon, Peggy Nelson, Alison Park-Douglas, Joe Pemberton, Robert Reeves, Beverly Sobelman, and Nat Ward.

Many thanks to my editor, Lee Harris, for the countless minor edits and major suggestions that helped sharpen the power dynamics and character drama in this story. Lee's notes included so many questions that I wondered if I had gone truly off the rails by even turning in the manuscript, but in the process of systematically addressing them, by clarifying key elements or cutting superfluous ones, the world of this book finally had a chance to become as specific and real on the page as it was in my head, where I'd been carting around versions of these "folk tales of the Building" for decades.

Kudos to my copy editors at ScriptAcuity Studio, who really had my back on this book, after I turned in revisions in a doc that was so deranged, it didn't appear as though I'd even used a word processor. Thanks to my cover designer, Jess Kiley, for delivering such an evocative piece; and much appreciation and many thanks to everyone involved in marketing, promoting, and shipping this book.

And finally, thanks to Susie, for keeping me company and keeping me sane when I was drowning in revisions on this book; and thanks to Jen, love of my life, who witnessed more of my inexperienced, bewildered flailing than anyone else and still continued to believe in me.

As I write these acknowledgments, I'm mere days away from my fiftieth birthday. Approaching that milestone perhaps explains the wistfulness I'm feeling as I gaze back across years of history and try to wave at everyone I can see. Too many good memories, not enough capture glasses.

Scotto, May 2022